P9-AGH-163

The Embassy House

By Nicholas Proffitt

GARDENS OF STONE
THE EMBASSY HOUSE

The Embassy House

Nicholas Proffitt

Bantam Books
Toronto • New York • London • Sydney • Auckland

THE EMBASSY HOUSE
A Bantam Book / June 1986

Grateful acknowledgment is given for permission to reprint "Whiffenpoof Song [Baa! Baa! Baa!]." Words by Meade Minnegerode and George S. Pomeroy. Revision by Rudy Valee. Special lyrics by Moss Hart. Music by Tod B. Galloway. Copyright © 1936, 1944 [renewed 1964, 1972] by Miller Music Corporation. Reprinted by permission.

Library of Congress Cataloging-in-Publication Data

Proffitt, Nicholas, 1943–
The embassy house.

I. Title.
PS3566.R643E43 1986 813'.54 85-48234
ISBN 0-553-05128-8

Published simultaneously in the United States and Canada

Bantam Books are published by Bantam Books, Inc. Its trademark, consisting of the words "Bantam Books" and the portrayal of a rooster, is Registered in U.S. Patent and Trademark Office and in other countries. Marca Registrada. Bantam Books, Inc., 666 Fifth Avenue, New York, New York 10103.

PRINTED IN THE UNITED STATES OF AMERICA

FG 0 9 8 7 6 5 4 3 2 1

In memory of

Robin S. Cassell, KIA, Vietnam, July 1967
William Douglas Booth, KIA, Vietnam, May 1970
and
Alexander Shimkin, MIA, Vietnam, July 1972

Acknowledgments

The author's thanks go to:

Kevin Buckley and Ron Moreau, guides and guardian angels in that emotional minefield called Vietnam, who taught me how to see, and how to feel.

And to:

Tran Tuong Nhu, for keeping me honest

"E," for doing the right thing

Jim Hoagland and Peter Jennings, for their early support

E. T. "Tommy" Baysden, Jr., for his experience

Rita and George, Joanne and Chuck, Barbara and Tom, Pat and Bill: for their sustenance and companionship

Aaron Priest, for his encouragement and good counsel

Linda Grey, for her wisdom and kindness

—N.P.

Author's Note

This is a work of fiction and with the obvious exception of a few historical figures, its characters are inventions of the author. But many of the agencies, programs, procedures, and operations described in these pages are based upon actual agencies, programs, procedures, and operations.

THE EMBASSY HOUSE

PROLOGUE

THE OLD MAN WAS SEATED on a wooden table, his scrawny legs spread wide in a V, his ankles lashed at the corners with loops of synthetic cord. He was naked and a knife, the kind the Americans called a K-bar, had been stuck through his scrotum, down low and away from the testes where the skin was loose and wattled like the skin on the neck of a chicken. The point of the blade fixed the old man to the table as surely as a pin held an insect to a collector's board. It was not as painful as it looked; it was the *idea* of it that hurt so.

The old man wept quietly, with as much dignity and as little movement as he could manage. His eyes were shut in a moist squint and his mouth worked, but he made no noise; a victory of sorts.

Even so, pain and terror rose like twin vapors off his sweat-slicked skin, giving up a metallic scent as tangible, as real, as the fishy odor of *nuoc-mam* that came through his dilated pores and mingled with the stink of the thin dribble leaking from his rectum to produce an acrid musk, a miasma that filled the hut like a foul fog.

An American with hair the color of fine beach sand, so closely cropped that it resembled a skullcap, watched from a corner. His long face, gaunt and yellow, the hue of ancient parchments, was bunched with distaste. He squatted Vietnamese style, back on his heels, his feet flat, his rump barely off the floor. He held a submachine gun by its pistol grip, his elbow propped *en pointe* on his thigh. He wore loose-fitting black pajamas and sandals made from old tires.

A few feet from the American stood an unusually tall Vietnamese with his arms folded across his chest, a chest broad and bare but for a single bandolier. His back rested lightly against the thatch wall and his face was empty and impassive, shut tight as a graveyard gate. It was a wide, flat, smooth face, the color of burnt butter.

Another Vietnamese half-stood, half-sat at the table, one foot on the packed-dirt floor, one buttock on the table. He watched the old man's face closely, taking his pleasure there, smiling genially and waggling the handle of the knife with a playful finger. A dozen more Vietnamese, all heavily armed, lounged outside, watching over a squalling woman and six quiet, wide-eyed children. Now and then, one of the men would poke his head in the door for a quick peek, then pull back to brief the others. They all wore the loose-fitting black pajamas and the sandals made from old tires.

The silence in the hut's single room was ruffled only by the old man's roupy breathing. It was a suffocating silence that gathered strength with every heartbeat. It created an ear-popping pressure, like that at the fringe of a typhoon, the kind that drove more sensitive animals mad and could do the same to men if it went on too long.

The American was first to fidget, first to concede that there was need of some kind of relief. His agitated face held the conviction that if this tableau were not soon broken they all could spend eternity precisely like that, forever locked in place. But just when he seemed about to speak, the tall Vietnamese gave a brief nod and the man at the table grasped the knife firmly by the handle and worked it free. There was surprisingly little blood.

The tall Vietnamese pushed away from the wall and came at the old man, moving languidly, without haste, a creature confident of its quarry, a cat advancing on a crippled bird. As he approached the table, his empty face changed, the blank page first dissolving, then reconstituting and filling with a miscellany of emotions: admiration, sympathy, even affection.

"It is time, old one," he said softly, soothingly. "It is time for you to talk to me. You have shown great courage today, but there is no need, no reason, for you to endure any more. No one could ask more of you. But it is time for you to talk to me now."

The old man continued to cry silently, but he opened his eyes, looking to verify the new note of kindness in the quiet voice, alert to any sign of salvation.

"Tell me first about this strange room you have under your house and how it came to be there," the tall man said, nodding at the large hole in the center of the hut floor where a set of crudely hacked steps descended into darkness. The hole had been hidden with plywood topped with dirt. It had taken the Provincial Reconnaissance Unit less than a minute to find it beneath the family's sleeping mats, and only a few minutes more to bring up the large earthenware urns full of cooked rice, the B–40 rockets, the bangalore torpedoes, the worn canvas knapsacks stuffed with medical supplies.

The old man did not answer right away. He was looking down between his legs in morbid fascination, assessing the damage. He seemed vaguely reassured by what he saw there. He looked back to the tall man, careful not to let his eyes meet those of his tormentor, his *savior,* lest it be interpreted as disrespectful. He smiled a shaky smile. It was not a friendly smile, not even a smile of relief, but rather the deferential smile the Vietnamese so often show to the powerful, to those with a say in their lives; a nervous, experimental smile full of request, asking for patience and understanding and, above all, mercy. "It belongs to the other men," the old man said in a tremulous voice.

"Tell me about the other men," the tall man crooned.

"The other men come at night," said the old man, his voice steadying. "They say they are going to make a place under our house, a place to put things. They say if we make trouble about this they will kill our buffalo so that we cannot work our fields. They say that if we tell of the place under our house they will kill us, too; they will cut off our heads so that our spirits will wander and never find peace."

"How many of these other men come?"

The old man answered quickly, almost eagerly, his resistance jettisoned as though he could not imagine now what had made him cling to it so tenaciously, so foolishly. A wise man did not fear that which was out of sight when there was something to fear right in front of him. He shrugged thin, tired shoulders and said, "Sometimes one or two, sometimes five or six, sometimes more."

"How often do they come?"

"Why, whenever they please, of course," the old man said with a bravado unthinkable only a few minutes before, clearly amazed at the question, a silly question.

The tall man gave no sign of being offended. "And how long do they stay?" he asked.

The old man shrugged. "Sometimes only a short time. Sometimes a long time. And sometimes they stay all night, until the sky turns the color of a bonze's robe, a monk's robe."

"And what do they do here when they come?"

"They eat our rice and our *mam* and collect taxes from us!" the old man said, indignant at the injustice, the very thought of it. Then, in a more subdued voice, he said, "And some nights they gather many villagers together in one house and talk to us."

"What kind of talk?"

"Such talk! *Troi oi!* All about *liberation movements* and *struggle groups* and *historical contradictions!* A simple man like myself can make nothing of it. They say that the men in the government are bad men, and that these bad men have given our country to the foreigners and that the foreigners want our rice and our rubber and that one day the foreigners will have taken everything and then they will leave and there will be nothing left for our own people." The old man stopped abruptly, cast skittering eyes toward the American squatting in the corner, and flashed his wan, placating smile again; a scattershot smile, sprayed imprecisely in the American's direction.

"What else do they talk about?" the tall Vietnamese asked softly.

"*Oi,* such confusing talk!" The old man shook his head in rueful apology for his lamentable ignorance. "I am only a simple farmer. I know nothing of such things. I do not know what I am supposed to make of these things they speak of, or what I am supposed to do with them."

"Do you believe those things you *can* understand?" the tall man asked, no threat in his tone. In fact, he seemed amused, although he did not smile.

The old man pursed dry lips and shook his head sagely, nobody's fool. "They tell us they are our friends, but they threaten to kill our animals, and us too, if we do not give them everything they want. They say they want to help simple farmers like myself, but then they say they want to take my third son to help them fight the government. My third son is only fourteen. Even the government's army does not yet want him, and the army is very greedy and always hungry for more soldiers. I tell the men who come at night that I need my son to help with the harvest. They say that they need him more, to help them with *their* harvest, the harvest of our freedom."

"Noi len di." Speak louder.

The command came from the corner where the American squatted. The old man had almost forgotten the American. He had been so mesmerized by the understanding manner of the tall Vietnamese, by the hope the gentle voice held out, that there had been no one else in the hut, in the world, but the two of them.

He had also been preoccupied with his own performance. It was all true enough, of course—he didn't know much, he was but a simple farmer. But he knew enough to know that it was always prudent to play the bewildered peasant. It was a stock character, a safe character, one that these men could comprehend, one they could be comfortable with.

The voice from the corner was neither angry nor cruel, but it was unexpected. It startled the old man and his fear returned to prowl the hut. He closed his eyes and smiled his inappropriate smile again, sending it out into the room without specific target, for whoever might accept it, man or spirit, and said nothing.

The American spoke again, in English this time, to the tall Vietnamese. "Ask him why he didn't go to the government soldiers in the village for protection."

When the question was translated, the old man opened his eyes and, careful not to let them stray toward the American, answered in an accommodating, louder voice: "Even though there are many soldiers here, the other men still come at night. When night comes the soldiers hide in their forts and do not come out until daylight. The other men come into the village and do as they please. They ask for rice and *mam* and you dare not say no. Then you dare not report to the village chief or to the soldiers about the giving. Then maybe the giving is found out later, and then you become VC in the eyes of the government."

A self-pitying whine had crept into the old man's voice. His grievances stacked up and he forgot to be afraid, forgot to hide behind his simplicity. "That is the trouble, I say!" he complained querulously. "At night the other men come. In the daytime the Saigon soldiers come. The Saigon soldiers visit the families who have relatives with the other men and frighten them so the families will invite them to one big feast after another. If you are really poor you must borrow money to buy food and drink for them, because if you do not they can cause you trouble. During the daytime we feed the soldiers. At night we feed the other men. We have nothing left to feed ourselves!"

The American spoke, again in English, to the tall man. "We're wasting time, Dang. Get him back on the track."

The tall Vietnamese nodded and asked the old man, "Do you know where these other men are during the day?"

The old man hesitated, then, fully committed now, said: "Yes. My son has told me. Twice the other men have taken him to their camp for more talk; to *educate* him, they say, for the day when they will take him from me. Their camp is in the Swamp of the Spirits. A bad place."

"Trai cua ho cach day may cay?" the American asked. How far away is their camp? He stood with a fluid movement. The American was tall, even taller than the tall Vietnamese. The old man felt as if he were in a forest, the U Minh Forest where his brother lived and where he had once gone to visit.

Never before had the old man heard a foreigner speak his language so well, with every inflection, every tone in place. He was as astonished as if he had met a dragon on the path to the paddy, one that could speak the human tongue. The old man answered the strange creature's question, but gave his reply to his countryman. "Five, maybe six kilometers."

"Phia dong, phai khong?" asked the American.

"Yes," mumbled the old man, again giving his answer to the tall Vietnamese. "To the east."

The American came close and the old man could smell his foreign smell. Even through his own stink he could smell it. He had seen Americans before, but he had never been so close to one. On the rare occasions when the American soldiers came to his village, the old man kept clear of them. The children had told him, with much giggling, that the Americans had hair on their arms, like monkeys, and the old man, looking for a safe, neutral place to put his eyes, now saw that it was so.

The American took a map covered in acetate from a case, unfolded it, and spread it on the table. *"Ta o dau,"* he said, pointing.

The old man showed him, keeping his eyes glued to the lines and squiggles of the map. He had begun to tremble once again, a reaction that shamed him but one he was powerless to control. He was afraid he would faint from the smell, from the *closeness* of this foreigner. He feared the closeness more than he had feared the knife, even more than he feared the other men. In fact, had it not been for this American with his pale eyes and pale hair, hair the color of harvest rice bleached white by the sun, the old man would have been unable to distinguish between these men and the others. These men dressed and acted just like the other men. And just like the other men, they had the sour smell of death about them.

The American asked many questions about the map and when he was finished he gave the old man a small, polite bow and said in a proper tone of respect: "I thank you for your help, Uncle, and I am sorry for all of the trouble we are causing you." Then, in English and to no one in particular, he said softly: "I hate this fucking job."

They took the old man with them when they left, making a show of it, herding him with loud curses and threats to one of two waiting helicopters, unmarked and painted black. Then both machines lifted off, headed west to make the rest of the villagers think that the PRUs were returning to their base in the province capital.

Ten kilometers out they set down next to a small stand of banana trees and off-loaded the old man and a single PRU nursemaid to watch over him. Then the helicopters lifted off again and circled back, flying contour, hugging the ground, and taking care to stay out of earshot of the village.

The old man had told them that the Viet Cong came into the village almost every night now, and it was vital for the PRU that they come this night too, that the enemy keep to the pattern. If the VC found out that a Provincial Reconnaissance Unit had interrogated the old man and had taken him back with them for further questioning—and they would find out the instant they returned to the village on another proselytizing mission—they would move their camp, and the intelligence that had led to the old man would be wasted, just one more job for the Embassy House shredder. One more blown mission. One more target that somehow had slipped the noose. One more post-op debriefing session full of questions without answers, mildly censorious and vaguely accusatory, put with sliding glances. One more hand-wringing report sent up to Saigon, carefully worded to avoid assigning blame, with anemic verbs and cringing adverbs, more question marks than periods.

They had the pilots insert them into a narrow strip of heavy jungle about two hours' walk from the trail that linked the old man's village and the Swamp of the Spirits. The black helicopters, looking for a place to land, could find no break in the sea of treetops, so they hovered over the canopy like mutant hummingbirds while the PRU lowered themselves into the verdant swells on ropes.

Once aground, the men hacked their way to the edge of the tangled growth, slung sandals and ammo belts around their necks, and slipped into the network of canals that webbed the Mekong Delta ricelands like cracks in a shattered windshield, wading through the mud-colored chest-high water. It was easy going, it was quiet, and it left no track.

They made good time. They would have made even better time if they had not had to climb ashore every half-hour or so to rest their arms, their muscles trembling from holding weapons above their heads.

Using the canals, they spent less than thirty minutes on firm ground before interdicting the path, and when the scouts had pronounced it free of foot traffic and booby traps, the men sank into the chin-high foliage along its edge and began to go over their weapons to make certain they were dry. Only then did they bother to remove their leeches, the once-thin black strings now grape-colored and swollen to the size of a maharajah's ring finger.

The tall Vietnamese named Dang checked the hang of the sun and spoke in a low voice to the American, whose name was Gulliver: "We have one hour of light left. How do you want to do this? An X and the usual way?"

Gulliver shrugged and smiled. "It's your team, Dang, not mine. How do you want to do it?" They spoke in English, the language they most often used around the other members of the team, the language of leadership.

Dang did not smile back; Dang never smiled. But there was a teasing note in his voice. "You are a terrible adviser, Sandman. You never advise."

Gulliver smiled again and said, "My policy is to advise only when I think my counterpart needs my advice."

"And did your counterpart need your advice with the old one back in the village?" Dang asked in the ironic, slightly mocking tone he so often used, the tone that should have been accompanied by a smile but never was.

Gulliver grew serious. "Maybe. I didn't think what you did back there was absolutely necessary. The old man would've told us what we needed to know without all that business with the knife. The Special Branch report said he wasn't hardcore VCI."

Dang shook his head and said in mild rebuke: "*Everyone* is part of the Viet Cong infrastructure one way or another. The old one was afraid of the other men and we had to make him more afraid of us. There was no time for the easy way. But you knew that. Were you not thinking of the consequences of yet another mission failure? Did you not push me to hurry him?"

"Yes, but after he began to talk, not before. Once you got him going, it looked like he'd never stop, and we didn't have time for Nguyen's Nutshell History of the War. But it was *after* he started talking, Dang, not before. And *I* didn't tell anyone to stick a K-bar through the poor fucker's nuts."

The tall Vietnamese shook his head again, registering disappointment. "Ah, the lines of distinction you Americans like to draw. As if they will save your troubled souls."

"Fuck you," Gulliver said without anger.

Dang put a hand on Gulliver's shoulder and said calmly: "Do not squander your emotions, my friend. The other men do not spend theirs so foolishly. Sometimes your fastidiousness makes me wonder if I made a mistake in leaving them."

"If you *have* left them," Gulliver said, partly in jest, partly not.

Dang ignored the bait, just as he ignored it every time Gulliver tossed it out. He stared back with flat soot-black eyes and said: "I am serious, Sandman. You are no child when it comes to such things; no *cherry,* as you like to say. You know the rules. You must put away this silly Western idea of fair play. It will be your ruin. You waste too much time on questions that have no relevance here."

"And you waste too much time showing off that Western education of yours. You're the one who's wasting time now. Set up any goddamn way you want. *That's* my advice."

Gulliver watched as Dang positioned an X-shaped ambush, admiring the way his counterpart arranged mines, rifles, and machine guns to spin a murderous web of interlocking fields of fire. What he had told his friend the moment before—and despite all the verbal fencing, Dang *was* his friend, perhaps the only real friend he had left—was true. He rarely had to advise his team leader. Captain Dang was the finest field commander he had ever worked with, Vietnamese or American. If the other side had many more like him, they were all in for a long, sad war.

While Dang finished deploying the ambush, Gulliver got on the radio to give the team's coordinates to the fighter pilots sitting at the ready in their planes on the tarmac at Binh Tuy, their own radios tuned to the PRU's classified frequencies. In the event tactical air support was needed, Gulliver had the authority to scramble the jets with a single code word.

He also radioed the coordinates to the black helicopters which now waited on the ground back where they'd left the old man. If it went bad and a hot extraction became necessary, he wanted no mix-ups. He did not want the helicopters out doing a grid search in the dark while the team was being gutted.

Dang was back a few minutes later, shaking his head in disgust. "This team of ours is worthless, Sandman. They must be told how to do everything. Everything!"

Gulliver grinned. "You say that every time out. This is the best

PRU team in the Delta, probably the best in-country, and you know it."

Dang spat. "Then you had better memorize the writings of Comrade Ho Chi Minh, my friend. It will be required reading under the new government."

Gulliver laughed. "C'mon now, Dang. They're not too bad, considering. Try to remember what they were like when we took them over. Think about that first mission, then tell me that we haven't done a pretty good job of training. They're a lot better than the thugs you find in a lot of the other teams."

"Perhaps the *hoi chanh* among them might be salvageable," Dang conceded reluctantly, "but only because they were first trained by the other men. The others, murderous scum untimely ripped from the womb of Saigon's jails, are beyond teaching."

"Paroled common criminals, ex-VC—and ex-VC who abuse Shakespeare," Gulliver said, grinning. "Who else could you get to do this kind of dirty work?"

"Disgraced American army officers." There was no smile where there should have been. Gulliver sometimes wondered if there was something wrong with the nerves in Dang's face, an old wound perhaps. He laughed for them both.

While Dang moved up, scouting for a spot from which to launch the "snatch 'n' snuff," vanishing into a bush near a sharp bend in the trail, Gulliver pulled on a black knit cap, used a camouflage stick to paint up, and found a place for himself at the cross hairs of the X. He chambered a round into the Swedish K, cursing himself for not bringing his twelve-gauge duckbill instead. Just because the agency's cowboys thought that the Swedish K and the Uzi fit their image was no reason for him to carry one. Such toys had their uses, but for close work in heavy bush the duckbill was better. You could clear a landing zone with a duckbill. All shotguns were banned by the Geneva Convention, of course, but then so was everything else connected with PRU work. Besides, the people he was going to use it on had never signed the Geneva accords.

Gulliver checked the luminous dial of his steel Rolex. Time to lock 'n' load. He reached inside his pajama top for the waterproof bag taped to his ribs and shook out a handful of pills. He popped them into his mouth and washed them down with a sip from his canteen. Then he nestled into his hiding place and waited for it to happen.

Lying in wait, all ears and eyeballs, the speed slowly taking hold, the dark settling slow and soft over him like a black silk parachute, Gulliver felt loose, felt fine. This was the part of it he still loved: the bushcraft, the hunt, the setting of the trap . . . the *professionalism*. Here under the black parachute he could imagine he was back with the Special Forces, back before the dirty tricks, before the cowboys took over. At times like these he was a soldier again, not some goon for the spooks. And the PRU team was no longer a motley collection of misfits and renegades, but his old Montagnard striker team, loyal and brave. Though he was going to have to kill someone in the next few hours, and though he did not love that part of it and never had, this was as close as he could get to honest soldiering anymore. This was the only part of it that could still make him feel clean.

Gulliver could feel his heart speed up, fueled by the flow of adrenaline through its valves. His temples began to throb, pulsing in and out with every breath, and his cranium felt as if it were ballooning, expanding to make room for his mushrooming brain. His every nerve and organ seemed to jump, adjusting to new realities as his senses expanded, turning into calibrated antennae that magnified every sound, every sight, every smell. Gulliver grinned a skull-like grin. The pills were kicking in.

Gulliver had long since convinced himself that there was legitimate reason for the pills. They did not dull the motor skills, but rather fine-tuned the senses to an extreme pitch. They gave a man his own personal radar, even as they rendered him sufficiently incoherent in case of wounding or capture, turning him goofy just long enough to give the rest of the team time to switch to an uncompromised plan. Each PRU wore a syringe of morphine on a chain around his neck for the same purpose, along with a small tin of cyanide capsules for emergencies. But Gulliver knew there was another, better reason for taking the pills. Later, when he came down from them, he would not remember the killing.

In a final triumph of will over chemistry he cleared his mind of its accumulated garbage, took a deep breath, held it, and exhaled slowly. Again. A third time. Then he relaxed and let the pills, a mix of Benzedrine and Dexamyl, take over.

With a clarity that was almost painful, Gulliver's ears pulled in the thousand or so rustlings and scurryings that filled the *silent* jungle with a cacophonous, ear-splitting din: bats with wings as loud as carpet-beaters against the thick clotted air, clubfooted insects stumbling like drunks across the littered jungle floor, waterfalls of rank sweat cascading down his face in a hissing spray, rappelling spiders hitting the bottoms of their drops with a bang, the drone of mosquitoes overladen with their cargoes of malaria and dengue and hemorrhagic fever; the rude geckos, chittering monkeys, cranky kraits, obstreperous vipers, antsy ants. Gulliver's eardrums thrummed like a plucked guitar string. He could even hear the labored breathing of the hundred-foot-tall sack trees, *Antiaris toxicaria,* wheezing as they worked to produce the poisonous sap the VC would someday use to paint the bamboo stakes at the bottoms of their punji pit traps.

And his *eyes*! His eyes were twin telescopes, infrared Starlite scopes. His pupils were a foot, a *yard* in diameter. He had Superman's eyes! The black parachute slowly dissolved and the light came so bright, so intense, he had to squint against it. He could see everything! He could see *through* everything, *into* everything, right through to the core of the earth, right into the soul of Vietnam, right into the black heart of the war itself. For one brief moment, Gulliver felt that he was on the brink of some momentous insight. But he had been on the threshold of such breakthroughs before, and this time, as always, nothing came of it. His pinwheeling eyes were out of control, keeping tabs on everything, *seeing* nothing. They refused to settle on any one thing long enough for him to focus, long enough to get a fix.

The only thing Gulliver could not hear, could not see, for all his pulsing antennae, for all his chemically induced sensors, was the team lying in ambush. He and Dang, despite his friend's professed scorn, had trained them well.

There were seven of them, coming by the book, in single, silent file, with proper, prudent intervals. Their fine trail discipline would have done credit to a Special Forces A-team. The Sandman himself might have trained them. They were good, very good, but they never had a chance.

Afterward, Gulliver remembered that much anyway. His boosted senses had picked them up a long way out, in spite of their wonderful technique. He knew how many, how far off, how the poor doomed bastards parted their hair. He just *felt* it. The pills were wonderful.

As for the rest of it, he could only assume that it had gone down the same as any other snatch 'n' snuff. No sweat, routine, SOP, standard operating procedure.

Dang would have let the first few go by, their sandaled, whispering feet passing only inches from where he crouched in his bush. He would have waited for the cadre leader, the one carrying the map case stuffed with manifestos and directives from COSVN, the Central Office for South Vietnam, the VC high command. When that one rounded the bend, momentarily out of sight of the others, Dang would have popped up and hit him full in the face with the Mace. The aerosol nerve agent was Gulliver's idea, brought with him from Special Forces, who, in turn, had taken their cue from the stateside police. It cut down on the chances that an errant gunshot would prematurely spring the ambush or alert any other enemy elements in the neighborhood. Dang would have simultaneously used his free hand to deliver a numbing chop to the cadre's carotid nerve and would have had his man tucked snug in the bush before the next man in file came around the bend. There were times when proper intervals were not so prudent.

That was the snatch. The snuff sometimes meant that the snatch was executed on the spot, or a little later perhaps, after a field interrogation. It depended on the mission.

His man in hand, Dang would have triggered the ambush. Those not killed outright in the lethal X's first fusillade would have been polished off with single shots behind the ear, or maybe a K-bar dragged across the throat. The Air America choppers, the same two black Hueys that inserted them, would have swooped in a moment later to fly the team and its prize home, back to the province capital and to the Embassy House. Home and in the rack by first light. No sweat, routine, SOP.

The next day, after he had slept off the crash from the pills, Gulliver found that it had indeed gone just so. There had been no PRU casualties and no VC survivors aside from the cadre, who had been turned over, along with his map case, to the National Police Special Branch and to the interrogators of the Provincial Interrogation Center. The old man had been ferried home as soon as the operation was completed, safe and sound save for a nasty case of blue balls.

For Gulliver, the details of what had happened during the ambush itself were fuzzy. The pills had made them fuzzy and the pills would keep them fuzzy. They always did. That was why he took them.

Book One
Sandman

1

CAPTAIN JONATHAN GULLIVER HAD ALWAYS BELIEVED that one of the few conveniences of military life was that you rarely had to wonder about people. You could read a man in uniform the way you would a chart. It took most of the guesswork out of human relations.

When Swain first walked into Gulliver's office a week before the Tet holidays, he seemed as easy to decipher as the top line on an eye test, proof-on-the-hoof that Gulliver's Law worked, that what you saw was invariably what you got.

And what Gulliver saw was both familiar and reassuring: a young bullock of an officer, strappingly fit, guilelessly gung-ho and, by all appearances, undoubtedly competent if not necessarily bright.

Swain's milky-colored, bleached fatigues were tailored to fit snugly across wide shoulders, a solid trunk, and strong thighs. The single silver bar of a first lieutenant garnished his collar tips, and cloth Airborne wings were sewn above his pocket. There was a Ranger tab on his shoulder, just over his MACV patch, and on the other shoulder was the insignia of the 173rd Airborne. And the Combat Infantryman's badge took its proud place over the jump wings. This time at least, Gulliver thought, they'd had sense enough not to send another cherry.

The condensed professional biography Swain was wearing fit tongue-and-groove with the white-sidewall haircut and the porcine face with its heavy jaw, stubby nose, and narrowly spaced eyes under simian brows. It was a stupid face with a touch of the brutal in it. Good soldier, thought Gulliver.

Gulliver began to revise both his first impression and his Law almost at once. Swain did not bother to render a hand salute or any of the other military courtesies. He just ate up the distance between the door and the desk with two hungry strides, poked out a sausage-fingered hand, and said breezily: "Hiya. You must be the Sandman. I'm Harry Swain." Then he plopped, uninvited, into the straight-backed wooden chair in front of Gulliver's desk and began scooting it around noisily to take best advantage of the feeble stir of air from the sluggish three-bladed ceiling fan, grousing all the while about the lack of air-conditioning.

Gulliver's cramped first-floor office and his living quarters on the second floor were the only two rooms in the sprawling Embassy House villa that were not air-conditioned. Gulliver did not like air-conditioning; its constant hum too easily masked the small, seemingly insignificant noises that could prove important. Nor did he like people he did not know using his old Special Forces nickname. Gulliver didn't think he was going to like Harry Swain much, either.

A moment later he was sure of it. When Swain settled at last, he heaved a sweaty locker-room leer across the desk at Gulliver and said without preamble, but with a waggle of his apelike eyebrows: "I hear you're the man to see for solid intel, Sandman. So how's the gook gash supply around here?"

Gulliver blinked, too stunned to respond immediately. He checked Swain's eyes, looking for a joke. It was like looking into a sheet of tinfoil, a crinkly shimmer without backing or depth, a reflection from a dry wasteland. He felt a foreboding wash over him. Those bastards in Saigon had done it to him again, he thought, fighting back a rising gorge. He found his voice and choked: "What?"

"Gook gash. You know . . . bimbos," Swain said obliviously. He leaned back in his chair, one hand absentmindedly cupping his crotch. "The word in Saigon was that the spook houses let a man keep a gook broad on the premises. That so? What's the SOP here?"

"I'm not in charge of SOP around here," Gulliver said evenly, "so yes, it's so—women are allowed in the villa."

"*Number One!* What're the house rules?" Swain asked with a grin, giving his genitals a playful squeeze, so obviously pleased with the information in Gulliver's response that he missed the accompanying tone of disapproval.

Gulliver tried doubling the dosage. "House rules say you can have a woman share your quarters, but she's restricted to your living area, the kitchen and dining room, and the common room. She's got to be checked regularly for venereal disease by the Embassy House doctor, and she's got to be run through the box before she moves in, then once a month after that."

This news, too, seemed to please Swain. He grinned and wagged his bushy eyebrows again and asked, "What's this *box* they get run through? I'm kinda fond of runnin' through *boxes* myself, if you know what that means."

Gulliver knew. It meant they had sent him a cunt-hound. "The polygraph," he said in a strained voice. "Everyone gets put through a lie-detector test once a month."

Gulliver wasn't bothering to hide his distaste. Strictly speaking, of course, he was in no position to stake out the moral high ground. But Nhu was different. She was no whore, no *bimbo*. And he had never brought her to the Embassy House, not even for dinner. Except for Dang, no one at the Embassy House even knew she existed.

"Number One idea," Swain said seriously, giving it his stamp of considered approval. "We don't want double agents runnin' all over the place, like in that Green Beret case."

Again Gulliver was momentarily speechless. Was Swain baiting him? Did he know about his role in the Vuong Affair? He checked Swain's face again and saw only earnestness. No, no trouble there. But what *was* in the face was almost worse. They've sent me a cowboy, Gulliver thought bitterly. First it's a kid who's never seen combat, a *cherry*, now a cowboy commando who thinks he's in an Ian Fleming novel.

"A green beret is a hat, Swain—the men who wear it are Special Forces," Gulliver said at last. "Now, what say we get to work, okay? What kind of orders are you packing?"

Swain held on to the serious look. The hyper eyebrows arranged themselves into a knot of concern. "Jeez, Sandman," he said in a scolding voice. "Loose lips sink ships and all that. Of all people, you should know they never cut written orders for assignments like this. I thought they briefed you about me."

Swain was walking the thin edge of insubordination and enjoying it, Gulliver saw, wasting little time in loosening the tight collar of military protocol. Not once had Swain called him Captain or Sir. He would have only two months out of uniform and he seemed determined to make the most of this holiday from Army stricture.

Lieutenant Swain probably was a good soldier, Gulliver

thought. The merit badges seldom flat-out lied. The man was a paratrooper, a Ranger, and a combat veteran, and Jake Gulliver, being all those things himself, knew just what a soldier had to put into each and just what he got in return. But all too often something happened, even to good soldiers, when they were taken out of their natural setting and given over to the Central Intelligence Agency. They put their good judgment and common sense on hold, like salesmen at a convention. Gulliver had seen it happen time and again.

Gulliver, too, could have taken such liberties when he first came to the province, seven months back. Major Ansell, the province intelligence officer and a career Army man who, like Gulliver, had been seconded to the agency because of his special skills, had taken a shine to his new PRU adviser and had invited a loose familiarity. But Gulliver had refused to play either the spy or the civilian with his P officer. He didn't give a rat's ass for either role. Until the day *Major* Ansell was killed, *Captain* Gulliver never called him anything more chummy than Major or Sir. Gulliver's steadfast adherence to Army chain-of-command formality was one of the few ways he still had left of going on record with the fact that he had never accepted, would never accept, being shanghaied by the CIA. Not after what they'd done to Special Forces. To Colonel Sculler. To Jake Gulliver.

Gulliver gave Swain a chilly look. "I know you aren't carrying written orders, *Lieutenant,* and I *have* been briefed by the agency base chief in Can Tho. *I* know what your orders are. What I'm now trying to find out, just so there are no misunderstandings, is what you think your orders are. I want to know who briefed you and exactly what they told you."

"Jeez, Sandman," Swain whined, "I've had so many fuckin' briefings I can't remember who said what. In Saigon there was MACV and the company. Then in Can Tho there was CORDS and the company again. So which do you want to hear about?"

The company? Swain was already starting to pick up the cute cowboy lingo, Gulliver noticed. It was a bad sign. In as calm a voice as he could muster, Gulliver said: "I've already had a rundown on what they told you in Can Tho, Swain, so I want to hear about the Saigon briefings. But before you tell me anything, I'll tell you something. I'm Captain Jonathan Gulliver. I let friends call me Jake, but there are only a handful of men I let call me Sandman, and you're not one of them. You may get to parade around out of uniform for the next sixty days like some kind of civilian, but you're not a civilian, Swain. You're still in the United

States Army and I'm still your superior officer. You call me Captain or Sir."

Swain was staring at Gulliver, his mouth slightly ajar, his piggish eyes wider than mere pencil points at last. He was utterly flabbergasted at this suggestion that Gulliver might not be all that taken with him. It was a possibility that had never occurred to him. Everyone liked Harry Swain. Everyone. His size and temper guaranteed it.

Gulliver could see confusion, then a dark anger blotch Swain's face. Then something more flooded that arid expanse—a hitch of caution. Swain was remembering the story behind the nickname. If he knew about the nickname at all, he would also know how Gulliver came by it. It was not something Gulliver was proud of, but it could come in handy at times.

Swain was angry but tried to cover it. He held up both hands as if to ward off any unfortunate misunderstandings and smiled what was meant to pass for a winning smile. He looked like a schoolboy caught smoking by a teacher. He said: "Jeez, uh . . . Cap, I was just trying to be friendly."

"I don't need any more friends, Swain. What I need is someone to turn this asshole job over to," Gulliver said, refusing to be charmed.

Swain stowed the cardboard smile and, his anger fully visible, said, "If that's the way you want it . . . Captain."

"That's the way I want it," Gulliver said. "Now, tell me about Saigon. Start with the embassy."

"The company session was short," Swain said truculently, still feeling grievously wronged. "Since I was only going to be on loan to them for a couple of months, they weren't all that interested in me. It was mostly just a formality."

"Who'd you talk to?" Gulliver asked.

"Only one biggie, a guy in counterintelligence ops named Steelman. He didn't think much of PRUs. He said PRUs are just contract killers. Hired hit men, he called 'em."

"I know the man," Gulliver said with an acidic look that for once had nothing to do with Swain. "When it comes to hit men, he should know. Anybody else?"

The leer crawled back onto Swain's face. "Yeah, a tall redhead on the fourth floor who deals with minorities. She said she knew I wouldn't be working for the company once I took your place, but she'd still appreciate it if I'd pass along anything good I picked up on the main religious group down here . . . uh, that's the Hoe-ah Hay-o, ain't it?"

"Hoa Hao," said Gulliver. "You pronounce it 'Waa How' ".

"Whatever. Man, that bimbo was some looker. Legs clear up to her ass and great knockers. I'd like to have taken a run through *her* box."

"She works minorities?" Gulliver asked brusquely, before Swain could elaborate.

"That's what she said."

"Was the name Teacher? S. Teacher?"

"Yeah, that was it. Sally Teacher. You know her?"

Gulliver shook his head. "Not really. I've had a couple of rockets from a spook in Saigon by that name, always signed S. Teacher. I just didn't know it was a woman, that's all."

"It's a woman, all right," Swain said, brows moving up and down. "With more time I'd have laid my move on her. She puts on a queen-of-the-manor act and that's the kind that's always hot in the sack." The eyebrows did their little dance again. All Swain needed was a pair of thick glasses and a long cigar and he would have looked like Groucho Marx getting off a risqué one-liner, Gulliver thought. "Tell me about the MACV briefing," he said.

Swain shrugged his big shoulders. "They just told me I was to spend a couple of months learning the ropes, then take over as PRU adviser when the province team makes the switch-over to the new system and the new guidelines."

Gulliver nodded. "What did your briefers tell you about this province?"

The big man gave another exaggerated shrug, and Gulliver, repelled and fascinated at the same time, wondered about the single nerve that seemed to link Swain's brain, loins, brows, and shoulders.

"They said it's pretty quiet in the Hoa Hao districts, but that there's still pockets of Indian country," Swain was saying, "and how this is one of the few remaining provinces where the Phoenix program, including the PRU team, is still supervised by the CIA. They told me they're turning the whole ball of wax over to the gooks and the advisory role over to MACV. They call it Vietnamization. I call it bad news." Swain paused, then said, "My MACV briefer told me that the first guy they sent down to relieve you got blown away. That so?"

"Yes, it's so," Gulliver said flatly. He saw a grinning freckled face, open and friendly, achingly American; a Norman Rockwell face. What was the cherry's name? Peer. That was it. Lieutenant Edward Peer. He had even looked like a cherry, the fruit kind, with that brick-colored hair and those ridiculous freckles. ". . . Back home in South Bend my friends call me Fast Eddie because I shoot a mean game of pool. What? You mean you never saw Paul Newman in *The Hustler,* sir? Where've you been, Captain?" Places where movies are few and far between, kiddo. Gulliver saw the boy's body sunk headfirst up to the armpits in the Bassac River, elbows crooked out like a crab's legs, fingers splayed like frog's feet on the mud bank where dirty water lapped at them. Fast Eddie Peer looked as if he'd just flopped down for a quick dunk—some Hoosier kid cooling off in a quarry pond on a hot summer's day. It wasn't until they took hold of his ankles and pulled him out that they saw he had no head. There wasn't another mark on him. It was Dang who found the head, fifty meters off in a tree, hanging by the mouth on a broken-off branch. With no blood to back them up, Fast Eddie's freckles had faded away. The boy's eyes were popped wide and crossed almost comically, sighting down the branch as if it were a rifle barrel. Gulliver could still see it clearly. The pills had been no help there. No help at all. "Why do you think it's bad news for the agency to give up Phoenix?" Gulliver asked, somehow knowing in advance what Swain's answer would be, or at least what it would add up to: a question of accountability.

"Jeez, how can you ask?" Swain said with a surprised look. Then he shrugged. "Hell, I guess since your team still runs under the old setup, maybe you don't know what's been happening around the rest of the country."

"Maybe I don't. Why don't you fill me in." Gulliver kept his voice level, trying to camouflage the sarcasm.

"Roger that!" Swain said with enthusiasm, pumping his pelvis to scrape his chair a few inches closer to Gulliver's desk, the set of his features announcing that he was now, at last, ready to get down to business.

Gulliver saw that he needn't have worried about masking his sarcasm, or anything else. Swain was as immune to nuance as a fakir to fire. Those amazing eyebrows, strung along the baseline of his shallow forehead like smooching caterpillars, telegraphed his every move, his every attitude. To Gulliver, they appeared to be working hand-in-glove with what civilians sometimes called a military mind, meaning that rigid set of mind in which all conclusions, all convictions, were strictly by-the-numbers, products of rote Army classwork or training manuals, never anything arrived at through the brain's own built-in circuitry. The big man's ardent purposefulness, his pell-mell manner of attacking the matter at hand, amused Gulliver almost as much as it pained him. Harry Swain was so relentlessly, so incorrigibly *Airborne*! All-the-Way-Sir! Can-Fucking-Do!

"For starters," Swain said earnestly, "in every province where the company's already turned Phoenix over to the gooks and the advisory duty over to MACV—and that's almost all of 'em—everything has gone down the toilet. The amount of hard intelligence coming in has dropped off and the number of VCI neutralized has dropped with it. Half the time the target gets word he's on the hit list before the PRU can mount the operation, and he's long gone when they come to pick him up. But what can you expect when every gook in the Phoenix chain gets cut in on ops planning? I mean, Jeez, *mamasans* in the market know as much about missions as the PRU themselves."

Gulliver shrugged. "We're not immune to that sort of thing either, Swain. Your almighty company may still advise Phoenix here, but we have to clear PRU ops with the province chief's office, Special Branch, and the Province Intelligence Operations Coordinating Center. And I might as well tell you now as later that we've had an unusual number of missions blow up in our faces in the last few months. We suspect our operations are being compromised."

Swain registered concern, but he shook his head. "Maybe so, but I've seen the numbers on this team and they're still better than in those provinces where the spook houses have been closed up and the advisory duty turned over to MACV. Besides, at least you can work on your prisoner once you lay your hands on him. An IO with MACV is handcuffed. He can't raise his voice without proper clearance. I had nuns in parochial school who could instill more fear than the average MACV interrogation officer." He shook his head at the crying shame of it, then, in the portentious, slightly smug tone of the insider, asked: "You ever hear of MACV Directive 525–36?"

Again Gulliver had to stifle the sarcasm. "Why don't you tell me about it."

Swain pumped his hips again, scooting his chair flush with the edge of Gulliver's desk, his thick legs bowed along the sides as if he were asaddle a horse. At this point-blank range his close-set eyes looked almost crossed. He dropped his voice a notch, to a level more appropriate to classified information: "Directive 525–36 is the reporting requirement on the abuse of the laws of land warfare. You probably never heard of it because you work at the province level, and the provincial interrogation centers, being under the company's umbrella and all, aren't bound by it. But what it says is that MACV advisers can't engage in assassinations, torture, or other violations of the rules of land warfare, and that any time you see anybody bend the rules, gook or American, you gotta report it. Now, I ask you, Cap, ain't that a bitch?"

"Yeah, a bitch." Gulliver remembered the look—half-amused, half-pained—on George Cameron's face and he heard his own voice quoting with precision from Military Assistance Command Vietnam Directive 525–36: ". . . If an individual finds the police-type activities of the Phoenix program repugnant to him, on his application, he can be reassigned from the program without prejudice." Six months ago, hardly a month after Major Ansell's death, and Cameron, the new P officer, already weary of his PRU adviser's bad attitude. "For God's sake, enough already, Jake. You're wasting your time, and mine. Those guidelines are for MACV personnel and so is the bail-out option. For the zillionth time, you don't work for MACV anymore. Like it or not, you work for the company, and you aren't going anywhere, with or without prejudice, until we find *you* repugnant and toss you out on your ass." Cameron shook his head in exasperation, but there was a fondness in his voice. "And these half-assed ploys to get reassigned are growing repugnant to *me*. Now, go outside and play cowboys and Indians and let me get back to work, or you'll be terminated with prejudice, all right. *Extreme* prejudice. Out, out, out!"

"When I was with the 525th Military Intelligence Group in Saigon I was hog-tied by 525–36," Swain was saying, "so I know it like the Act of Contrition. Directive 525 for the 525th MI. Funny, huh?"

"Yeah, funny."

Swain rattled on, relishing being in the know. "Now, just between us, I know the district-level advisers get around 525 by walking away from an interrogation when it's time to get rough and letting their gook counterparts handle it. A man can't report what he can't see. But in Saigon there were so many Boy Scouts around, we couldn't even do that. In short, Cap, 525–36 is the pits, and I'm not too thrilled with the thought of going back to it. Then on top of everything else, they told me that once I'm back under MACV and their bullshit rules, I won't even be allowed to go with my PRU on missions. So that's why I'm sorry MACV is taking over, and that's why I plan to make the best of the next couple of months while I'm under company rules."

Gulliver eyed him silently, then said, "All I want from you in the next sixty days is for you to keep your eyes and ears open and your mouth shut. *I'll* fill out your dance card. And now that you've told me about your briefings, you can tell me about you. And you can start by telling me what makes you think you're qualified for this kind of work."

"Be glad to, *Captain,*" Swain said, matching Gulliver's arctic tone degree for degree. "But if it's all the same to you, *Sir,* I'd appreciate it if you didn't treat me like some kind of greenhorn. I been doing this kind of work ever since I came in-country. It's just that I've been doing it for the Army rather than the company. And I'm damn good at it . . . *Sir.*"

For the first time since Swain walked through his door, Gulliver was marginally impressed with the man. He had Swain pegged for a bully, and most bullies could easily be bullied. Nor had he thought Swain intellectually capable of sarcasm.

"How about if I tell you how good you are after I've seen you work?" Gulliver said curtly, not *that* impressed. "No matter what kind of stuff you've been doing, you've got a big surprise coming if you think it prepared you for the kind of work we do around here. Airborne and Ranger training is good, but it's not near enough. What else have you done?"

Swain was belligerently proud of what he had done, and his tone said as much. "I started my first tour as a rifle platoon leader with the 173rd in the Central Highlands," he said. "After eight months of line duty I went to my brigade's CRIP platoon—Combined Reconnaissance and Intelligence—a unit set up to coordinate recon and intel-gathering between the 173rd and the Vietnamese units in our area of operations, and that was one hairy AO. We basically did the same kind of stuff your Provincial Reconnaissance Unit does. We had Kit Carson Scouts and other ex-VC types, *chieu hois.* We even had some PRUs working with us, and quite frankly I didn't think they were all that hot shit."

Gulliver declined to take up the gauntlet. He did not necessarily disagree with Swain's assessment of PRUs. Most of them weren't all that hot shit.

When Gulliver didn't say anything, Swain continued: "The CRIP platoon wasn't all gook, like your bunch. It was a mix of Americans and gooks. That's probably why we were good. The gooks would fuck things up and we'd fix it."

Gulliver nodded. Swain might not be someone he wanted to go drinking with, but with CRIP experience he was infinitely more welcome than that cherry Saigon had sent him last time. It wasn't that Gulliver hadn't liked young Peer. He had. A damn sight more than he was going to like Swain, he'd wager. It was just that Fast Eddie had only managed to stay alive less than a week, thereby postponing Gulliver's departure. Gulliver knew all about the CRIP platoons now being used by line units; he had helped train the cadre for the first one. And while they were not as terror-oriented as a Provincial Reconnaissance Unit, they were as good a prep school for PRU work as a man could find.

Swain was still beating his own drum. "I really enjoyed CRIP work, so I signed on for another tour. Sure enough, soon as the ink was dry the fuckers transferred me. I'd been doing more and more straight intel work, so some genius assigned me to MACV in Saigon—to the 525th Military Intelligence Group, like I mentioned before."

"What did you do with the five-two-five?" Gulliver asked hopefully. Swain was a cretin, but he was looking better all the time.

"I worked in the Combined Military Interrogation Center as an IO, an interrogation officer. I picked up some really interesting techniques and I got some experience in working with gook counterparts, because we worked real close with the Military Security Service, ARVN's military intelligence. They were a bunch of useless fuckers, but I figured what the hell, it always looks good on your record if you show them you can work with gooks."

Gulliver smiled tolerantly at Swain. Horny Harry was no prize, but he was Gulliver's ticket out—out of the Embassy House and out from under the cowboys' thumb. Given Swain's background and experience, there was no reason the transition should not go smoothly. Gulliver's only concern was to keep Swain alive long enough to get himself away. And that could prove tricky if Dang were anywhere around the next time the word "gook" passed Swain's lips.

Swain followed Gulliver out into the hard heat of the compound, squinting against noon's white glare, feeling content and excited. His just-completed tour of the Embassy House villa had confirmed what he'd guessed from the start: this new assignment was going to be prime duty. P-r-i-m-o. Number One!

The villa was a two-story French colonial house made of buff-colored stucco, its roof covered with corrugated red tiles. Across the front was a deep veranda packed with wicker and bamboo furniture—rockers, couches, tables. The double front doors opened onto a large living room furnished in more wicker and bamboo. It was a wide, open, airy room, even with the wooden shutters, which were backed with steel plate, shut to keep the cool, conditioned air from leaking away.

The living room, Gulliver had told him, was a kind of common room, open to all, the social center of the Embassy House. Along the wall opposite the front door was a bamboo bar with half a dozen stools, a long mirror, and four rows of shelves holding as many and as varied liquors as an officers' club back in the World. There was an American refrigerator, too, and when Swain had peeked inside he'd been greeted with the soothing sight of ice-cold beer—Heineken, Carling's Black Label, and his favorite, San Miguel from the Philippines.

The common room had contained a complete entertainment center: a state-of-the-art stereo system with complementary records and tapes, shortwave radio studded with exotic knobs and dials, bookcases packed with paperbacks, regulation-size pool table, and, in one corner, a movie projector pointed at a screen permanently fixed to the wall. In that one room, Swain spotted all the comforts of home.

The rest of the ground floor was taken up by a clean and spacious kitchen, a large dining room, a communications room, and four offices. Of the offices, Gulliver's was the smallest and the most spare. That of the province intelligence officer—the P officer's name was Cameron, Gulliver told him—was by far the most comfortable, with a sofa, a couple of armchairs, and a modern wood desk instead of the gray government-issue metal desk he had seen in each of the other three. The villa's windows were made of shatter-proof Plexiglas, Swain noticed, the openings protected by steel bars.

The radio room in particular intrigued Swain, with its jumble of consoles, code books, toggle switches, and running wires. Gulliver showed him a bank of scrambler telephones and referred to the radio system as the "Diamond Net." Swain saw a paper shredder and a receptacle with a hand-lettered sign reading: "Burn Bag." Gulliver said it was for the incinerator on the roof. Just being in the cluttered room, wrapped in a feathery cocoon of old secrets, made Swain feel powerful and potent—*in the know*.

The villa's upper floor housed nothing more thrilling than a half a dozen large bedrooms, each with its own bathroom and small sitting area. These were the living quarters for the Embassy House's four permanent resident advisers and two guest rooms, one of which would be Swain's home for the next two months.

Except for the kitchen staff, which had been busy fixing what looked like enough chow for the New Orleans Saints, the villa had been empty when they went through it. Gulliver had introduced him to the house's two gook cooks, one a perfectly round jolly-faced woman called Chi Ba—which was gook talk for Sister Three—the other a rail-thin old bat called Chi Hai, Sister Two. Swain knew that gook women often were called not by their proper, given names, but by their order of entry into the world. He knew this because he'd nailed his share of Chi Bas and Chi

Hais during his two tours in-country—and he'd had Sisters Four through Ten as well.

But if Swain's new home was Number One inside, outside it was Number Ten. The fleeting, unfavorable first impression he'd had on arrival earlier in the day was now verified by a closer inspection as he and Gulliver stepped out of the shade of the veranda and into the sun-blasted swept-dirt square of the compound.

The grounds were as ugly as that gook cook, resembling any fire base Swain had ever seen in the Central Highlands, with all the standard clutter in all the standard shades of brown—from the tan of the sandbag revetments to the roan of the rusting metal shed roofs to the tepid turd-brown of the earth itself, which had been scraped flat as a parking lot. A few spindly palm trees had been left standing to provide a little fractured shade, but these too were more brown than green, their fronds coated with a thick russet dust. Even the resident dogs, kept around as rat-catchers according to Gulliver, had dun, dirty coats.

The compound square was neatly framed by a fifteen-foot-high masonry wall strung top and bottom with whorls of concertina wire, and derricklike observation towers, sixty feet tall and capped with blockhouses, anchored the four corners. Big klieg lights and M–60 machine guns were mounted in each tower, and sandbags had been stacked shoulder-high around their bases. All the outbuildings had sandbags around the portals, and at the more strategic points—each entrance, the base of the towers, the main gate—were fifty-gallon drums filled with more sand to provide additional firing posts. It was hard to believe that this brown scab was part of the war's most valuable and contested prize: the lush Mekong Delta, Indochina's rice bowl.

The guard posts at the main gate and in the towers were manned by squat dark-skinned troops dressed in tiger-striped camouflage uniforms and armed with Swedish K submachine guns. They definitely were gooks of some sort, Swain saw, but they did not look Vietnamese or even, despite their swarthiness, like Khmers—Cambodians. They were coarse-featured, more primitive than your average gook, like aborigines or some race of slant-eyed Cro-Magnons. He asked Gulliver about them.

"Nungs," Gulliver said. They were ethnic Chinese from North Vietnam who had fought with the French against the Viet Minh and now served as the CIA's Gurkhas. "They have the same kind of relationship with the spooks that the Montagnards do with Special Forces," he said, "but I wouldn't trade you one Yard for a dozen Nungs. They're mercenary bastards. But loyal enough, I guess, as long as they get paid on time."

They passed close by a guard post. The sentry followed Swain with arrogant eyes, openly sizing him up. Swain stared back challengingly, and decided that he didn't like Nungs any better than he liked the rest of them. A gook was a gook was a dink was a slope.

The tour was beginning to bore Swain. He wanted to get back to the villa, back to the air-conditioning and to one of those cold San Miguels. But Gulliver, like some dumb bedouin traversing the Rub-al-Khali, the Empty Quarter, ignorant of even the existence of cooler climes, forged ahead, seeming immune to the wrenching heat, not even perspiring.

They had been outside less than five minutes and already sweat was soaking through Swain's fatigues. For all his time in the tropics, he'd never gotten used to the heat. It could get bad up in II Corps at times too, but not like this. This Delta heat made him suddenly nostalgic for the cool mountain air of the Central Highlands.

Conceived, born, and reared on the edge of a bayou, Swain knew the heat shouldn't bother him like this, but it did, and it always had. Maybe when his military obligation was done—260 and a wake-up!—he'd head for mountains again. Someplace cool, like Colorado. Aspen maybe, or Vail, some swank place like that. Both those towns were said to be chockablock with willing women, snow bunnies, and hippie chicks who believed in free love. Roger that! He'd definitely have to give Colorado a look.

Unless, of course, he could sign on full-time with the company. That was his new ambition, and if he made a good showing over the next sixty days, made a good impression on the P officer, Cameron, and on that guy Steelman in Saigon, he would have a shot at it. Whether or not Gulliver liked him didn't matter. Gulliver was a lifer and a loser . . . Army, not company.

They came to a small building made of poured concrete. Inside was a generator. "This is our power supply," Gulliver said. "There's another generator shack over behind the villa with a backup unit. We can't risk using the local juice. It goes on and off like the refrigerator light in a jock dorm. Besides, if we plugged in to local power we'd be vulnerable to attack. A ten-year-old with a jackknife could cut us off in a minute."

Swain did not smile. He had not appreciated the crack about jocks. He wondered if Gulliver knew he'd played college ball, wondered why Gulliver had such a hard-on for him. Swain had no explanation for Gulliver's hostility. Jeez! Both were Airborne-

Rangers and blooded veterans; you'd think that would count for something. He had only tried to be friendly back in Gulliver's office. There had been no call for the sorry prick to get snotty and pull that Mickey Mouse rank crap. Gulliver was not even in uniform, for Crissakes! He was wearing faded Levi's, a short-sleeved bush shirt, and a holed pair of tennis shoes.

Gulliver still looked like a soldier, though, Swain had to admit, with those wide shoulders and narrow waist, and the long muscles that looked like knotted ropes. Gulliver's skin seemed darker than it really was because of the way the jaundice coloring was set off by the blond, almost platinum-colored hair and the pale blue eyes. Gulliver must have had malaria or hepatitis a dozen times over to get skin that color, Swain thought. It looked like ivory stained Oriental style, by long immersion in tea. Gulliver's strange coloring, together with the haunted face, made him look like some Bataan Death March survivor, or a color caricature of the Grim Reaper himself. All in all, Swain concluded, Gulliver was one spooky-looking bastard.

Swain sneaked another look. Had it not been for the hair, eyes, and height, he told himself, Gulliver could pass for a gook. Gulliver had to go six-two or -three, and about 165. At LSU he'd have made a flanker if he carried a normal weight, say 190 or so. Swain, a much bigger man at 225, had played tight end for the Tigers—one hell of a blocker and tough up the middle on the quick slant patterns. He pictured himself, old Number 85, putting a murderous hit on Gulliver. Welcome to big-time college football . . . *Sir.* He could not help grinning at the thought.

Swain did not like Gulliver and it was not because of the man's churlishness. It had begun even before they'd met. In Saigon, he had heard Gulliver's name over and over, every time, it seemed, that he told anyone of his upcoming transfer to the Delta. He had grown tired of hearing about the great Sandman, about how wonderful, how bad-ass Gulliver was.

First it was Belew in his section at the 525th. ". . . Holy shit, Swain, you really gonna work with Gulliver? The Sandman himself? That guy's a fuckin' legend, man. They say he's got more than fifty confirmed solo kills, most of 'em behind the lines, while the poor shit was sleepin'. That's why they call him the Sandman. That dude puts them to sleep forever, man. I ain't sure if I should envy you or pity you, Swain. Working with the Sandman would give me the creeps. You piss off the Sandman, you better start sleepin' with your eyes open."

Then Major Silverstein, his MACV briefer. ". . . Pay close attention when you get down there, Swain, and you might learn something. One of my Academy classmates worked with Gulliver in Special Forces and has some wild stories about him. There was one time when he was with SOG, the Special Operations Group, and he made a HALO jump—one of those high-altitude, low-opening jumps—into North Vietnam and took out a colonel whose troops had been giving our DMZ outposts fits. This colonel had his HQ about fifty klicks north of the D. The Sandman jumped in, got through the wire, tiptoed into the colonel's tent, and cut his throat while he was asleep. Then, cool as ice, he gathered up all the papers he could carry, took a roll of snapshots of the situation maps showing where the NVA were bivouacked, and snuck back out to meet his extract chopper. All in the space of two hours! At dawn, about the time they were finding the colonel's body, we were hitting their troop emplacements with arc lights, B–52s. The estimates were that we bagged a third of the NVA 308th Division that day. It's a shame Gulliver got into such deep shit with MACV during the Sculler case. He sounds like one hell of a soldier, one hell of a man."

Finally, there had been that company operations officer, Steelman. Steelman had not talked about Gulliver in hushed, cathedral tones, as if he were some kind of Superman. It was obvious that Mr. Steelman did not like Gulliver much, either. ". . . Gulliver is nothing but an assassin, Swain; a hired gun for the company. He is a liar and a troublemaker, like so many of those Green Beret types. I'm delighted that you will be taking his place down there. We don't need Gulliver's kind in the company, and if I have anything to say about it—and I do—he won't be getting another posting when the Phoenix changeover is completed."

Steelman had made it sound like a death sentence.

Swain had not told Gulliver about that segment of his conversation with Steelman, or about what Steelman had said when Swain had asked about his chances of getting picked up by the company when his military service was done. ". . . You mean staff? Hmm, well, why not? A man with your background might make a good hire, Swain. But of course it all depends on how you do in the short time you're with us in the Delta."

A thoughtful look had come into the CIA man's face then, and after a pause he had added: ". . . I've a splendid idea, old boy! Why don't you keep an eye on Gulliver for me? Shoot me a weekly memo; what he's doing, who he's seeing, anything that might indicate his attitude toward the program. It can be a dose of on-the-job training for you. You'll be my penetration and I will be your control. That way I can see just what kind of operative you would make for us. Do a good job for me, old boy, and I promise to do everything I can to help you climb aboard when your military service is over."

Swain had eagerly agreed and they had talked for another hour, setting up a reporting procedure, Swain already feeling like an *operative,* like a company man. The jargon that rolled off Steelman's tongue, delivered with an almost limey accent, only fueled his growing excitement. *Penetration,* and *control,* and *sources and methods,* and *cutouts,* and *dead drops!* Swain had left the embassy on fire, his ambitions swathed in mufti, impatient to shed Army twill for company seersucker.

Thinking of the interview as he tailed Gulliver through the fried compound to the next stop on his interminable tour, Swain was impressed all over again with the handsome, assured CIA man. Steelman had been wearing an Italian suit that had to have cost five hundred dollars, and Eye-tie shoes, too, and a tie Swain had recognized as a Skull and Bones tie because he had once fucked a girl from Sewickley whose father had one just like it. Swain could see himself like that someday, dressed in expensive clothes, sitting the way Steelman sat, with a leg thrown casually over the arm of a chair while he smoothed back lank hair, worn fashionably long. That Steelman was a class act, the kind of man who could be extremely helpful if he were on your side, and extremely harmful if not.

Gulliver was leading the way into a long, low building, an equipment storehouse of some sort. Swain was making little effort to disguise his boredom . . . when they came upon a room that caused his disinterest to evaporate.

"These are all sanitized weapons," Gulliver explained, pointing to several bins stacked with an assortment of guns. "The serial numbers have all been filed off so they can't be traced and they aren't registered anywhere in the world. You can see we mostly have Uzis, Swedish K's, and the Browning 9mm pistol. We use the Browning as a sidearm because the ammo is compatible with both the Swedish K and the Uzi. They're nice-enough toys, but most of our PRUs carry the M–16 for regular ops and the AK–47 for missions in Indian country. In profile the AK makes us look like VC . . . and it always works."

Swain played with the weapons, slamming home bolts and tracking imaginary targets, until Gulliver held the door open and pointedly cleared his throat. Swain reluctantly put down the Uzi he was fondling and followed Gulliver back out into the baking compound.

They passed by a large shed sided with sheets of stamped metal that read, over and over, row upon row: "Budweiser." But

Swain's guide did not explain it, did not include it in the price of the tour. He seemed even to avoid looking at it.

Gulliver was leading the way toward yet another long, low building constructed of yet more poured concrete and painted in yet another pastel. Swain didn't much care what this new building housed. He was sick of this familiarization tour. He trudged on only because he was looking forward to getting out from beneath the Delta sun.

But when they finally stepped inside, he found the air even more stifling than it had been outside; it was full of the smell of dirty men and dirty laundry and tinged with the unmistakably foul odor of *nuoc mam,* the ubiquitous gook fish sauce.

Swain blinked against the sudden gloom; then his eyes adjusted and he saw they were in a rude barracks. A string of GI cots lined either side of the long room, stripped-down bunks without sheets, blankets, or pillows, nothing more than bare sandwich-thin mattresses set on top of springs. A droop showed below most of the frames, discreet depressions caused by the weight of slight sleeping men clad only in skivvies. A few men sat cross-legged on their cots cleaning Kalashnikov rifles, and a few more were cooking over small one-burner hot plates. They were all gooks.

"This is the PRU barracks," Gulliver said, leading the way down the center aisle. Swain followed, meeting the flat stares of the men who were awake and wrinkling his nose at the stench.

The PRU troopers were all short, slight men with lean but well-muscled bodies. Most of them wore their hair longer than was usual for gook troops, and some wore bandannas around their heads like sweatbands, Green Beret-style. Many wore a single gold earring. There was no mistaking them for anything other than irregulars.

Those PRUs who were dressed were wearing black pajamas, the same kind Viet Cong soldiers wore. And all of them, Swain noticed, had that same skeletal, scarecrow look that Gulliver had, as if they had just come from a POW camp where the food was both bad and scarce.

The two Americans walked clear to the end of the barrack before Gulliver stopped at the last cot in line, a spare bunk like the others. A Vietnamese soldier was sitting on the bed expertly sharpening a K-bar with an Arkansas stone. When he looked up and saw Gulliver, he put the knife aside and stood.

This one was nothing at all like the others. The only time Swain had seen a gook this tall was once in a *National Geographic* photograph of a Red Chinese Army honor guard. This slant-eyed bastard had to go a good six-one at least. Like the rest of them, he was wearing black pajamas, the bottoms only, and his chest and stomach were ridged with muscle. He was good-looking—for a gook—with a smooth, clear face that probably camouflaged a good ten years, Swain guessed: unlike Gulliver, whose tracked, ghoulish face made him look forty-two when, as Swain knew from his briefings, he was only thirty-two.

Swain was just thinking that this gook had the gentle, namby-pamby face of a schoolteacher or a poet . . . when he saw the man's eyes. They were so startlingly out of place in the peaceful face that they made Swain involuntarily suck in his breath. They were deep, deadly eyes, bottomless and rifled like a gun barrel, a couple of piss-holes in the snow. They were the most implacable eyes Swain had ever seen. The last time he'd seen eyes even remotely like them, they were in the face of a swamp nigger with whom he'd traded hard words in a bar just outside Monroe, Louisiana. The nigger's eyes had been like these in that split second in the alley, just as he put a seven-inch blade between Swain's third and fourth ribs.

"Lieutenant Swain, I'd like you to meet Captain Dang," Gulliver was saying. "Captain Dang is our PRU team leader."

Almost involuntarily, his eyes still locked to the two hot rivets in the Vietnamese's face, Swain put on his widest grin, stuck out a hand, and said: "Hiya. I'm Harry Swain. I'm right pleased to make your acquaintance, *Dai Uy*."

Swain had used the Vietnamese word for "captain" and that surprised him. He despised the language and its hard, grating tones, an ungreased wheel of a language. He knew only half a dozen Vietnamese words, and never used any of them unless he had to—like when he was working on some refugee bar girl fresh off the paddy and not yet familiar with massage-parlor English. He did not know what made him use one now.

Dang took Swain's hand but did not match his smile. His lips barely moved as he said in perfect English: "Welcome to the Embassy House, *Trung Uy*."

For a second, when Dang came back with the Vietnamese for "first lieutenant," Swain thought he had heard a laugh, a mocking in the quiet voice, but when he checked Dang's face, ready to take umbrage, ready to put this gook fucker in his place, there was nothing to resent. There was nothing there.

After the introduction, Gulliver and Dang ignored Swain and talked as if he were not there, switching easily between English and Vietnamese, using the language that best suited the thought. Swain followed along where he could, full of resentment when they spoke gook, reading it as a deliberate ploy to leave him out. His ire only deepened when he detected a special quality in their voices and gestures, an undeniable air of mutual respect and affection, one that Gulliver had yet to show him. Their tone was one of light bantering, and while Dang never did crack a smile, there was something close to one in his voice.

Swain felt excluded, snubbed, then cursed himself for the feeling. He didn't want, didn't need, a damn thing from either one of these assholes. But telling himself this did nothing to soothe him and his resentment grew when he heard Dang call Gulliver "Sandman." He lets a fucking gook use his nickname but not me, a fellow American and brother officer, Swain thought with a welling of bile. He could not believe it! He stood there fidgety and impatient, anxious to leave, sweating and seething in the crude airless barrack.

"Coughlin's counterpart over at Special Branch told him we really hit the jackpot with that snatch we made the other day," Gulliver was telling Dang, in English. "Major Do says the cadre we brought in was loaded down with documents. Gave us a good fix on the 18–B Battalion."

Dang shrugged briefly and said nothing.

"Goddammit, Dang," Gulliver said with an exasperated grin. "I'm paying you a compliment. Show a little pleasure, for Christ's sake. It wouldn't kill you."

Swain noted with satisfaction that Gulliver was having as little success in eliciting a proper response from this mum gook as he himself had had a moment before.

Gulliver added softly, almost to himself: "Christ knows we've been hunting those bastards long enough."

Dang merely shrugged again and said, "Finding the 18–B will not help the old one."

Gulliver looked surprised. "The old one? You mean the old man from the mission? You know something about the old *papa-san* I don't?"

"I have my sources too, Sandman," Dang said chidingly. "Your CIA is not the only well of useful information."

Gulliver held up his hands and laughed. "Okay, okay! So what do your sources say? Has the old man decided to sue us after all for failing to read him his rights?"

"No," Dang said softly. "*My* sources say the other men came for the old one after we returned him to his village. *My* sources say that the other men kept their promise. They cut off the old one's head, then put it on a pole in front of his house for all the village to see."

Mention of a beheading piqued Swain's interest. He was about to ask what they were talking about when he glanced at Gulliver and thought better of it. Gulliver's face had gone to stone; a new tint, cadet gray, lay over the ocherous hue of the quinine. He looked like a day-old corpse.

Gulliver did not speak for a long moment; then he said in a quiet, tight voice: "We killed him, Dang. Me and you. We might as well have gone ahead and used the K-bar on him when we had what we wanted."

"We did not kill him," Dang said firmly. "The other men killed him. The men who come at night killed him. We did only what we had to do. Nothing more, nothing less."

Swain saw that Dang's smooth face had gone blank again. Then he watched Gulliver watch Dang. Gulliver seemed to be foundering, but there was nothing in Dang's face for him to grab onto, just as there had been nothing in it for Swain a few moments before.

"What about the boy? Number three son?" Gulliver asked.

Dang shook his head. "They made him watch, and then they took him away. They cannot use him as a fighter now—they would never be able to trust him—but they will find a way to use him. Then they will kill him."

"I was going to talk to the province chief about the kid, maybe suggest keeping an eye on him until he was old enough to draft. To keep him out of their clutches."

"Then he would have died anyway," Dang said. "Next year. Or the year after. Or the year after that. Killed by the same men. Nothing was changed but the timing."

Gulliver stared at Dang, then slowly turned and walked off without another word.

Swain trotted after him, catching up as they went back out into the glare. "Hey, wait up," he said breathily. "What was all that about back there?"

Gulliver did not answer him; he just kept moving toward the villa as if he had not heard the question.

Swain swore and fell back a few paces. There he trailed, eating dust kicked up by Gulliver's ratty sneakers, sighting in on Gulliver's back, peevishly noting the lack of sweat on Gulliver's shirt, and nursing yet one more grudge.

2

STEELMAN WAS STANDING in her office doorway again. With her back to the door, Sally Teacher could not see him, but someone was there, and if anyone was there it was he. These late-afternoon visits of his were becoming a habit. She could feel his eyes stroking her back.

She turned and there he was, leaning coolly against the jamb in that loose, arrogant way he had. She did not know how long he had been standing there watching her type, his lips set in the thin curl that was almost a sneer, his lazy eyes at half-mast and slightly mocking.

"Hello, Bennett. What can I do for you?" she asked, her tone all business, her annoyance at the interruption artfully disguised.

No one in the Central Intelligence Agency's vast Vietnam station ever called Bennett Steelman IV anything but Bennett or, more often, Mr. Steelman. Anything folksy or familiar, like "Ben," was out of the question. Not even lapdog-friendly people, glad-handers meeting him for the first time, ever for a moment considered calling Bennett Steelman IV "Ben."

"You can let me buy you dinner tonight," Steelman said in his reedy, peremptory, patrician voice; his Boola Boola voice, someone in the embassy—a Harvard man, no doubt—had called it. "We'll go to the My-Canh floating restaurant and watch flares light up the other side of the river as we sup on langoustine from Vung Tau and prawns à-la-sugarcane. How does that sound?"

"It sounds scrumptious," Sally said, "but I'm afraid it also sounds impossible. I've three sitreps to finish tonight, all of which have to be edited by Hooks and laid on the chief of station's desk first thing in the morning."

Steelman came all the way into the office and flopped down in the lone visitor's chair, hooking one long leg over the arm, his head lolling back in unconscious imitation of his fellow Yalie, William F. Buckley Jr. Steelman always flopped, never sat. There did not appear to be a bone in the man's body.

Steelman brushed long, straight hair away from his eyes, looked down his slender nose, and said with a feigned pout: "These interminable excuses of yours are beginning to grow exceedingly tiresome, Teacher old girl. You have been here three months, yet you still seem to lack an appreciation of my considerable charms. Have you any idea what that does to my reputation, to say nothing of my ego?"

"Your reputation needs no help from me, Bennett, and I seriously doubt that *anything* could dent your ego," Sally said. "Not even armor-piercing RPGs."

Steelman laughed. "My word! Rocket-propelled grenades, yet. You've begun to pick up some of our quaint vernacular. Who says women don't make good spies?"

"Everyone in this station, including the COS," she said. "He'll be right if these reports aren't on his desk on time."

"Our chief of station is rarely right," Steelman said. "What are you working on that's so crucial to our national security?"

"I told you, three sitreps. Well, to be honest, they're only five-hundred-worders, but even short situation reports take time and it's going to take me most of the night to finish them. Scott wants them as crib notes for the dog-and-pony show at tomorrow's mission council meeting."

"That's all very interesting, I'm sure, but it doesn't tell me what they're about, old girl," Steelman said.

"I wish you wouldn't call me 'old girl.' It's too near the truth. I'm almost thirty."

Steelman sighed theatrically and said: "First you toss cold water on my reputation as a *galant* by refusing all my dinner invitations; now you rub salt in my wounds by making sport of my renowned skills as an interrogator. Are you or are you not going to answer my question?"

"What question was that, Bennett?" Sally asked sweetly, batting long eyelashes, an innocent chautauqua heroine.

He laughed in appreciation and asked again, very slowly: "What . . . are . . . you . . . working . . . on . . . Miss . . . Teacher?"

"Oh, *that* question. I'm doing the latest crazy antics of those lovable cartoon characters, the Cao Dai, the Hoa Hao, and the An Quang Buddhists."

Steelman rolled his eyes. "How awful. But I'll pretend interest; why don't you give me a summary of what you propose to say . . . in twenty-five words or less."

Sally shrugged. "The same old song. They're all behaving themselves, more or less, as well they should, considering the substantial brib . . . er, *subsidies* we dole out to them. Except for the An Quang, of course. As we *all* know, the ranks of the Buddhists are rife with reds, overrun by National Liberation Front subversives."

"Don't laugh, old girl," Steelman said seriously. "It's true enough. The pagodas are full of infiltrators. Once they shave their heads and don the robes, you can't tell one from another. Ho and Giap could be in there posing as monks."

Sally Teacher laughed again and shook her head. "Come on now, Bennett. Let's not exaggerate. It may be true that many of the bonzes, the younger monks, are opposed to President Thieu, but that doesn't make them communists any more than being a Democrat opposed to Nixon makes one a communist."

"Oh, Sweet Jesus! Don't be so naive," Steelman said with real annoyance. "The An Quang Buddhists are communists."

Sally stuck to her guns. "They are *nationalists,*" she insisted. "For the most part, they are religious men who only got involved in politics in the first place because of Saigon government excesses, and who've since been forced to the left by Thieu's restrictive policies."

Steelman sighed heavily and turned suffering eyes to the ceiling. "Thus spake three whole months of accumulated wisdom and experience." He shook his head sorrowfully and said in a patient professorial voice: "Listen, old girl. In Vietnam, words like 'leftist' and 'nationalist' are no more than synonyms for 'communist.'"

Sally did not have time to argue if she wanted to get home before midnight. "You sound just like Joe Alsop," she said, getting in one last shot, then quickly added, "but you also sound just like our chief of station, and that makes what you say gospel. If that's the line the Supreme Spook insists on, then that's the line the Supreme Spook will get from me. After all, who am I, a mere woman, to cause trouble?"

Steelman ignored her sarcasm. "That's the ticket, old girl.

Realpolitik. President Nixon is proud of you. Director Helms is proud of you. I'm proud of you."

"I'm so proud you're proud. Go be proud of me someplace else. I've got work to do."

Steelman complied reluctantly. He carefully unwound his rubber-band body from the chair and slouched toward the door. When he reached it, he turned, pursed aristocratic bloodless lips, and said in a soft voice: "Just for the record, Teacher old girl, I happen to *know* that the An Quang pagoda is little more than an NLF front organization. For the last three years we've had a penetration in place at the highest level of the Buddhist leadership . . . on their policy-coordinating council."

Sally's eyes widened and blood coursed into her face. "A penetration? . . . Three *years*?" she asked in disbelief.

Steelman nodded. "One of my best Vietnamese operatives, who also just happens to be a legitimate monk and a trusted *ancien régime* An Quang leader."

"Wh-Which one?" Sally asked with a sputter.

Steelman wagged a reproachful finger and clucked: "Tsk, tsk. You know better than that, old girl. That information is strictly on a need-to-know basis, and I'm the only one in the station who needs to know."

"At least tell me who else knows you have a man planted on the council," Sally demanded.

Steelman shrugged. "That's different. Scott, of course. And a few of my people in counterintelligence operations."

"God damn you, Bennett Steelman! I'm the reports officer for the sects! The minorities are *my* area of responsibility. Mine! How do you think it makes me look, not knowing something like this, when it seems that everyone on the fifth and sixth floors knows? I'll tell you how. Like a damn fool. Why didn't you tell me before this?" She was furious.

"But, Teacher old girl, I had planned to tell you. Weeks ago. Over dinner." Steelman threw back his head, laughed, and disappeared down the hall.

Sally continued to stare blindly at the vacant doorway, unwilling, unable to get back to her work, work now tainted, rendered even more trivial and suspect than before by Bennett Steelman's casually thrown grenade. What else was there that she didn't know? Didn't *need* to know? Their secrecy was one more gratuitous insult, one more slap in a face already puffy from such blows.

How typical of that preening ass Steelman, and of that nebbish Scott, Sally thought. Even her immediate supervisor, Hooks, saw her as little more than a nuisance, forced on the station and on him by the Langley home office, a little lady agent, to be pampered and jollied, a decorative addition to the fourth floor, like the etchings of Chinese calligraphy that hung on his office wall.

Sally had been sent to Vietnam to be a case officer, to run agents just like the big boys. Instead, she found herself doing "woman's work," housekeeping chores. After three months she was still a reports officer, compiling reports from field agents, discarding the garbage and the tired speculation, old intel in new dress, the obvious stuff from the "paper mills," the inflated, faked intelligence from local informers looking to justify their spot on the payroll.

Just temporary, they said; just until she was familiar with station SOP, they said. So every day she made up the station report, sending it upstairs to Scott for approval or additions, then on to "the big shed" in Langley, where the interesting bits were added to the interesting bits from the DIA and NSA daily reports and included in the President's intelligence briefing. And every day Hooks or Steelman or Scott would pat her on the back and promise her a case of her own to run. When? Soon, real soon.

For perhaps the hundredth time in the last three months, Sally felt like crying. While she would be the first to admit she lacked country time, she knew as much about Vietnam as any of them, more than most. True, it was book knowledge rather than experience, but knowledge was knowledge, wasn't it?

It had been a circuitous route that had taken her from an exclusive girls' school in the Virginia countryside to the CIA, via Paris, courtesy of an indulgent father who chose to reward his little girl's aptitude for French with a year at the Sorbonne and a generous monthly stipend.

There Sally had met a number of Vietnamese students, and taken one for a lover. It was her first sexual experience, and noteworthy for that, but the only lasting thing to come of it was a fascination with Vietnam. She had kept up her French studies, but added courses in Vietnamese, taking language and literature and eventually focusing on comparative religion in Southeast Asia.

When she returned home to Washington, she entered the foreign-service program at Georgetown, graduated with honors, and was all set to take a job at State, on the Vietnam desk, when an old friend of the family, a retired deputy director of intelligence, suggested that she consider the agency instead. Sally was just what the company needed, he said, someone who spoke both

French and Vietnamese and who knew something about the political situation in Indochina.

Given the high level of her recommendation, and the way the CIA old-boy network operated, there had been no problem at all. Besides, the timing was right. The women's movement was beginning to assert itself everywhere, and even the CIA, the last word in chauvinism, was feeling the pressure.

Sally made it clear from the beginning that she had no intention of languishing away at Langley, chained to a desk in DDI, the research-and-analysis branch. After going through JOT, the junior-officer-trainee program, she'd been assigned to the Vietnam Task Force. Eleven months later her request for Vietnam was approved, and after another month of "reading the cables," poring over the cable traffic between Saigon and Langley to familiarize herself with the situation, she was on her way.

It was only after arriving in-country that Sally learned how few of her colleagues spoke Vietnamese. Three or four of the younger people. Of the more experienced agents, those who had a language at all spoke one of the "important" languages, Russian or Chinese. Nor did it take her long to look around her and discover how well she measured up. She was a good analyst, meticulous and sober-minded, and a talented report writer, a skill with as much outsize importance at the CIA as at any other government bureaucracy, one that had lifted countless drones above their true levels of competence. Like the COS, Tom Scott.

The thought of her station chief made Sally feel a bit better, and a good deal more worthy. The schmoo-shaped Scott always reminded her of one of those toy punching bags, the kind that popped back upright after a stiff bop on the nose. She could see him sitting idle in his sixth-floor office, a befuddled, talcumed lord awaiting messengers from his barons; at mission council meetings with his fistful of crib notes; showing the flag at diplomatic social functions; the Supreme Spook, credited or blamed by the conspiracy-minded Vietnamese for every zig and zag in their nation's fluctuating fortunes, all while the clever Steelman ran the station for him.

Sally was no drone. The company would not have bucked a long-standing rule and sent a woman to Vietnam had she been. Oh, she knew about the rumors that accompanied her transfer, how the chief of the Vietnam Task Force approved the transfer because she was his mistress . . . how she'd slept her way up the pole, all the way to Vietnam, which, for all its hardship, was still the glamour stock at the CIA. All untrue.

Even so, there had been no way to squelch the talk. Such gossip rarely bothered Sally, and it never surprised her. It was common baggage for any woman who traveled up the company ladder. Conveniently forgotten or disregarded were her strong academic performance at school, the fact that she had been heavily recruited by State as well as the CIA, her hard work since making the decision to go with the company. The truth was that the agency was still an exclusive men's club, the last great male preserve left in government service.

There had been rabid resistance to her assignment, both at Langley and in Saigon. The most common complaint (nothing personal, of course—they'd have the same objection to any woman) was that Sally would not be tough enough for Vietnam, physically or emotionally. Just look at the burnout rate.

Sally thought that she was tough enough, whatever "tough" meant. It was not as if she had been put through the Farm at Camp Peary and sent to Vietnam as a field agent. Her station colleagues seemed to define "tough" as the bicep-flexing style of the operatives she had seen on their visits in from the provinces—contract people for the most part, former city cops or Green Berets decked out in cowboy boots with pointed toes and bush shirts covered with useless pockets and epaulets, swaggering through the agency's embassy offices, flirting with all the *round-eye* American secretaries while their Tu Do Street whores patiently waited outside in agency motor-pool Ford Pintos. Later they would be found swapping war stories and drinking themselves stupid in the bar at the Duc Hotel, the agency's make-do Hilton, their wrists ajangle with exotic tribal bracelets, the butts of their Browning pistols bulging conspicuously, flaring the tails of their safari shirts.

It amused her that this strutting, mannered style seemed so dashing to the station's sedentary pencil-pushers, that so many of them adopted it as their own; career analysts whose jobs rarely took them out of the embassy; brainy, slack-bodied men who had not fired a weapon in years, and then only on the company firing range back in Virginia. A puerile bunch, Sally decided. Still, if that was to be their criterion, she would just have to prove them wrong.

If they gave her a chance, of course. Stashed behind a desk, riding herd on a smattering of largely docile minority groups provided few opportunities to prove her point. She was well aware that if she did not fight for herself, no one else would do it for her. There was no shortage of men trying to get into her pants in Saigon, but precious few supporters.

Steelman's smirk still seemed to shimmer in the doorway, his taunting laugh hung in the air. Sally tore the paper out of her typewriter, inserted a clean sheet, and began to type furiously, her anger and humiliation evident in the deep indentations the striking keys left on the paper:

TO: Mr. Thomas Scott
Special Assistant to the Ambassador

FROM: S. Teacher

It has come to my attention that this station's operations section has succeeded in placing a penetration agent into a major religious group at the policy-making level. For this, Operations is to be commended. Less commendable is the decision not to inform me of this operation and to deny to me the input from a very valuable intelligence resource. To me, this would appear to be a clear breach of sound intelligence practice, to say nothing of the professional discourtesy involved. More important than protocol, this lack of access makes it impossible for me to do my job in an effective manner. I consider the whole affair an unforgivable breach of faith, in me and in the research and anal . . .

Her flying fingers stilled. Two thoughts stopped her. One was that such a memo would seem unprofessional. To Scott it would sound hysterical, a typically female reaction, and proof that Sally Teacher was indeed in the wrong job in the wrong place at the wrong time.

Equally disturbing was a suspicion triggered by the last words she had typed. She had assumed that since Steelman had not told her of his penetration agent he had also neglected to inform anyone in Analysis, and that was unlikely. He could play games with her, but not with Jerry Hooks, an officer of parallel rank. Which meant that Hooks, too, had elected to keep secrets from her.

Fighting back the tears that threatened, Sally tore the page from the machine, rolled it into a tight ball, and threw it against a wall. No one was there to see it if she did cry, of course, but she battled the urge nonetheless. It was *their* idea of how a woman would react.

The thought that Jerry Hooks had known all along hurt. More than anyone, he had seen her work, had read her reports, had some idea of what she could do. He had even, grudgingly, complimented her on several jobs, and had been assigning her more significant tasks lately. He still disapproved of her being in Indochina in the first place, of course, but Sally thought she had detected a softening there, some evidence that she had begun to change his mind.

The urge, the *need* to cry surged in her awhile longer, then ebbed, leaving in its place a cold anger that shook her anew with its force. She got to her feet, grabbed her purse, and started for Steelman's fifth-floor office, determined to confirm this new betrayal.

She went to the express elevator, the one that did not stop at the first three floors where the ambassador and the State Department FSOs—the foreign-service officers—had their offices, then changed course and headed for the stairs. She punched the code into the computerized lockbox, swung open the heavy metal door, and took the stairs two at a time. She punched the code into the box on the fifth-floor landing and, ever mindful of duty, made sure the door locked securely behind her.

The secretaries had gone for the day and there was only a lone marine guard on the floor, an almost bald teenager who recognized her and said shyly, "'Evenin', Miz Teacher," then eyeballed her long legs and switching buttocks as she brushed past without responding.

She found Steelman sitting in his normal loosey-goosey way behind his desk, a leg thrown over the arm of his chair, his forelock hanging over one eye. He was scowling when she came through his door, but when he saw her he sat up properly and his grimace turned into a smile. "Why, Teacher old girl, what a nice surprise! It's not often I'm graced with a visit from you. Change your mind about dinner?"

"I have a question," Sally said, ignoring his question. "Did Hooks know about your penetration?"

Steelman leaned back in his chair, head lolling on the hidden spring in his neck, nose in the air. He brushed the shock of hair away from his eye and finally nodded.

"That son of a bitch," she said quietly.

Steelman smiled again and shook his head. "You're wrong, old girl. *I'm* the son of a bitch. I asked Hooks not to tell you, to hold off until I could fill you in myself."

Sally digested this, then sagged, her rigid carriage collapsing as some of her anger drained. She hadn't realized how tightly wound she had been until that moment.

"You *are* a son of a bitch," she said.

"Yes, I know," Steelman said agreeably. "But I really did want to tell you all about it myself. I still do. And I'd still like to do it over dinner. What do you say?"

"I have to finish those sitreps," she said uncertainly, her righteous anger and indignation beginning to give way to curiosity, to expediency.

Steelman gave her a thin smile, a victory in the lazy eyes. "The information I have for you will undoubtedly mean you'll want to change at least part of your report anyway," he said smoothly. "We can talk about it over a quick supper at the My-Canh. I promise to have you back to your dreary reports in no time at all."

"All right," she said, "but let's make it Aterbea's."

"When we get back, I'll even help you finish up."

"I said all right, Bennett."

Steelman just sat there for a second with a reassuring look on his face, still selling. He seemed, for the briefest of moments, unsure of what to do or say next, surprised that she had acquiesced so readily. "Yes. Well. Good. The Aterbea it is," he said at last. With an abrupt motion he gathered up the manila folder on his desk. Steelman always kept his desktop clear except for a single manila folder. It was a bit of business that the chief of station, Scott, also had adopted recently. A stunt of intimidation.

She watched him roll his chair to his file cabinet and spin the combination lock. "Does that file have anything to do with your Buddhist monk?" she asked as he put the folder in the safe.

"No," Steelman said, shutting the drawer and twirling the dial. "It's a Special Branch interrogation report on what appears to be a high-level VC cadre from M-R Four."

"Appears to be? You have doubts?"

"I always have doubts, old girl," Steelman said, putting on his jacket. "And I especially have doubts about this one."

"Why is that?" Sally asked, not really interested but anxious to find a neutral topic of conversation. She was already beginning to question the wisdom of her decision to go out with him, afraid that in getting his inch, Steelman would press for his mile.

"Two reasons, really," Steelman said as he ushered her toward the door. "First, the intel gathered from this cadre does not jibe with my other sources. The prisoner himself is saying nothing, but according to documents captured with him, the Viet Cong 18–B Battalion—a sapper unit—is presently regrouping and refitting in the Seven Mountains of Chau Doc province. I don't buy it. A reliable agent we've infiltrated into the VC underground tells us that the 18–B is near Sadec, in Vinh Long province."

They stepped into the elevator. Sally said, "It sounds like an innocent-enough discrepancy; VC units have been known to move. You said two reasons. What's the other?"

"The other is the fact that this intelligence bonanza was raked in by Jake Gulliver's PRU and I'm naturally leery of anything that involves Captain Gulliver."

Sally mused: "Gulliver . . . the Delta. That name's vaguely familiar. I think I've had a report or two from him. Isn't he the one they call the Sandman?"

Steelman gave her a quick look, his eyes narrowing, then nodded. "Yes, he's the one." They stepped out into the lobby and crossed to the marine-guard kiosk to sign out.

"What's your problem with Gulliver?"

"A long story, old girl," Steelman said. "Perhaps I'll tell it to you someday. Maybe the *next* time we have dinner."

Aterbea's was one of the more popular restaurants among Westerners in Saigon; it had good food, was centrally located on Nguyen Hue Boulevard, and was efficiently run by Saigon's Corsican mafia. The little bistro had been a favorite of the intelligence community since the 1950s, and for that reason Bennett Steelman did not often go there. But since Sally had asked for it, and since it was their first date, he was more than happy to indulge her.

Steelman studied the wine list with disdain and selected an off-year Montrachet; not a promising wine, but at least it was French, not the usual Algerian.

"I can recommend the clams," he said with a gourmand's smooth assurance. "It's a *spécialité de la maison* and they do them with a topping of cheese and garlic that's really quite decent."

Sally nodded hastily. She would have agreed to anything to be rid of the waiter who was standing at her side, giving a demonstration of how fresh and lively the seafood was this evening, his thumb and forefinger clamped on the eye stalk of a plump crayfish which wriggled in pain. She had been about to order the creature just to put it out of its misery.

It was a busy evening, even for the Aterbea. Every table was occupied and the tumult of a dozen dinner conversations joined with the din of flatware to fill the place with noise. Casually, but carefully, Steelman ran a practiced eye over the room and saw a typical weeknight crowd: MACV officers, embassy people, civilian construction workers from companies such as RMK-BRJ. And, of course, their whores.

Reminded of whores, he saw that the press corps was well represented, sitting at two tables, separated by twenty feet and a full generation. At one sat a group of old Indochina hands, older men, of largely conservative bent, most of them decent-enough sorts, or at least not entirely traitorous. MacArthur of the Los Angeles *Times,* Shaplen of *The New Yorker,* Merrick of *U.S. News,* Beech of the Chicago *Daily News*. At the other table were the Young Turks, cynical and hysterical, bleeding-heart liberals with fat expense accounts, making reputations off the war they professed to despise, Steelman thought with contempt. Buckley of *Newsweek,* Greenway of *Time,* Whitney of the New York *Times,* FitzGerald of the *Atlantic.*

Steelman had little use for any of that seditious lot, especially the good-looking and serious-minded FitzGerald. As the daughter of a former high-ranking company man, one would have thought she could find something positive to say about the war effort. Then again, Steelman remembered, her father had not been enamored with the Vietnam adventure either.

He knew everything about them—who slept with whom, who played the black market, who frequented the opium dens of Cholon—while they knew nothing about him. Bennett Steelman IV was listed in the mission phone book as a junior political officer. He knew the reporters played games, how they tried to separate CIA wheat from State Department chaff by studying the embassy prefixes, searching for fourth-, fifth-, and sixth-floor numbers; but his ops people all had State prefixes, and Steelman himself even kept a dummy office on the third floor, complete with a nameplate on the door and a mess on the desk. If the press had a State Department directory, a "stud book," and knew how to read it, they wouldn't have had any trouble, he thought with an inward smile. Legitimate "Staties" had "FSO"—foreign-service officer—after their names, while the company people were listed as "FSOR"—foreign-service officer reserve. He wondered what the ladies and gentlemen of the press would say if they knew that one of their number, one of the most vocal critics of the war, was a company operative, or that several of their Vietnamese staffers were Special Branch agents.

All things considered, he thought with satisfaction, the Vietnam station handled the media rather well. The important bureau chiefs were granted an audience with Tom Scott from time to time, aware of who Scott was, unaware that the chief of station fed them only what Bennett Steelman advised him to feed them. Some of the correspondents had their own sources in the station, but Steelman knew who those sources were. He kept sensitive material away from them, or used them to leak that which he wanted leaked. It worked out well for everyone.

Steelman's smug reverie was interrupted when Sally said, "I don't know what you're smiling about, but it's certainly a welcome change. You've been preoccupied and moody ever since we left the embassy."

"Sorry, old girl," Steelman said with a sigh. "For the most part, it's been rather a trying day."

"How come?"

"Oh, this and that. Mostly the scintillating news that one of our people in the Delta has disappeared."

"An American? Do I know him?" Sally asked with alarm. She had not heard anything about it.

"It was a Vietnamese stringer, strictly low-level."

"What happened?"

"We don't know," Steelman said. Then he shrugged. "The usual cycle, I imagine—we find them out, they find us out. As I said, the unfortunate soul in this particular case was not up to anything important. It's not so much the *who* as it is the *where* that bothers me. He was working Jake Gulliver's province, and that's one more snafu in a long line of snafus in that territory."

"What do you mean?"

"The Phoenix program seems to be in trouble down there. I don't know that Gulliver had anything to do with this one, but a lot of the foul-ups have involved his PRU team."

"What kind of foul-ups?" Sally asked.

"All kinds. The promising lead that leads nowhere. The arrest order that does not result in an arrest. The ambush that gets ambushed."

"Sounds like simple incompetence," Sally said. "So fire him."

Steelman smiled grimly. "Our Captain Gulliver is guilty of many things, but incompetence isn't one of them. Besides, there's more to it than that. I've been dogged by a sense of *déjà vu* lately. The developing pattern of mission failure in that province is all too reminiscent of a similar incident in which Gulliver was involved. Not directly, but on the fringe, as in this case. Gulliver often seems to be on the fringe of company calamities."

"What incident was that?" Sally asked.

He shook his head. "I really can't go into it."

After a long day of going over boring agent reports on the in-fighting within the Cao Dai sect, Sally was interested. Besides, like so many of those in the company's service, she was naturally nosy, with a personal taste for intrigue that would have earned her the sobriquet of busybody had she been merely a curious civilian rather than a professional snoop. The only threat to a near-compulsive academic performance at Georgetown had been neither men nor social activities, but an addiction to day-time soap opera. Sally adored gossip.

She changed tack. "Like I said before, fire him."

"He'd like that," Steelman said with venom. "The worst thing I can do to him is leave him where he is. That will have to do until I can find a way to put him away for good."

Sally saw that he meant it. His anemic lips were pursed in distaste and there was a subtle suggestion of color in his normally sallow complexion. She was surprised at the depth of his antipathy for this man Gulliver, that anyone could get to the distant, unflappable Steelman. It made her even more curious.

"You said you would tell me about the trouble between you and Gulliver. So tell me."

"I said *perhaps* I would tell you the next time we had dinner."

"You're being a tease. It's not fair to keep bringing up the man's name if you're not going to tell me."

Steelman laughed. "I've been accused of many things, old girl, but fairness is not one of them."

Sally batted her lashes and said sweetly: "Bennett *old boy,* when was the last time someone threw a glass of wine in your face in a public place?"

He laughed again. "You know, I really think you would."

"You bet your ass I would. So tell me."

"I can't. It's classified."

"I'm cleared."

"Not high enough."

"You insult me, good sir. I'm cleared top-secret," Sally said with sublime indignation, still playing the game.

Steelman looked at her without smiling, and repeated: "Not high enough."

When she realized he was serious, her eyes widened. She was silent a moment, then asked: "Would it have to do with a code-word classification . . . something like, say, *Sandman*?"

He smiled. "You're quite the little spy, old girl."

Sally shrugged. "It's not too difficult. I figured they had to call him that for some reason."

"And that's another of my bones to pick with Gulliver. Code-word classifications are supposed to be inviolate, so secret no one's supposed to know they exist. Yet Gulliver's designation began making the rounds from day one. Only four people were cleared for *Sandman:* the chief of station, the chief of operations, Gulliver's up-country control officer, and Gulliver himself. He had to have told someone. I'm sure of it. Probably his old Army buddies in Special Forces."

"Well, if you honestly can't tell me about it, I won't press you anymore," Sally lied.

Steelman sighed. "I don't suppose there's any in-house security reason for not telling you; God knows there are enough people in the station who know, or think they know. I'm surprised you haven't already heard it on the grapevine."

"I don't seem to be on the grapevine. Nobody tells me anything around here," she said cuttingly, including him in her indictment.

Steelman ignored the gibe. "And I'm somewhat reluctant to be the first," he said. Then he shrugged and added, "But since it's only a matter of time before you hear it anyway, you may as well get the correct version . . ."

He paused while a waiter delivered their food. It was a different man, but he had the same fawning manner and servile smile as their original waiter, who now tortured the crayfish at another table. When he was gone, Steelman said: "Gulliver, a.k.a. the Sandman, is . . . was . . . an assassin."

"An *assassin?*"

Steelman, his mouth full of baked clam, nodded.

"Who for?"

" 'Who for?' Where *did* you go to school, old girl? Oh yes, Georgetown. The fathers should get a ruler across the palms. It just proves what I've always suspected: Jesuits are clever enough but they do not possess first-class minds. It's a shame there are so many former Jezzies in the company."

"Spare me the Boola Boola bullshit," Sally said with a groan. "Okay, okay, for *whommmm?*"

"That's better. For the record, he was still with Special Forces, attached to the Special Operations Group, or, as John Q. Public knows it, if he knows the innocuous cover name at all, the Study and Observation Group. But *we* ran SOG and *we* ran the Sandman."

"As an assassin? Do we *do* that sort of thing, Bennett?"

"Come now, old girl," he said impatiently. "I really don't feel like getting into a philosophical debate on the moral ramifications of political assassination. Suffice it to say that this is a war and that you are in the big leagues now. Do I have to give you the standard oration on how the fate of the Free World hangs in the balance?"

"I . . . I suppose not."

"Good."

Sally was shocked, but not too shocked. She had heard things. She supposed this was what they meant by being tough enough for Vietnam. "Who were the victims?" she asked.

"The Sandman was used only against carefully screened targets, top-level communist cadres, military and civilian."

"But why did people have to be killed?" Sally asked. "Why not just arrest them?"

Steelman shrugged. "There were a variety of reasons why we couldn't take them out legally. In some cases the target was too well wired with GVN officials, with enough protection to prevent arrest, or enough clout to beat the rap. Even when people were convicted and sentenced, they would often be back on the street after only a few months in custody. We did not want to take that chance with the truly dangerous ones. In other cases it was a target who kept to the supposedly safe side of a restricted border . . . I can see a look of revulsion growing on your beautiful face, but rest assured, there was *never* any question about a target's guilt. Whatever the case, whenever it became imperative that we, ah, terminate someone, the job went to one of a handful of specialists. The Sandman was . . . is . . . such a specialist."

"He does sound repulsive," Sally agreed with a little shudder. "But in all fairness, if he was just doing what he was told . . . I mean, you can't hold it against him if we ran the show."

"I don't," Steelman said. He took a dainty swallow of the Montrachet and wrinkled his nose. "I should have brought a bottle of my private stock," he murmured.

"Then why do you dislike him so?" Sally asked.

He put down the glass and studied her, sifting the pros and cons of saying anything, measuring out a precise dollop of information to divulge. Then he said abruptly: "Tell me what you know about what the tabloid press called the Vuong Affair."

The demand caught Sally by surprise; it did not seem germane. She shrugged and said, "Not much. Just what everyone on the street knows, what was in the *Post* last summer. The story got good play in Washington, probably because a couple of D.C. lawyers were on the defense team."

"So what does everyone on the street know?"

"Let's see: a group of Green Berets in some hush-hush unit were charged with the murder of a Vietnamese national, an agent working for them. It came out when one of the men got the guilts and wrote to his parents, who passed it on to their congressman. There was a stink, then the charges were suddenly dropped. The accused denied any wrongdoing and no body was found. The alleged murder victim simply vanished."

"The alleged murder victim had a name. Nguyen Tu Vuong," Steelman said. "But go on."

"I don't think I can go on," Sally said. "All the press accounts were highly speculative. No one seemed to know much for certain, and if there was any inside stuff floating down the halls at Langley, it missed me. The victim allegedly was killed because he was a double agent, working both us and the North Vietnamese. And, of course, there was the not-so-veiled suggestion that we, the company, had ordered the Green Berets to kill him when it was discovered he was working both sides of the street."

"That is a damn lie," Steelman said, his voice breaking in anger. "The company got dragged into one of the military's internal political squabbles. The brass at MACV and the Joint Chiefs had been looking for an excuse to rein in the Special Forces for a long time, and the Vuong Affair gave it to them. The Regular Army has never liked elite units, Special Forces in particular. But JFK adopted the Berets, made pets of them, got the publicity mill going—all that romantic manure. So long as Kennedy was Commander-in-Chief, the Pentagon did not have nerve enough even to suggest the disbanding of Special Forces, and by the time he was dead, the Berets were heroes, firmly entrenched in America's mind and folklore. The Army discovered that it still had to move with caution if it was going to go after Special Forces. The brass had to find just cause. They found it in the Vuong Affair. As it turned out, there was no trial, but the publicity created a climate in which MACV could phase the Green Berets out of the war. And they have done so. The Special Forces' border camps are being Vietnamized or abandoned and the troops shipped home. By the end of this year, by December 1970, there won't be more than a handful left in-country. And good riddance."

Sally was stunned by his strident outburst. She coughed to cover her unease, and asked: "Why wasn't there a trial?"

"There was no trial because the prosecution had no case; no body, no murder weapon, no evidence. And they had no case because the defense insisted the Central Intelligence Agency testify. We refused, of course. We had no choice. We could not, and would not, allow some circus ringmaster of a lawyer to start asking wild questions about covert CIA operations in Vietnam with the world's press taking down every word. Even though it was the company, not the Army, that was ultimately damaged by Vuong's death, officially we were quite willing to let the matter drop. It was the Army who elected to make an issue of the case, the Army who tried to use it to jerk the chain on their own mad dog. It backfired."

Steelman's face, suffused with angry blood, glowed like an overfed farm stove and he was gripping his knife and fork as if they were weapons, his knuckles showing chalky white. Sally had never seen Bennett Steelman IV lose his composure. She did not understand it now. His was an unexplained, and seemingly unjustified, rage.

"I can see how you'd think it a mistake for the military to make an issue of the case," she said, "especially after it went public. But it didn't go to trial and the station didn't have to testify, so why are you still upset? And why do you say we were the ones damaged? What did that man's death have to do with us?"

Even before the final question in her string was fully out, Sally could see a transmogrification begin. As suddenly as it came up, the blood left Steelman's long face, restoring it to the hue of the marble floor in the lobby at Langley, a mausoleum color. His eyes, which had been rather frightening, but alive at least, turned back to painted glass, the always focused, room-tracking gaze of a mounted trophy. He even gave her a brief smile, a dead thing that looked as if it had been chipped from a polar floe.

"Nguyen Tu Vuong was not Hanoi's agent," he said with a new voice to match the new face, one under such tight control it rendered the mask futile, fooling no one. His words could barely get out around his implacable fury. "He was my agent."

"Yours?"

"That is correct. He was keeping an eye on the Special Forces for me, for us. And it is my conviction that when his Army agent-handlers discovered that he was a company employee, they cavalierly decided to kill him for it."

"But why?"

"Who knows? With Green Berets it could have been for the pure sport of it. But my guess is that they wanted to make a point; they wanted to send a message to the company, to me. A warning to the company to keep its nose, and its fingers, out of Special Forces' affairs."

"But that's . . . that's horrible! It's insane!"

"Very shortsighted of them, indeed," Steelman agreed. "I have at my disposal so many ways of exacting reparations for their hairy-chested arrogance, their gratuitous insult."

His words were final, the closing of a door. For Sally, the horror lay in the casual taking of a human life; for Steelman, she realized with a chill, it was in the personal affront. She felt suddenly squeamish, and tried to channel the conversation in another direction. "I'm confused. Exactly what was that unit?"

"It was called the B–40 Detachment," he said, "and it came under the authority, but not the direct command, of the Fifth Special Forces Group commander, Colonel Sculler, one of the eight later arrested. The detachment was made up of U.S. Army

Military Intelligence officers in Green Beret uniform, a few legitimate Green Beret intelligence people, and a company of mercenaries."

"But we ran it, right?" Sally said.

"Wrong."

"Oh. I had the impression it was a SOG thing and that the company ran it."

"No. It was not SOG, and we had no direct operational control or input. We did make ourselves available to the B–40 on a consultation basis in the event they needed our help. We had, we thought, an understanding; they were supposed to keep our base chief in Nha Trang advised of what they were doing. They did not. That was why a penetration was sent in."

"What *were* they doing?"

"They ran intelligence nets in Cambodia and Laos. But not North Vietnam—everything north of the Ben Hai River was SOG, run by us. The B–40 used Vietnamese civilian agents controlled by the MI agent-handlers on the team. The Saigon government knew nothing about it, of course, for security reasons."

"But what—?"

Steelman held up a hand. "First let me finish giving you what background I can. Last spring, things began to go wrong on the Cambodian border. Several experienced agents vanished or were killed in a rash of strange *accidents*. Several of the cross-border operations, HALO drops mostly, were ambushed. It was quite similar to what's now happening in Gulliver's area of operations. In any event, the problem was in two specific sectors, one run by a Special Forces intelligence noncom, the other by Vuong. Both were taken to Nha Trang and questioned. The B–40 interrogators used sodium pentothal, the polygraph, God knows what else. According to Special Forces, their man was cleared, while Vuong was revealed as a double agent."

"But you don't buy that," Sally said, taking a cue from his mocking tone.

"Most certainly not."

"What did they do about it?" Sally asked, her elbows on the table, her food forgotten. She was enthralled; she felt as if she too were a player in the tale. But not wholly so. She too was an employee of the Central Intelligence Agency, the raw material of espionage fiction, but in truth, the most dangerous thing about her job was the ever-present threat of a bad ink stain on a good blouse.

"Ahh, now, that is where the road forks," Steelman said. "The Truth sits at the end of the right path, or the left path, depending on the fork taken, on whom you choose to believe. The B–40 people claimed that when they discovered that Vuong was a double, they went to Colonel Sculler, who in turn went to the company's regional base chief in Nha Trang for guidance, and that our man said . . . and I quote . . . 'Terminate him.' "

"Kill him?"

"If I'm not mistaken, that is the accepted translation," Steelman said with a touch of sarcasm in his voice.

Sally ignored it. "And so they did."

"And so they did."

"But that's not what happened?"

"No. What happened is that the B–40, without consulting anyone, planned a phony operation that included Vuong. Once in the bush, he was shot in the back of the head with a gun manufactured in the communist bloc. The body was put into a body bag, weighted down, and dumped into Nha Trang harbor."

Sally Teacher felt a small shudder run through her body, a tremor that was almost sexual. Her dinner lay half-eaten, her appetite long gone. She was horrified, of course . . . but also, undeniably, a little thrilled.

This was a side of the business Sally hadn't really seen before, of which she was far more ignorant than the average reader of spy novels. She had heard wild tales, of course, at company parties, over cocktails at agency watering holes, but she had always dismissed them as war stories, as part of the one-upmanship game those on the covert side loved to run on those on the staid overt side. Or the line of some company Romeo, some GS–12 trying to impress her enough to get lucky, hinting as how he was only home on R-and-R after a harrowing escapade in Bogotá or Bucharest, fudging the details if she pressed, saying, "Don't ask, I can't talk about it." Sally knew full well that the bulk of intelligence work was done by the analysts, those who spent their lives poring over Soviet corn-production reports, not dangling over the Urals under a black parachute. But in Vietnam, such tales seemed more plausible. It was a country, a war, where anything seemed possible. She believed Steelman. The uncharacteristic emotion in his voice and face dispelled all her doubts.

For the first time, Sally felt a slight tug of sexual attraction toward Steelman—unfocused and unburning, but there all the same. It was simple enough to explain; she suffered the occupational disease of the company careerist: an obsession with raw information. Intelligence was power, and of all those in the Vietnam station, Steelman knew the most. He seemed to know *every-*

thing. Even the crumbs he had just passed along made Sally feel omniscient, a vault for terrible secrets.

But while she was fascinated, she was also confused. The story seemed incomplete. "I still don't see what any of this has to do with Captain Gulliver," she said. "Was he a member of this B–40 Detachment?"

"No, but he was working with them at the time," Steelman said. "He was on loan to them from SOG when the Vuong killing happened. The B–40's agent net had generated several targets for elimination in the Cambodia sanctuary area, and the Green Berets came to us for a specialist. They rejected the first couple of people we offered, but accepted Gulliver, probably because he was a Green Beret himself and had, in fact, served with Colonel Sculler in the past. Even so, they didn't trust him completely—after all, he was attached to the company—so they waited until he was out on another job before they went after Vuong."

"But that means he really didn't have anything to do with the murder," Sally said.

"Not directly, no."

"But indirectly . . . ?"

"Yes," Steelman said.

"How?"

Steelman sighed. "Gulliver got involved after Sculler and the seven other Berets were arrested, during the Article Thirty-two hearing, the Army's pretrial investigation. He approached the defense team and told them that he could substantiate the defendants' story, that he personally had heard the agency's base chief in Nha Trang issue the order to terminate Vuong. The lawyers ran him before the board straightaway, of course, where he was permitted to spew out his lies."

"But why would he say something like that?" Sally asked.

"To save his Green Beret buddies, of course," Steelman said with contempt. "He tipped his hand when he delivered a touching testimonial to Sculler, how Colonel Sculler was the finest officer and man he'd known in more than a decade of military service, *et-cetera, ad nauseam*. Then he gave those uncleared Army clowns a full briefing on the Sandman Project, detailing specific jobs—all supposedly to show how the company's Nha Trang base chief, who also just happened to be the Sandman's control officer, specialized in eliminations, how the killing of someone like Nguyen Tu Vuong would be right up his alley. Gulliver's voice broke in all the right places and the hint of a tear appeared in the corners of his experience-hardened, yet sensitive eyes at exactly the right moment. Oh, it was a masterful performance, I can assure you." Steelman's voice dripped poison.

"Did the board believe him?" Sally asked.

Steelman shrugged. "Since the case never went to trial, we'll never know. But when the Nha Trang base chief took the stand, those Army clods treated him as if he were a slug that had just crawled out of their dinner salad."

"Oh my," was all Sally could say.

"Oh my, indeed," Steelman echoed. Then he smiled grimly. "But the Sandman did not emerge unscathed himself. His little performance did not win him many fans. His military superiors were displeased that he tried to torpedo their putsch against Special Forces, for trying to take Sculler and the rest off the hook. The company was displeased that he blew the whistle on the Sandman operations, that he let the Army get a glimpse of the agency's dirty laundry. It was suggested to him that he resign his commission. He refused and hinted that he would go to the media if we tried to force him out. He was told that he'd be subject to prosecution under the National Security Act. He said he didn't care, that he'd do it if he were not released from SOG. What this champion of justice was doing, old girl, was trying to swap a promise of silence for a more palatable job. So the Army and the company got together and voted to bury him in the PRU. With all his hand-wringing over the Sandman missions, we thought he would refuse and resign—after all, the jobs are not dissimilar. But to our surprise, he took it."

At last Sally understood. Nodding, she said, "Well, I can see why you don't like him very much."

Steelman shook his head. "You only think you can. I do dislike him for what he did to the company, but I hate him for what he did to me."

"To *you*?"

"To me. You see, old girl, *I* was the base chief in Nha Trang at the time of the Vuong Affair. *I* was the Sandman's control officer. *I* was the one he accused of murder."

Sally had not seen it coming. She did not know what to say. After a pause she said, "Obviously Gulliver's story was not taken seriously. It doesn't seem to have hurt you. You were brought to Saigon to be a section chief."

Steelman nodded. "Once the gossip completed its rounds, it enhanced my reputation in some respects. It's never a bad thing for an operations officer to be labeled ruthless. The field agents think I'm a god, and my Saigon staff is scared to death of me. But it did hurt me, old girl. Badly. Vuong was killed in my sector, on my watch. It's all in my file. I doubt I'll be getting a station of my own someday."

"But they promoted you."

"They had to. They had to visibly defend me, and hence themselves. Obviously I could not continue on in Nha Trang, home of Special Forces, but to have punished me would have been tantamount to admitting company culpability."

"Surely Washington didn't believe Gulliver?"

"Who knows?" Steelman said with a shrug that said *he* did. "I know that many of the generals, even those who most wanted to curtail the Special Forces, believed him, believed that I set up the whole thing and left the Berets, the *Army,* holding the bag. The Army doesn't like Gulliver, and didn't like his testimony, but his effort served to remind them that however much Special Forces had sinned, they were still Army, and the Army takes care of its own. Even when it's a matter of meting out punishment, they don't much appreciate civilian interference."

"What do you care what the Army thinks?" Sally asked.

He gave a bitter laugh. "Do you know how many generals there are in Washington? They sit on the National Security Council, they lunch with the President, with senators, with the Director. I was in trouble as soon as those blundering Army asses decided to make a *cause célèbre* of Vuong, more so after it got out of control, when the lawyers and the press made a circus of it. The Army began looking for a scapegoat and we were handy. They said the CIA had botched their case, first by its involvement, then by its refusal to testify. Langley ignored them, but it didn't appreciate the heat. No, I've gone as high as I'll go. There was a chance to contain the damage until Gulliver came along. The minute he opened his mouth, my career went to stalemate."

"I can't believe it, Bennett," Sally said, believing it. It might not be fair, but what he had said was probably true. "You're too good at your job, too valuable to be overlooked. Doesn't ability override everything else?"

Steelman, his lips pursed ruefully, shook his head. "I thank you for your kind words, old girl, but I'm afraid the world doesn't work that way."

This time, Sally did not contradict him. "Isn't there anything you can do about it?" she asked.

"I can make sure it doesn't happen again," he said. "I think I'll go down there sometime in the next few weeks, for a personal look at the team's operation. I don't know what's going on, but I intend to find out. As I said, I don't like the feeling of *déjà vu.* And I know something about Gulliver, about his . . . ah . . . associations . . . that lends credence to my concerns. I can't go into all that, but I can tell you I'm not about to let Gulliver finish the job on me. He's not going to destroy what's left of my career."

"Do you really see a connection between what's happening there and the Vuong case?" Sally asked skeptically. "It sounds like you're reaching."

Steelman held up his hands. "All I know is that there's a pattern here that's disturbingly similar to the one on the Cambodian border in the weeks before Vuong's murder. Was it coincidence that the trouble in Vuong's sector started about the same time that the Sandman started working in that area? Perhaps. Perhaps not. I honestly don't know. What I *do* know is that I'm going to look into it."

Sally said, "Well, all *I* know is that everything you've told me has been fascinating in a gruesome sort of way. Now that you've got me hooked, I hope you can keep me posted."

Steelman smiled, a real smile by his standards, with the barest breath of warmth in it. "Oh, I can do better than that, Teacher old girl," he said. "I can take you with me."

"Take *me*? With *you*? To the Delta?"

"Why not? You've been here three months and have yet to get out of Saigon. It's time you saw some of the countryside. Besides, it's Hoa Hao territory. Wouldn't you like a firsthand look? We can set it up for you to meet with a few of the Hoa Hao leaders; you can put a few faces to those names you stick into those boring sitreps. What do you say?"

Steelman had again taken her by surprise. "Well, I . . . I don't know," she stammered. "I . . . I don't know if Hooks would let me go. Or the chief of station." Sally was intrigued with the idea, but for some reason she could not explain, her mind cast about for obstacles.

He brushed aside her objections as easily as he did the hank of hair that had fallen across one eye. "Leave it to me; I can fix it with Hooks and the COS just like that," he said, snapping his fingers.

"Well, I . . . Okay! Great! I'd love to go."

"Good. It's settled. Now, how about coffee and dessert? The peach melba is usually good. Or perhaps the flan?"

Steelman turned in his chair, searching the room for a waiter. When he saw one and made eye contact, he snapped his fingers again and called loudly: *"Garçon!"* It was Bennett Steelman IV at his most imperious. The waiter came running, already starting to smile nervously.

Sally looked around and saw their original waiter making his resolute way toward the kitchen, a sour look of betrayal and abhorrence on his face. He had one arm extended in front of him, his hand as far from his body as he could get it, as if he were carrying something unspeakably foul. Then she saw that he was indeed ushering something quickly from the room, a plump, unmoving object. It was the *spécialité du jour,* the hapless crayfish, a victim of one pinch too many.

3

QUYNH NHU'S HOUSE WAS at the back of a long alley that spoked from the hub of the busy main street of the province town. It was not a proper house, rather a large flat, three spacious ground-floor rooms adjacent to a tailor shop which specialized, as most did these days, in military uniforms.

Nhu stepped carefully along the tight alley, so as not to break the circles of customers who squatted in front of the soup stalls lining either side of the crowded passage. She made her way slowly, pausing now and then to chat with vendors and patrons, avoiding the bold, hungry looks of the ARVN soldiers. She was wearing a brocade *ao dai,* and gusts of furnacelike air, trapped in the dead-end alley and panicking in short-lived dervish dances, fluttered the long panels of her tunic, making her resemble a rare species of butterfly.

The alley seemed to writhe like a wounded snake with people and clutter—wheeled food carts; teetering piles of crockery; flower stands; squat wood stools; steaming kettles of *che;* plastic crates of Ba Muoi Ba "33" beer, and *Co-ca;* blocks of dirty ice, dying slowly in puddles; sleeping mats laid out in urine-marked doorways; lame dogs, flyblown and jut-ribbed; bicycles and motor scooters parked against the peeling whitewashed walls.

Nhu did not mind. The gaudy, noisy life of the street was one of the reasons she still lived here. She drank in the gabble of voices, the whoop of greetings and good-byes, the pungent food smells, the sweet bouquet of flowers, the cries of half-naked children, the clatter of pan covers, the tick of chopsticks against the sides of rice bowls . . . the *life* strewn in her path.

She listened to the slow whir of soothing, imprecise Delta accents and felt, as sudden and as final as a dagger in her breast, a stinging pang of homesickness for her village, her people. In these southern faces, these southern voices, she saw and heard her family, her friends, her ancestors, all the ghosts of her old life. They were here in these simple alley people, the majority of them refugees from shattered Delta villages much like her own. She saw them in the crones with black-painted teeth and gums reddened by betel nut; in the frail, ancient men with cataracts, stick-thin and dressed in cast-off uniform parts; in the barely pubescent girls with prematurely lined faces, an infant already at the breast. They bought and sold, ate and drank, laughed and gossiped—and pulled at Nhu's heart.

Making slowly toward home, Nhu eavesdropped on their excited chatter, the voices full of anticipation, abuzz with plans and preparations. Most of the talk concerned the coming holiday, Tet Nguyen Dan, but all talk of Tet and Canh Tuat, the Year of the Dog, stopped when they spied her. Their faces lit up and they called to her in invitation and held up their offerings, their tributes: bowls of *pho,* cups of *che,* sticky sweets, bunches of cut flowers, Tet candles.

Nhu was popular with all the people of the province town, but she was cherished by those who lived and worked in this alley. They appreciated that she still lived here in her modest set of rooms despite having the means to live far more comfortably elsewhere. And, as ever, they were captivated by her beauty, her grace, her fame. To have a Cai Luong actress living in their midst gave a glitter to their alley, to their lives. It gave them a minor celebrity of their own.

As Nhu passed, the women waved and snatches of the most popular Cai Luong songs popped into their heads. They heard the songs on the radio, over and over until they knew the repertoires by heart, the way the English once knew Gilbert and Sullivan. Many of the alley people attended the theater itself as often as their purses allowed, and for much the same reason that they went to the cheap karate films at the cinema—to take themselves out of the war and out of their disrupted lives for a few hours, to substitute their real pains for the imaginary troubles in the plays put on by Vietnam's reform theater, the national soap opera that was Cai Luong.

"Eat!" they cried, holding up bowls of *pho,* rice cakes, steaming cups of *che*. "You must eat something!" they cried, lifting fly-speckled muslin covers from pans of sweets made of sticky rice. *"Co Nhu oi!"* they cried. Come and chat with us!

Nhu smiled a sweet apology and played the role expected of her, shaking her head demurely, tapping the crystal of her wrist-watch with a slim, long-nailed, regretful finger to tell them she did not have time to linger today. "Next time," she promised, and to cushion the blow she allowed them to press upon her a plate of sweets and an armful of flowers.

That she often did stop to pass the time with them gave the alley people pleasure and pride, and the feeling that they were, in their own small way, artists all. They adored her for it. And when Nhu's Cai Luong troupe, one of the forty national ensembles scattered throughout Vietnam, played the province town, she would dispense free tickets among them. They adored her for that, too.

In fact, Quynh Nhu could do no wrong in their eyes. The alley people begrudged her nothing—not her fame, not her physical beauty, not even her American lover, the gaunt pale-haired one who was rumored to be a dangerous man but who always was so polite and reserved when he spoke to them so fluently in their own tongue. And when outsiders—most often the Vietnamese soldiers who came to the alley for soup or uniforms—made crude, disparaging remarks about Nhu and her American, they all stoutly defended her. It was only to be expected that a great beauty such as their Nhu would be taken by one of the rich and powerful Americans, and it was only to her credit that she had chosen to go with one of the uncommon good ones.

When Nhu, one more triumphant performance behind her, finally closed her door on the alley, she put down her gifts and leaned for a moment with her back against the door and pressed delicate tapered fingers to her temples. A headache was gathering strength behind her eyes.

She was tired, inside and out. At times it seemed as if she spent her every conscious moment in a never-ending play; on stage, in the streets, in the alley, even—through sheer force of habit—when she was alone. She could safely step out of character for a few quiet moments only at times like this when she was closed off in her rooms where it was safe to unlock her secret doors so that the real Nhu—Nhu Quynh, not Quynh Nhu the actress who'd transposed her name to match that of a beautiful flower—could come out for air, for a stretching of limbs. But today she would not have long offstage, perhaps an hour. She had no time for headaches.

Through the thin wall Nhu could hear the animated murmur of preholiday activity from Mr. Tho's tailor shop next door. In the weeks before Tet, Tho and the rest of the country's tailors dropped their preoccupation with uniforms and turned full attention to the civilian trade. Tet was a time when all who could afford it bought new clothes.

Nhu herself had two *ao dais* on order with Tho for Tet. One would have a traditional mandarin collar and the other a boat neck, what often was called the Madame Nhu Look, named not for Nhu the Cai Luong star, but for Nhu the sister-in-law of the late President Diem, the woman who had popularized it. *That* Nhu had fled the country when her husband and Diem were slain in the coup of 1963, but her *ao dai* was still in favor with moderns.

Tho had promised the garments for tomorrow, and Nhu was confident they would be ready on time; the tailor was prompt, and as predictable as the storyline of one of her plays. He would deliver the *ao dais* personally and, despite entreaties, would accept no payment. Then Nhu would offer him a block of theater tickets, and these he would readily take, there being no loss of face in an honorable exchange of services between professionals. Only when the transaction was complete would they get down to their real business. Mr. Tho the tailor and worshiping fan would disappear, and Comrade Tho the struggle-group commander would take his place.

Nhu took up the sweets and the flowers and placed them on the altar of her ancestors. She went into the bedroom and rummaged through a bedside drawer for the packet of Salems Gulliver always kept there, then returned and put it on the altar next to a framed photograph of a young man. The sweets were for whoever might be hungry, but mostly for her mother, who had had a notorious sweet tooth. The mentholated cigarettes were for her brother, who had fancied them—so much so that Nhu was certain he would still want them even though he knew now that it had been the Americans who had taken his life.

Although Tet Nguyen Dan would not begin for yet another week, Nhu was ready: new clothes were on the way, Tet candles were on the altar, her larder bulged with food, her house was full of flowers. And in keeping with custom, she had paid her debts so as to start the Lunar New Year with a clean slate.

But in other ways, her painstaking preparations were sham. She knew that certain of her associates would find it odd, and not a little amusing, that she should observe Tet with such bourgeois convention. After all, Tet was a time for family, and Nhu no longer had a family. Tet was a time for laughter, and Nhu had no laughter left in her. Tet was a time to cleanse the heart of hate and anger, and Nhu's heart was still choked with both. And Tet was a time to forgive one's enemies, and Nhu would never do that.

She knew she profaned the idea of Tet, that she observed the old rituals strictly from habit, a conditioned reflex of a former life, one that had known many happy holidays. Since that content time, come to an abrupt end only two years ago—although it seemed far longer than that—she had spent Tet by herself, shut up with the restless spirits of her ancestors. No longer was Tet a celebration of a new spring, a new year. Now it was a painful reminder, mere accent to her loneliness. Her ancestral spirits were of little help. They made for sad company, polluting her house and her heart with their nagging reproach, their unavenged deaths, their unavenged lives.

Nhu felt them there in the room with her, premature and unwelcome Tet visitors. The pressing weight of their presence forced her to her knees before the altar. She bowed with the proper respect and pressed her palms together. Their sadness commingled with her own behind her eyes, where the pain now threatened to crack her skull. She fought her pain and her burgeoning despair the way she always did, the only way she knew how—with her art. From a source even deeper than the pain, she plucked a poem, written by a fifteenth-century emperor, and to take her mind off her throbbing head, her throbbing sadness, she chose not to recite it plain but to convert it to song, inventing a music to go with the words.

I shudder whenever I think of existence
Sent into life, I go back to death
Intelligence, idiocy: joined together under nine feet of earth
Riches, poverty: a pot of rice cooking!
To struggle? Before my eyes, clouds dissolving
To suffer? Behind my body, very heavy mountains!
Vainly I question Heaven
Yet, I strive to live, listening out for Fate!

Despite her pain and sorrow, or perhaps because of it, Quynh Nhu had set herself a difficult task. Even without the complication of music, the poem was artistically demanding, calling for great discipline. It was a poem of the eight-line form called the *Bat Cu,* and there were very strict rules of composition. In each of the eight lines there had to be seven monosyllabic words, or *feet*. In each line, pauses marking a rhythmic point of division had to come after the fourth foot. The rhyme had to be the same throughout and the tone of each word fixed. The introduction was always posited in the first two lines and the conclusion in the final two, leaving it to the middle four lines to convey the poem's message.

Nhu sang the poem quietly, in a strangled whisper, so that none of the alley people outside might hear her sadness and become distressed for her, so that Tho the tailor's Tet business bonanza might go unspoiled. She sang the poem three times through, composing a fresh melody for it each time, and with each rendition a new timpani of tears appeared at the corners of her eyes.

The exercise helped. Her sad poem acted as a leech which drew the heart's foul black blood to it. The pain in her head faded considerably, and some of her sadness with it.

Nhu looked at her wristwatch, a gift of burnished gold Gulliver had brought from Saigon, and saw that in exorcising her headache and her heartache she had used up her free hour. She hurried to her bathroom, stripped, and sponged her body. She put a touch of expensive French perfume—another gift from Gulliver—at her throat, at both wrists, and between her breasts, then put on a loose silk robe.

She returned to the front room and moved to a window, inching back the bamboo curtain to peer down the alley. And there he came, head and shoulders above the tumult. She saw him stop and talk to a soup vendor, both men laughing over a joke, then to a flower seller; saw him pick out a bunch of flowers and politely argue when the merchant, a young girl whose blush Nhu could plainly see from her distant vantage, refused to take his money. The girl, pretty under her dirt—no doubt a Cai Luong star herself in her daydreams—knew who the flowers were for. They all did. Nhu saw him surrender with grace, paying for the flowers with a smile and a *cam on,* a thank-you. The flower girl stared wistfully after him as he continued on toward Nhu's door.

She had the door open before he could knock, and when it was closed he stepped up behind her, moved her fine-textured waist-long hair to one side with a rough finger and kissed the nape of her long neck. "You smell better than these," he said, handing his bouquet around her slim body with a snaking arm and pressing the flowers to her breasts.

She turned and faced him and kissed him properly on the mouth, then, holding his drawn face between her hands, looked at him closely and announced: "You are so tired."

"Does it show that much?"

She nodded and led him by the hand to a settee with a lacquer frame. When he was comfortable she knelt before him and pulled off his shoes and socks and began to massage his feet. "Your operation was a long one this time, *Anh* Jake," she said, using the term that lovers used, calling him older brother. They conversed in Vietnamese. Nhu had some French but not a syllable of English, and Gulliver spoke abominable French. "You have not come to see me for more than a week. When did you return?"

"This morning."

She knew it was a lie; he had gotten back three mornings ago. She nodded in sympathy and said: "It is I who must leave now . . . tomorrow. We have two performances before the holiday."

"Where?"

"Both in Rach Gia. I will be gone two days."

This time it was Gulliver who nodded in sympathy. "Rach Gia. The end of the world."

Nhu shrugged and said without complaint, "We are a regional troupe. We must bring the theater to all of the people. The people of Rach Gia need diversion as much as those in Can Tho or My Tho or here. They need it more."

"Do you think it's safe for you and your players to go there?" he asked. "The provincial compound in Rach Gia was mortared twice last week."

Nhu shrugged again and said, "We do not perform in the provincial compound."

"I still don't like it," said Gulliver. "Things aren't good in Kien Giang province. Half your audience will probably be VC."

"So long as they enjoy our humble offering," Nhu said. Then, changing the subject: "Are you hungry? Let me make you something to eat."

"No, please, I'm not hungry." He reached out and put a hand on her shoulder to keep her from getting to her feet. He saw her eyes widen in alarm and he laughed and said quickly, "I'm sorry, Nhu. I keep forgetting. I've disturbed the genie who resides on your shoulder." He touched her other shoulder to offset the bad luck and said, "There. That should fix it."

"I am not superstitious," Nhu said with grave dignity.

"You are the most superstitious person I know," Gulliver said, the laughter still in his eyes. "It's quite all right. I'm superstitious too."

"Well, *I* am not! Superstitions are for the ignorant."

"Then why do you always jump when I touch your head, the place where your spirit lives?"

"I do not."

"And why is there a mirror on your front door?"

Nhu said nothing.

Gulliver was delighted. "It's there so that if a dragon tries to get in he'll see his reflection and he'll think that there's already a dragon in the house and go away. Right?"

"I am not superstitious," Nhu insisted.

Still chuckling, Gulliver said, "Have it your way. It's bad luck to contradict a lady."

"Will you eat something?" Nhu asked again, uncomfortable with his teasing.

Gulliver shook his head with regret. "I can't. I can't even stay very long. That's really what I came to tell you. There's a dinner at the Embassy House tonight. The province chief and the rest of that bunch are coming. It's a command performance and I have to be there."

"Do you have time for your pipe at least? It will relax you."

"Yes," Gulliver said. "There's always time for my pipe."

Nhu smiled at last, rose in one graceful motion, and went to the bedroom. She returned with a straw mat, a hard pillow, and a sarong of thin Cambodian batik with a herd of stylized elephants trooping along the hemline. She put the mat and the pillow on the floor and went back into the bedroom while he shucked his clothes and wrapped on the sarong.

When Nhu returned, carrying a pipe and a large lacquered box, Gulliver was already on the mat, his head on the pillow. Nhu sat cross-legged on the floor beside him and opened the box while he ran an admiring finger along the pipe stem. It was made of ancient ivory the color of a nicotine stain, much like Gulliver's face, and was decorated with silver filigree.

Nhu fired up a small Bunsen burner and began heating the tip of a long needle-thin stick over its flame. When it was hot she dipped the stick into a crud-encrusted bottle, then put it back over the hissing flame. Back and forth, back and forth, Nhu twirled the stick, the brown-black sticky ball at its tip fattening with each spin. Nhu watched the growing ball, aware that Gulliver watched her. His beautiful eyes, similar in shape to the Eye of God that adorned a Cao Dai cathedral, grew pensive as they combed her face. But she was an excellent actress and she knew that he saw only what she wished him to see—a serene face, placid as a dead lake on a windless day.

She packed the gummy ball into the hole at the bottom of the pipe's bowl and held that over the flame, then handed the pipe to him, keeping a supportive hand on it, close to the bowl.

Gulliver took the pipe in one hand, near the mouthpiece, and began a long, gurgling draw, the sound of a straw at the bottom of a milkshake. He finished it in two long inhalations, then rolled over onto his back, his face to the ceiling, one arm thrown across his eyes, while he waited for her to pack another. "My replacement came today," he said, his voice dull and muted, trapped in his armpit.

Her eyes did not leave the flame. The only sound in the room was the whisper of her skilled hands—dipping and rolling, dipping and rolling—as she spun the opium on its stick.

At last she said, "Your replacement has come before."

"I know, but this one looks like he might make it."

After a pause she asked, "When would you leave?"

"In about two months."

"Where would you go?"

"I don't know. It's up to them. It's always up to them. Some other part of Vietnam, perhaps. Or . . . home."

"America?"

"Fayetteville, North Carolina, is what is listed as my home of record. And that's where my old unit is now posted."

"You must be very happy," she said, no comment in her voice.

"Not altogether."

"You hate your job," she stated.

"But I'm not Willy Loman. I don't hate my territory."

"I do not understand that."

"I'm not sure I do either."

The pipe was ready and she fed it to him like a mother quieting a baby with a milk-swollen breast. This one, too, was dispatched with two practiced breaths, and when she began to fix a third, Gulliver said: "That has got to be the last. I have to keep a clear head for tonight."

"Such a practical man . . . for an eater of dreams." She said it with a small smile, but Gulliver's news whorled in the air between them like the haze from the pipe.

As usual, Gulliver had no idea what she was thinking—about the prospect of his leaving, about anything. Far from being inscrutable, Gulliver found most Vietnamese easy enough to read. They were not a truly devious race, but were rather straightforward in their legendary indirectness. Not that he would claim really to know them, only that he usually knew what they were thinking, if seldom how, or why. It was merely ironic that the only Vietnamese he could not read at all were the two closest to him—his counterpart and his mistress.

What did he really know about Nhu beyond the healing in her

hands, the calming in her voice? Who was she? Different things to different people, he guessed. To Cai Luong fans she was a star. To him she was myth as much as mistress, a maker of pipes, a sanctuary, his escape from that other Vietnam. And to his colleagues, men like Harry Swain, she would have been something else entirely had they known about her—Jake Gulliver's bimbo, his gook gash.

She was all those things, and none of them. All Gulliver really knew was the here and now of her. Of her past, he knew only that she came from a village on the outskirts of Ben Tre and that her family had been wiped out during Tet '68, when the U.S. Army found it necessary to destroy the town in order to save it. The Ben Tre Cai Luong troupe had been away on tour when the communists launched their nationwide offensive, left stranded while its home was leveled. Suddenly orphaned, a troupe without a town, the cast had spent the next year on the road, living out of trunks, moving from place to place before settling on a new home base, setting up shop in the province town barely a month after Gulliver himself arrived.

He had met her soon after, through Dang, his new friend and counterpart, another recent arrival. Dang had cajoled him into going to the theater one night and there she was, center stage, an exotic vision of Oriental womanhood.

Gulliver had no memory of the play itself, a production as foreign to him as *Guys and Dolls* would have been to Dang. He had been oblivious of the skirling music, of the elaborate sets and extravagant costumes, lost in that voice, that face. He sat entranced as Nhu went through her role in the pattern that was to become familiar to him, starting off in a normal conversational tone, segueing into verse as the action heated, finally breaking into unexpected song, gamboling at the top of the scale with ease, her voice pure and high, as hypnotic as a snake charmer's flute. Thoroughly smitten by the end of the first number, he'd thought her the most alluring creature he had ever seen.

After the show, Dang had taken him backstage to meet the troupe manager, an old friend from university days, and found him talking with the actress. Nhu addressed Gulliver directly only once during that first meeting, to compliment him on his Vietnamese, but her musical voice, seductive even in mundane conversation, stayed in his head, as ineradicable as a catchy jingle.

For the next month he had played stage-door johnny. He saw her every performance, leaving the running of the PRU to an amused Dang, bribing chopper pilots so that he could trail her around the Delta Cai Luong circuit. He stormed her as if she were an enemy bunker complex, giving her no rest, cutting off all avenues of escape. During the show there he would be, sitting up front, his snow-capped head sticking up out of the black-haired sea around him, as conspicuous as a swan among ducks. After the show there he would be again, waiting at her dressing-room door, a constipated look on his gaunt face, a bouquet of flowers in his rough hand. Quynh Nhu had been, by turns, irritated, amused, touched, and, finally, overwhelmed.

"What is he like?" Nhu asked.

Gulliver, lost in reminiscence, started. "Who?"

"Your replacement."

"Oh. The Ugly American."

"You once told me that you were the Ugly American," she said with a smile.

"That was before I met Swain. He redefines the term."

"Is that his name? Swain?"

"Yes. Harry Swain."

"Is this Ugly Harry Swain a strong man?"

"Strong how?"

"Strong enough to survive until it is time for you to go away. The last one was not strong."

"I think so, but I don't know for certain. I'll find out in two days' time," Gulliver said.

"How will you find out?"

He hesitated and Nhu did not know whether it was because of the opium, which slowed the brain's response, or if he was reluctant to tell her. Sometimes he spoke freely to her about his work, other times not. There was never any way for her to know beforehand which it would be.

"We're going into Chau Doc province," he said at last, almost mumbling. "We ambushed a VC team on our last mission, killed six and captured one, along with some papers leading us to believe that a sapper unit we've been after is in the Seven Mountains. We're going in after more intelligence, to get a fix on their deployment. I'll get a chance to see how Swain moves in the bush."

Nhu handed him the third pipe and he drew it down with a hunger that startled her. She had seen his dosage grow from five or six pipes to ten or eleven in the six months they had been together. Three pipes would not be nearly enough to ease his troubled mind and spirit this evening. He would want to make love to her before going off to his feast. She began to prepare herself for it.

"Let's not talk about Ugly Americans," Gulliver said. "Let's not talk about anything ugly. In America it is said that music soothes the savage beast. Your voice is music, Nhu. Soothe me with one of your songs . . . or a poem."

"A poem about what? About love?"

"I thought all Vietnamese poems were about love," he said with a tight smile.

"No, not all," Nhu said seriously.

"Anything. I don't care. What comes into your head?"

She closed her eyes for a moment, then opened them. "A poem about a marriage. An unhappy marriage. One that was arranged for a young village girl by her mother."

"What makes you think of that one?" he asked, searching her face for meanings. It was maddeningly clear.

Nhu shrugged and said nothing.

"I don't care what it's about," he said, giving it up. "I just need to hear the sound of your voice. It's always soothing, but especially when you sing or recite poetry. It changes then. How can I describe it? Like a warm, soft rain. A monsoon rain on the back of a swan."

"Perhaps you should recite poetry to me," she said.

"Please, *Em,*" he said, almost begging, using the term of endearment that could mean "dear" or "child."

"All right," she said quietly. Then:

> My mother was greedy for
> A basket of steamed glutinous rice
> A fat pork and Canh Hung taels
> I told her to refuse
> She mumbled and brought me in
> Now my husband is short
> And I am tall
> Like a pair of unequal chopsticks

Gulliver stared oddly at her, looking neither relaxed nor enchanted by her poem. "And just what is that supposed to mean?" he asked.

Nhu stared back with solemn eyes; then she spread her hands like a holy man imparting a blessing or a parable and intoned: "Everything . . . and Nothing. You must always remember that nothing is what it seems, that there are circles within circles, wheels within wheels . . ."

Gulliver hooted and lunged for her.

It was an old joke between them, something she had once said when he had asked her opinion of some baffling political development, asked what it meant. It was shortly after they had first met, back when she was still leery of becoming involved with an American and inclined to play games with him, testing him to see if his grounding in her culture went beyond a mere command of the language, feeding him a steady diet of twaddle disguised as ancient Oriental wisdom—Confucius played by Johnny Carson.

Delighted with her joke, Nhu squealed and tried to roll away, but his arms were wrapped around hers, pinning them as he made growling sounds and nuzzled her neck. Her hands were trapped between their wriggling bodies, down near his crotch, and she grabbed for whatever she could reach. When she found his penis, Gulliver yelled *"Troi oi!"* They were both giggling madly, but through the thin material of the sarong, Nhu felt his penis go bold with blood, its thick stalk pulsing in her tiny hand, its head throbbing against the batik and making the elephants dance along the hem.

As she began to stroke him, Gulliver tightened his grip and began to gnaw on her neck with sucking, painless bites. Nhu suddenly went wide-eyed and limp and assumed one of her many stage roles and one of her many stage voices, a voice that had always amused Gulliver, an innocent young girl's tinkling singsong: "Oh, please, Great Dragon, please do not eat me! Who will support my aged and crippled mother if you eat me? Spare my life, O Dragon, and I will transport you to heaven! I will make love to you!"

The gnawing stopped. "And how can I be certain you will not trick me and try to run away, Young Virgin?" the Dragon asked with a low growl, maintaining its tight hold on her.

"Oh, I swear it! I do! On the graves of my ancestors!"

The Dragon thought it over. "But it is dinnertime," it said at last, unconvinced. "And at dinnertime *someone* must be eaten. It is written. And you are the only one here."

"With the utmost respect, I suggest that is not strictly true, O Great Dragon. *You* are here. And if it is written that someone must be eaten, *I* will eat *you*!"

Gulliver laughed and relaxed his grip. He raised his hips accommodatingly as Nhu pulled up his sarong, and when it was bunched around his waist, she took the head of his penis into her mouth. It was an American way of lovemaking, one he had introduced to her, but not one she particularly enjoyed, and after only a few minutes she disengaged and pulled him on top of her. He did not object.

When he entered her, Nhu inhaled sharply and then let loose a little bark as he pushed all the way in. He began to move in long, rhythmic strokes and she felt each of them like a bayonet thrust in her belly.

As Gulliver worked above her, Nhu felt a pang of guilt, of sacrilege, shoot through her, as though she were indeed coupling with a dragon. The image came to her unbidden, but powerfully, filling her head, triggered by the realization that she was making love with an American under the very eye of ancestors killed by American bombs, in the presence of a brother shot in the back by American soldiers. As with most Vietnamese, the dragon was no mere myth, no vague symbol to Nhu, but as real as any buffalo that ever worked a field. A contradictory creature, at times benevolent, at other times malevolent, but always powerful, always larger than life. A beast capable of great nobility, but even then—especially then—potentially dangerous. Like America itself. Like her *Anh* Jake.

The idea of making love with the dragon frightened her, but at the same time it fired her escalating excitement. Her legs were hooked over Gulliver's shoulders, and when she looked into his yellowed, straining face she saw the head of a camel, the horns of a buck, the eyes of a demon bulging in their sockets. His ears were those of a buffalo and his neck and body those of a snake. She pushed in panic against his bunched arms and felt the carp's scales under her hands, and when she glanced down to the end of his arm she saw the paw of the tiger and the claw of the eagle. She was fornicating with the Dragon!

The enormity of her sin struck her with a violent force. But even as her brain exploded with it, there was no denying a simultaneous detonation in her loins. The storied power of the Dragon was evident in every stroke as it plowed roughly into her belly, over and over. She could feel the scalding penis inside her, monstrous and pink out of its sheath, and felt herself coming to orgasm. She tried to hold back, sure that if she did not, both her offense and her damnation would be sealed.

She yelled out—*"Oi! Oi!"*—and began to buck wildly. The Dragon, mistaking her terror for passion, rumbled low in its armored neck and doubled its effort.

Nhu tried to speak, tried to call a halt to this unholy act, but no sound came from her throat. The only sounds were of ragged breathing and the wet slap of bellies. She was only vaguely aware that even as her mind screamed its protest, her pelvis was in revolt, pumping back at the beast. And as she felt the cataclysm below start to unfold, she convulsed and pulled her monstrous lover to her, running frenzied hands up and down its back, over the eighty-one scaly points along its spine. Then she arched her back, screamed, and had her release, her mouth open in a perfect O, her damp eyes helplessly locked to the animal's own wild face, where long barbels hung from the corners of its gasping mouth, where the brilliant, glittering wink of a precious stone shone from under its bright, lolling tongue.

It took a few minutes for their breathing to return to normal and for the last palsied tremors to run their course.

At last Gulliver got up to dress. Nhu rolled over onto her stomach, the weave of the straw mat showing in a red pattern on her back, and began to sob quietly.

"*Em,* don't cry," he said, tucking in his shirttail.

When she kept on, he knelt on the floor beside her and ran his hand along her back and over the suede skin of her compact buttocks. He could feel the heat still rising from the moist, matted terminus where the two perfect moons came together at the bottom.

"Please don't cry. We both knew this time would come," he said, misreading her tears. "We still have two months."

When she still did not respond, Gulliver sighed and got to his feet. He looked down at her shaking back and said in a soft voice, "*Em,* I've got to go now. I'll see you when you get back from Rach Gia. We can talk about it then." He bent, kissed her softly between the shoulder blades, and left.

Nhu lay there awhile longer, unsure of who or what she was crying over, her body aching, her head thick as elephant grass with so many thoughts, each at odds with the next. She hated her weakness, and her strength. The trouble was always the same . . . there were so many roles. She had played so many characters, she could no longer remember what was real. Plays within plays . . . circles within circles, wheels within wheels.

The room had grown dark. Night had fallen over the town, coming early to the back of the alley, where the only direct light was at midday when the sun was straight overhead. Nhu's fluttery weeping abated, then ceased. The sweet clinging odor of opium still lingered in the room.

Finally she rose, locked the front door, and lit the Tet candles, padding naked past the electric light switch, not yet ready for full illumination and the accusatory stares of her ancestors. Skirting the altar, she went into her bathroom and urinated, placing her small feet on the large footmarks and squatting over the hole in the floor that was her toilet. Then she filled a chipped enamel basin with warm, soapy water and vinegar and squatted again, douching herself thoroughly. When she finished, she bathed and perfumed her body once more and put on a fresh silk robe.

When she returned to the front room, he was already there, sitting still as a headstone in the murky light of the candles.

Nhu started with a sharp intake of breath and her hand flew to her throat. She glanced at her door. Still locked. "H-how did you get in?"

"There are ways. It doesn't matter," he said evenly. He sniffed ostentatiously and added in the same neutral tone: "The stench of your coupling is still strong. Open a window."

Nhu, humiliated, complied without comment. To change the subject, she asked, "Are you hungry?"

"Yes. But I will eat later. When duty is done."

He ran his eyes around the room, taking in the candles, the flowers, the altar, and its pile of offerings. "I can see that Quynh Nhu is all ready for Tet," he said.

"I am well aware that you consider it a silly business," she said, both defiance and defensiveness in her voice.

He merely shrugged. "Who am I to say? Even the other men, who are said to be godless men, observe Tet and call a truce."

"With one exception, Mau Than, the Year of the Monkey," Nhu said, a catch in her voice.

"Yes, with one exception," he said softly.

"We must not forget the exception," she said, making her point unnecessarily, her voice tight with emotion.

"None of us will forget that Tet, *Em*. It was a costly one . . . for everyone," he said gently, watching her closely, knowing that she, of all people, would not forget the Year of the Monkey. Her memory was what made her so valuable.

"But this Tet and the Year of the Dog are still several days away," Nhu said, a new, hard edge to her voice.

"Yes, several days away." Then, after a pause, he said, "The bait has been swallowed whole."

"I know. He told me about the captured documents."

Neither of them said anything for a moment; then Nhu murmured, "It is a great tragedy about the . . . bait."

"The one who was captured was a volunteer, specifically trained to endure interrogation."

"The six men who died were not volunteers," Nhu said cuttingly. "Or were they specifically trained to be corpses?"

"There have been thirty years of sacrifice, Nhu," he said sharply. "I should not think that you, above all, would need reminding."

"It is still a great tragedy that men had to die," she insisted.

"What is done is done," he said calmly. "Now, listen to me. The news I have is for Comrade Hoa Binh of the regional coordinating committee. Comrade Hoa Binh only. Do not tell Tho. Tho is authorized only to give you information, not to receive it from you. He does not know about me, and he must never know. Now: in two days' time, a twenty-man PRU team will go into Chau Doc, to the Seven Mountains, to hunt the 18–B Battalion."

"I know. He told me that, too."

He looked at her in cold appraisal. "It seems I can tell you nothing new. I am impressed. But then, you have always had very special talents."

Nhu squirmed under his hard glance. She pulled her robe tight to her body, looked away, and asked: "What will happen now?"

"That is no concern of yours."

"Will he be killed?"

"Comrade Hoa Binh is tired of waiting for you to do it."

She paused, then said, "It is only that he will be gone in two months' time anyway."

"That is two months during which we would have to suffer *his* special talents."

"It is only two months," she repeated weakly.

"A moment ago you spoke like one of the avenging angels found in their Scripture. Now you talk like . . . like a woman." In his mouth it sounded like something weak and shameful. "Is the American so powerful a lover he makes you forget what his people and their puppets did to your parents? Your brother?"

"No, I have not forgotten!" Nhu said heatedly. Then, in a calmer voice: "But he had nothing to do with the deaths of my parents or my brother. He is different, not like all the others. You have said so yourself."

"I know what I said."

"Can't you help him?" she asked, unable to keep the plea out of her voice.

When he did not answer, she added: "I believe him when he says that he hates his work."

"I believe him too," he said quietly. "But he is very good at it, nonetheless. And to Comrade Hoa Binh, that makes him dangerous."

Nhu, biting her lip, did not respond, and he shrugged and said: "In any case, such decisions are not ours to make." When she remained silent, he made a sweeping gesture toward the Tet decorations and added: "Besides, is not everything in the lap of fate? A proper bourgeois, a religious person like yourself, should know that."

"Why must you always mock me?" she asked.

He rose and came to her and slipped the robe from her shoulders, then put his hands over her small dark-tipped breasts, massaging them gently. Her nipples hardened under his touch. "I do not mock you, Nhu," he said in a whisper. "I would never mock perfection."

He stepped away from her and began to undress. Even in the dim, wobbly light of the Tet candles, Nhu could see his face clearly, in every detail. Had the room been as black as the inside of a tiger's belly she would have been able to see it clearly. They could pluck both her eyes from her head and she would still see it. It was burned deep in her brain, her heart, her very soul. A wide, flat, smooth face, the color of burnt butter.

4

THE EMBASSY HOUSE'S FLEET of Ford Broncos had been sent out into the province town to collect that evening's dinner guests, and now the returning vehicles were stacked up at the gate, their headlamps stabbing deep into the compound, their cargoes being carefully checked against a manifest by unsocial Nung sentries.

The four tower searchlights—each one forty inches in diameter and as fulgent as half a billion candles—were lit up as well, one targeted with blinding inhospitality on the activity at the entrance, the other three trained outward, sweeping the bulldozed approaches to the compound, on the lookout for party crashers.

The Nungs manning the tower machine guns were alert and nervous; the last attack had come just six months ago, on an occasion much like this one, during a party. The P officer, Major Ansell, had been killed, along with four PRUs and two Nungs. The survivors still laughed when they remembered the sight of the then-new PRU adviser, Captain Gulliver, working the .50-caliber mounted on the villa's roof, bare-ass-naked, his private parts flopping wildly, bouncing up to slap his belly with every buck of the machine gun. It was funny . . . now.

After verification at the gate, the Broncos pulled up to the villa one by one to deposit their loads, like limousines arriving at a Hollywood premiere. The drivers, Nung warriors pressed into service as chauffeurs and chafing at the insult, manned the doors for their passengers with stiff, exaggerated salutes; the PRUs riding shotgun piled out with a matching panache, their fingers in the trigger guards of their M–16s.

The CIA province team, Gulliver and Swain included, had gathered on the veranda in a welcoming party. As the ranking resident, Cameron was playing the role of official host and greeter. The P officer's perspiring face had the roseate, slightly stunned look it got whenever he had too much to drink. He was already half-drunk, had been since lunch.

Gulliver made no effort to welcome the arrivals. He hung back near the door that opened onto the common room, a forced smile of sociability on his face, as out of place as a grin on a cadaver. The music from the loudspeakers just inside the door beat insistently in his ears, an unrelenting combustible noise that joined forces with the opium he had taken earlier to fill his head with a volatile, disorienting gas.

In retaliation, his head was playing games with the rest of him. Now and then it would float off his shoulders to sail overhead like a scanning falcon, his mind's eye detached and a little bemused as it took in the convivial scene, watching Cameron and the others step up to greet the guests with firm handshakes and limp jokes, the white-jacketed servants close behind with nervous smiles and trays heavy with highballs.

From his disembodied vantage, Gulliver could rubberneck without comment, the ill-at-ease Jake Gulliver under scrutiny along with the others, as disapproving of his own deportment as of any. He had not had time for a shower, and Nhu's smell, rising off his body like a hissing steam, was still strong, a sensuous blend of incense, perfume, and sweat.

Gulliver grinned inanely and shook a hand that came his way without noticing whom he was greeting. Then he shook his head to reunite his various parts. His eyes, back where they belonged, flitted about for an ally, but Dang was nowhere in evidence. He had not seen his counterpart all afternoon, not since his midday visit with Swain to the PRU barracks.

The drivers had been briefed to deliver their passengers in ascending order of rank—with the last, grand entrance reserved for Colonel Minh, the province chief—and their collection run through the town had been carried out with the synchronized precision of a military operation. Accordingly, Majors Do and Ngoc, the provincial commanders of the National Police Special Branch and the National Police Field Force, were first to arrive. Of equal rank, they were simultaneously ferried up the circular driveway from opposite directions, their drivers cutting engines at the same instant, stopping nose-to-nose at the foot of the steps with neither enjoying so much as an inch in advantage. It was a drill the Nungs had practiced all afternoon.

Major Do of Special Branch, a veteran policeman trained by Interpol and too Europeanized to worry about insignificant matters of face, was first up the steps, sweeping impatiently past Major Ngoc of Field Force, who hung back, determined to have his petty protocol victory.

The sensible Major Do was in mufti this torpid evening: wash-and-wear slacks and a shirt made from banana-leaf fiber. More in tune with his calling was a Walther PPK–38 that rode in a holster fixed to his belt, its pearled grips clearly visible through the fibrous, gauzy fabric of his shirttail. The pistol was a gift from President Thieu and it was rumored that Do never went anywhere without it, not even to bed.

Major Do was a whippet of a man, with a narrow frame and a skinny, feral face. Everything about him was thin. He had a thin nose, thin lips, a thin Gilbert Roland mustache—the solitary vanity of an otherwise no-nonsense personality—and he combed his thinning hair straight back, cementing it down with an uncharacteristic thick lading of brilliantine. Major Do always made Gulliver think of a sleek and dangerous animal, the illicit issue of a breeding experiment gone awry, a cross between a wolverine and a Doberman.

Major Ngoc followed, the quick antidote to Major Do. In spite of the sticky night, Ngoc was resplendent in a woolen dress uniform gleaming with brass and an impressive array of medals, most of which had been awarded *to* Major Ngoc *by* Major Ngoc. His precisely creased trousers were bloused into glossy U.S. paratrooper boots and he wore a powder-blue beret and a matching scarf. He'd ordered that the same color-coordinated accessories be issued every man in his command, squandering funds Saigon had earmarked as a rations supplement for his men's families. Ngoc was as vain as Do was homely, as thick as Do was brilliant.

Cameron introduced the two officers to Swain, who'd been stuck to the P officer's side like spruce tar all evening, and Gulliver heard Swain laugh loudly at something Major Ngoc said—much too loudly, given the usual caliber of the major's wit. Swain was enjoying himself, as excited as a puppy at a picnic.

Ngoc helped himself to a whiskey and lingered to chat with Cameron and Swain, while Major Do, who disapproved of strong drink, took a *Co-ca* and joined his counterpart, Bill Coughlin, a one-time Philadelphia homicide detective now on contract with the agency. They moved away from the others and whispered in French—some postscript to the day's business.

Next to arrive was the PSA, Colonel Edward Sloane, the province senior adviser. The "Colonel" had been retired from the U.S. Army for more than a year, but he still appreciated a salute when he could get one. He got one this evening from Major Ngoc, complete with a Prussian heel click. He would not get one from Gulliver. Gulliver had little use for any of the American country team officials, and none at all for the PSA. Sloane was the most incompetent person, civilian or military, Gulliver had seen in his nearly seven years in-country—the embodiment of the misplaced Rotarian abroad. Gulliver did not understand how any man could spend two full tours in Vietnam without learning at least something about the country and its people. Even the fact that Sloane had spent both years in the climate-controlled tomb of Pentagon East, the labyrinthian MACV headquarters at Tan Son Nhut, could not explain it.

In his loud aloha shirt and matching smile, Sloane looked more like a mainland tourist at a Don Ho concert than the highest-ranking American official in the province. He bellied up to the small group clogging the head of the steps and greeted each man there with singular warmth, his elastic grin expanding improbably when Cameron introduced him to Swain. The PSA shook Swain's hand with unquestionable sincerity, patting it with his free hand to lend an emphasis to his welcome. Then he took a gin and tonic from a hovering servant—bestowing a quick politician's smile even upon the lowly houseboy—and clapped a friendly, gathering arm around Ngoc's epauletted shoulders, mindlessly disturbing the genie residing there. Sloane was said by many to be the most friendly and considerate man in the province. Had he known of the genie, or even that Vietnam had genies, he surely would have found some other way to show his delight at seeing Ngoc.

Sloane liked and admired Ngoc, as he did any Vietnamese who spoke English. Like many Americans, he equated a command of English with competence. The reverse also applied; he was uncomfortable with Vietnamese who did not speak English. It was his litmus test, and it explained why he thought highly of Ngoc and the province chief, Colonel Minh, but not Major Do, who not only lacked English but also compounded his insult to the United States by speaking French.

Gulliver smiled as he watched Sloane daub the group with bonhomie. He knew, as Bill Coughlin knew, that Major Do had excellent English. Do simply chose not to reveal it to most people. It kept his dealings with men like Colonel Sloane to a minimum.

Cameron was just sneaking a concerned look at his watch when the province chief's Bronco came through the gate and up the driveway at last, his personal bodyguard trailing close behind in an open jeep with M–60 machine guns mounted front and back. Except for Chuck Riesz, adviser to the Provincial Interrogation Center and busy this evening with a prisoner, and Dang, who should have been there but was not, the cream of the province Phoenix program was now gathered at Embassy House. One round could get us all, Gulliver thought . . . and the world would be a better, and safer, place for it.

Everyone except Gulliver and Major Do made a fuss over the province chief's arrival, even Coughlin, who left Do in mid-sentence to worm a path through the cluster at the head of the steps. The abandoned Do joined Gulliver by the door, the two of them trading glances and brief strained smiles.

Colonel Duong Van Minh took great pains to let everyone, and his American allies especially, know how demanding his duties as the highest government authority in the province were, and how hard he worked to discharge them. As a personal and political crony of President Thieu, Minh did not need the approval of the Americans to hold on to his office, but it could only please Doc Lap Palace that he had it. His adviser and counterpart, the considerate PSA, Colonel Sloane, rarely mentioned Minh in correspondence with Saigon without tacking the adjective "tireless" in front of his name.

To reinforce the impression that while a meal with his American friends was always a delight, it came only at expense of an impossible schedule, the colonel had come directly from his office in the provincial compound without stopping by his villa for a change of clothes. His workaday uniform of combat fatigues was stretched over his corpulence like a sausage casing, and his bloated circumference was girdled by a web belt supporting the weight of a .45-caliber automatic. Minh's pistol, like Do's, also was a gift from the President, but in keeping with the discrepancy in rank, its grips were made of unblemished ivory rather than mottled mother-of-pearl.

Minh waded into his boisterous welcome as though elected and not appointed to office, shaking hands all around, doling out his winning smile, his proud gold tooth reflecting the limelight. The scene made Gulliver think of a Mafia chieftain at a funeral. He saw Minh laugh, setting 260 pounds aquiver, all except his eyes, which remained lost and secret, buried in the fatty folds of his moon face. His hail-fellow-well-met manner was not unlike Sloane's, but Minh used his to mask a good mind. It was a mind more cunning than intelligent, but for Vietnam's soldier-politicians, one was as good as the other. First among Gulliver's many beefs with the weak, unsuspecting Sloane was that the PSA was no match for his crafty counterpart. It meant that the other Americans had to spend more time on their toes.

They spent an hour on the veranda. Gulliver, drinking beer from the bottle, spoke only when spoken to, which was not often. His head had conquered its wanderlust, but he did not feel any better. He wished he were back with Nhu, with his head in her lap while she massaged his temples, the way she often did after he'd had his pipes.

Her response to today's lovemaking had been uncommonly violent. His talk of leaving had something to do with it, no doubt. He could still hear the sound of her weeping, as awful as a scalpel's silent scream; it was the first time he had ever heard her cry.

Maybe he should have done it differently, rationed his news, done more to prepare her. She was an artist, after all, sensitive by definition. But he had never thought of her as being vulnerable in that way. It was always Nhu who was in control, who did the comforting. Besides, it wasn't as if there had been talk of love between them. Need and release, yes; curiosity and discovery, yes; but never love. He was not one to confuse exoticism with love, and neither was she. There came a point where exoticism ruled out love. From the onset they had agreed upon the impracticality of a shared future. He came from a country that acknowledged only the future, she from a country that could not even presume to have a future. She did not want to go to America. He could not spend forever in Vietnam.

From inside came the polite tinkling of Chi Ba's dinner bell and the crowd on the porch began a slow migration toward the dining room. They crossed through the common room, still loud with talk and laughter, chugging down the dregs of their drinks, clearing palates in anticipation of the superb dinner wines for which the Embassy House was renowned.

Gulliver came last, a trailing spark in the tail of Colonel Minh's comet. He was stalling. The evening crouched ahead like a ravenous wolf. He would rather be out in the paddies laying in an ambush than at that table, where an ambush of a different sort awaited. Colonel Minh had been eyeballing him, and while he had not said anything, Gulliver knew the province chief was only conserving ammo until his target was in range across the lemon chicken. Then he would fire his chiding questions about the blown missions, a kindly father scolding a prodigal son, all done with a smile that never got through the fat to the eyes.

That last snatch, with its good intel on the 18–B, would temper the criticism, but it would not deter it. Minh was covering his ass with Saigon by laying it on the PRU—and the Americans were covering theirs by going along with him. Sloane and the others, fearing contamination, had kept clear of Gulliver all evening. Only Major Do had braved so much as a smile, and only because Special Branch, which proposed most PRU targets, had been wounded by Minh's verbal ricochets.

Gulliver was just setting his half-finished beer on the bamboo bar and steeling himself for the treacherous passage into dinner when Dang walked through the front door and into the common room. Gulliver was so happy to see him he did not laugh at Dang's costume—a flowered sport shirt, chinos, and sandals—although it was funny to see Dang in civvies.

"Here comes the cavalry, a day late and a dollar short as usual," Gulliver said gruffly. "Where in the hell have you been? I could have used a little company tonight."

"I could have used your company tonight, too, Sandman," Dang said with what passed for a smile, his lips pursed as if he had been eating alum.

"Where have you been, anyway?"

Dang paused, then said, "On . . . a mission."

"A mission? What mission? There weren't any operations scheduled for today."

Dang paused again before answering: "A special."

"Awww, Jesus Christ! Not again!"

Dang shrugged and nodded.

"Who was the target this time?" Gulliver asked hotly.

"Do you really want to know? Does it matter?"

"Fuckin'-A I want to . . . No, no, you're right. It doesn't matter. I don't want to know. What I want is to break Minh's fat neck."

"Colonel Minh does not have a neck," Dang said.

Gulliver had been introduced to Minh's "specials" soon after his arrival in the province. One, then another, and another, targets not quite right, unlikely members of the Viet Cong infrastructure—an Indian bank officer, a prominent local businessman, an ARVN battalion commander—all marked for elimination.

Minh's special snuff orders always came down the same way: Captain Bich, Major Do's deputy at Special Branch, would hand-deliver it to the PRU barracks at the Embassy House, an unmarked envelope containing a name, an address, and a picture for positive identification, usually taken with a zoom lens. The order was never signed.

It was the absence of an authorization signature that first had drawn Gulliver's suspicion, but when he had tried to confirm the hit with Cameron, the P officer's ocherous boozer's eyes had filmed over with evasiveness.

"Uh, yeah, uh . . . it's, uh . . . aw, fuck it. Look, Jake, don't worry about authorization. Just do it, okay? Trust me. It's legit," Cameron had said finally.

"What do you mean, legit?" Gulliver had asked. "Nothing is legit without a signature. Who says it's legit?"

"Special Branch." George Cameron's vein-stitched eyes had wandered the room.

"*Who* at Special Branch?"

"The top banana himself. Major Do."

Gulliver could get no more from Cameron, so he had tried to check it out himself, making the short trip across town to Special Branch headquarters in the provincial compound to see the police chief.

Major Do had been uncomfortable, but he'd confirmed the order. "It is a special order from the Province Intelligence Operations Coordinating Center," he said, holding up both his hands to show Gulliver just how tied they were.

"Can I see the finger card on this man?" Gulliver had asked. Under Phoenix program rules, only three accusations were needed to brand someone as VCI, a part of the Viet Cong infrastructure. With the first accusation, a "finger card," a Special Branch file, was started. No other action was taken; there was no investigation into the validity of the charges, nor into the possible motives behind them. Once three people—any three people—fingered an individual, he or she was PRU meat, fair game for arrest or elimination. It was a lousy system.

Then it had been Major Do's eyes that wouldn't stay put. Like Cameron, the policeman seemed to look everywhere except at Gulliver. "There is no card," he had said at last.

"There has to be a card," Gulliver insisted.

"Not when the order comes through the PIOCC direct from the province chief's office," Do had replied as a matter of fact.

"The province chief?" Gulliver had paused to let Major Do's words, and their implications, sink in. Then he'd asked: "Was your order signed by anyone? Because mine sure wasn't."

"No. It came to me as a verbal order from the PIOCC. And it came to them as a verbal order from Colonel Minh himself."

Gulliver paused again, then asked: "Will you sign mine?"

Major Do showed Gulliver a thin raised eyebrow and an equally thin smile. "Don't be foolish. Of course not."

Gulliver had suspected as much. He made up his mind. "I cannot and will not commission any of my people to terminate anyone, VCI or no VCI, on the basis of a verbal order."

"I am sorry," Do said, sounding truly sorry. "I do not like it any more than you do, but I cannot disobey a direct order from a superior. And neither can you."

"We'll see about that." Gulliver had been nearly out of the police chief's office when he stopped, turned, and asked: "Tell me something, Major . . . who's the target?"

For the first time, the policeman had looked straight at Gulliver. He smiled a wan, pained smile and said: "Rest assured that he is a highly dangerous man, Captain. He is a business rival of the province chief. A clear menace to our republic, one that must be disposed of as expeditiously as possible, *n'est-ce pas*?"

Gulliver had gone back to Cameron, but it hadn't changed anything. "I don't like it any more than you do, but there's not a thing I can do about it," Cameron had told him, echoing Major Do. "It's an order from Special Branch who says it's an order from the PIOCC who says it's an order from the province chief himself. The rulebook says that's good enough for us. The Viets run the Phoenix program, Jake. Our job is simply to advise . . . and consent."

"They run Phoenix, my ass!" Gulliver had shouted. "If it wasn't for the CIA, there wouldn't *be* a Phoenix program. And what rulebook? There are no fucking rules!"

Cameron had tried to calm him: "Jake, c'mon. Nobody's asking *you* to do it. I know the deal was that you wouldn't have to do this kind of job anymore. You and Dang just pick a good man or two and give 'em their marching orders. But it's gotta be done. Period. Either you get the ball rolling or I will."

Gulliver had turned on his heel for a dramatic, storming exit when Cameron stopped him. "By the way, if it's the lack of a finger card that's bothering you, Major Do called right after you left his office. He said to tell you they've found a card, and it's got the required three signatures."

"Golly gee, Buffalo Bob, that was quick. And very handy. Who'd they get to sign it?"

Cameron had grinned sheepishly and shrugged. "What can I

tell you? Three low-level street cops . . . White Mice. But it's good as gold, Jake."

Gulliver had briefed Dang, who selected two PRUs to act as assassins. Then he had written a memo to "cowboy central" in Saigon, with a drop copy to the agency base chief in Can Tho, detailing the facts and recommending an investigation into Phoenix program abuses in the province. George Cameron had declined to forward it.

When Captain Bich appeared a couple of months later with another envelope, another "special," this one gussied up with a proper finger card and its three signatures, Gulliver refused to take delivery. He went round and round again with Cameron, then wrote another memo to the Saigon station. That one, too, wound up as fodder for the shredder, its overwrought protest scattered to the heavens in a belch of ash and smoke from the rooftop incinerator. That time, Cameron himself arranged the details of the hit with Dang.

Gulliver had checked around, questioning PRUs and other advisers, and discovered that the PRU had always been used as the private instrument of the province chief, a personal goon squad for looting and extortion. It had been like that before Minh, and would be like that after Minh. It was like that all over Vietnam. By the time he was done, he had heard more than enough about the PRU and the Phoenix program.

The PRU, Gulliver had learned, was a modern incarnation of the CTU, the "counterterror units" formed in the mid-1950s during the Diem regime and run by CIA advisers. The idea was sound—to beat the VC at their own game—and the tactics simple: quick raids into Viet Cong hamlets, random torture of villagers to gain intelligence, swift execution of identified VC leaders. And it worked. With their mobility and freedom from ethical restrictions, the CTUs enjoyed an advantage over conventional military sweeps.

To motivate these irregulars, the CIA put head prices on targets and turned its back on looting. The spooks' cavalier attitude toward the rules gave the CTUs the impression there were none, and the excesses grew. Instead of bringing in VCI suspects, the troops began to shake them down. If they paid, they lived; if not, they died on the spot. The game worked so well that noncommunists were invited to play; after all, a wealthy merchant was VCI if the CTU said he was VCI. And as the teams answered only to the province chiefs, the province chiefs grew rich, spreading just enough of the take among the troops to keep them in line, pocketing the rest.

"Those were wild and woolly days, Jake, days of taking ears," George Cameron had told him. "We knew it and the bad guys knew it, but nobody else knew or cared, so it was okay."

By 1967, after too many years of taking ears, it was no longer okay. Instead of scaring the VC away from the people, the CTUs were scaring the people away from the government. Saigon's newspapers began to bugle their concern, and when the counter-terror units were denounced in the Assembly as "a bunch of thugs," the CIA, quick to spot a public-relations problem, "disbanded" the CTUs, changing their name to PRUs and quietly slipping them into the new Phoenix program.

And just as the PRU rose from the ashes of the CTU, the Phung Hoang program—Phoenix in English—hatched out of a new CIA plan to save Vietnam, one that was going to root out the VC with counterterrorism and *root in* the government with public works projects. Called CORDS—Civil Operations and Rural Development Support—the plan's goal was to bring VC cadre in alive, to be exploited for intelligence. But as so often was the case, the CIA found it more than the Vietnamese could handle. The primary problem was bureaucratic: who was to be considered a VC cadre? The local village chief who only served part-time, often under duress? Or hard-core communists with full party membership? The PRU, Phoenix's enforcer, went for a scattershot approach, picking up anyone who might be a suspect. And when the jails were filled to overflowing, they began taking the law, such as it was, into their own hands.

It wasn't long before the Phoenix program and the PRU took on the same bad odor as the CTU. Even CIA people began calling it the Phoenix pogrom or the Blackened Bird.

So the CIA moved to disown the monster it created. With the onset of Vietnamization, a new station chief, Tom Scott, arrived from Langley with orders to phase the company out of Phoenix. The Vietnamese could have it all to themselves, and the U.S. Army could advise them. That was why the embassy houses were being closed, and why Swain had come to replace Gulliver.

Gulliver had heard a few horror stories about the PRU when he was with Special Forces, but he did not know the full of it until he saw for himself on his initial outing as a PRU adviser. It also had been the first time out for the new team leader—Captain Dang, who'd just been transferred from duty on the Cambodian border, where he had been serving as chief of Kit Carson Scouts for an American infantry division. Both men had been stunned by the team's total lack of professionalism and discipline, and sickened by what they witnessed on their first operation.

The mission had been to snatch and to snuff two VC tax collectors living in a Hue Duc district hamlet. According to the Hamlet Evaluation Survey it was a B hamlet, effectively controlled by the Saigon government. The HES, as usual, had been wrong. The ten-man PRU team had to shoot its way into the ville when it arrived just after midnight, and shoot its way out when it left just before dawn. But in the interim, before the Viet Cong regrouped and brought up reinforcements, the PRU had the run of the place.

The two targets had been quickly located and dispatched. Then, before Gulliver and Dang quite knew what was happening, their troops had gone berserk. They surged through the tiny hamlet like Tamerlane's horsemen, going hut to hut, stealing everything of value. They murdered anyone who raised a voice in protest. They raped women. They shot water buffalo just for the inconvenience of it.

Gulliver and Dang had run from hut to hut too, pulling their troops out by the hair, booting them out with savage kicks. One by one the rampaging PRUs were collared and herded to the hamlet center and made to line up before a distraught hamlet chief, who wept and shook with fright and anger. His people stood behind him, hurling curses, and stones when they could find them in the broom-swept dirt street.

Long after the shooting stopped, the night air was still noisy with a sound like that of feeding birds. From almost every hut came the shrill keening of grief, punctuated from time to time by a sharp scream of new, grisly discovery.

Gulliver had been grateful for Dang's help in restoring order, but it was only after the men were finally corralled, looking sheepish and spotted with the blood of their victims, that he had an opportunity to take the first full measure of his new counterpart.

When Gulliver had finished screaming at the men, having used every Vietnamese epithet he knew, Dang had singled out two men and had them kneel before the hamlet chief. One had been dragged off a ten-year-old girl. To pass the time while waiting his turn, the other had used his K-bar to cut the throat of the little girl's squawking father.

The two PRUs had smiled nervously, questioning fate for having been chosen as examples, sidling glances at each other, and trying to guess how much pay they would be docked, the penalty always exacted by the previous team leader, Captain Thanh.

Without a word, the new team leader, Captain Dang, had shot the first man through the brainpan.

For one stunned moment the second man had gaped dumbly at the hot geyser that spurted from the massive hole in his friend's head. Then he'd quickly added two and two, got four, and begun to cry, turning a beseeching face to Gulliver and sobbing: "*Dai Uy,* please! What have we done wrong?" Before Gulliver could tell him, Dang fired again, spattering pieces of the man's brain all over the hamlet chief. The villagers, mollified, had roared their approval.

Gulliver did not sanction Dang's instant justice, but he understood it, and he never doubted its effectiveness. He and Dang had spent the next several weeks on intensive training of their team, and while they noticed a certain sullenness on the part of some of the men, they'd had no more trouble like that first time out. When one man was overheard complaining that he could not live on his pay, loudly advocating a return to the good old ways, he'd been promptly returned to Saigon, to Chi Hoa prison, where he had been serving time for murder when released for PRU work. That had put an end to any open grumbling.

Gulliver had no way to know if Colonel Minh was involved in PRU extortion, and he had waited to see what kind of heat, if any, came down the chain of command. If Minh was involved, the new SOP had to be playing hell with his earnings ratio.

Perhaps because he was clean, more likely because he was subtle, the province chief hadn't seemed to notice the change in methods. Except for an odd evil eye cast his way, Gulliver hadn't had any trouble from Colonel Duong Van "Medium" Minh, so-called to distinguish him from the well-known politician Duong Van "Big" Minh and the respected ARVN general Tran Van "Little" Minh. No trouble until Captain Bich had appeared at the Embassy House with his unmarked envelope, his "special."

Gulliver had toyed with the idea of going over Cameron's head about Minh's "specials," but in the end he had not. He had never pulled an end run on a superior in his life. Besides, he suspected that both the CIA base chief in Can Tho and the operations people in Saigon knew what was going on. Bennett Steelman was a nasty bit of work, but he was not stupid. He would know. Cameron would have cleared it with him.

And so Gulliver had kept his misgivings within channels. Confronted with Cameron's refusal to forward his memoranda, he had written no more of them. But neither had he accepted any more envelopes from Captain Bich. The next time Bich came around, Gulliver again refused to accept delivery, and again Cameron had been forced to make the arrangements with Dang.

After that, the "special"-delivery system had bypassed Gulliver altogether. Captain Bich no longer came calling. On Cameron's instruction, he took his envelope directly to Dang. And since Dang did not discuss the details of these special missions, and since no written records were kept, Gulliver still did not know how many "specials" had taken place during his tenure. All he knew was that every so often Dang would vanish without a word, for a few days or a few hours.

As he had this afternoon.

"Ah, to hell with it. I'm just glad to see you," he told Dang now, meaning it.

He did not blame Dang. The little Gulliver knew of his friend's background was enough to see how his own Occidental angst must seem silly. Dang had thus far managed to survive in a harsh world, one that had been at war on the day of his birth and was likely still to be at war the day of his death. Dang knew no other existence. But he did not agonize over it, he endured it; he did not question assignments, he completed them. Dang was a soldier, a professional, and professionals did not write memoranda on their orders. They executed them. To the letter.

For Dang, things were simple, Gulliver guessed. In a war that had lasted thirty years and could go on for another thirty, all things became part of the business of survival, and survival came easiest for those who saw the world in black and white. Gulliver knew that for Dang there were no grays. Gray was the color of self-indulgence, of weakness, a dangerous color—a civilian color.

Gulliver often wished that he could see things as simply as Dang seemed to, as he himself once did. Why shouldn't he? After all, they were not civilians. They were professional soldiers, and a professional's pride was the timber shoring their friendship. They were so alike in other ways, in the way they worked, for example, each so attuned to the other's skills of bushcraft that they were able to dispense even with hand signals. They communicated as if by telepathy, all the more remarkable because each was used to working alone.

But Dang certainly did not look the professional soldier this evening. Gulliver could not hold it back any longer. He laughed. "Jesus Christ, Dang. If you don't look like a clown in that getup."

Dang looked down at his wild shirt. "I was told to come in civilian clothes," he said simply. "This is all I have."

Gulliver grinned. "And you're all I have in the way of reinforcements at the moment. Maybe Fat Minh will be so busy laughing at your costume he'll forget all about giving me a hard time. In any case, it's time to lock 'n' load and join the party. C'mon, I'll take point."

He led the way into the dining room.

Had it been a purely social evening, ladies would have been welcome. Atypically, the Embassy House had but one in permanent residence, a handsome middle-aged woman Coughlin had imported from Hue. Her name was Tuyet and she was said to have once been a teenage concubine of the Emperor Bao Dai. But because business came before pleasure, Tuyet dined alone in Coughlin's rooms and the usual protocols were in force.

As host, George Cameron sat at one end of the table, while the ranking guest, Colonel Minh, was at the other. Gulliver found his spot in between, flanked by Coughlin and Major Ngoc. He had hoped to slide into place unnoticed and unremarked, but his tardy entrance interrupted the province chief in the midst of a monologue, and everything stopped until he was seated. Then Minh smiled like a cherub and said in his odd, high-pitched English: "Is *so* very good of you to join us, Captain."

Before taking his seat across from Gulliver, Dang paused at the province chief's chair to whisper into his ear. Medium Minh smiled, nodded with satisfaction, and resumed his story, something to do with the odds the town's fortune-tellers were giving on the likelihood of another Tet offensive.

"My astrologer tell me nothing will ruin this holiday," Minh said. "VC bad hurt last time. Not strong enough to try more. VC finished in Delta."

"You had better hold on to that fortune-teller of yours, Colonel Minh, because he sounds like a good man," Sloane said good-naturedly from his place beside the province chief. "His prediction matches up with what U.S. intelligence resources have been telling us. If your boy would like a job, I think I can get him into J–2 in Saigon."

Minh smiled indulgently. "He make *boo-coo* more money from me. Why he trade for army pay, eh?"

Everyone around the table laughed appreciatively, except Gulliver and Dang. The province chief noticed.

"You not believe in astrology, Captain Gulliver?" he asked with a Buddha-like smile, a fleshy oracle.

"No, sir, I don't," Gulliver said firmly.

"Ahhh. Maybe *that* is your trouble."

Gulliver sighed inwardly but decided it was best to play dumb. "What trouble is that, sir?" he asked innocently.

"The trouble you have accomplishing your mission here," Minh said, still smiling. "Maybe I have my astrologer come see you before you go to pick up communists. He maybe tell you when to stay home, if you would be wasting your time."

Gulliver said nothing.

"You waste *boo-coo* time, is it not true, *Dai Uy*?" Minh pressed, still smiling and looking around the table to gauge the impact his remarks were having on the others. "Six times in three months, if my information is correct. And I believe it so."

Gulliver debated whether to ride it out or say something in self-defense. No one else at the table seemed willing, or able, to help. Coughlin was preoccupied with spooning up soup, obviously hoping no one would be so gauche as to remind Minh that it was Special Branch which had set up all those targets who had not been at home when the PRU came calling. Major Do, who supposedly didn't understand a word of English, was being careful to appear bewildered. Major Ngoc, who did understand English, *was* bewildered. Colonel Sloane was thinking that it might be wise to get his own deep concern over PRU failures on the record in his next dispatch to Saigon, just to be on the safe side. And Swain was trying, with little success, to conceal a smile in his napkin, openly enjoying Gulliver's discomfort.

Only Cameron had any honest sympathy in his face. For all his sins, the P officer was a meek drunk, wistful and sentimental, something of a weeper. All his studied cynicism fell away when he was looped, replaced by a tremulous, almost touching vulnerability. He became a peacemaker when he drank, his fear of discord multiplying with every jigger he downed. It was a switch on the way alcohol affected most people.

Cameron now smiled a placating smile and tried to rescue both his subordinate and the mood of his dinner: "Well, now, they really didn't do too badly the last time out, did they, Colonel? That was nice work, Jake . . . Dang."

Gulliver shot Cameron a look of gratitude.

Dang paid them no mind. He busied himself with the first course, *cha gio,* liberally anointing the spring rolls, filled with pork and crabmeat, with *nuoc-mam* and feeding them into his face one after another. He could afford to ignore Minh's barbs because he was never included in the province chief's criticism of the PRU, even though he was the team's leader. There had been no failures on any of Minh's "specials"—like the lawmen in the American cowboy films Minh loved so, Dang always got his man.

Besides, Minh had made up his mind that the problem was a security leak inside the Embassy House, an arbitrary conclusion that neatly took his own headquarters off the hook. And to avoid criticizing Cameron—a career CIA officer who might influence the funding for the Phoenix program—he had decided to put the blame on Gulliver, the soldier merely on contract. He knew that Gulliver had tried to cause trouble over the "specials."

The expensive whiskey and good wine had put Colonel Minh in an expansive mood. He decided to grasp Cameron's proffered olive branch. "You are quite correct, Mr. Cameron. If we can locate and destroy the 18–B Battalion, then Captain Gulliver has not wasted all his time. We shall know if this is so the day after tomorrow, eh?"

Chi Ba and Chi Hai brought the rest of the meal: pork, followed by tripes swimming in a sauce of coagulated blood, and, more in line with the American palate, "seven kinds of beef," strips of tenderized buffalo wrapped in lettuce leaf and rice paper.

Table talk was light and sociable, the failings of the PRU forgotten for the moment. Colonel Minh had been in Saigon earlier in the week for consultations with the President, and he passed along some of the more innocuous palace gossip, as well as the President's assessment of how the war in Military Region Four was progressing, as if they who fought it did not know. As expected, compared to the high level of activity in the Central Highlands and up in Eye Corps near the DMZ, the Delta war slumbered.

They were just finishing dessert—lichees and papaya, a disappointment for the Vietnamese guests, who'd hoped for the creamy American ice cream the Embassy House had flown in from Saigon—when Chuck Riesz came in. He looked exhausted. Ever since Dang and Gulliver had brought in their VC cadre, Riesz had been at the Provincial Interrogation Center almost around the clock, supervising the interrogation sessions and sleeping on a cot in an adjoining cell. The most idealistic of all the CIA officers assigned to the Embassy House, Riesz had, after Gulliver, the most unsavory job.

"How did it go tonight?" Cameron asked him.

"Zilch. Absolutely nothing," Riesz said, pulling up a chair and helping himself to a cup of coffee. "It's a good thing he had those papers on him because I don't think we'll get another thing out of him. I've never seen anyone stand up to questioning like this guy. He's a tough bird."

"There are very many ways to loosen the meat on a tough

bird," the province chief interjected, smiling another Buddha smile at Riesz, his gold tooth catching the candlelight.

Riesz shook his head. "I *know* all the ways, sir. They're not going to work on this guy."

"How rough has it gotten?" Cameron asked, his fluid eyes wincing, already shrinking from the answer. Gulliver marveled at how a sober Cameron could have no qualms about going along with Minh's "specials," the murder of people whose only crime had been to cross the province chief's commercial path, while a sloshed Cameron quaked at the very thought of violence.

"We haven't laid a glove on him," Riesz said. "When you know what you're doing, you don't have to."

"What have you tried, Mr. Riesz?" Minh asked.

"Everything, sir. We started with the Arabic method and went from there."

Swain piped up. "What's the Arabic method?"

Riesz noticed Swain for the first time, and his eyes panicked behind his spectacles. "Jesus H . . . !" He turned to Cameron. "Who the hell is he? Should he be hearing this?"

"It's okay, Chuck. Meet Harry Swain. He takes Jake's place for MACV when we switch. Until then, he's company."

"Oh, well, welcome aboard." The two men reached across the table to shake hands, and Riesz said: "Under MACV rules you won't be able to use it, Harry, but in answer to your question, what you do is this: strip your prisoner naked, bandage his eyes, and tie him to a hard chair placed in the middle of a soundproof room. Then just walk away and leave him to sit for half a day."

Swain looked disappointed. "What's so bad about that?"

Riesz smiled ruefully. "After four or five hours the guy is totally disoriented. His senses aren't getting any input. His initial mild discomfort goes through pain to bad pain to nothing, just numbness. After a while he thinks he's back in his mother's womb. That's when you tiptoe back in and start your questioning in a soft, soothing voice—a voice out of the dark unknown. By then he can't tell where the voice is coming from. It seems to come from everywhere, from nowhere. It's like it's coming from inside his own head, inside his *soul*. The poor guy thinks he's in there all alone with his God."

Swain looked skeptical, and Riesz, with a boyish smile, said, "A technique like that is a lot more effective than pulling fingernails, if that's what you're thinking."

Swain grinned sheepishly. That was exactly what he had been thinking. But he was still not convinced. "Okay, but you just admitted it didn't work," he said, making his point.

Riesz nodded sorrowfully. "And I don't understand it. The Arabic *always* works. Christ, when I came back to start my questioning, he was as bright-eyed and bushy-tailed as when I'd left him six hours before. It was amazing."

"What else did you try?" Cameron asked.

"You name it, we tried it. Cuban, Chinese, Soviet, a few tricks the French found to be useful in Algeria. I'm telling you, George, we took this guy around the world in eighty *ways*."

They all laughed at the pun, but Riesz was not trying to be funny. He was genuinely discouraged. It was inevitable. He was an ardent young man, only twenty-six, slim and intense, who still used such phrases as "domino theory" and "American hegemony" and "hearts and minds." It was always something of a shock to him whenever his country or his company training let him down.

"So what are you going to do with him?" Gulliver asked.

Riesz shrugged. "My counterparts at the center are going to try once more tonight using more, ah, direct methods. They won't work on this guy but they want to try. Then we'll ship him to Saigon and they can decide what to do with him."

"Before you do that, why don't you ask him if he'd like to *chieu hoi*," Gulliver said. "He sounds like the kind of man we could use in the PRU. In fact, he sounds like the spitting image of Captain Dang here."

They laughed, even the province chief. All except Dang, of course, but even he smiled in his own way, his black eyes glinting above an unmoving mouth.

It was after midnight when they moved to the common room for their planning session. But first Cameron doled out party favors—a carton of Marlboros each for Minh and Ngoc, both of whom liked American cigarettes, and a carton of Gauloise for Do. They lit up and found chairs around the poker table.

Gulliver, who had been assigned the planning, suggested they keep it simple: two teams of ten men each, one under Dang, the other under himself with Swain along as observer.

He laid out the basics of his plan.

—They would fly to Tinh Bien and then proceed by foot, scouting first the nearest, then the next nearest of the Seven Mountains. Dang's team, code-named "Dog Catcher One," would move clockwise around the base, Gulliver's "Dog Catcher Two" counterclockwise, linking up halfway round.

—They would carry the special CIA radio, the RS–1, and enough PIRs—patrol indigenous rations—for five days.

—They would avoid all contact with enemy units of more than

a half-dozen, and if discovered would call for immediate extraction.

—They would hunt individual VC, officers or message runners, those with access to information. They would take them alive, interrogate them in the field, and terminate them.

—They would continue to "snatch and snuff" until they had what they needed: the 18–B's complete order of battle and map coordinates for all its various elements.

—The information would be radioed to "Dog Pound," the forward command post set up in Tinh Bien district capital and manned by Coughlin. When the intel was in hand and collated, the 18–B would be subjected to air strikes from American and VNAF squadrons out of Can Tho and Binh Tuy. Then Major Ngoc and his Field Force strikers would alight in coordinated CAs, combat assaults.

And it all had to be done within the next week, before the Tet cease-fire went into effect.

When Gulliver finished, Colonel Minh spent a few quiet moments with his eyes closed, going over the plan in his head, searching for holes. It worried him that Cameron had given the planning responsibility to Captain Gulliver, whose recent record for running successful operations was not very good. But Gulliver was the acknowledged military expert, and the province chief could not find any glaring flaws. Perhaps one of the others had. He opened his eyes and looked to each of them, and one by one they nodded their approval.

"Then we are agreed," Minh said with a sigh, pushing back his chair and getting up with a grunt. "Major Ngoc will fly to Can Tho tomorrow to coordinate support with M-R Four headquarters."

Cameron turned bloodshot eyes on Swain and said: "We're not giving you much time to get the lay of the land, are we, Lieutenant? I'm afraid your first PRU op could get a little hairy."

Swain grinned. "No sweat, sir. Number One! That's just the way I like 'em. Harry's my name and hairy's my game."

Behind Swain, Gulliver groaned inwardly and he and Dang exchanged a glance. But Medium Minh beamed at the new man and invited him to lunch at provincial headquarters the next day. It was an unusual offer. Swain accepted.

Cameron got to his feet, staggering and nearly tipping his chair. But he recovered nicely and, with no unsteadiness in his voice, said to Minh: "I know it's late, Colonel, but we've got a new movie in the house if you'd care to stay. A western."

Colonel Minh's eyes lit up with interest. "John Wayne? Randolph Scott?"

"No, sir. It's a new one, called *The Wild Bunch*. I think you'd enjoy it; it's got lots of bang-bang." Cameron did not seem to mind violence, even when drunk, as long as it was confined to celluloid.

"I watch," Minh decided. He smiled, gold tooth flashing.

Cameron went off to get a houseboy to work the projector and returned to find his party scattering. Majors Do and Ngoc said their good nights and left as they had come, simultaneously but separately. Riesz went to the kitchen to forage for leftovers before going back to the Interrogation Center to oversee the final session with the prisoner. Coughlin said good night and went up to join the patient Tuyet, who had once waited for an emperor. Minh, Sloane, and Swain refilled cognac snifters and settled in for the movie. Dang left without a word to anyone.

The noon-to-midnight drinking seemed to catch up with Cameron in a single instant. One moment he looked fine, the next poleaxed, his face suddenly gone bloodless and beaded with sweat. He swayed uncertainly, then mumbled a slurred, all-encompassing good night, and unsteadily climbed the stairs, using the banister to pull himself along.

Alarmed by the P officer's pallor, Gulliver followed at a discreet distance. When he got to the top of the stairs he tiptoed down the hall and tapped on Cameron's door. There was no response. He tried the knob and the door swung open. Cameron was not in the sitting room or bedroom, but Gulliver could hear a gagging sound from the bathroom, a desperate retching that went on and on.

He crossed the suite and pushed open the bathroom door. Cameron was on his knees in front of the toilet, both arms wrapped around the bowl.

"You all right?" Gulliver asked.

Cameron was too sick to be startled, by Gulliver, by the indignity of his posture, by anything. He nodded weakly.

Gulliver took a washcloth, wet it with cold water, and started swabbing Cameron's forehead and the nape of his neck. "Why do you do it, George?" he asked softly.

"Vietnam, Jake, Vietnam." Cameron used a finger to clear a string of bile from his chin, and got shakily to his feet. "The booze helps me hang on. I'm an old man. Most men aren't old at fifty-four, but I am. Except for one tour in Laos and one in Thailand, I've been in-country twenty years, and I was too old for it when I got here."

Gulliver said nothing. Cameron did look a good fifteen years older than his age. He even had an old man's age spots.

"Jesus, Jake, sometimes it feels like I've been out here my whole life. It was all right when I worked with honorable men, men like Des FitzGerald when he was DDP in the East Asia Division. He warned them about Vietnam, but they wouldn't listen. And Ed Lansdale. Did I ever tell you that Lansdale was the model for *The Quiet American*? Did I tell you how I came in-country with the very first team, with Lansdale and Lou Conein, under the cover of the Saigon Military Mission?"

Only a hundred times. "No, you never did, George."

"Goddamn right I did! I've seen it all—the defeat of the Frogs, partition in fifty-four, the coup against Diem. That was Conein's operation. Old Three-Fingered Lou. I ever tell you how he'd meet with the generals upstairs at Ramuntcho's, planning the coup?"

"No, you didn't, George," Gulliver lied.

"Damn right! Saw it all! The revolving-door governments, the Buddhist Uprising, the bonzes setting themselves on fire, Tet sixty-eight, all the whiz kids fresh out from Langley with their whiz-kid ideas, like this . . . this fucking Phoenix crap."

Cameron's eyes teared. "Things have changed, Jake. I've changed too. I had to. Because the company changed. I don't know these new people. I don't like them. Why can't they just go back where they came from and leave me alone?"

"Why don't you quit?"

"You know why. I'm retiring next year. I'm taking an early out after twenty-five years. Damn near full pension."

"If you keep this up, you won't be around to collect."

"Oh, I'll collect. The fuckers owe me. Vietnam cost me my family. My wife divorced me ten years ago this week; said she couldn't take it anymore—the separations, the company. Now it's my kids. I got two daughters. Didn't know that, did you?"

Gulliver hadn't known that. "No, I didn't."

"Goddamn right! But they hate me. My girls hate me. They say they're ashamed of me. Their own father! They go to peace marches and carry signs about CIA criminals while I pay their college bills. Oh, I'll collect, Jake. Because the company owes me. Goddamn right!" Cameron began to cry.

Gulliver helped him into bed, tucking him in under the mosquito netting as if Cameron were a child. From a ceiling corner a gecko watched, its tongue flicking, zeroing in, testing ranges. An unsuspecting insect made its slow way across the whitewashed wall, heading straight for the lizard, straight for oblivion.

Gulliver had doused the lights and was about to leave when the lump in the bed stirred and said: "I know how you feel about the company, Jake, but you never saw us in the old days, when it was just Lansdale and Conein and me and a few other good people. We had us some men then. Honorable men."

"Sure," Gulliver said gently. "Try to get some sleep, George."

"Me too, Jake. I was an honorable man too. You should have seen me then, Jake. I was hell on wheels."

"I know. I know you were, George. You go to sleep now." Gulliver shut the door and went downstairs.

The movie was just starting. He sat in the back, alone and unnoticed. He had seen the film when it first came down from the embassy in Saigon, but he wanted to see the opening scene again, the one where the children played in the dust, huddled around a scorpion tethered to an anthill. He saw the scorpion writhing in the ocean of ants, its stinger wild and useless, pounding the barb deep into its own back as it tried to strike back at the fiery, the maddening, pain. He saw the children laughing and poking at the creature with sticks. He saw the scene through, then rose quietly and went up to bed.

He slept fitfully, naked under a slow fan, balling and soaking his sheets, dreaming of sad old men. There were two. One drank too much and snored in another room, dreaming his own dreams, of younger days and younger men. And one wandered the land of spirits, roaming headless, in sightless search of heaven's door. Gulliver did not know their names, just their faces, tired and afraid and in pain and slippery with sweat. Just two lost, sad old men who had asked little enough. Only to be left alone.

5

SWAIN HAD JUST LEFT Colonel Minh's headquarters when he saw her. It was the tits that got his attention. They seemed to jump at him from clear across the compound. Harry Swain had never seen tits that big on a gook. If they were genuine, she could stack up with any round-eye he knew.

Swain, headed for his Bronco for the drive back to the Embassy House, changed course to get a better look. As he grew closer, he saw that the woman had a face to match the body—a perfect valentine, with eyes like teardrops laid sideways, and a wide, pouty mouth. She was the best-looking gook he had ever seen.

The very sight of her was like an extra dessert, Swain thought, a perfect cap to the meal he had just consumed. The lunch with Colonel Minh had been a great success: good food and good talk, mostly about Gulliver, whom the province chief did not seem to like any more than Swain did—but this made it even better.

He tried to think of a slick opening line as he made a wide circle and came up on her blind side, but the best he could do was: "Hey there, little lady."

The woman whirled around at the sound of his voice. "Oh, pardon, sir. Please to tell me where I am to take my request for employment?" she said in decent English. "My papers are all completed."

"Employment? Papers?"

"Yes, please, sir." She was nervous. Her eyes blinked in time with her tripping heartbeat, and a small white-knuckled fist clutched a batch of papers to the bodice of her *ao dai,* tight against her amazing chest, ruining Swain's view.

"I don't know what you mean, doll," Swain said.

"I am told to come here . . . to ask for work in the office of U.S. Aid . . . as secretary," she said with a slight stammer. "It say in newspaper U.S. Aid need Vietnamese lady who speak good English. I speak good English. I work the typewriter. I work very hard, make good secretary."

Swain grinned. "I'll just bet you would. But the USAID office ain't here. It's in the CORDS compound, the American compound. This here's the goo . . . uh, the provincial compound."

"Oh. I make the mistake. I am so sorry." She smiled an embarrassed smile, her eyes wide with confusion. "Where am I to go, please?"

"Back out the gate and hang a left, then maybe a couple hundred yards and there it is," Swain said. "It's not far."

Hang a left? Yards? The woman was still confused, but she dared not ask the American to repeat his directions. He would think her stupid and he would tell the other Americans and she would not be hired. She stood uncertain and unmoving, smiling nervously at the huge American.

Suddenly he took her by the upper arm and said: "C'mon, I'll give you a ride over there. My vehicle's over here." He began to guide her to it.

"Oh, no, sir! Please not to trouble. If not far, I walk," she said with alarm, tugging against his grasp, digging in slippered heels. It was unseemly enough for a proper woman to be seen talking with an American, much less riding around town with one.

Swain did not let go. "Hey, little darlin', if you want to work for Americans you've got to think American, and rule number one is never walk when you can ride." He was leading her to the Bronco, his grip like the mandibles of a pliers on her slender arm, so powerful that he was hardly aware of any resistance. Whey they reached the vehicle, he opened the door and effortlessly lifted her up and in with one big hand.

She went along—partly because he had said it was only a short way, partly because she wasn't certain she could find the U.S. Aid office on her own, but mostly because she did not know what else to do. She did not want to offend this American, or any American, for fear of losing out on one of their highly prized, highly lucrative jobs.

"What's you name, honey?" he asked as they pulled away from

the compound. A QC, the ARVN military policeman at the gate, stiffened and threw the Bronco a grandiose salute, confirming for her the American's importance.

"Mai," she answered tentatively. "Nguyen Thi Mai."

"Mai. Mai." He tasted the name. "That's a pretty name."

"*Cam on*. I mean thank you."

"A pretty name for a pretty lady," he said with a grin, showing his big teeth like an animal, not covering them with a hand as was polite. He was staring openly at her breasts.

Nguyen Thi Mai did not know how to respond and so did not. Her face, the color of weak tea, darkened to the shade of strong wine and she turned to the window, feigning an interest in the wash of people, automobiles, cyclos, and bicycles that eddied along the province town's congested main thoroughfare. She shivered in the air-conditioner's icy blast, but her face was hot. She was unnerved by the rude directness of this big American's tongue and eyes. She hugged herself, crossing her arms on her chest like a corpse laid to coffin, fanning her application forms in front of her breasts in a futile effort to hide them.

Her breasts! Her disfigurement! Mai had been ashamed of them since her twelfth year, when, almost overnight, they had pushed up out of the flat plateau of her slender trunk like magical mountains. In a race of small-breasted women, they made her a freak. She had suffered the whispers of the marketplace and the insults of soldiers who did not know she was a decent married woman of good family. She was aware that her breasts made her look like a whore, like one of those women who went to Bangkok or Taiwan to have their breasts made huge, like those of the shameless American women she had seen when, in curiosity, she had peeked into an American magazine that her eldest son had hidden away.

The American spoke again, making her jump. "How about going out with me tonight? We can have dinner or something. Wouldn't you like that?"

"Yes," she said, responding to the negative question as most Vietnamese would, meaning yes she *wouldn't* like that.

"Outstanding! Number One!" he said with another toothy, uncovered smile, reaching over to pat her knee. "We can eat at the villa where I live, then we can see a movie. You like American movies, don't you? After that, maybe I'll show you my quarters, where I sleep." He wiggled the bushy eyebrows that made him look like a giant forest monkey.

"Oh! No!" she said quickly, anxious to clear up the misunderstanding. "No can go with you. I am married woman. I am not *Co* Mai! I am *Ba* Mai . . . *Mrs.* Mai . . . wife of Mr. Trung."

"Hey, no sweat, doll. I didn't figure a woman who looks like you would be running around loose. We'll work up a good story to tell your husband."

"It is impossible, sir. Please. I am married woman . . . *Ba* Mai . . . wife of Nguyen Khac Trung," she repeated stubbornly.

Swain frowned. "So who's whatzizname . . . this guy Trung you're married to? What's he do? What kind of work?"

"My husband work at military hospital. It good job but pay *ti-ti* money. I have children, need *boo-coo* money. So I go to ask work in office of U.S. Aid, make *boo-coo* money." She babbled in panic, her English slipping badly, falling apart along with her composure.

Swain smiled, relieved that she was not married to some gook bigshot. "Look, honey. I know the top people at USAID. I could put in a word for you and get you that job . . . if you say you'll go out with me tonight."

"No! I married woman. *Ba* Mai," she said firmly, finally, deciding she didn't want to work for the Americans after all. Americans frightened her. She would take the clerical job her husband had found for her with the Social Democrats, the Hoa Hao party, in which he was active. It wouldn't pay as well, of course, but there would be no complications, no Americans who resembled giant monkeys and who made rude, improper advances to respectable women.

Swain did not have enough time to come up with a fresh approach; they had arrived. The American compound was called Palm Springs by mission personnel and, besides USAID, housed the offices of the province senior adviser, the deputy PSA, and the refugee officer. Colonel Sloane and his staff lived in a collection of prefab houses and Conex trailers—crude accommodations by American standards, but impressive to most Vietnamese. Mai did not even glance at her posh surroundings.

He pulled up to the USAID office and Mai got out without a word. She went inside, but stayed close by the door and did not approach the Vietnamese secretary, who looked up briefly from her *Ladies' Home Journal,* then went back to it.

Mai peeked out a window and saw the Bronco make a U-turn and drive out the gate. She waited another two minutes, then left the office and the compound, walking out into the street and flagging down a cyclo, a rickshaw welded to the back of a motorcycle. She gave the driver her home address, then leaned back in the seat and closed her eyes, utterly exhausted.

Swain was waiting for her, sitting in a blue-and-yellow taxi less than half a block from the compound gate. He had stashed the conspicuous Bronco up a side street. When he saw her step into the cyclo, he tapped the driver on the shoulder and motioned for him to follow.

They inched through the center of the capital, a typical province town, with jammed streets and blue exhaust haze and block upon block of two-story concrete buildings with iron shutters. Most of the town's citizens lived over their shops, entombed in sickly pastels. The thousands of refugees had set up house where they could, on sidewalks and in alleys.

They passed by the provincial compound again, and Swain was reminded of his luncheon with Minh. The colonel had been friendly and complimentary, saying how glad he was that Swain was going to replace Gulliver. Swain had asked him about the PRU problems he'd mentioned during dinner the night before, and the province chief had filled him in on the details. How it seemed that whenever Special Branch managed to identify a big fish—a VCI cadre above the rank-and-file level—the catch would invariably slip through the PRU's net. And how, since the trouble had begun when Gulliver came to the province, the only possible conclusion was that the PRU adviser was doing something wrong. And if it was a security leak within the PRU, as Minh suspected, then it was Gulliver's job to find and plug it, and that was something he had been unable to do.

Swain made a mental note to put Minh's dissatisfaction with Captain Gulliver into his report to Steelman. It would be his first report for the CIA man, and he was pleased that he would have something of substance to include.

Mai's cyclo kept to the main boulevard until it cleared the edge of town, then turned toward the Bassac River. There was a break of five or six kilometers in the dense packing of houses and shops, the sides of the road giving way to rice paddies; then the urban sprawl started up again, thick as ever. They were entering an outlying suburb.

Swain's taxi driver spoke a brand of Pidgin English and was using it to pepper his passenger with offers of assorted personal services. Did American Sir want to change money? Buy Buddha Grass? Heroin? Boom-Boom? Swain told him to shut up, then, as he saw Mai's cyclo slow, barked in the same breath: "Slow down! Stop here!" The driver slammed on the brakes and pulled onto the shoulder of the street, which was cramped and unpaved and full of potholes.

"Where are we?" Swain asked, looking around. They were in a

modest neighborhood, parked in front of the sandbagged entrance to a small police substation. The flag of the Saigon government, piss-yellow with three thin red horizontal bands, hung limply from a rooftop flagpole.

"This place name Senh Tien," the driver said. "Senh Tien is Vietnamese name for thing for making loud music. How you say in English . . . drum? Yes, like drum!"

"Why do they call it that?" Swain asked idly, watching Mai pay off the cyclo drive and go into a two-story house made of pastel-painted concrete block, no different from the other places on the street but for the fancy grillwork on the windows and the fact there was no shop at street level.

"Very many Hondas here, very many small children here," the driver was saying. "It very noisy all the time. Same as drum."

Swain checked his watch and saw that he had run out of time. The PRU team was leaving for the Seven Mountains that night and he had to get his gear in shape. And he still had to write up his report for Steelman and take it to the drop, a tailor shop off the province town's main drag.

"Same as you," he said to the driver. "Take me back to town, and keep quiet."

The driver shrugged, started up, and made a narrow U-turn. As he pulled away, he looked into his rearview mirror and saw that his passenger had turned around in his seat for one last look up the street. When the surly American turned back to face the front, he was grinning.

6

THEY LANDED at the Tinh Bien military airfield in what the U.S. Air Force meteorologists had forecast as the night's darkest hour, the hour just before dawn. The weather boys had used a million dollars' worth of sophisticated high technology to confirm the wisdom of a hoary bromide.

The USAF C–130, in full war paint, came in on a darkened runway without landing lights. The skipper, a CIA pilot more accustomed to flying STOLS—the short takeoff and landing craft—brought her in as if she were his Pilatus Porter. He did not stop, just throttled back and made a turn at the end of the strip while the crew chief lowered the rear hydraulic hatch. The PRUs disembarked from the still-moving plane on the run, gear flouncing, with barely enough time to clear the tarmac before the airplane came hurtling by on its takeoff run. It had spent less than a minute on the ground.

The airfield was strung along an edge of Tinh Bien City, a district capital, which was itself strung along the eastern bank of the Vinh Te Canal. The canal, a misnomer since it was as long and wide as most major rivers, formed the border with Cambodia all the way to the Gulf of Siam. The PRUs were not given a chance to sample the limited pleasures of the shabby border town; they were formed up and marched away before any informers in the vicinity of the airfield had an opportunity to look them over. While every possible precaution had been taken to ensure that the plane was not seen to land, it was unlikely that its visit, short as it was, would escape notice altogether. The Lockheed C–130 Hercules was arguably the noisiest propeller-driven aircraft in existence.

Waiting for them at the otherwise deserted terminal was an American army officer, a Captain Karsten Prager, who was familiar with the AO, the area of operations, and who would be their guide for part of the way. Prager, the adviser to the local Ruff-Puffs, the Regional and Popular Forces, was not part of the Phoenix program apparatus. All he knew about this mission was that he had to get these pajama-clad men to the far side of Ba Chuc village without them being seen.

Prager watched with interest as the PRUs blackened their faces and taped down loose equipment, then led them to a hole cut in the perimeter fence. They passed through one at a time and waded into an adjacent paddy. The immediate objective was a seldom-used path Prager knew, the first link in a maze of interconnected dike trails that would keep the PRUs off the main road between Tinh Bien and Ba Chuc, the last population center they had to skirt before they could lose themselves in the foothills of the Seven Mountains, the Seven Sisters.

The PRUs came to the end of the paddy and, without having to be told, lined up at the bottom of the dike wall in order of march, then scrabbled up together. Once on the narrow dike path, they picked up the pace to a brisk walk.

Prager, at the point, was thinking that if they could maintain the pace they should have no trouble in reaching the backside of Ba Chuc village before daybreak. The first of the four hamlets that made up Ba Chuc was five kilometers from Tinh Bien by highway, and only three klicks by the route he had mapped. He doubted that these troops would find the pace a problem. He was impressed with the discipline of these PRUs. They had crossed the paddy as quietly as any men he had ever seen. Twice he had to look over his shoulder to make certain they were still there and following, and twice found himself eyeball-to-eyeball with the team commander, Captain Dang.

As a rule, Prager did not think highly of PRUs; he found them no better than hoodlums. But this bunch seemed different somehow; certainly different from his own ragtag Ruff-Puffs, who crossed this same paddy twice a week on routine sweeps. His boys tried hard, but they couldn't cross their eyes without making a racket. This Dang and that adviser of his, Gulliver, had to be given credit for a bang-up job of training.

Captain Prager was not new to his district, but he had never worked with these particular PRUs before. They were not from Chau Doc, his province capital. Yet there was something about Gulliver that tugged at his mind's sleeve. He was sure he had heard the name before, but couldn't remember where.

And then he could. The Sandman! He was walking point for the goddamn Sandman! It had all happened well before his time, of course, but some of his Ruff-Puffs, the older ones, still talked of how the Sandman had come to town to pull the plug on General Blood. "Well, kiss my ass and call it Mother," he whispered to himself. The goddamn Sandman!

The captains at the ends of the file—Prager in front, Gulliver in back—were thinking along parallel lines. After positioning Swain in the middle of the column, Gulliver had taken the drag position, but his mind was farther back than that. Six years back.

Prager's route let them bypass Tinh Bien district town completely, and that was just jake with Jake Gulliver. He had been to Tinh Bien only once before, in the monsoon season of 1964, but he had two reasons to remember it—one good, one not so good. Tinh Bien was where he'd met a bona-fide Special Forces legend, Captain Larry Thorne. It also had been the jump-off point for his first Sandman mission.

Gulliver could still picture Thorne clearly, despite the years—a grinning, genial giant who could, with equal ease, crush a beer can or a man's skull with one hand. He had heard of Thorne before their meeting, of course; there wasn't a man in Special Forces who had not. Thorne, a native Finn, had won a Mannerheim Cross for his exploits against the Russians, for leading a small ski patrol behind Soviet lines and wiping out a three-hundred-man Red Army convoy. Later he had gone behind Russian lines again, this time with German commandos, and that was where he'd been when WWII ended. Thorne had fought on for a few days more so he could surrender to the Americans rather than the Russians, but then busted out of his American POW camp, worked his way to the United States, and after changing his name, enlisted in the U.S. Army. He had been a natural for Special Forces, gaining notoriety in field exercises at Bragg as the mock guerrilla leader "Charlie Brown."

When Gulliver met Thorne at Tinh Bien, the big Finn and his small Civilian Irregular Defense Group—a mixed bag of Montagnard and Hoa Hao troops—were working hard to clean up the district, a VC stronghold. With his skills, Thorne had not really needed Gulliver's help, of course, but neither he nor his CIDG troops were authorized to cross the Cambodian border, and that was where his big problem was bivouacked: a charismatic Khmer bandit chief who had put his private army of mercenaries at the disposal of the local Viet Cong in exchange for the privilege of collecting tolls from sampans using the busy Vinh Te Canal.

So Gulliver had come to Tinh Bien under agency auspices and under agency cover, identified only by a single code-word classification: Sandman. The proud Thorne had been miffed, but he was a professional, and he had grudgingly cooperated with this Sandman character they'd saddled him with, turning over what intelligence he had on General Blood's dispositions and even wishing the interloper luck as he watched him slide into the murky waters of the Vinh Te on a moonless night.

When the Sandman took a chair opposite him at breakfast the next morning, Thorne could only choke on his corn flakes and sit there as the Sandman briefed him. When he'd found his voice again, he had used it to demand proof that the mission had been accomplished. Gulliver had reached under the table and hauled up a still-damp ruck full of papers and personal belongings, including a diary and a bloodstained nightshirt.

"To damn-hell with spook-shit," Thorne had boomed in his fractured English. "What is your damn-name, man? Who are you? I'll bet you the boots you are Special Forces. Yes? Tell me! Tell me or I will haf to kill you!"

Gulliver, still resentful over having been put to work for the CIA, and not thinking any more highly of "spook-shit" than Thorne, had shrugged and told him . . . and found himself enveloped in a life-threatening hug, effortlessly jerked off his feet by Thorne, who had rounded the table in a flash, roaring: "I knew it! Too damn-good to be the damn-spook! Goo-leever, you damn-fuck Sandman, I luf you!"

Gulliver had hung around Tinh Bien for a few days more, long enough to get wind of the marketplace rumor that General Blood's army had suddenly melted away, leaving the local Viet Cong perplexed and considerably weakened. He had spent those days resting, if getting drunk with the volcanic Thorne could be called restful. The two had become friends in that short time, with Thorne liable to wrap Gulliver up without warning in a laughing, bone-crushing bear hug, his arms like pythons. Even after all this time, it was hard for Gulliver to accept the idea that Larry Thorne, survivor of a hundred hopeless predicaments, was dead, his chopper lost over Laos less than a year after that meeting. Thorne's body was never found, so there had been no proper memorial, but his name had been enshrined nonetheless, kept alive in Special Forces lore.

The legendary Larry Thorne had been discreet with the story of the Sandman and General Blood, but before he was killed he'd told enough people, the right people, to start Gulliver down the road to becoming something of a Special Forces legend in his own right. The silent shadow who put people to sleep. The Sandman.

The Sandman. The ghoulish tag, the inspiration of some faceless CIA operations planner, had become Jake Gulliver's nickname despite his bitter objections to it—starting with Thorne, who told a select few, then spreading like a cancer once everyone figured it was okay to talk about it, after he left SOG, the Special Operations Group. People moved around a lot in-country, and had too much empty time to fill up with empty gab, Gulliver thought. It was probably inevitable that the growing supply of Sandman stories would be passed around like dog-eared comic books, person to person, place to place, outrageously exaggerated with each retelling.

Gulliver had heard the nickname used in various ways by various strangers: in adolescent awe by young troops wishing to be acolytes; in mocking challenge by bad drunks who didn't think the Sandman looked so tough to them; in false joviality by outsiders, non-Special Forces officers trying to mask an uneasy fear of him. Gulliver had done all he could to stop it from being used at all—a cold glare usually worked, or a polite but unsmiling request when hard looks failed—but it had been like trying to piss into a typhoon without getting wet. Nicknames were as much a staple of Vietnam as heat and mud, and when even the Vietnamese troops knew your nickname, Gulliver had to concede, you were fighting a lost battle.

But a man had to draw a line somewhere, and Gulliver had told Swain the truth; he did let only a few men use the name to his face, men of uncommon ability, men he respected and admired. When such men used the name, it was not in awe or belligerence or fear, but in respect for Gulliver's skills, and he could accept it on that basis. Thorne could call him Sandman. Dang could call him Sandman. Swain could not.

Thinking of Swain, Gulliver squinted into the easing gloom and saw that Swain's head was sticking up a good foot higher than the heads of the men in front and back of him. Off to their flank, he could see lanterns sputtering on. They were nearing a hamlet. He began to work his way toward the middle of the file, toward Swain, moving with care past the others on the narrow dike path.

They were not two hours into the operation and already both of Swain's feet had started to blister from the chafing of the rubber-tire sandals. Before leaving home, Gulliver had advised Swain to put on boots, arguing that anyone who got close enough to notice his footwear would see by his size and features that he was an American. Swain had obviously heard a challenge in the suggestion and had insisted on wearing what everyone else wore. It had been a mistake. The big man was laboring, and Gulliver now made things even worse for him by telling him to lower his six-foot-four-inch profile as they passed Ba Chuc. Swain groaned but complied, bending his knees awkwardly and waddling comically along the dike top like a crippled duck.

Returning to his place at the end of the file, Gulliver dragged some air deep into his lungs and looked around. Dawn was breaking like the Creation itself, out of the South China Sea in the east, daubing the chill morning air with whorled colors that danced at the edge of the world. The string of PRUs was just passing by the last of Ba Chuc village's four hamlets, keeping to the dike paths, a prudent eight hundred meters from the nearest hut. Smoke from cooking fires corkscrewed up from the cluster of huts along the edge of the paddies, climbing a short distance, then flattening out to hang like a parasol over the hamlet. The huts nestled under it like lions taking the shade under the canopy of a giant acacia tree.

A few industrious families were already moving into the fields, husbands and wives together, the children up on the family buffalo, taking reed switches to the dung-encrusted rumps of beasts reluctant to begin another day of toil. A few of the figures in mollusk hats paused, a hand shading their eyes as they tried to make out the line of men who crossed their fields in the distance. Tonight, Gulliver knew, those of keen sight, those who could make out the black pajamas and the silhouettes of AK–47s, would tell their neighbors of the Viet Cong who had passed through that morning.

The PRUs were out of the paddies at last, moving through groves of mango and jackfruit trees, the ground ahead of them rising and falling like the swell of a benign sea. The sun, a burbly, runny yolk, was fully above the horizon and already beginning to assert itself. Directly to their front squatted Nui Giai Mountain, the most accessible of the Seven Sisters, and just beyond, Nui Dai and Nui Tuong, both still dark and forbidding, not yet touched by morning light.

They walked another two kilometers, then stopped for a five-minute break while Captain Prager said good-bye, wishing them good luck and good hunting. Rather than try to retrace his steps and risk being seen by the farmers of Ba Chuc, he would stay there until the PRUs were deep into the foothills. Then he would call for a chopper to pick him up and take him home to his Ruff-Puffs. Dang and Gulliver thanked him for his help and started the troops up again, the two of them at the point, going over the plan one last time.

When the column had gone another three kilometers, Dang stopped it again. Gulliver signaled up the RTOs and had them ring Coughlin at the command-and-control center at Tinh Bien airfield. When the radios had been checked, Gulliver advised Dog Pound that they were ready to split up. The two teams of strikers, Dang's Dog Catcher One and Gulliver's Dog Catcher Two, gave each other a thumbs-up and moved out in opposite directions, hugging the base of the mountain.

Gulliver left Swain at mid-column and remained up front with his new point, Sergeant Phuoc. At forty-five, the team sergeant was Gulliver's oldest and most experienced man, a veteran of the Viet Minh war against the French. It was said that Phuoc had been with General Giap's army at Dien Bien Phu, but the taciturn NCO would only smile whenever the subject came up, neither confirming nor denying the story, and no one pressed him for a straight answer. The PRU was a bit like the French Foreign Legion in that regard—no one dug too deeply into a man's past. All Gulliver really knew about Sergeant Phuoc was that he had come to the PRU from Con Son, the infamous prison island off the southern coast, and that underneath his pajama top, across his chest and back, were the raised signatures of his jailers, the welted grid of the whip.

The PRUs moved into the mountain's shadow, the heat no less oppressive for the shade. If it was this bad this early, Gulliver thought, the rest of the day would be a ball-buster.

Sergeant Phuoc kept them off the obvious trails, using them only when there was no way around, always watching for trip wires. Gulliver and Dang had spent the night before at the Embassy House going over "hot spot" maps, the infrared imagery readouts furnished by MACV J–2 at the request of the Saigon CIA station. They had agreed on the routes to use and where to meet. If neither team got a good snatch opportunity, they would meet halfway round Nui Giai Mountain just before nightfall. The next day they would scout Nui Dai, then Nui Tuong and so on, working through as many of the Seven Sisters as they could, until they found the 18–B or ran out of time.

The last sign of civilization literally was a sign, made of wood, now rotted, adorned with a skull and crossbones, and a hand-lettered proclamation: *Vung Tu-dia*. Deadly Ground.

Of the sign's veracity, Gulliver had no doubt. Signs and portents did not usually spook him, but he was getting a bad feeling about this place and this mission. He thought about breaking open the bag of pills taped to his rib cage, but did not; he made it a rule to use the pills only at night, when the senses needed help. His nerves could use some help now.

The PRUs went through the hot morning and into the hotter afternoon without finding fresh spoor of their enemy. There was the trace of an old cook fire here, stone-hard feces and sandal prints there, but nothing to spark excitement. And yet Gulliver grew more jumpy as the day wore on, unable to shake the feeling they were being watched.

In a way, that did not surprise him. The Seven Sisters were rumored to be enchanted mountains, inhabited by spirits and full of magic. It was said that there were golden temples on the summits, and hermit monks who chose to pray closer to heaven, away from the temporal world below. But Gulliver had yet to meet anyone who had made it to the top and returned to confirm the stories. Anyone who lived atop the Seven Sisters was conditioned to seeing few visitors. The expansive belly of the cordillera, the stretch between the peaks and valleys, was the exclusive fief of the Viet Cong.

Proof of their possession was all around, anywhere one cared to look, manifest in the scars left by the efforts to dislodge them: bomb craters filled with stagnant rainwater and busy mosquito beds, napalm burns still dusted with white ash, smashed trees with fire-blackened trunks and deformed limbs, still pointing fingers of accusation at the sky, from whence their destruction had come.

To keep his mind off spirits and signs of war, Gulliver went down the file and back, checking on the men. They were holding up well in the heat—except for Swain. While he still looked like the athlete he once was, Swain had clearly suffered from his tour of duty behind a desk. He was out of shape and wilting. "Humping the ruck" was tough enough for a man who did it all day every day, Gulliver thought. A year's layoff was like starting all over again, like a cherry just coming in-country.

Swain had lost his spot in the middle of the column and was

now back near the tail, huffing hard and stumbling every few steps, his feet rubbed raw by the tire sandals, just as Gulliver had predicted. Gulliver had been unable to find any pajamas to fit Swain's six feet, four inches and 225 pounds, and so had made do with the largest pair available. The hem of the trousers hit Swain at mid-calf, and his arms shot a foot through the barrel of the sleeves. He brought to mind Dr. Frankenstein's monster, or Li'l Abner dressed in his Sunday-go-to-meetin' clothes. But Gulliver saw no point in worrying over Swain's costume; nothing would make him look like a VC. What worried him was Swain's physical condition.

"You want me to call a break?" Gulliver asked him.

Swain, his face white and drawn, wheezed: "Don't . . . worry 'bout . . . me, Cap. If the gooks can . . . hack it so . . . can I."

"Suit yourself." Gulliver rejoined Phuoc up front.

He waited fifteen minutes for appearances, then called a ten-minute chow halt. The men uncoupled the plastic bandolier tubes holding their PIRs—the patrol indigenous rations—and squeezed a serving of dehydrated rice and fish into their canteen cups. They added a little water, sprinkled on a few drops of *nuoc-mam,* and ate. They ate like dogs, gobbling the food, holding their cups up to their mouths and scooping the glop in with their fingers. Then, after a good belch and a pinch of black Vietnamese snuff, they resumed the march.

It was two hours later that Gulliver decided to check on Swain again, when the PRUs quietly passed up word that the new *Trung Uy* had dropped too far behind, dangerously behind. With an audible sigh, Gulliver began working his way toward the rear.

It had cooled off considerably, the sun's gassy ball now well down behind the mountaintop. Gulliver's team was almost halfway around, drawing near the rendezvous point. They had not seen a single soul since Ba Chuc village, nor anything to indicate that the 18–B Battalion was using Nui Giai Mountain. Neither, apparently, had Dang's team. Dog Catcher Two and Dog Catcher One had been unable to establish direct radio contact because of the mountain mass between them, but Dog Pound was reporting no luck for Dang, either.

The PRUs of Dog Catcher Two were beginning to relax, to cut themselves a little slack. The only contact today would be with Dog Catcher One, and that was fine with them. Most of them wanted nothing more than a good night's sleep. They had been on the move since midnight of the night before and they were exhausted.

In fact, Sergeant Phuoc was in the middle of a yawn when the sniper's bullet hit him in the throat.

The round took Sergeant Phuoc in the hollow at the base of the throat, and he would have strangled on his own blood had a command-detonated mine not shredded him like a soaked tissue in the very next instant. The bullet that killed him was incidental, a signal to trigger the mine.

The mine, an American-made Claymore, threw seven hundred steel balls fifty meters down the track in a sixty-degree fan, killing the next man in line—the slack—and the two right behind. In the wake of the blast came a trailing lull, a moment of reverberating paralysis, a ringing in the ears that blocked out everything, even the hysterical screeching of the monkeys. Then both lips of the trail blew up in a hawking expectoration of automatic weapons fire, as if Satan himself were clearing his throat.

Gulliver had just reached the end of the line—where he'd found Swain struggling two hundred meters behind the appointed drag, his chest rolling like a heavy surf, his feet bloody in the unfamiliar sandals—when the sniper triggered the round that triggered the mine that triggered the ambush. Swain was in a sorry state, but his inability to keep up saved both his and Gulliver's lives. They were clear of the firestorm's eye.

When the mine went off, Swain jumped like an outsize cat, diving for the sanctuary of a circle of boulders on the apron of the path, his exhaustion replaced by a heady brew of terror and adrenaline.

Gulliver, just as quick, sprinted toward the shooting. He got as far as his drag man, who now lay dead across the trail, before being stopped by an RPD—a Ruchnoi Pulymet Degtyarova machine gun—working from a well-camouflaged spider hole. He emptied both barrels of his shotgun at the enemy gun crew, snatched up the fallen PRU's radio, and ran back to the natural rock fortress where Swain waited.

They were quickly joined by a third figure, Gulliver's radiotelephone operator Ti-Ti, who arrived panting, winded from aping Gulliver's madcap dash. The tiny RTO had had to take twice as many steps as Gulliver to get up the trail and back. He was less than five feet tall and had the unfinished face of a boy, even as he neared middle age. He'd been given his nickname—Vietnamese slang for "little"—by Gulliver himself, and he wore it like a medal.

Gulliver had been dubious when Ti-Ti first volunteered to be his personal RTO, joking that the radio outweighed him. But the lilliputian *chieu hoi* had proved hardy and fearless, never tiring and never more than a step from Gulliver's side in action. Ti-Ti idolized the tall American, and they meshed on the job like the gears in Gulliver's Rolex. Now, his eyes glued to the trail ahead, Gulliver reached back a blind hand and Ti-Ti, like an operating-room nurse, slapped the handset into it.

"Dog Pound, Dog Pound, this is Dog Catcher Two; over."

"Dog Catcher Two, this is Dog Pound; over." Even with the channel hiss, Coughlin's calm voice was recognizable.

"Dog Pound, we've stepped in some shit. I don't have a visual fix, but from the fire volume it sounds company-size, maybe more. You better bring up the air and a dust-off. I got at least one KIA and anticipate *boo-coo* casualties; over."

"Copy on tac and medevac. What is your position; over?"

"Stand by . . . we are one thousand meters north of our last-reported coordinates; repeat, one-zero-zero-zero-November of last radio fix; over." Gulliver's words came slow and level, bereft of exclamation points.

"Copy. One klick north of last fix. I'll give you A–37 Dragonflies with napalm. A little dab'll do ya; over."

"Negative; repeat, negatory. Nape's nice, but Ol' Victor Charles is sitting right in our lap. We're too mixed together for fixed wing or arty. We need gunships; over."

"Roger, Two. Choppers you want, choppers you got. I'm scrambling the eggs for you now. Do you want to pull up your team; over?"

"Roger . . . if I've got anybody left to pull. You'd better jerk the chain on Dog Catcher One as well. We've been blown sky-high; over."

"Roger, Two. Our last fix on One puts him less than two klicks from you. You were just about to rendezvous. I'll get him moving on the double. He can help you hold on there, then we'll pull the both of you up at the same time; over."

"A big roger on that, Pound. We can use the help; over."

"Roger . . . uh, stand by . . . just got word that your birds are up. ETA is seven minutes." Then, after a pause, Coughlin said: "Hang tough, Jake . . . we'll get you home. Pound standing by; out."

Gulliver stayed on the frequency to monitor Dog Pound and Dog Catcher One, but the command post was having no luck in raising Dang's team. After a few more unsuccessful tries, Gulliver broke back in, his voice lined with concern. "Pound, this is Two. Where the fuck are they; over?"

"Damned if I know. We had 'em on just a bit ago. They may

have been jumped too, but it can't be so bad they can't get off a call. Let me try again; out." Coughlin's voice had lost much of its lassitude. There was a forerunner of panic in it.

Gulliver listened in as Coughlin tried Dog Catcher One a few more times, getting only freq noise for his trouble. Then Coughlin rang him back: "Two, Pound. No luck with One. ETA on your birds is now five minutes; repeat, five minutes; over."

Exactly five minutes later, two VNAF Huey Hogs and two American-piloted Cobra gunships were *thwack-thwack-thwacking* overhead, looking for something to kill. Gulliver spent those five minutes like a wastrel, on a series of futile gestures.

He had only a dim idea of the tactical situation, unable to see what was happening up ahead, unable to tell by ear who was shooting at whom; his PRUs carried AK–47s, same as the VC.

Nor could he raise anyone who could tell him. The last of the team's radios was up front, but he got no response to his calls. He kept at it, in Vietnamese, in case they could receive if not transmit: "Team Two, this is Top Dog Two. Close air support in four minutes; repeat, tac air in four minutes. Mark your targets with yellow smoke; repeat, pop yellow smoke to mark your targets. Do you copy; over?"

Nothing. No acknowledgment. No yellow smoke. He tried a few more times without success, then decided to have another go at reaching them on foot.

He stayed off the trail this time, circling instead. He hadn't gone ninety meters when he saw three VC hiding behind a big rock, facing the path, their backs to him. The closest cover was a large bramble bush and he crawled into it.

The bush was full of long, sharp thorns that reduced his pajamas to confetti and left him scratched and bleeding in a dozen places. He wriggled to the fore and poked the shotgun's snout through the bramble wall. The VC were unsuspecting, the nearest two whispering with their heads close together, like schoolgirls in class. Gulliver killed them both with a single barrel, then dropped the remaining man with the other.

He backed from the thicket and was down on one knee, the sawed-off twelve-gauge broken open for reloading, when another VC hove into view, coming at a run to investigate the shotgun's unfamiliar report. The soldier saw Gulliver a second before Gulliver saw him. He brought up the muzzle of his AK, then hesitated when he saw the black pajamas and yellowish face. It gave Gulliver time enough to snap the gun shut, trigger both barrels at once, and blow a hole the size of a bowling ball through the man's brisket. Then he reloaded again and took off in a hunched run, back to the refuge of the rocks.

He found Swain alone, working the extra radio. "Where's Ti-Ti?" he asked, breathing hard.

"Jeez! I thought he was with you, Cap. He took off after you."

"The crazy little shit!" But there was nothing to do but wait for him to turn up. Ti-Ti was tough; he'd make out fine.

"What's going on up there?" Swain asked, his voice calm, his tone conversational. He even managed a grin to go with his next question: "How 'bout we just charge the fuckers and kick ass?"

Gulliver gave him an appraising look. Swain had not yet ventured from the protection of the rocks, but neither had he panicked, not since being spooked by the ambush's first big bang. Now he seemed as unconcerned as a Guernsey at pasture. The merit badges had not lied after all, Gulliver thought. Gulliver's Law did work: you do get what you see. If anyone had lost his cool, he himself had. His hands still shook from his encounter with the VC. He wasn't used to working without the pills, he told himself in excuse. It had been nearly a year since he'd killed a man without the pills.

Gulliver shook his head. "The percentages suck, Swain. If anyone's going to get their ass kicked, it's us. And I don't know what's going on up there. My gut tells me they're all dead."

Swain started to nod in agreement, then cocked his head. "Jeez! No they ain't, Cap. Not all of 'em. Listen!"

The ground fire had fallen off to a sporadic hiccuping. Gulliver listened in the spaces between bursts. At first he heard nothing; then, in the next space, he heard it, a faint tremolo: *"Dai Uyyyyyyyyyy! Dai Uyyyyyyyyyy!"* He cupped an ear and it came again. *"Dai Uyyyyyyyyyy! Dai Uyyyyyyyyyy!"* It was a quavery, graveyard sound, high and haunting, like the wail of a Taureg woman ululating.

"Jesus Christ! JESUS FUCKING CHRIST!" Gulliver said in a hoarse whisper. "It's Ti-Ti! He's hit!"

Gulliver tensed, quivering like a bird dog, trying to locate the sound, which now, in the firing's ebb, came clear and unrelenting, a shrieking full of pain and urgency that burned a hole in his brain. He had to stop it!

He was about to rush out when Swain grabbed a dangling remnant of his ruined pajama top and pulled, jerking him off balance and bringing him down hard.

"You sonofabitch!" Gulliver screamed. "Can't you hear him calling? Captain! Captain! He's calling me! *Me!"*

"You can't help him now, Cap," Swain hissed. "Listen!"

Gulliver listened, heard nothing, then realized that was what Swain had meant. The shooting had stopped.

"They're using him for bait, Cap," Swain said, his voice urgent. "They're just waiting for someone, for his *Dai Uy,* to come get him."

Swain was right, of course. Gulliver closed his eyes and tried to blot out Ti-Ti's heartrending cries. *"Dai Uyyyyyyy! Dai Uyyyyyyy!"*

"DAI UYYYYYYYYYY!"

Both men jumped and looked around wildly, their hearts hammering. The sound, loud and searing, had come right out of the earth, right from under their feet!

"DAI UYYYYYYYYYY!"

For a moment Gulliver thought the sound was coming from inside his own head . . . then he spied the radio on the ground. Ti-Ti, a good man to the end, had held on to his radio, had even had the presence of mind to depress the transmit bar so that his hero, his *Dai Uy,* would hear his plea, would come to save him.

"DAI UYYYYYYYYYY!"

Gulliver turned a stricken face to Swain, horrified, tears welling in his eyes. Even Swain looked uncomfortable.

The radio crackled again, but instead of a harpy's cry it was Coughlin, no trace of tranquillity left in his voice. "Two, this is Pound! Who's making that godawful racket? Is somebody singing? What the fuck's going on up there; over?"

"DAI U—"

Gulliver reached down and switched off the radio. They could still hear it, of course, but now mercifully muted, no longer on top of them like a musty, smothering blanket. They slumped wordlessly, avoiding each other's eyes, trying not to hear.

Ti-Ti's cries grew progressively weaker, but it was not until the thudding sound of approaching helicopters began to drift up from the valley floor that they stopped completely. There was one sustained burst of AK fire, then . . . silence.

There was no time to mourn. Gulliver turned the radio on and spoke to the pilots, relaying an imprecise description of the area he wanted them to hose down. He had not seen any VC since his foray out, but he could hear them now, poking into bushes, scuttling over the rocks like crabs in a tidal pool, hunting for food, for *Dai Uy.*

"No sweat, Dog Catcher," drawled a Southern voice, one of the Cobra pilots. "We ain't hurtin' for targets. Got me an eyeball fix and shitload to choose from. I can see the bunch of heathens I want right now. I'm goin' in."

The lead Cobra came in on its run, its twin six-barrel miniguns each spitting out rounds at four thousand per minute in a rousing overture, a prelude to the loosing of its pod-mounted rockets. But before it could touch them off, up from the bush below came a rush of 37mm cannon fire, along with three SA–7, heat-seeking missiles, fired in tandem. One of the SAMs flew up the Cobra's exhaust and the ship exploded in a fireball.

Gulliver, who had clambered up a boulder to watch, stood speechless. What was the 18–B—a sapper battalion—doing with this kind of antiaircraft capability? The radio he had dragged up with him fell mute, crackling one minute with the laconic jargon-peppered patter of professionals at work, hissing like a doused match with empty static the next.

Then the channel reignited with disbelieving voices.

"HOLY SHIT!"

"DU MA!" Motherfucker!

The second Cobra had been drafting behind the first, all ready to deliver the knockout punch in a one-two combination. Its pilot, temporarily blinded by the fireball that consumed his running mate, threw his stick over hard and flew straight into a locustlike swarm of ground fire. His craft seemed to hit a wall in the sky; it stood stock-still, shuddering. The last sound he heard, just before his ship cartwheeled into a rock outcropping, was the rattly sprong of shearing metal as his main rotor coupling disintegrated.

Before the last of the debris fell to earth, one of the Vietnamese gunships had turned for home. The remaining VNAF pilot hovered uncertainly at a prudent altitude, then made a decision and a lazy turn and fluttered after his friend.

A single speck was left in the sky, the dust-off chopper which had been waiting for the gunships to clear a landing zone before coming in on its medevac. It was close enough for Gulliver to see the red cross on its nose. He radioed it.

"Dust-Off, Dust-Off, this is ground commander. Thanks for sticking. I don't know where all the ack-ack came from, but it's sited well away from us. I'll put out some smoke for you and you can drop down, hook us, and be out of here before they can react. How does that sound to you; over?"

The answerback came in Vietnamese, without formal radio procedure: "It sounds as if you are in a very unsafe place, Captain Gulliver."

Gulliver frowned, puzzled: a Vietnamese pilot, one who knew him by name. It had to be one of Medium Minh's boys out of the province town. But all Minh's pilots knew English and were under orders to use it on joint operations. If this guy knew him, he might also know that Coughlin spoke French but not Vietnamese, and that would mean he did not want Coughlin monitoring the conversation.

Gulliver answered in Vietnamese, his voice wary. "You're right, my friend. It is a little unsafe. But not too unsafe for a tiger like yourself, eh? Uh, whom am I talking to?"

"As you said, Captain . . . a friend."

"Good, good. Glad to hear it. Uh, how does my proposal sound to you . . . friend?"

"It still sounds very unsafe, Captain. If I should lose my craft, it would be very big trouble. Even if I survive, it would be very bad for my record. There is much at stake here, for if I were to be grounded because of a foolish decision, I would lose my flight pay, and that would be very hard on my family. This is a very difficult decision for me, my friend; yes, very difficult."

Very, very, very. Gulliver was beginning to understand *very* clearly.

"Yes, I can see the difficulty," he said, trying to keep his voice ingratiating and full of sympathy, even as his lips curled back to bare his teeth.

Swain had been ignoring what he could not understand, but the contrast between Gulliver's wild facial expression and his kindly tone piqued his curiosity. He gave Gulliver a questioning look.

Gulliver ignored him. "Perhaps it would help if you had insurance against such calamity," he suggested to the pilot.

"Insurance! But of course! That is the solution!" the pilot responded with enthusiasm, as if Gulliver had come up with a brilliant and original idea.

"How much insurance would you need?" Gulliver asked.

The reply came promptly. "Two hundred thousand piasters, payable to my go-between immediately upon your safe return."

Gulliver did some quick arithmetic in his head. At the official exchange rate of 118 p' to the dollar, that would be nearly $1,700—even if he went the black-market route, at the current rate of 400 p' to the dollar, the "Bank of India" rate, it would cost him $500. He'd be damned if he'd pay, but he would have to deal with this bloodsucker later. First he had to get himself and Swain out of here. "That sounds reasonable," he said pleasantly.

"Excellent!" the pilot crowed. "If you would be so kind as to mark your position, Captain."

"I'm popping purple smoke . . . friend."

Gulliver unhooked a smoke grenade from his VC rucksack,

found a sufficiently wide spot on the trail, and released the spoon. There was just room enough for the Huey to put down.

It was a windless day and the smoke rose straight up in a lavender column. Gulliver saw the chopper bank sharply and come for it. At the same time, he heard faint shouts from up the trail—the smoke would also serve as a handy beacon for the Viet Cong. But he was not unduly worried; the Huey should win the race easily, with time to spare.

The helicopter was just going into a flare, preparatory to setting down, when the terraced slope directly above the Americans' laager came to violent life: two 37mm guns, their pom-poms in full spate, gushing twin rivers of tracer fire which converged toward an X, trying to put the red cross painted on the chopper's nose in the confluence. The target dipped sharply as the pilot goosed his craft, powering away. He made altitude and was on the radio a second later.

"*Du ma!* It is more unsafe than we imagined, Captain. I am afraid that two hundred thousand piasters is not enough insurance."

"I agree," Gulliver said with a hollow laugh, trying to cover a sinking feeling. "Let's double it to four hundred thousand. What the hell . . . let's make it five hundred. That's a lot of money."

"I'm afraid you are not understanding me, Captain. Money is no longer the issue."

"One million piasters."

"I am sorry."

"Goddammit! You can't leave us here!" Gulliver yelled, no longer concerned with masking his anxiety. "At least stay in the area. We'll work our way out of here, back toward the valley floor, away from the guns. You can pick us up farther down."

"Too dangerous. It's getting dark. Perhaps we can do business together another time, my friend." The helicopter, already moving away, picked up speed, growing smaller in the cloudless sky.

Swain, whose eyes had been moving back and forth from Gulliver's angry face to the helicopter to Gulliver's angry face to the helicopter, finally realized what was happening. Panicking, he stood up and waved his arms like a marooned sailor, shouting after the vanishing helicopter, as though the pilot could hear him and be swayed. "HEY! HEY! COME BACK! HEY, YOU FUCKIN' GOOK SLOPE FUCK! HEY!"

Swain turned a flummoxed face toward Gulliver and asked, whispering now: "Jeez, Cap! Where the hell is he going?"

Away to the front and on their flanks, Gulliver could hear the shouts of the VC, growing louder as they homed on the smoke.

"Home, Swain," he answered with weary resignation. "He's going home."

"J-jeez, Cap! What're we gonna do?"

"We're going to die."

The VC were on both flanks, cooing to one another as a way of staying in touch, about to close their circle. It was get out now or die there in the rocks.

Gulliver slipped into the radio harness and tugged at Swain's sleeve. "Let's move," he whispered.

He had to say it twice more. Swain's face had gone dead. He was fully upright, peering wide-eyed over the top of a big rock, staring with morbid fascination at the soldier who came slowly down the main track, his head swinging side to side, a mere hundred meters away. Behind the point man were another dozen men. The Viet Cong were running a cordon-and-search maneuver, the flankers trying to flush their prey into the firepower of the patrol on the trail.

Gulliver shook Swain again, more roughly, and whispered: "Swain, c'mon! We've got to get out of here!"

Swain came out of it with a shudder, but his eyes never left the enemy point man. In slow motion, like a zombie, he raised his Uzi, steadied it on the rock, and drew a bead.

Gulliver slapped the weapon away. "No!" he hissed. "It's too late for that! It'll give 'em a fix! Let's go, goddammit! Now!"

They left the rocks, staying low and moving at a quick but quiet walk, fighting the urge to run. Gulliver led them away from the trail, playing it by ear—literally—trying to find a link of silence in the VC's chain of soft chatter, a spot where the circle was not yet complete. He had turned off the radio; an incoming call from Coughlin now could prove fatal.

To Gulliver's surprise, Swain was doing fine, moving smoothly and silently with newfound grace, despite the torn feet. He was going strictly on adrenaline and instinct and training, Gulliver knew, impervious to his aches and pains.

They were quiet and careful, but not too careful. There was no time to stop and mull options, no time to feel their way through. Gulliver pushed on unhesitantly. He too was going on adrenaline and instinct and training, but also on experience. He had been in such spots before, and he knew that it was simple enough. Either he was right or wrong. If right, they had a chance . . . if wrong, they did not. About the only good thing one could say about war was that it pruned things back to the roots.

When they had gone three hundred meters, Gulliver knew they

would make it. They were outside the cordon's line of containment, they had good cover—a combination of rocks and heavy growth—and full darkness was no more than half an hour away. It was now just a matter of working down to the bottom of the steppe, finding a good place to hole up for the night, and calling a cab in the morning.

The silence of the monkeys at a time of evening when they were usually the most vocal should have told Gulliver differently. He was just giving Swain a helping hand down the slick face of a deep ravine carpeted with loose rocks when a machine gun opened on them. The first burst chiseled a gouge from the rock next to Gulliver's head, salting his face with a stinging shower of flint chips. The next series found the mark. He felt a burn in his side, as if he had been touched with a soldering iron.

When the shooting started, Swain let go of his handhold and fell the fifteen feet to the gully floor, landing heavily but more stunned than hurt. He was up on a knee, shaking his head to clear it, when Gulliver landed squarely on top of him.

Gulliver lay sprawled across the unmoving Swain for a moment, taking inventory. He put a hand to his side and it came back covered with blood. The wound was painful, but not critical. The round had entered from behind, glanced off a rib, and exited. At least one rib was cracked or broken, but the bullet had gone through clean, clear of organs. His head was fairly clear too—enough to notice that besides holing him, the round had carried off his pills. A dangling strip of adhesive and a flap of cellophane were all that remained of his supply of painkillers.

The shooting had stopped. Somebody would be on the way over to tally up the score, Gulliver knew. He had to move.

He struggled free of the radio harness and checked on Swain. No visible wounds, a strong pulse . . . he must have been knocked out in the fall, Gulliver told himself. He took Swain by the feet and began to drag him down the ravine, his hands slippery with blood, his own and that from Swain's feet, a double helping of steak tartare. Swain's head bounced along the stony ground, but Gulliver could not help that—he had his own problems. Moving Swain's deadweight was like trying to pull a tractor, and with each tug a new flash of pain shot through Gulliver's side, making him dizzy.

When he thought he could pull no more, he kept pulling, looking for a way out of the gully. It would have to be a cut in the wall; getting Swain up a side was out of the question. Getting *himself* up was out of the question.

He pulled another fifty meters before finding it, a gap opening onto a stretch of flat ground dotted with brush. He dragged Swain through it and across the flat, until he feared he would pass out, then hauled himself and his burden into a swatch of tangled growth.

Swain was still out cold, but breathing easily. Gulliver tore away what was left of his own pajama top and, squirming inside a cramped cage of bramble, fashioned a crude dressing for his wound. He had lost a great deal of blood and had to fight off dizziness. When he had finished doctoring himself, he lay back exhausted, sucking for air. It was only then that it occurred to him they were unarmed. He had lost the twelve-gauge in the fall. Both it and Swain's Uzi were back there on the ground with the radio—and their negligent owners were dead men unless he could come up with something.

Gulliver tried to think. The machine-gun crew—gunner and loader—was probably just that, a lone crew, one of several set up along possible escape routes, in case the prey slipped the noose. They would have alerted the main element by now, but for the next few minutes at least there would be just the two of them. Hope flickered, died. So what? Without a weapon, it might as well be a regiment. No brilliant ideas, no tricks of the trade came to him. The storied Sandman was coming up empty.

For Gulliver's pursuers, the smart thing to do, what the Sandman would have done, was to wait for help before starting their search. But they did not wait, and they compounded the error by splitting up. Gulliver heard someone, some *one,* and when he squinted through his window of thorn, he saw a single VC soldier going from bush to bush, stabbing into each with a rifle-mounted bayonet.

The soldier did not seem worried about being ambushed. He and his comrade had undoubtedly found the dropped weapons. Had there been more light, he could have followed the blood trail right to Gulliver's bush. As it was, he would find it soon enough by simple process of elimination.

Gulliver, his mind growing fuzzy, could not think of a countermove. He was too weak to overpower the man. All he could do was lie there and hope the probe missed the mark. He felt Swain stir and clamped a hand over the big man's mouth, his brain screaming: "NOT NOW, ASSHOLE!" Gulliver had never felt so helpless. He wanted to weep with frustration.

It was almost fully dark, but Gulliver clearly saw the VC soldier silhouetted against the sky, saw him approach the bush, saw him raise his rifle, saw a glint of moonrise on the long bayonet.

Gulliver shut his eyes and imagined that he could still see . . .

see the bayonet find his heart . . . see the dull red smear on the blade as it was withdrawn . . . see the triangular-shaped puncture hole, the signature of the Chinese bayonet, in his chest . . . see the white wisp of his soul as it flew out and up and away. He was losing consciousness, slipping under, the combination of blood loss and a last-ditch defense mechanism of a mind reluctant to witness its own end.

But before the veil could fully drop he heard a clatter, then a gargling sound. He forced open his eyes—a tenet of his training had been the quick and accurate identification of unfamiliar noises. But his furred brain did not quite know how to interpret what it saw. The VC soldier had dropped his rifle, and his hands clawed at something behind him. A K-bar was sunk to the hilt just under his armpit. The blade made a rasping sound as it turned and slowly withdrew, scraping bone on the way out. A thick gout of blood bubbled after it, as if a bung had been removed from a wine cask. Gulliver could make no sense of it, until the man slipped silently to the ground, unveiling his killer. "Fucking . . . cavalry," Gulliver croaked. "Day late . . . damn dollar . . . short . . ." He tried to struggle up.

"Ngoi yen!" Be still! Dang slipped the K-bar back into the sheath he wore under his pajama top, at the small of his back, and tore at the bush. *"Dau o dau?"* Where are you hurt?

Gulliver shook his head and said: "Watch . . . yourself. One more . . . somewhere close."

"He, too, is dead," Dang said. He found the wound on his own, dusted it with sulfa powder, and retied the dressing. He pulled up the chain that hung around his neck, uncapped the morphine syringe, and deftly popped it into Gulliver's thigh.

The drug hit Gulliver like a hammer. In seconds his pain went away and the world went soft and dreamy, with everything vague, more felt than seen. His problems, so pressing just a moment before, no longer seemed insurmountable or even very important. Morphine was a revelation! Better than the pills! Better than opium! He grinned a goofy grin.

Dimly, as if from a great distance, Gulliver heard Swain moan once and struggle to a sitting position. Swain was woozy himself, trying to get his bearings. The first thing he saw was Dang, then the body of the Viet Cong soldier.

"Dang! Where . . . Who . . . Jeez! Where did he come from? Who greased him? You?" Then Swain noticed Gulliver, saw the blood on his torso. "Uh-oh! How is he?" he asked Dang.

Gulliver giggled. "How's Harry? Is it hairy enough for Harry?

Harry's . . . my name and hairy's . . . my game." He giggled again and hummed: "I'm Just Wild About Harry . . ."

"Can mau," Dang answered Swain. Using Vietnamese with Swain was the only indication that Dang might be rattled.

"What?"

"He needs blood," Dang said in English. "He is in shock from the loss of blood. You have good size, *Trung Uy*. Are you strong enough to carry him?"

"Jeez, I don't think so," Swain said in a whining voice. "My feet are in pretty bad shape."

Dang gave Swain a stony look. "Then I will carry him. Here, take my weapon. We must go now."

Gulliver felt himself being lifted in a fireman's carry, hung over Dang's shoulder like a rolled-up carpet. The ground started moving under his dangling head, scrolling past like a boring movie, a Warhol movie. In spite of the jouncing, there was no pain. He felt like laughing because there was no pain. But he did not. Even now his training was at work, insisting on silence. He settled for a drowsy grin.

He laid his cheek against Dang's broad, warm back and closed his eyes. He felt happy. Safe. In good hands.

7

THE GARRISON WAS STILL AT BREAKFAST when Jake Gulliver returned to the Embassy House, just twenty-four hours after being carried unconscious into the province town's military hospital. He had the driver swing around the villa and take him straight to the PRU barrack.

The barrack was nearly deserted, with only a handful of men in evidence, but it seemed even emptier than that. The bay rang with funereal quiet, echoing like a freshly robbed grave. The twenty bunks had already been stripped, their mattresses rolled up. On top of the mattresses someone had laid out snapshots of the missing, giving them up for dead.

Gulliver walked slowly down the center aisle, using the cane he'd been issued at the hospital. When he came to the end of the line and saw that Dang was not there, he turned and walked slowly back to the center of the barrack. Then he signaled the men who were there over to him, and told them what little he knew about what had happened on the mountain.

The PRUs heard him out stoically, their faces betraying nothing. They were rough men in a rough trade, not given to emotion. The former criminals among them, paroled murderers and thieves, generally cared for no one but themselves. The former VC soldiers, the *hoi chanh,* knew better than to form strong attachments to comrades who might be dead in a month, a week . . . tomorrow.

Gulliver had known better too, but he had let it happen anyway. When he finished briefing the men, he sat for a while on Sergeant Phuoc's footlocker, looking at the photograph of the team sergeant, then spent an even longer time at Ti-Ti's bunk. He looked at the boyish face in the picture, and heard the tiny radio operator's cries for help. When they grew too loud to bear, he got up and left the building.

He found Dang—along with Cameron, Swain, Riesz, and Coughlin—in the common room sitting around the same poker table where he had so confidently outlined his plan for them only three nights before. It looked as if they had been at it most of the night. Coffee mugs and dirty ashtrays sat around the rim of the table, and maps and readouts were strewn over the felt surface like so many busted flushes.

George Cameron, an unhealthy breakfast in front of him, a jelly glass and a bottle of vodka, jumped up when Gulliver walked in. "Jake! You're out! How are you feeling?"

Coughlin pulled a chair up for him, and Gulliver eased himself down with care, trying not to wince. "Just two clean holes and a couple of cracked ribs," he said. "I was lucky." He looked at the mess on the table. "Conducting an autopsy?"

Cameron sat back down heavily. "Jesus, Jake," he moaned. "We can't figure out what went wrong. All we know is that it went real wrong." Cameron looked tired and scared.

Gulliver glanced over at Dang. "For your team too?"

"If anyone had gotten out, we would have heard by now," Dang said in a flat voice. "No one got out."

"Just you," Gulliver said softly.

Dang stared back, his eyes unfathomable, like two black marbles. "Yes. Just me. The same way it was just you and the *Trung Uy* who got out."

Gulliver nodded. "I seem to remember that we have you to thank for that."

"You got that shit right, Cap," Swain said with feeling.

Dang merely shrugged.

"The hot-spot maps don't show a thing, Jake," Cameron said, picking one up, then dropping it back onto the table. "These pictures were taken the night before the ambush, and there wasn't a damn thing on that mountain then."

"Something sure as shit was there the next night," Swain chimed in.

Gulliver turned to Cameron. "I can see you've decided to take the scientific approach, George," he said. "You pose the anomalies while Swain here states the obvious."

It took Swain a moment to realize he had been insulted. Then he flushed. "Hey, what's obvious, Cap, is that your plan went blooey," he said heatedly. "We were supposed to find the 18–B; they weren't supposed to find us."

"Unless sappers have started carrying 37-*mike-mike* guns and SAM–7s in their rucksacks, it wasn't the 18–B who hit us, Swain," Gulliver shot back. "It was a main-force element, one that wasn't supposed to be there. Don't blame the plan, blame the intelligence."

"The intelligence was yours too, Cap," Swain said. "Who was it who brought in that cadre and his documents?"

"That's quite enough bickering, gentlemen," Cameron said sternly. "It's unprofessional and unproductive."

"Is that going to be the line, George?" Gulliver asked quietly. "That the plan was bad?"

The air of authority left Cameron's face. He took a sip from the jelly glass before answering. "Sloane and Minh are pissed off, Jake," he said with a you-know-how-it-is shrug. "Especially Minh. My guess is that he's going to come after you on this one."

"Come after me how?"

Cameron glanced at the others. Coughlin was staring at the wall. Riesz was feigning interest in an imagery readout. Swain and Dang were watching Gulliver. "Let's talk about it later," he suggested.

"Let's talk about it now, George," Gulliver said. "Come after me how?"

The P officer sighed. "Minh wants you gone, Jake. Out of his province."

"He tell you that?"

Cameron nodded. "And Colonel Sloane has been kind enough to relay his counterpart's sentiments to Saigon."

"They approved the plan," Gulliver said. "Both of them."

Cameron nodded again. "I know that, Jake. All of us did. But look at it from Minh's point of view. Half his PRU force has been wiped out and the palace is on his ass. He's on the rampage and looking for someone to pin it on. You're handy."

Gulliver said nothing for a moment; then: "Well, I've got my after-action report to fill out." He got to his feet and looked at Dang. "Captain Dang, when you're through here, could I see you in my office?"

Dang nodded.

Gulliver turned back to Cameron. "Just out of curiosity, George, who did Sloane call in Saigon?"

"Steelman."

When Gulliver did not respond, Cameron added, "Steelman wants a full briefing. He's flying down this afternoon."

"He's coming *here*?" Gulliver said in a strangled voice.

"Yes, I'm afraid so. We're in for a heavy shitstorm, Jake."

The two men stared grimly at each other, until Gulliver set his cane on the table and started walking, awkwardly but unaided, toward the hallway leading to his office.

Gulliver spent only a few minutes working on his report before giving it up. He had much to think about, but nothing to say. The ambush remained a mystery.

He had a theory about such things. Gulliver's Law Number Two: when there are no easy answers, the next best approach is to pose hard questions. But even that proved to be more than he could handle. The news that Steelman was coming was an insurmountable distraction, a prospect which filled his stomach with a bile he could almost taste.

He looked up and saw Dang in the doorway, watching him, waiting for an invitation to enter. Gulliver had the feeling that Dang had been there for some time.

"Dang. Come in and sit down. Shut the door."

When Dang was seated, Gulliver wasted no time. "What happened on the mountain?"

Dang shrugged. "You were there. They were waiting. Our intelligence, the cadre's documents, it was all a lie."

"No shit," Gulliver said impatiently. "You know what I mean. What happened to Dog Catcher One?"

"The same thing that happened to you," Dang said. "First a big mine, then machine guns and rocket-propelled grenades from all sides."

"How did you avoid getting caught in it?"

"I was far in front, scouting. They let me go by so they could surprise the main column. Then they sent four men after me. I killed them."

"That's how it happened? Just like that?"

"Yes, my friend. Just like that."

Gulliver said nothing for a moment, then asked: "Did you know that Pound was trying to reach you while we were getting the shit kicked out of us?"

"Yes, he told me."

"Why didn't you answer?"

"You would have to ask my radio operators that question. I did not take a radio with me on my reconnaissance."

"Why did you leave your own team to help us?"

"There were too many VC between me and my people," Dang

said. "There was nothing I could do for them, except perhaps die with them. And I am not one of Minh's cowboy film heroes, my friend—I was not concerned with helping you, but with helping myself. I was looking for a passage off the mountain when I heard the machine gun fire on you. It was fate that I happened to be close by."

When Gulliver fell silent again, Dang said: "I do not understand the reason for these questions, Sandman. Or why you are so angry."

"Goddammit, Dang!" Gulliver exploded. "We just lost half our fucking team. We just lost twenty men. Twenty! Why aren't *you* angry?"

"What would be the use of anger?" Dang asked calmly. "I am sad, but not angry. And neither my sadness nor your anger will change things."

"Jesus," Gulliver said wearily. "No Eastern philosophy today, okay, Dang? I'm not in the fuckin' mood."

"These things happen, Sandman."

"Not to me they don't. And not to you either. We're too good."

"Without reliable intelligence, a soldier's skills are useless."

Gulliver shook his head and laughed bitterly. "It must be nice to have a homily for every occasion, an answer for every question."

"I have no answers," Dang said with another shrug. "Like you, I have only questions."

Gulliver sighed. He was suddenly anxious to be rid of Dang. He wanted, needed, to be with Nhu. She would be back from Rach Gia today. She would comfort him; she would make his pipes.

"All right, no more questions," he said. Then he paused, remembering something. Even though all the PRUs were required to sleep in the barracks, a few of them had families living in a collection of squalid shacks beyond the compound, in the shade of the palms at the edge of the bulldozed clearing. He asked one more: "Did any of those men keep families here?"

Dang nodded. "I think yes, perhaps two or three."

Gulliver had a vision of wailing wives and questioning, wide-eyed children, of a little boy with black eyes, large and liquid. "Will you go talk to them? I don't think I'm up to it."

"Yes, of course," Dang said. "It is my responsibility in any case."

"Tell them that since no bodies have been recovered, the men will be carried on the books as MIA," Gulliver said, "and that their salaries will be accrued. I'll see if I can fix it so some of the money can be released."

Dang nodded and got up to leave. He had his hand on the doorknob when Gulliver said, "Dang, tell me one more time it happened the way you said it did."

"It happened the way I said it did, Sandman."

Gulliver stared at him for a moment, then nodded. "Okay, go on and talk to the families. And, Dang, thanks for bringing me home."

Sally Teacher was just sitting down to her first chore of the day, thumbing through the local papers, when Bennett Steelman poked his head into her office and announced: "If you still want to go to the Delta, be ready in one hour."

"An hour!" she protested. "But you said sometime in the next few weeks! Couldn't you have given me a little notice?"

"Afraid not, old girl. Something's come up."

Sally noticed that Steelman, always impeccably groomed, had not yet shaved this morning. "What is it?" she asked.

"I returned from Danang late last night to the news that one of our Provincial Reconnaissance Units had been chewed to bits. Guess whose."

"Oh no! What happened?"

"No one's really quite sure," Steelman said, his voice sounding pinched. "Acting on obviously tainted information, Gulliver's PRU went into Chau Doc province to look for that sapper battalion I told you about, the 18–B. The communists were expecting them. It was a fiasco."

"But I thought you told me that the . . . 18–B is it? . . . was someplace else," Sally said, confused.

"It is. We've confirmed that it's in Vinh Long province, right where *my* man said it was. We don't know who it was that Gulliver bumped into, but we know it was not the 18–B. It was a regular main-force outfit, and a sizable one at that, with antiaircraft guns, surface-to-air missiles, the works."

"How big a fiasco?" Sally asked.

"Total, I'm afraid. Two U.S. helicopters and their crews lost, twenty PRUs missing and presumed dead, and one American adviser wounded. Gulliver himself."

"Oh dear. Badly?"

"No. Unfortunately."

Before Sally could say anything more, Steelman glanced at his watch and said, "You now have fifty-six minutes. I'll meet you in the parking lot. If you're not there, I'll leave without you." He turned and walked off.

Sally locked up her office, went home and packed a bag, and was back at the embassy in forty-five minutes.

Steelman said little on the drive to the airport, only that they would be stopping at Can Tho before continuing on to the province town; Steelman was paying a surprise call on Tom Patton, the company's Delta base chief. For most of the ride he sat slumped and silent in the corner of the seat, and Sally thought it best to leave him alone with his mood.

It was a few minutes past noon when they left from the sprawling Tan Son Nhut air base, flying out of the isolated, restricted Air America terminal. The agency airline had laid on a Beech Twin Bonanza for the chief of counterintelligence operations.

As they lifted off and gained altitude, Sally looked for landmarks. She could see the stately twin spires of the Roman Catholic cathedral rising up from the roundabout in front of the PTT, the post and telegraph building. Her villa on Nguyen Du Street was only two blocks from the church, but before she could find it they were across the Saigon River and over lush wetlands. Sally thought she had never seen anything so green.

She did not have long to enjoy the view. They spent only a short time at cruising altitude before the pilot began his descent into Can Tho. Sally was aware that both Can Tho and the province town were less than a hundred miles from Saigon, but it was still a full day's drive when the ferry crossings and military checkpoints were factored in. Besides, all CIA officers—especially one of Steelman's rank—were under orders to stay off the roads unless it was unavoidable.

While Patton did not know that Steelman was coming, his duty officer did. Early that morning, Saigon had telephoned with instructions to arrange transportation for the chief of operations and to find and secure a decent local restaurant for his lunch. The duty officer was ordered to say nothing of this to anyone, and to omit the call from his logbook.

An air-conditioned Ford Bronco met them at the airfield and delivered them to Patton's air-conditioned office in the CORDS compound. Sally practically had to trot to keep up as Steelman breezed by Patton's flustered secretary and into the base chief's office with the air of a slum landlord touring his holdings.

Bennett Steelman did not give the startled CIA officer time for pleasantries, did not even pause to introduce Sally. He dropped into a leather chair with a whoosh of cushion air and asked in a tone that matched the frigid room temperature: "What is going on with Cameron's bunch, Tom? To be specific, with Gulliver's PRU?"

"I . . . I'm not sure that I know, Bennett," Patton said. His smile of welcome was frozen in place, slow to catch up with Steelman's mood and out of synch with the apprehension that was already beginning to settle over the rest of his face.

"It is your job to know, Tom. And if you were doing your job I would not have had to take time out from my schedule to come down here and do it for you."

Stunned, Patton looked from Steelman to Sally and back. He tried to speak but Steelman held up a hand. "No. I don't want excuses, old boy. What I do want are copies of all the operational progress reports, field information reports, and after-action reports filed by Cameron's shop in the last six months. And I want a list of all agents recruited during that same period . . . every Vietnamese you have entered on a central agent record card. Miss Teacher and I are going to lunch now. We should be about an hour. When we've finished, we will be returning to the airfield. I expect you to be there with the materials I've requested." With that, he unwound his elastic body from the chair and strode out of the office.

When they boarded the Beech an hour later, Steelman was carrying a large box of papers. He took his seat and started skimming through them, wholly absorbed. He did not utter a word to Sally during the short flight to the province town.

As they disembarked, Sally saw that this time Steelman had let the province team know he was coming. Another Bronco was on hand to meet them, along with a perspiring provincial intelligence officer. And this time Steelman was gracious enough to introduce her. As Sally took George Cameron's hand, she noticed that it shook. She put it down to age—the man looked old enough to be her grandfather—and she blamed the vicious sun for the splotches that lay high on his vein-burst cheeks like wildflowers in a mountain meadow.

Cameron made a fuss over Sally, flirting shamelessly but innocently, taking pains not to let his watery eyes linger on her shape, even though the belted jumpsuit she wore showed it off to spectacular advantage. The P officer beamed at her and his words of welcome sounded sincere. He insisted on carrying her overnight bag and vanity case. Sally liked him.

As they rode along in air-conditioned comfort toward the hot-looking haze that marked the center of the province town, Cameron reviewed the arrangements, chattering on like a riled blue jay, clearly nervous and trying not to show it. He sat in front beside the Nung driver, his body twisted around in the seat so he could talk face-to-face with his passengers.

"Bennett, you'll be staying over at Palm Springs—the CORDS compound—with the PSA. Sloane wanted it that way and I thought it best to let him have his way. Colonel Minh, the province chief, also offered, but I had to decline. He didn't want our PRUs or Nungs camped out on his lawn, and I wasn't about to trust your safety to his private goons. Also, there wasn't enough time to run a security check on his household staff. I'm putting Miss Teacher up at the Embassy House. You should be comfortable there, Sally."

Sally nodded and was relieved to see that Steelman, too, was nodding. She felt vaguely reassured by the idea that they would be spending the night in different compounds. She had given Steelman the benefit of the doubt, but the possibility that he might have a dirty weekend in mind had occurred to her.

Cameron had wondered as well, Sally saw. He was watching Steelman closely for a reaction to the sleeping arrangements. When he saw no more annoyance in Steelman's face beyond that which was always there, he breathed an almost audible sigh of relief and went ahead with his briefing.

"I don't see any problems on the meetings you asked for, Bennett. You're seeing Minh and Sloane this afternoon, and the house briefing is laid on for tomorrow morning. You're all set too, Sally. The province chief has arranged for you to meet with a few of our local Hoa Hao tonight."

Steelman spoke up for the first time since leaving the airfield. "What about Gulliver? Is he well enough to attend tomorrow's team meeting?"

"Jake? Sure, Jake's okay if he doesn't move around too much. He's still got a lot of pain from the ribs, but they're wrapped good and tight and he can get around the house okay. Lieutenant Swain is filling in for him. They were both lucky to come out of it alive. If it hadn't been for our PRU team leader, Da . . ." Cameron caught a cold look from the back seat and he switched gears as abruptly as if Steelman had thrown a switch. ". . . but I guess you don't want to hear all this now. Plenty of time to talk later. Besides, we're here. Home sweet home. I thought we'd drop you off first, Sally."

The compound had been well prepped. The Nung sentry at the entrance saluted smartly as one of his colleagues swung open the heavy gate. Half a dozen other Nung soldiers lined each side of the driveway in a makeshift honor guard, and a cluster of household servants in white jackets waited on the villa's veranda to take Sally's luggage—ten willing hands for two small pieces. Sally and Steelman were out from under the sun and into the cool common room a few steps later. Only George Cameron, who'd sat smack in the blast of the Bronco's air-conditioner the entire drive in, was sweating.

While a servant took Sally's cases upstairs, the three of them sat down for a cool *citron pressé* served by Chi Ba.

"I didn't think you would want the whole team to meet you," Cameron said, "so everybody's either still at work or holed up getting their briefings ready for tomorrow."

Steelman said nothing.

"I thought we'd have a family dinner here at the house tonight, Bennett; just us company folks," Cameron rattled on. "Colonel Minh has arranged for a local doctor named Loan to feed you, Sally. This guy Loan is one of the Hoa Hao movers and shakers here, and he's invited a bunch of other Hoa Hao leaders to a dinner in your honor. They've been told only that you're with the American embassy, a kind of goodwill emissary from Ambassador Cave. Even Minh thinks you're State Department. It would never occur to him that we have female spooks."

"Thank you, George. That sounds wonderful," Sally said quickly, sensing that Cameron was desperate to talk about anything but the one thing that had brought Bennett Steelman to the province. She felt sorry for him and wanted to help. "But when you say leaders, what exactly do you mean? Are these people going to be church leaders or party leaders?"

With a look of enormous gratitude, Cameron laughed and asked: "What's the difference?"

She laughed too, conceding his point. The Hoa Hao sect had always been as much a political movement as a religion. Spiritually, Hoa Haoism was a kind of poor man's Buddhism, teaching that inner faith was more important than external trappings, that gaudy pagodas and elaborate ceremonies were not necessary for the worship and glorification of God, and neither were fancy weddings or funerals or anything else that caused financial hardships for the people. On a more temporal plane, the sect's objective was an unchanging one: military, political, and economic control of its traditional home areas.

"The way the Hoa Hao see it, what's good for the church is good for the party and vice versa," Cameron was explaining to Steelman. "They have a history of opposition to just about everyone—foreign devils like us, the communists, whichever government happens to be in power in Saigon at any particular time. Of course, as Sally can tell you, all they really care about is their own . . ." He stopped abruptly.

Bennett Steelman had come quickly to his feet and was staring fixedly over Cameron's shoulder. Sally turned too, following his eyes, and saw a man bare to the waist except for a heavy wrapping of bandages standing at the bottom of the stairway, staring stiffly back at Steelman.

Cameron scrambled to his feet, threw a wistful look in the direction of the bar, where the rows of bottles ran as straight as soldiers on parade, and said in an overly hearty, unconvincing voice: "Why, Jake! Come in! Come in! Join us!"

The man moved toward them, walking slowly, favoring his right side, his eyes never leaving Bennett Steelman.

"Sally, this is Captain Jake Gulliver, our PRU adviser," Cameron said. "Jake, meet Sally Teacher, the loveliest spook in all Vietnam, ha, ha."

Gulliver did not even glance in the woman's direction, and Cameron hastily added, "Uh, I believe you already know Bennett Steelman."

Steelman, his thin lips curled in a travesty of a smile, spoke first. "Hello, Sandman," he said softly. "It's been a while."

"Not long enough," Gulliver said evenly. "And the name is Gulliver. There is no Sandman. He no longer exists."

Steelman, holding on to the maimed smile, did not reply. After an awkward silence, Gulliver turned to Sally and said, without offering a hand: "Pleased to meet you."

His face said differently. Sally saw a contempt in his eyes and, after a puzzled moment, realized with a jolt that this man clearly thought she was along as Bennett Steelman's plaything. She reddened without cause and nodded curtly. She did not smile or get up.

Sally thought him the oddest-looking man she had ever seen. His wolfish face was a yellowish orange-brown, like a pomegranate left too long in the sun, and the creases in his cheeks reinforced the impression of a rotted fruit. His pale eyes seemed colorless, opaque like an albino's, and were set in deep sockets, giving him a ghastly countenance. His short hair was almost pure white, and Sally had the feeling it had gone white quickly, overnight even, as if from a bad scare. Maybe he'd paused at a mirror, she thought uncharitably. He was thin but marbled with muscle. It ran along his chest and arms in strings that quivered occasionally, as if electrical charges were passing through him. A blood spot the size of a quarter had begun to seep pinkly through the dressing around his waist. He wore jeans and sandals and a tribal bracelet on one wrist. He matched precisely the sketch Steelman had drawn for her: he looked every inch the professional killer.

"Well . . ." Cameron said in the resounding lull, a note of desperation in his voice. He turned to Sally. "I'll show you to your room." He swung back to Steelman. "Then we'll get you settled in over at Palm Springs."

The news that Sally and Steelman would be spending the night in different places registered on Gulliver's face. The flicker of surprise was gone almost as soon as it came, but Sally caught it. She gave him a brief, stony smile.

"I have some personal errands to run first," Steelman said. "Just have my bag sent over to Colonel Sloane's. I'll be along shortly. And I'm afraid I won't be able to join you for dinner this evening. I have other plans."

"Huh? Oh, yeah, sure, whatever you say, Bennett. Uh, how well do you know our little burg?"

Steelman shrugged. "Not very well."

"Then maybe I'd better go with you. We're no Washington, D.C., but we're big enough to get lost in."

"I'll manage," Steelman said curtly. "What you can do is provide me with a vehicle and a driver."

"Oh sure, whatever you want." Cameron, his priorities in place and raring to complete his tasks, looked apologetically at Sally. "Uh, I'm sure Jake here would be more than happy to show you to the guest room. Wouldn't you, Jake?"

Before Gulliver could answer, Sally said: "I'm certain I can find it by myself. You go ahead. I'll be fine."

"You sure? Okay, uh, great . . . great. End of the hall, the last room on the right. I'll see you all later," he said and, sweating more heavily than ever, rushed off to find a car and driver for the chief of operations.

Steelman walked Sally to the stairs, a proprietary hand on the small of her back. "I won't see you until morning, so have a pleasant evening, old girl," he said. "You can tell me all about the Hoa Hao tomorrow. *Ciao* for now."

Sally climbed the stairs and paused uncertainly at the top. What had Cameron said? The right?

She poked her head through the first door she came to and saw a small suite as overfurnished as a spinster's parlor, crammed with chairs, side tables, and wardrobes. She also saw unmistakable evidence of occupancy. A man's personal belongings were strewn about and the walls were papered with girlie-magazine centerfolds. Draped over a tufted chair was a military blouse with a name tag reading "Swain." The name rang a bell, and Sally nodded to herself, vaguely remembering the rather unpleasant young Army officer who had dropped by her office in Saigon.

The door to the next set of rooms had George Cameron's name stenciled on it, and the room after that was Gulliver's. There was no name on the door and, when she cracked it open and peered in, no conveniently marked article of clothing, but it had to be Gulliver's. The lair matched the animal.

Sally stepped inside and looked around, curious about how someone like Gulliver, someone like the Sandman, lived. It was a Spartan chamber, compulsively tidy and totally bare of nonessentials. The sitting room was empty except for a single straight-backed wooden chair. In the bedroom beyond, there was nothing more than a spare bunk rigged with mosquito netting and an army footlocker. There was a ceiling fan, but no air-conditioning unit, and all the windows were open wide. The air inside the room was as dankly oppressive as the air outside. It was, Sally decided, about as close as one could come to living out-of-doors while still being bracketed by four walls.

She backed out of the room, turned . . . and almost fainted. Captain Gulliver was standing right in front of her, his arms folded across his bare chest, an amused look on his face.

"It's the next one down," he said quietly.

Sally had no idea how long he'd been standing there; she had not heard a sound. All she heard now was her own pounding heart. She was startled, but even more embarrassed.

"Oh . . . uh, thank you . . . I . . . I didn't . . . Thank you. . . ."

She could feel the heat on her skin as she brushed by him and ducked into the guest room.

She crossed to the window air-conditioner and turned it up. Her face was still on fire, on the brink of combustion. Retracing her steps, she locked the door, turned and put her back against it, and whispered: "Damn."

8

GULLIVER SHOOK OUT A HANDFUL of pills, hesitated, then put all but two back in the bag. He took them with tepid tap water that smelled and tasted of sulfur, splashed some water on his face, and rose up to look into the mirror above the sink. The naked man staring back was a stranger, but vaguely familiar, an unsavory-looking character with hard, taunting eyes. There was a smile, faint and cruel, on the stranger's face as he watched Gulliver watch him while they both waited for the pills to do something about the pain in their side.

Gulliver waited stoically, almost comfortable with the pain now. Dr. Loi, the Embassy House doctor, had prescribed two tablets every four hours, and he had taken only two. He felt inordinately proud of himself.

Through the common wall separating their bathrooms, he could hear the woman from Saigon moving around. He heard her drop the seat and use the toilet, her stream loud and bawdy, heard her run a bath and give out a little moan as she slid into the hot water, heard her splash and hum. It all came as clearly as if he were sitting on the rim of her tub waiting to scrub her back.

Gulliver closed his eyes and watched her lather up, saw soapy hands heft heavy breasts, then slide down the long body like chamois over porcelain. The inner turmoil he had felt at seeing Steelman again had ruled out a conclusive look at her downstairs, but he had not missed the swell of breast and the skin the color and texture of country cream. The first two buttons of her jumpsuit had been artfully left undone.

He felt a cold burn, like that of a dog's nose under the bedcovers, and looked down to see that he had an erection and that it was poking the sink. He wasn't surprised. He had been randy ever since the ambush, and the thought of Sally Teacher laving herself just beyond the tip of his phallus made him a little dizzy. He had not been with a white woman in nearly seven years.

Gulliver took hold of himself with both hands and began a rhythmic pull, rocking heel-to-toe, slow and easy, mindful of his wound and of the fact that he was still chafed and raw from the session with Nhu earlier that afternoon.

He closed his eyes again and saw Sally Teacher's white, cretaceous body buck under him, banging back, no spongy give to it, so much more substantial than the fragile, honey-hued Vietnamese bodies he was used to. Here was no yellowed autumn leaf, dry and brittle. Here was a solid frame, one that did not threaten to crumble under his weight. A Made-in-America body, a Body-by-Fisher body, a Timex-watch body . . . one that could take a licking and keep on ticking.

His eyes fluttered open and he had a glimpse of himself in the mirror. The ribald Paris postcard in his seething head dissolved, replaced by the one he now saw in the glass: a man up on tiptoes, his face as suffused with blood as his penis, contorted and lost in slack-mouthed lust.

That snapshot made way for yet another, one of a young Jake and his buddies standing in a melon patch, howling and hammering on one another in slapstick glee as Ulysses "Yule the Fool" McAlister masturbated. "Loping the mule" they called it. That was before they had taught Yule how to have sex with a melon—even more hilarious, because when he was done he would always eat the melon, jism and all—but still it was enough to break the monotony of a Carolina summer's day. The amiable mongoloid would grin the askew grin of the idiot at them as he flailed away, a glistening rope of drool on his chin, his eyes rolled back to show only the whites, an animal's bark issuing from his lopsided mouth.

Yule the Fool had looked very much like the strange man Gulliver had just seen in his mirror.

Gulliver let go of himself in disgust. What in the hell was the matter with him? He wasn't sure, but guessed that it was some sort of reaffirmation-of-life syndrome at work, a heightening of the procreative impulse after a close brush with death. The animal, made freshly aware of its mortality, instinctively rushing to reproduce, to ensure the survival of the species.

It made a certain sense. He was always abnormally horny right after an operation, and ever since the ambush, since he had come to in the hospital, he'd been in what could only be called a sexual fever. The nurses who had tended him during his short stay had fled the ward red-faced and giggling to tell the others about the American who grew hard whenever a woman came near. He had even sprung a boner when they cleaned out the holes in his side and wrapped his ribs. Had he been a Vietnamese soldier, the nurses would not have batted an eye, but they did not get many American patients, and they must have found him a remarkable beast indeed.

There was nothing particularly remarkable about him now; he had gone flaccid. What had been the center of a universe only a moment before was now a mere hank of idle meat, and a sore one at that, a casualty of his afternoon visit with Nhu, when he had suffered yet another seizure of satyriasis.

He had found Nhu home from Rach Gia and unusually moody, erratic as a gypsy moth, veering without warning between mild euphoria and sudden weeping jags. She had opened her door to him and gone rigid, her dark eyes expanding like a stain on a blotter; then she had rushed to him, burrowing her face into his chest and banging his tender ribs, sobbing "*Anh* Jake! Oh, *Anh* Jake!" as if she had not expected to see him again.

She had been content simply to sit with him, to hold his hand and run her fingers along his cheek, but he had wanted, had demanded, more carnal evidence of intimacy. And when the pipes had helped numb his side, he'd had his way, browbeating her into complaisance, lying on his back while she straddled him and, with proper concern for his sore ribs, put her body, if not her heart, into her work.

He toweled off, wrapped on a sarong, and lay on his bunk, adjusting to accommodate his side. The two pills had not been enough, and his erotic exercise, his Yule the Fool imitation, had not helped matters. But he would not take any more pills until it was time. It had become a matter of pride.

To take his mind off the pain, he thought about what he had done in the bathroom. Nothing to be proud of there. He felt ashamed, as if he had been unfaithful to Nhu in fact as well as fantasy. He did not blame himself entirely. He also blamed the Teacher woman. The *loveliest spook in all Vietnam*. Steelman's slut. And he blamed the man in the mirror.

Then it came to him. He knew where he had seen the man in

the mirror before. It all fit: the tight, taunting smile, the undeniable air of superiority, the eyes full of mocking contempt and pity. The man in the mirror was no stranger. No stranger at all. It was his old sidekick—the Sandman.

It was the shock of seeing Steelman again that had led to the Sandman's unexpected and unwelcome visit, Gulliver told himself, hoping it was so. He had told Steelman that there was no Sandman, that he no longer existed, but he wondered. Could it be that the Sandman was still there inside of him, just biding his time, waiting to be unleashed, well rested and deadlier than ever?

Gulliver had not set eyes on Bennett Steelman in nearly eight months, not since the time of the Vuong Affair, and he had not expected ever to see him again. He had thought that would be the end of it. The life he had now was bad, but not as bad as the life he'd had back then, when all Steelman had to do was push a button and the Sandman was activated, coming to life like some sinister robot.

The killing of General Blood had been the start of it, the first of the Sandman missions, the first lurching drop in a fall from grace as final, as complete, as any since Adam was turned out of the Garden.

But hadn't it really begun before that, with a different crossing of a different border under different, yet similar circumstances—with the killing of a man with an equally colorful nickname: the Red Prince? *No*. That had been Special Forces, a military show from bore-hole to butt-plate. *Yes*. That *had* been the start of it. Special Forces may have done the job, but it was the CIA's idea. And when he got his man, he got their attention . . . and got his foot caught in their trap.

But if that was when and where it had begun to go wrong, how had it gone wrong after that? He had never been quite sure. The same way America itself went wrong, he guessed. A little at a time, one turning away of the eyes after another, until all the times you said yes when you should have said no added up to where you couldn't say no anymore . . . to where you had too much invested.

He thought about the face he'd seen in the mirror; far older than its years, discolored and lined, each and every compromise gouged in. It was the face of a vandalized piece of sculpture. The face of a used-up man. Where had his youth gone? Had he ever had one? Of course he had, he told himself irritably, but it seemed so long ago. He had been so young when he had first come in-country, a simple soldier, anxious to test his training, and convinced that the mission—to save the freedom-loving people of South Vietnam from Godless Communism—not only was worthwhile but also could be accomplished in short order. That was the kind of confidence that Special Forces fostered in a man in those early years.

He had been with Special Forces off and on, mostly on, since joining up twelve years before. And God how he'd loved it! Not only because it had been an alternative to becoming a tobacco farmer like his father and brothers, but because of Special Forces itself—romantic and adventurous, a chance to do demanding and important work. A man had to love it or it made no sense. The straight-leg Army, nonparatroopers, had a deep and long-standing bias against elite units, and an officer who pulled more than a tour or two was hammering nails in his career's coffin. That had never concerned Jake Gulliver much. As far as he was concerned, he had not joined the Army, with its structures and strictures. He had joined Special Forces.

He had been headed for the south forty when he staged his rebellion, dropping out of N.C. State a semester short of a degree, lying around the house until his father threatened to boot him out, then enlisting one morning, still half-drunk after spending the night before in a Hay Street bar getting shitfaced with a bunch of Special Forces noncoms from Bragg. He had listened wide-eyed to their wild stories, had envied their maudlin but touching camaraderie, and he had drawn the obvious and beckoning comparison between their exciting and unpredictable lives and the narrow furrow of a life that was waiting for him between the rows of golden leaf on a piss-ant tobacco patch ten miles outside Fayetteville, North Carolina.

From the day he took the oath on that hung-over morning in 1958, Gulliver's life had been anything but predictable. After basic there was Airborne and Ranger training at Fort Benning, and then the language school at Monterey, where he had been all set to study Mandarin when they had snookered him into Vietnamese instead—forty-seven long weeks of it. Even then the United States Army had seen a future for itself in Vietnam.

His first posting had been to the 101st at Campbell, but he put in for Special Forces as soon as he was eligible, the day he made sergeant. With a language and jump-qualified, he was taken at once, and after one more service school, at Fort Bragg's Special Warfare Center, a mere fifteen-minute drive from where he'd started, he had at last put on the beret.

In typical Army fashion, some personnel type had noticed Gulliver's language qualification . . . and sent him straight to Laos, where, of the many dialects spoken, none was Vietnamese. First it was to one of the A-teams helping to train the Royal Lao Army under Operation White Star, then to the highlands to help General Vang Pao organize his private army of Meos, and finally to the grassy uplands of the Boloven Plateau to work with the Kha tribesmen. Laos had been his initial experience with CIA control over Special Forces operations, but it had all seemed harmless enough at the time; something of a boon in fact, given the bottomless nature of the agency's purse.

In the year Gulliver spent in Laos there had been only one extraordinary episode. It started when a Pathet Lao POW told the Americans that his commander was a renegade prince of the Lao royal family. Like his cousin Souphanouvong, this blue-nosed black sheep had taken the *nom de guerre* of the Red Prince, and after engagements in Laos he would take his army into China for rest and refitting, to a base camp just across the border. Aware of the propaganda value such a leader would have to Hanoi, the agency asked the Special Forces detachment nearest the border for a volunteer to cross over and bag this Red Prince for them. The detachment commander considered the idea insane, but he had put it to his men caveats and all. To his surprise, Sergeant Gulliver, his best weapons specialist, volunteered.

Six hours after Gulliver crossed the border he was back, and the Red Prince was dead. Gulliver had found the Pathet Lao's perimeter security lax to the point of nonexistence, so confident were they of the inviolability of China's border.

The spooks had been delighted. There could be no medal for Sergeant Gulliver, of course; Laos was still very much a secret war then, and the very idea of going into China was enough to chill the blood of a Congress whose worst nightmare was that the Red Chinese would be provoked into entering the war. But the cowboys took note, squirreling away Gulliver's name for a rainy day. His Army superiors took note as well, tapping him for officer-candidate school. Gulliver himself put the whole thing out of his mind. It was just one more job that had needed doing. Had he known where it would eventually lead him, he would have followed the oldest rule in the book: never volunteer for anything.

Gulliver had been shipped home to Fort Benning for OCS, leaving only a few months before all U.S. military personnel were forced out of Laos by the Geneva Accords of 1962. He had had to wait more than a year to get back into Special Forces, until he made first lieutenant; Special Forces would not take butter-bar second lieutenants. Then it was back to Indochina, Vietnam this time, the system finally working, his experience in Laos and his language skills tailor-made for the Civilian Irregular Defense Group program.

CIDG had been the most rewarding experience of his life. He worked with the Rhade Montagnards at Buon Tong Bong in the Central Highlands, commanding a split A-team, six men rather than the traditional dozen, living among the people the way they lived, eating what they ate, teaching them how to defend and care for themselves. To Gulliver, CIDG was Special Forces at its very best, what Special Forces was all about.

It was still early on in the CIDG program and his team, Detachment A–212, used the excellent model established the year before at Buon Enao by the very first CIDG detachment, Captain Ron Shackleford's A–113. Gulliver and his NCOs armed their Yards with modern weapons and schooled them in village defense. They supervised the construction of stockades and punji traps. They showed the tribesmen where and how to clear fields of fire. They taught patrol and ambush techniques. No longer would the proud but primitive Montagnards have to bow before the Viet Cong as helpless supplicants, used as slaves, pressed into service as porters or suicide troops, only to be called *moi,* savage, for their trouble.

To augment the military assistance, the white soldiers in the green hats started a civic-action program. They helped the villagers build swine pens, a dispensary, a school, a new community long house. And, most effective in the campaign to win over the Montagnards, they themselves became Montagnards.

To a man, the Americans underwent the ceremony of tribal initiation . . . the dancing, the feasting, the drinking dry of chin-high urns filled with the yeasty, potent Montagnard home brew, nursing at the fat bamboo straws until they swooned and fell insensate to the ground, accompanied all the way down by the hoots and cheers of their new brothers.

Gulliver even took a Montagnard woman. As an honorary chief, he was invited to choose from among the unspoken-for girls. He begged off, until it was made plain that to refuse would be the gravest of insults. Giggling bare-breasted girls were paraded before the squirmy young officer until at last he picked one, a stinking but sultry beauty with long greasy hair, deep free-standing breasts, and skin the color of sable. And in a stroke he demonstrated both his good taste and good sense, having unwittingly selected a daughter of the village headman.

Gulliver had truly loved his Montagnards—loved their simplicity, their honesty, their loyalty, their bravery, and their eagerness to learn—and he still wore with honor and pride the thin copper bracelet of his tribal affiliation.

That he did love them made it that much harder to leave them seven months later when the Central Intelligence Agency came back into his life, this time to stay, plucking him out of idyllic twelfth-century surroundings with a twenty-first-century hand—the agency computer, which, in its search for a solution to the problem of General Blood, spewed out a name committed to memory two years earlier when the equally thorny problem of the Red Prince had been solved. Gulliver, J. S.

When he had disposed of General Blood, the Sandman was to all appearances forgotten, retired. The spooks still used Lieutenant J. S. Gulliver, but not the Sandman.

They had used Gulliver sparingly at first, then with increasing regularity, on a succession of equally unorthodox but more savory free-lance missions. But first they arranged for his transfer out of the Fifth Special Forces Group and into the First, although he did not join the First at its home base on Okinawa. Instead he had been attached to SOG, the Special Operations Group that was run by the CIA under the benign-sounding cover name of Study and Observation Group, as if it were nothing more than some harmless luncheon club for university dons.

As Gulliver understood it, SOG's primary function was to mount, deploy, and run harassment missions and agent networks north of the DMZ, in North Vietnam itself. But except for the odd limited-duration, task-specific, cross-border operation, he had no connection with that phase of it. He was something of a SOG floater, idle for much of the time in the beginning, brought into play only when a mission called for his special skills: border penetration, behind-the-lines intel gathering, downed-pilot recovery.

The jobs were varied, and if none of them produced the deep sense of accomplishment he had gotten while working with his Montagnards, he found some of them interesting, even fun.

To utilize his cross-training in communications, for instance, the spooks had him set up a black radio operation. Broadcasting from a powerful hidden transmitter in the South, his team would send phony messages to nonexistent agents in North Vietnam, instructing them to be at grids so-and-so for a parachute drop at such-and-such hour. These transmissions were broadcast in the clear without any codes, meant to be intercepted, designed to keep enemy troops hopping around the countryside on wild-goose chases.

The cowboys were so childishly pleased with the results, they had him do it again, transmitting from Laos this time, the message targeted against Khmer Rouge forces in Cambodia and against Cambodia's neutral head of state Prince Sihanouk, who, by his refusal to take sides, *their* side, had become a thorn in the CIA's side. The team had employed a dandy bit of business that time, a near-perfect imitation of Sihanouk's voice, electronically produced by an agency technician using the latest computer equipment. The fake voice was just like "Snooky's," breathless, squeaky, full of giggles and nervous energy. Aimed at the unworldly peasant, the broadcasts seemed to toe the party line, but were loaded with nuances designed to rub villagers the wrong way . . . as when the transistorized Sihanouk would encourage young women in the liberated areas to further the cause of anti-imperialism by sleeping with the valiant Khmer Rouge and North Vietnamese Army soldiers.

Black radio had been a gas, like an elaborate fraternity prank. A man didn't have to burn his clothes and scrape dried blood off his hands when the joke was over.

Nor had Gulliver much minded when he was assigned to the clandestine Special Forces/CIA joint operations that used him the way he'd been trained to be used, for honest soldiering.

In his role as honest soldier, he went to a Black Jack team, a special 150-man Mobile Strike Force company, where he commanded the Mike Force's extra recon platoon. They crossed the border and operated along the Ho Chi Minh Trail, planting booby traps, destroying caches, and conducting small ambushes. That led to more hush-hush work along the trail, in a project called Shining Brass. Working from a forward operations base at Khe Sanh, Gulliver took a team of three Special Forces men and nine Montagnards in and out of Laos to scout targets for U.S. bombers. Back home, the American public and the Congress were being told that U.S. troops were strictly forbidden to cross the border, but such deception did not bother Gulliver. Anything that allowed him to perform as a straight soldier he considered to be honest work. He would rather have been back in the Central Highlands with his CIDG team, of course, but all things considered, he was content, even happy. He was out in the bush and not behind a desk; he'd been given captain's bars; and the work, while it could get a tad hairy now and then, was fun.

It stopped being fun on a pewter-colored morning at Khe Sanh in 1967.

The day had started early for Gulliver, at 0400 hours, when a runner from the commo shack shook him awake rudely and handed him a rocket from Shining Brass command-and-control at Marble Mountain outside Danang. It was addressed to Gulliver, J. S., CPT, Commanding, Detachment A–111 Study and Observation Group, and was marked *UrgentUrgent* and *Eyes Only*. Everything else was in code.

The message was in two parts. The first ordered Captain Gulliver to relinquish command of the team to his senior NCO until a new officer could be assigned, effective immediately. From that point on, the message made no further reference to anyone named Gulliver. *Sandman* was not to disclose or discuss the circumstances of his relief with anyone. *Sandman* was to rendezvous with Air America helicopter 677B4, scheduled ETA at Khe Sanh combat base 0630 hours this A.M. *Sandman* was to liaise with a passenger on board, who would identify himself as *Razor*. *Sandman* was to place himself subordinate to *Razor*. *Sandman* was to have all personal belongings boxed up and at the chopper pad, prepared to accompany *Razor* on an immediate turnaround flight. *Sandman* was henceforth on TDY, temporary duty, attached to the United States embassy, office of the consul general, Nha Trang. *Sandman* was to acknowledge receipt of message. *Sandman* was to destroy message.

Sandman was confused.

Had his work for Shining Brass displeased the shining brass? That couldn't be; his team had done a good job. So why was he being relieved? Why was the Sandman being brought out of retirement after all this time? Why was he being seconded to Nha Trang, to an up-country consulate, a civilian show? Of course! Civilian . . . Air America . . . code-word identification. He must be getting old, growing senile. It added up, to a penny, which dropped. The spooks!

He had waited quietly at the edge of the pad, sitting on a worn duffel bag that held the sum total of his possessions. A light drizzle had begun to fall and his forest-green beret did nothing to keep the water off his face. With no military flights scheduled at that hour because of the fog, he had the pad to himself. He chain-smoked while he waited, cupping the butts to keep them dry, looking at the mist-masked mountains that circled Khe Sanh. Black, rain-heavy clouds curled around their tops like hunting dogs around a cabin stove.

He picked up the chopper a long way out, a dot of white in an ash sky. He field-stripped his cigarette and watched as the helicopter grew larger and larger and finally settled. He saw the door slide back, but no one emerged. The machine just sat there, its rotors turning slowly, its open door inviting and ominous at the same time, like the mouth of a cave in a storm. When it became clear that no one was going to get out, Gulliver shouldered his duffel bag and boarded.

Waiting inside was a lanky, loose-limbed man with long hair and languid features. He wore a safari suit and he had slug-white hands and clean fingernails. He did not offer one of these immaculate hands. He merely regarded Gulliver with hooded, disapproving eyes, then turned and rapped twice on the back of the pilot's helmet. The pilot, who had kept his eyes straight to the front throughout Gulliver's boarding, never once looking around, lifted off.

Gulliver was still full of questions about his abrupt transition, and more than a little resentful, but he decided to start off friendly. "Good morning. I'm Jake Gulliver," he shouted over the engine noise, offering his hand.

All the man shook was his head. "You're quite mistaken, old boy," he said. "You are not Jake Gulliver. You know the drill, and I suggest we run through it. Now."

Gulliver shrugged and said: "All right. I'm *Sandman*. Who are you?"

"Razor." Razor was frowning and his lidded blue eyes had frost on them. His nose was wrinkled and turned up, as if he had just found a month-dead rat behind the refrigerator.

Gulliver tried again. "Okay, Mr. Razor, now that we've done the Mata Hari routine, who are you in the real world?"

Razor regarded him with a shadow of a supercilious smile and said: "My name is Steelman. And I think you will come to discover that this *is* the real world."

"You a spook, Mr. Steelman?"

"I am the deputy consul general in Nha Trang," Steelman said priggishly, his bloodless lips pursed.

"You're a spook," Gulliver said wearily. "What about me? Am I a spook now too?"

"You are going to be a military attaché in the Nha Trang consulate," Steelman said, clipping off the words.

Gulliver sighed. "I'm a spook too."

"I don't like that word. It's a silly word, one bandied about among silly people—journalists and that ilk. Please do not use it again."

Gulliver shrugged again and changed the subject. "Where are we going? Nha Trang?"

Steelman nodded.

"What am I going to be doing once we get there? Besides serving as a military attaché, of course."

"Whatever I tell you to do."

Gulliver was set to ask another question when Steelman tilted back his head and closed his eyes. Gulliver watched him snooze for a while, or pretend to snooze, then stretched out on the cold steel-plate floor and went to sleep himself, using his duffel bag for a pillow. Both dozed intermittently all the way to Nha Trang. They did not exchange another word, not even during the brief stop at Marble Mountain, where they switched to an unmarked C–47 for the last leg of the journey.

Thus had begun the bad time. For the next two years Jake Gulliver sat in a tiny office in the American compound in Nha Trang with little to do, not even putting up a pretense as a military attaché. He became an invisible man, as isolated as a leper. Steelman specifically forbade him to fraternize with the officers from Fifth Special Forces Group headquarters just across town, even though he had old friends among them. He chose not to fraternize with any of the consulate personnel.

Day after day, week after week, he sat at a bare desk, keeping up with the ball scores in *Stars and Stripes,* playing chess with himself, doing push-ups and sit-ups behind a locked door. He went to the beach nearly every afternoon, and to the bars nearly every night. He was a prime source of income for a dozen whores, and for the Vietnamese doctor who specialized in venereal diseases. Gulliver's only friend was the *papasan* who ran the opium parlor where he discovered how easy it was to lose himself in shimmery dreams, where he could live in his head, surrounded by old friends. The pipe had the power to take him back to the Highlands and his CIDG team, back to his Montagnards, back to the sultry headman's daughter.

Every few weeks—sometimes six, sometimes ten—there would be a break in the routine and the Sandman would be put to work. Steelman would use his own key to let himself into Gulliver's office and lock the door behind him. Razor talked, Sandman listened. It was the only time they saw each other.

The Sandman missions were of a piece, instant replays of General Blood and the Red Prince. But just as in his solitary chess games, there were infinite variations within the play. Sometimes the Sandman's opponents were military, sometimes not. Sometimes they were across a border, sometimes not. The Sandman worked at night, he worked in daylight. He worked in jungled mountains, he worked on grassy plateaus. He worked in plush villas behind guarded gates, he worked in hovels at the end of garbage-strewn alleys. His head was full of schematics and blueprints, of entry points and escape routes. And he was as at home in certain urban neighborhoods—in Saigon, Quang Tri, Ban Me Thuot, Hue, Kontum, Dalat, Qui Nhon—as anyone born and raised in them.

Some of the assignments were easy, some were not. Once the Sandman took out a Hanoi agent who slept in a room full of snoring men in a safe house for communists on the run. The target was a different kind of sleeper, an aide to the mayor of a large provincial capital who'd come out of deep cover to assassinate his boss. The Sandman had had no choice but to go in after him. His prey had gone to ground and simply refused to leave the house.

That job had impressed even the hard-to-faze Steelman, but Razor did not remain a fan of the Sandman for long. When Gulliver knew beyond a doubt what the agency expected of the Sandman, he'd tried to smuggle a letter to the Special Forces Group commander requesting his intervention. He never found out if that officer could, or would, have helped; the letter was intercepted by a CIA plant at Group headquarters.

Steelman had fashioned the letter into a paper airplane and with a contemptuous flip of his wrist had sailed it onto Gulliver's desk. It landed among the chessmen, scattering the setup, a Modern Steinitz Defense arrayed against a Ruy López Opening.

"If you ever try anything like this again, old boy," he had said, "you will find yourself back in that East Jesus town you come from, up to your ankles in chicken droppings. Your military career will be over . . . *kaput . . . finis. Capisce?*"

Gulliver had not helped matters any when he replied with a nonchalance he did not really feel: "I'm really impressed, Steelman, *old boy*. You're one helluva linguist."

That exchange set the mood for the months that followed. Merely uncordial until then, their relationship disintegrated into one of open hostility. After the wayward-letter episode, the Sandman and Razor went through an unchanging vaudeville routine with each new mission: Gulliver would unlock his door some morning, anticipating nothing more than another boring day, and find on his desk a file containing the name of a target, its last known location, and any other pertinent intel the spooks had managed to collect. He would take the file straight back to Steelman's office, drop it on his desk, and announce: "Get somebody else. I won't do it."

Without looking up, Steelman would reach into a drawer, pull out two sets of papers, and slide them toward Gulliver. One was an undated resignation form with Captain Gulliver's name and particulars already typed in; the other was a set of courts-martial papers charging Captain Gulliver with refusal to obey a direct order in time of war and verifying that the accused had read and understood the charges against him.

"If you would be so good as to sign one or the other for me, please," Steelman would say pleasantly. Then he would go back to whatever he had been doing.

After a moment, Gulliver would retrieve the target file and leave.

So why hadn't he resigned? Gulliver told himself that it was the principle of the thing, that he was not about to let a man like Steelman, a civilian, run him out of the Army. But he knew the real reason. He did not resign because he could not come up with a satisfactory answer to the next question: And do what? Farm? Soldiering, for all its hardships, was his life. Go home? Vietnam, for all its horror, had become his home.

Gulliver knew that he was suffering from a bad case of *le mal jaune,* the Yellow Fever. He was hooked on Vietnam, as addicted to its cheap thrills as he was to its cheap opium. After seven years of riding an adrenaline high, he knew that if he went home now he would be like a diver who surfaced too quickly—he would die of the bends, of boredom.

So that was how it stood between Sandman and Razor until that final break, in the wake of the Vuong Affair. It was in the interim that he first tried the pills and discovered the beneficial side effects, how they fuzzed the details when the job was over. Once he had sampled their cleansing powers, the Sandman rarely ventured out without them.

The pills didn't always work, of course. There were odd moments from that time that had crystallized, that he still remembered as vividly as if he were in the instant of living them. There was one night in particular, a wet monsoon night, one that came back to him every monsoon season, triggered by the sound of rain on a roof. It was a night when the Sandman broke into a one-room tin-roofed shanty on the bank of the Perfume River in Hue; a night he had taken the better part of an hour to creep over six sleeping children so that he could murder their father in his bed.

He had a hand clamped over the target's nose and mouth and was pulling his K-bar across the man's throat, the blood coming like spray from a faulty fountain, when he looked over and saw a boy of about ten watching. The child did not move, did not make a sound. He lay curled in a ball, skinny knees pulled up to his chest, his palms pressed together to make a pillow between his cheek and the sleeping mat. His black eyes were large and liquid in the gloom while the rain beat on the tin roof and filled the shack with a drumming ran-tan.

Gulliver did not move either, *could not* move. He stared back helplessly, holding down the still-bucking body of the boy's father while he waited for the spasms to subside. The two of them—the man in blackface, the boy with the black eyes—watched each other for an eternity, neither of them moving, neither making a sound.

Gulliver could see a pulse hammer in the child's throat even as he felt it slow, then stop, in the father's throat. There was a soft sigh, barely audible over the night sounds of the sleeping family and the rain, as a last lung-load of air escaped through the scarlet vent that the Sandman had opened. Then both the father and the son slowly closed their eyes and did not open them again.

The Sandman left as silently as he had come, despite a trembling he could not control. Once outside, he knelt at the river's edge, intending only to wash the knife and his bloody hands, surprised to find that he started to cry instead. And then to vomit. He wept and heaved at the same time, doubled over with nausea and despair, one hand clutching his stomach, the other his heart. The K-bar slipped from his grip and sank like a stone in the Perfume's sluggish current. The rain came down in hissing sheets, pocking the river's surface, washing away the Sandman's warpaint. It ran down the gutters of his face in greenish-black rivulets, leaving only his tears still in camouflage.

9

GULLIVER THREW ON JEANS and a T-shirt and went out into the hallway. He fully intended to go back downstairs, but he turned the other way instead. By the time his head caught up with his feet, he had already rapped twice on the guest-room door.

Sally Teacher opened the door a crack, just wide enough for him to see her face change; she was as surprised to find him there as he was.

"Hello," he said, the only thing he could think to say.

"Hello." Her voice sounded wary, and she did not open the door any wider.

"I, uh, wanted to apologize for sneaking up on you the way I did. I hope I didn't frighten you."

"Well, you did."

"Yeah. I guess I did." She was wearing a formal-looking black dress. It made Gulliver feel as scruffy as he looked.

He tried a smile. "Listen, I really am sorry," he said. "But try to see it from my point of view. I mean, for all I knew, you were casing the joint, about to make off with one of my priceless antiques, or maybe one of my Picassos."

Sally Teacher, undoubtedly picturing his stripped-down, utilitarian set of rooms, laughed. It was a husky, unchained laugh. The door swung open another foot.

"Okay, I confess; you caught me red-handed," she said, still smiling. "But I couldn't help myself. You have such an impressive collection."

"Yeah." Gulliver, long out of practice, could not think of anything to keep it going. "Well, it looks like you're all dressed to go out. I won't keep you."

"I'm meeting a few of the local Hoa Hao this evening," she said. "They're sending a car for me, but it won't be for another twenty minutes."

She had an expectant look on her face and Gulliver knew that she had either just opened the door wide or slammed it in his face. He was not sure which, whether he should make a move or go away. So he just stood there, saying nothing and feeling thick and clumsy.

When she grew tired of waiting, she said: "That should be enough time for you to buy me a drink at that nice little bar I saw downstairs. I've been dying for one, but I didn't want to sit there by myself."

"Oh. Sure. Roger. That sounds good."

Gulliver waited in the corridor while she got her purse, then followed her down the stairs, his eyes swinging with her hips.

They crossed the common room to the bamboo bar and she took a stool while he went around behind the counter. "So what'll it be, then, miss?" he asked in a publican's brogue.

"I'd love a Scotch on the rocks, but you better make it a vodka-tonic instead," she said. "It wouldn't do to show up at a dinner with teetotalers smelling of whiskey."

"That's right. They don't drink, do they?"

"Nope. No alcohol, no opium, no gambling, no meat, no nothin'. The Hoa Hao are Buddhism's Baptists."

Gulliver smiled. "Sounds dull."

"It gets worse," she said lightly. "They don't condone arranged marriages or the selling of child brides either."

Gulliver winced. "Life without child brides wouldn't be worth living," he said as he served her drink and started to pour a bourbon for himself. "There's this one I've had my eye on. She's all of twelve, but it's okay . . . because she has the body of a ten-year-old."

Sally Teacher laughed and her eyes seemed to pulse, like a signal from a distant star, going from dark green to light green and back again. They reminded Gulliver of gemstones in candlelight. He took the opportunity to study her, and found her flawless. She had a wide, full mouth with dimples in the corners, a thin, straight nose, and a long, fluted neck which drew attention to her pale coloring. Over her nose and across the tops of her cheeks lay a light dusting of freckles the same strawberry color as her hair, which she wore to medium length. She was the colleen of every black Irishman's dreams.

"I've never met a lady spook before," he said, casting about for a topic of conversation. "I didn't realize we had any over here."

Sally sipped her drink and sighed her approval. "Unless they have someone in deep cover, I'm the only American woman in the station at the moment," she said. "But there are rumors that they're thinking of sending over another."

"That's good," Gulliver said, not knowing if it was or not, but thinking she would think so.

"Not necessarily," she said with a rueful smile. "I have mixed feelings about it. It would be nice to have someone to both shop and *talk* shop with, but they give me little enough to do as it is, way too little to divide in half. As far as my superiors are concerned, when it comes to meaningful jobs, the spy business is a man's game."

Gulliver shrugged. "You can't be in too bad a position," he said without thinking, letting more bitterness show than he intended. "You seem to have caught Steelman's fancy." He knew he'd made a mistake when he saw the look on her face.

"Bennett Steelman is my colleague, not my sugar daddy," she said sharply. "And a colleague is all he is."

"I didn't mean that," Gulliver said quickly. "I just meant that he seems to think highly of you, and—"

"I *know* what you meant, Captain, and if—"

"Miss Teacher please?" A slightly built Vietnamese man, flanked by two squat and scowling Nung guards, was standing at the double front door. He wore proper chauffeur's livery and a nervous smile of apology. He took another few hesitant steps into the common room, the Nungs moving with him like a double shadow, and said again, "Miss Teacher please?"

Sally nodded and the man said, "I am Van, driver of Dr. Loan. I have come for you please."

"And not a moment too soon," she said. She slid off the stool, picked her purse off the bar, and followed the driver out.

Dr. Loan's house was a large two-story villa in the town's best neighborhood, just two blocks from the province chief's house. The villa sat back from the street, behind a cinder-block wall and a well-kept garden, and looked like a smaller model of the Embassy House.

Dr. Loan himself was short and portly and gracious. He and Mrs. Loan, also short and portly and gracious, made Sally feel immediately at home. They took her around a living room generously appointed with Chinese antiques and introduced her to nearly two dozen men and women. Sally had little chance to match names with faces.

The guests seemed almost equally divided into two very distinct groups. There were the lay people, mostly members of the Social Democratic party and their wives, the men dressed in business suits, the women in formal *ao dais*. They laughed and chatted animatedly and held their glasses of fruit juice like cocktails. And there were robed monks, huddled together protectively in small knots, looking as if they disapproved of such secular sociability. They cast hard looks at everyone and everything, their suspicious eyes zipping around the room like auctioneers', scrutinizing the furniture and art as if trying to guess the prices.

When they went in to dinner, Sally found herself seated directly across from her host, Dr. Loan, and between the most important guests: a Hoa Hao senator and the province town's senior Hoa Hao monk. The bonze, a bald ancient man who did not seem quite sure of where he was or why he was there, had little to say. Sally talked mostly with Loan and the senator. Both men seemed delighted with the fact she spoke Vietnamese, and constantly used their chopsticks to pick out the choicest morsels from the giant platters of food and transfer them to her set of bowls.

The dinner itself was meatless, but excellent: cabbage leaves stuffed with rice and soybean, noodle dishes, spiced vegetables, baked fish, soups, and sticky sweets and coconut cakes for dessert. Sally minded her manners, careful not to leave her chopsticks stuck in her food or to let them touch or make unnecessary noise. And with each fresh course, she remembered to leave a little on her plate, to let her host know that there had been enough and that she was satisfied.

The senator, a courtly and loquacious man, told her that he spent more time at his house in Saigon than he did here in his constituency. When Sally told him that he was not unlike American senators in that regard, he laughed.

"Would you like to know the origins of our religion?" Dr. Loan asked Sally.

"Yes, please," Sally said, not wanting to deny him the pleasure of telling his story. She already knew the Hoa Hao history and was more interested in contemporary affairs, but she listened attentively.

The sect had been founded in 1939 by a young man named

Huynh Phu So who was born in the small hamlet of Hoa Hao in the That Son Mountains of An Giang province. Huynh Phu So was a sickly boy who had been placed by his father into the care of Tra Son, a monk widely considered to be a wondrous healer as well as a philosopher and teacher of Buddha's Way. Tra Son was never able to cure Huynh Phu So, but the young man lived with him until the old monk died. Not long after, Huynh Phu So rose from his bed one night and prostrated himself before the family altar. When he got back to his feet he was cured. From that day forward he declared himself to be a prophet and began to teach. He quickly became known as a miracle healer, and was so dynamic a speaker that before the year was out he had more than 100,000 followers. They called him "The Living Buddha." The authorities—the French were the prevailing foreign power of the day—called him stark raving mad and had him committed to a lunatic asylum.

"And do you know what happened while he was there?" Dr. Loan asked, already grinning with anticipation.

"Please tell me," Sally said, trying her best to sound breathless.

Loan laughed delightedly. "He converted his psychiatrist to the Hoa Hao faith and won his release on the spot!" All up and down the table, guests were smiling appreciatively; a few of them even broke into applause.

Sally smiled and quietly clapped too. "I know that An Giang is still predominantly Hoa Hao," she said quickly in an attempt to change direction, "but what about this province?"

The senator answered. "Here, too, the majority is Hoa Hao. The government's census figures are always suspect, of course, but it is estimated that seventy-two percent of the people here follow the Hoa Hao faith. The remaining people are traditional Buddhists, with a few Catholics among them."

"Are those figures reflected in the National Assembly?" Sally asked.

"The representation is quite fair," said the senator. "The province has two senators, both of us Hoa Hao. In the Lower Assembly, four of the five provincial representatives are Hoa Hao. So six of the seven assemblymen are Hoa Hao, members of the Social Democratic party."

Sally noticed that Dr. Loan was frowning and she had a good idea why. She decided to stir the pot a little. She put on an innocent face and said, "You must be very pleased with that."

"Ha!" Loan exclaimed. "Our most honorable senator and his SDP colleagues work hard, but their voices are lost in the Assembly. If they try to go against the government, Mr. Thieu's clique easily votes them down. Even when all of the minority parties agree to vote together, they can do nothing in the face of such numbers. We have no official power!"

Now the senator, too, was frowning. He wanted the woman from the American embassy to know the truth, of course, but the truth diminished his own importance. "What Dr. Loan says may be so," he said, "but even if our seats in the Assembly do not translate into real political power, it is more than we enjoy here at home."

This was what Sally was after: an unvarnished assessment of the sect's strength within the province itself. "What do you mean, Senator?" she asked.

"What the senator means, Miss Teacher," said Dr. Loan, "is that in our province, as in any other, the power of the province chief is absolute. It is the province chief who has the strength of the national government at his disposal, the province chief who controls the armed forces and the police, the province chief who controls the Phoenix program with its unlimited power to put people in prison, even to kill them. And in this province, the province chief is a Catholic. The chief of the Special Branch secret police is a Catholic. The commander of the Field Force is a Mahayana Buddhist. And all their deputies, and all their deputies' deputies, are either Buddhist or Catholic. There is not one Hoa Hao in an official position of power."

"It is President Thieu's system of maintaining control," the senator said. "First he puts all of the real power into the hands of the province chief, and then he puts one of his political cronies in as province chief. It is his insurance against coups."

"A very effective system," Sally agreed sympathetically. "But what can you do about it?"

"We can show Saigon that it is the Hoa Hao who command the loyalty of the people here, not the province chief," said Loan. "Our merchants can refuse to trade with the communists, or not. Our monks can urge our young men to accept the draft, or not. We can talk to the police when they seek information, or not. There are many ways in which we can help or harm the government. But if Saigon wants our cooperation in fighting communists, it must take Colonel Minh's boot off our necks."

"That is where you can help," the senator said, smiling at Sally. "Thieu does what the Americans tell him to do. If you can persuade him to give us the levers of power in those provinces where we have a majority, we will rid the Delta of communists for you. The communists cannot survive in a happy province, a content province, a free province—"

"A *Hoa Hao* province!" croaked the elderly monk sitting at Sally's side. She had thought he was asleep.

Loan, his face slightly flushed, was out of his chair. He lifted his teacup and said: "A Hoa Hao province!"

Up and down the table, guests were scrambling to their feet. "A Hoa Hao province!" they shouted.

They were looking at Sally. She thought of the province chief, a man she had not met, but the one who had, after all, arranged this dinner for her. With a small shrug, she pushed back her chair and raised her cup. "A Hoa Hao province," she said.

It was a few minutes before midnight when Dr. Loan's man dropped Sally back at the Embassy House. As she came through the double front door and headed for the stairs, she saw that Captain Gulliver was right where she had left him, standing at the bamboo bar. He did not say anything when she went past and started up the steps to her room, but she had the feeling that he had waited up for her.

The driver, a PRU, was doing double duty, serving as both chauffeur and bodyguard. An Uzi lay beside him on the seat, and a sawed-off shotgun loaded with double-aught buck was mounted to the dash in a fast-draw clip scabbard.

Steelman wrote the address on a slip of paper and held it up. The PRU reached for it, only to see it snatched away. When he dropped his hand, Steelman held the paper up again, like a man using a biscuit to train a dog. The driver leaned close, read it, and nodded. Steelman rolled the slip into a ball and put it into a pocket of his seersucker jacket.

A few minutes later the Ford Bronco stopped at the mouth of a long alley that spoked off from the hub of the busy main street of the province town. Steelman got out and ordered the driver to wait there with the vehicle.

Even at this late hour the alley was crowded, and he ran a gauntlet of beggars and vendors, turning down the chance to buy everything from model sampans carved from buffalo horn to black-market piasters to Park Lanes, the tailor-made marijuana cigarettes. He found the tailor shop at the end of the alley and went in.

The shop was busy, open late for a last-minute burst of business before the Tet holiday closed everything down.

"I would like to see Mr. Tho, please," Steelman said in English to a youth who was taking a customer's measurements. The young man, his mouth full of pins, nodded toward an old man sitting on a high stool behind an American cash register. There, in the lee of modern technology, he worked an abacus.

"Mr. Tho?"

The man's eyes came up but his fingers continued to fly over the counters. Before Steelman could say anything, the tailor shook his head and said, "Very much busy now. Please to come back after Tet." He looked back to the beads.

Steelman did not move. "Mr. Tho, I'd like some work done to my jacket . . . a secret pocket made."

Tho's fingers stopped. His eyes came back up to study Steelman. "Secret pocket?"

"Yes. It would only take a minute. A simple cut in the lining would do. You could do it with . . . a razor."

The tailor's face changed. He set the abacus aside and said: "You come. I fix." He got down from the stool, said something to an assistant in rapid Vietnamese, and led the way into the bowels of the shop.

They pushed through a succession of curtain partitions, past busy fitting rooms and stacked bolts of cloth. The shop seemed to go back for miles, a warren of rooms and hallways.

At last they stopped in front of a double-wide door and Tho took a key chain from around his neck and unlocked it. He motioned for his customer to enter and Steelman found himself in a comfortable, well-appointed room, obviously the tailor's private living quarters.

Tho relocked the door and asked, "Would you like some tea?"

"No," Steelman said, helping himself to a seat on a sofa set in a heavy, lacquered wood frame.

Tho took a chair opposite and beamed at him. "So you are Razor," he said.

"Yes."

"Allow me to say that I am both honored and pleased, but also surprised. Captain Bich said it was most unlikely that I would ever be granted the honor of meeting you." The tailor's English had improved dramatically.

"Unusual events sometimes necessitate unusual methods," Steelman said coolly. "I, too, have been surprised. But not pleased."

"Yes, I can understand that. How may I serve you?"

"You can answer some questions for me," Steelman said. "For starters, you can tell me who massacred our PRU team."

"The 97th Viet Cong Strike Brigade, also known as the Brigade of Steel. A most experienced unit."

"Why didn't you let us know it was there?"

"I did not know," Tho said, shaking his head in sorrow. "It was my understanding that the Brigade of Steel was in its home sanctuary, what you call the Parrot's Beak, in Cambodia. I learned of the ambush only on the day it was done, and the identity of the responsible unit only a few hours ago. I made an appointment to see Captain Bich early tomorrow morning, to tell him of what I have only just learned."

"But you are the struggle-group commander for this area. How could you not have known well in advance?"

Tho shrugged. "I know only what my superiors want me to know, and they want me to know only what I must in order to properly conduct their affairs in this one modest provincial capital. Do you not operate in much the same way?"

"Then how did you know that the 18–B Battalion was in Vinh Long and not in the Seven Mountains of Chau Doc?"

"Ah, most fortunate fate," Tho said. "I have a nephew in the 18–B who was kind enough to visit his old uncle. We had a nice talk. Yes, most fortunate fate. But you know of this. It was in the report I gave to Captain Bich." The tailor's voice was calm, serene. He sat perfectly still and spoke as softly, as carefully, as if he were in a cage with a tiger that had not been fed for many days.

Steelman said nothing for a moment. Then he said: "Tell me about Gulliver."

Tho held up his hands, a gesture that said he thought it safe to move now. "The pattern remains the same. He comes to visit the woman two or three times a week when she is not out of the city on one of her tours. They talk, he has his pipes, they make love. They are very noisy when they make love."

"When was the last time he saw her?"

"Today. About midday."

"What did they talk about?"

"The battle in the Seven Mountains. And his wound. Then he had his pipes and they made love. They were not noisy when they made love. I think they had to be careful because of his wound."

"What about before the ambush?"

"He came to see her two nights before."

"Did he tell her anything about the Seven Mountains operation on that visit?"

"He told her everything."

"What?" Steelman's face grew excited. "He told her! You heard him tell her?"

"Oh yes. I used the listening machine Captain Bich gave to me, same as always."

"Then we have it on tape?"

Tho shrugged. "Of course."

"Good, good! Good work, old boy! What have you done with that tape?"

"It is here, in this very room."

"Good. Good," Steelman said again. Razor was smiling, so Tho smiled too, pleased that Razor was pleased.

"Taking drugs . . . fraternizing with a VC agent . . . divulging classified information . . . there's enough to send him to prison right there," Steelman said, more to himself than to Tho.

"Of course, the recordings make it clear that he knows nothing of her illegal activities," Tho said incautiously.

The change in Razor was immediate. He stopped smiling and glared at the tailor. "Let me determine what the tapes make clear and what they do not," he said. "And speaking of her illegal activities, I've noticed that your reports have been woefully short on details."

"It is most unfortunate," Tho agreed sorrowfully. "Her troupe travels throughout the Delta and I am certain she is used as a regional coordinating cadre, but I have no proof for you. It is ironic that the woman is my superior in the chain, my only connection to the provincial committee, and that I found a placė for her next to my shop so it would be easier for us to trade information. Yet she tells me nothing, while I am to tell her everything. Whom she tells, I do not know . . ." The tailor paused for maximum effect before adding, ". . . All I know is that he has visited her a few times."

Steelman stiffened and sat upright. "What? Her control? You've *seen* him?"

"Alas, no. He comes seldom and always at night. But I have heard him in there with her. She makes love to him, too, but they are never noisy."

"Have we got him on tape?" Steelman asked excitedly.

Tho shrugged. "Yes and no. His voice is too indistinct to be of use. He speaks quietly, as if he knows someone might be listening. The times I have heard him, I have stayed at my window all night, trying to get a look at him when he leaves, but it is as if he does not leave at all. There is only the one door, but he does not use it. Yet he is not there in the morning." The tailor shook his head. "I have lost much sleep over this, watching, thinking, wondering how he can go in and out without being seen."

Razor seemed unimpressed with his sacrifice. "When was the last time he came?" he asked brusquely.

"Also two nights before the ambush, after the American had left. She made love to them both that night. She was very noisy with the American, very quiet with the other."

Razor had stopped listening. He was up and pacing the room. "I'll put a man in the alley . . . watch her place around the clock," he said, thinking out loud. "A soup vendor . . . or better yet, a beggar . . . a disabled veteran . . . an amputee for authentic cover . . . I'll give him a wife, children perhaps . . ."

"Yes," Tho agreed solicitously. "That is an excellent idea. I cannot watch all the time by myself. I have my shop to run, my game to play with the communists. And even I must sleep sometime."

Steelman turned to the tailor. "I want those tapes. The one where Gulliver tells her about the mission, and anything you have on this other fellow. We have technicians in Saigon who may be able to pick something off them."

Tho got up and walked to a wall. He removed a painting, a picture of a tiger feeding on a deer, and opened the safe hidden there. He took out two reels of tape and handed them to Razor.

Steelman hefted the tapes in both hands as if he could measure their secrets, their worth, by sheer weight alone. Then he smiled and whispered a soft promise: "First your VC whore girlfriend and then you, Sandman, old boy. First her, then you."

10

For the second time in as many days, Harry Swain sat in a parked taxi in front of the Senh Tien police station, under the drooping flag of the Saigon government, half a block from Mai's front door. His driver squatted at a soup stand across the street, taking his time, confident from the experience of the day before that he had at least another hour in which to have a bowl of *pho* and catch up on the war news.

He was wrong. Swain glanced at his watch with mounting irritation, knowing he should probably be starting back to the Embassy House. With Gulliver out of commission, Cameron had made Swain acting PRU adviser, and Steelman's briefing was scheduled to start in forty minutes, at nine A.M. on the nose. He decided to give it another couple of minutes.

A minute later he was glad that he had. Mai herself did not emerge, but her husband did; at least Swain assumed the man was her husband. Nothing special there as far as he could see. Your run-of-the-mill dink: thin, short, and ugly as sin. Trung looked to be considerably older than Mai; certainly no competition for a young stud in the prime of life.

Swain said her name aloud, savoring it. *Mai*. Now, there was a gook word that wasn't ugly, he acknowledged. *Mai*. She filled his imagination and he could not say why; he had never been partial to gook broads. But then, he'd never seen a gook broad who was stacked like Mai. If proof of his infatuation was needed, he'd had it when he spotted the Teacher woman at the Embassy House the afternoon before. Sally Teacher was a fox, but Swain was no longer interested, would not have been even if he hadn't pegged her for Steelman's woman, strictly off limits. She suddenly seemed gross and ungainly compared to his Mai.

Swain had tried to figure out what it was about Mai that had gotten to him, but he could not explain it. All he really knew about her was her name, where she lived, and that she was afraid of him. But that was enough. That was good. When a man had a woman afraid of him it meant that he was always on her mind, that he had power over her, and it meant that sooner or later she was his. Face it, he told himself with conviction, at heart, women wanted to be pushed around.

He had learned that lesson back in Baton Rouge with that snooty cheerleader, Amy Sue Cummins. She had given him a hard time too, until that Saturday night when LSU beat 'Bama and, still riding the high, he had called her on her prick-teasing ways, dragging her into the equipment room and throwing her onto the mountain of dirty towels and sweaty jocks. A couple of quick shots to that face she was so proud of had quieted her down fast. After that, he'd had her anytime he wanted. She would go wall-eyed with fear whenever he came near her, just a-shakin' like a dog shittin' peach pits, but she had never made the mistake of saying no to Harry Swain again. Of course, after Harry Swain gave them a little lovin' they no longer wanted to say no. Amy Sue Cummins had never said a word to anyone about that first time. She knew the score. If she had tried to holler rape, it wouldn't have taken him five minutes to round up a dozen teammates to swear on a pile of King James Bibles that she put out for the entire offensive line.

Swain waited as long as he could, then went to fetch his driver, who was halfway through a bowl of noodles. They had just gotten back into the taxi when Mai came out of the house and started down the block. Swain jumped out of the taxi and ran, catching up before she reached the corner, materializing suddenly at her elbow, saying: "Hey there, pretty lady. Where you goin' in such a hurry?"

The blood left her face so quickly Swain was afraid she might faint. He took her by the arm, just in case, and was stunned when she jerked it away violently and began to yell. "No! No! No! You go 'way!"

"Jeez! I ain't gonna hurt you," he said in a placating voice. "I just want to have a little talkee-talkee."

"GO 'WAY! *Ba* Mai! *Ba* Mai!" She yelled at the top of her lungs, standing stiff as an andiron, her arms rigid at her side, her tiny fists balled pugnaciously, her mammoth chest heaving like a bellows.

"Jeez!" Swain felt the onset of panic. A crowd had begun to gather, closing with hostility, and two policemen came to the door of the substation to see what the ruckus was about.

He tried to calm her. "Hey, I just want to talk. There's no call for you to go wild on me. Jeez!" His tone was that of an aggrieved victim; he felt thoroughly misunderstood.

Mai kept yelling and the crowd began to mutter. One of the policemen was walking toward them. Swain bolted. He ran back to the taxi and ordered the driver to *di di mau,* to haul ass. Moments later they were rattling back along the road to the province town, the driver maliciously running over every pothole he could find, incensed at being suckered into paying for a full bowl of *pho* and being given time to eat only half, and no more charmed by his fare's conduct than those in the crowd had been.

The driver's fit of pique went unnoticed. Swain was too busy puzzling over Mai's bizarre behavior. He wanted her to fear him, of course, wanted her to feel and to acknowledge his power, but she was being ridiculous about it. He could not understand it.

Swain sighed. Round-eyes were hard enough to figure, he told himself righteously, so how could a man be expected to figure gook broads? Nevertheless, he tried for the rest of the ride back to the Embassy House.

He was ten minutes late, but George Cameron was too busy to scold him. Cameron was in the middle of his briefing when Swain came in, a briefing complete with maps, slides, charts, and telescoping pointers: number of VCI estimated, number of VCI identified, number of VCI neutralized. As he passed by on his way to the back of the room, Swain thought he caught a sour smell coming off the P officer's skin, a combination of nerves and last night's whiskey.

The Embassy House team was packed into Cameron's office. The air, pushed around and around the same tight confines by the overworked air-conditioner, reeked of cigarette smoke and a musty smell of slept-in clothes.

Swain saw that Steelman was sitting up front, at center ring, like the *presidente* at a bullfight. So was Gulliver, Swain noted peevishly, while he, Coughlin, and Riesz had to stand. Gulliver was milking his wound for all it was worth.

Swain had been grudgingly impressed by the way Gulliver had performed up on the mountain, but he did not credit the Sandman with saving his life. As far as he was concerned, if Gulliver had not fallen on top of him and knocked him cold, he would not have needed saving in the first place. Nor had he necessarily agreed with Gulliver's tactics, his decision against making a stand and fighting back. Swain considered the whole episode shameful in fact. They still didn't know how many of their PRUs were dead, how many wounded or taken prisoner. They had not been able to retrieve a single body. Harry Swain had never left a friendly body on a battlefield in his life. It was disgraceful.

Swain had been more impressed with Dang, even if he was a gook. It was Dang who had saved both their asses; Dang who had led them out of the shit; Dang who had a confirmed kill on the day. Gulliver claimed to have greased four, but Swain had seen Dang's kill with his own eyes. He looked around the room for Dang but could not find him. It was an all-American meeting: no gooks allowed.

Cameron was still at it, a boring barrage of statistics. Swain dozed with his eyes wide open, a trick he'd learned in college, while leaning against the wall, a trick he'd refined in the army.

He straightened when he heard his name. George Cameron had finished and was looking his way.

"Harry, I'll repeat what I was telling Jake before you came in, because it concerns you too. We've got some long days and nights ahead of us, holiday or no holiday, if we're going to get a new batch of PRUs trained before we have to close up the house and hand everything over to the locals and MACV. Mr. Steelman has said that he'll push buttons in Saigon to get our replacements to us as quickly as possible . . . and I want to thank you again for your help, Bennett . . . but we have to do our part too. Jake is well enough to conduct whatever training can be done here in the compound, but it's going to be up to you and Dang to shepherd the new men through their bushwork."

Swain nodded. "No sweat, sir. You can count on us. We'll do a Number One job for you." Out of the corner of his eye he saw Steelman smile approvingly.

Cameron noticed too, and he aped the gesture, adding *sotto voce:* "Outstanding . . . outstanding."

Swain glanced at Gulliver and saw that he was staring back, a faint smile on his face. Fuck you, Sandman, Swain whispered to himself.

Cameron addressed the room at large. "As for the rest of you, I hope you took to heart what Mr. Steelman had to say at the top of the meeting. I'd like to amplify his message. It's imperative that we leave our Vietnamese allies with a viable Phoenix program. The war we in this room fight is a quiet but important one, because the Viet Cong infrastructure is the whole point of the war. No less an authority than General Vo Nguyen Giap, Hanoi's top military strategist, has been quoted as saying that the VCI is the one battlefield element in the South he could not do without. Well, I say fuck Giap. Our job is to *make* him do without it."

Swain, starting to get fired up, applauded. He felt as if he were back in the LSU locker room at half-time. After a moment of hesitation, Riesz and Coughlin joined in.

Delighted with the response, and obviously hoping that Steelman was taking note, Cameron continued with a flushed face: "Phoenix works! Of the 63,229 VCI estimated in-country, 37,388 have been identified. But we have to do even better. The VCI have been eliminated in only 239 of the two thousand active villages. And while we have eliminated a lot of small fry, we've not been as successful in identifying and eliminating the top cadre. But with the solid apparatus we leave behind, our province chiefs and police chiefs should be able to—"

Steelman cleared his throat. Cameron looked down at him, then at the others, and saw that he had lost them as quickly as he had gotten them. The recitation of dry statistics they already knew had torpedoed his momentum and he stumbled to a stop. ". . . Uh, yes, well, I'm confident our Vietnamese friends will now be able to deal with the problem. . . . Uh, Bennett, do you have anything to add?"

"Yes, I do. Take a seat, George."

The worried look was back on Cameron's face as he and Steelman traded places. Steelman sat on a corner of the desk and stared at each of the team members in turn for a moment, then began speaking in a voice that cut like a laser:

"As most of you know, six months ago I was asked by the special assistant to the ambassador to take on the task of phasing out our direct participation in the Phoenix program. That process is nearly completed. I did not then, nor do I now, agree with the decision to turn the supervisory role for Phoenix over to the U.S. Army. George is quite correct when he says that Phung Hoang is the most important program of the war, and experience would suggest that the U.S. Army is not up to such a responsibility." He looked straight at Gulliver.

"But this was a policy decision, made by the director of intelligence and the President himself, and so I accepted it. After all, I am a professional, and professionals know that disagreeable tasks are part and parcel of any job." Again he directed his remarks at Gulliver.

"My caveats aside, it is important to me, personally and professionally, that the transition go smoothly and according to plan. I am pleased to be able to say that in a majority of provinces it *has* gone smoothly and according to plan. I am less pleased to have to say that this province does not seem destined to become a member of that majority."

There was a pause while Steelman threw Cameron a pointed look. Cameron reacted to adversity the way he invariably did; he began to perspire.

"I knew that all was not well here, but it's even worse than I had thought. During the flight down, I looked through the paperwork of the last six months. I was sickened by what I read. The recent record of this house is abominable. It is one of sloppy intelligence work, of miscalculation, of one bungled operation after another; all culminating, of course, in the annihilation of half of this province's PRU platoon."

He paused again to sweep the room with a disgusted look, then went on. "And what am I to tell my superiors? That we've turned over a Phoenix program that is in good shape in every province but one? Every province but a Delta province which, because of its Hoa Hao influence, has historically been among the most pacified? I can't do that. I *won't* do that."

Steelman's voice was a reedy flute, its notes hard-edged and pure. The others stared sheepishly at the floor, bowing before the barely controlled fury in it; except for Gulliver, who watched Steelman in the same way that he always watched Nhu when she was onstage, following the story line but also judging the performance itself.

Steelman looked down at the sweating Cameron. "You do know what happened to you on the ambush, don't you, George?" he asked.

Panic washed through Cameron's face. He looked like an unprepared schoolboy caught by a pop quiz. The sweat was now plainly visible on his forehead, a beaded crown of thorns.

After a painful silence, Steelman answered for him. "You were set up, George."

"S-set up? By who . . . ?" Cameron stammered, looking around as if the guilty party might be in the room.

"By a clever and resourceful enemy, George," Steelman said with a great show of patience. "But they had help, of course. It's clear they knew the overall plan, as well as which trails the PRU would take. Now, the question is, where did that help come from? Where is the leak?"

"The leak?" Cameron echoed.

Patience exhausted, Steelman snapped: "As a provincial intelligence officer, you make a fine parrot. Yes, the *leak*. Who knew the plan? Who knew the routes?"

Cameron finally caught up. Once he did, he spoke with a surprising confidence; George Cameron had been an excellent intelligence officer once upon a time. "I'm afraid that road doesn't go anywhere, Bennett," he said. "Or, more accurately, it goes everywhere. It was Jake's plan, but everyone in this room knew it. So did Sloane and Minh, and Do and Ngoc. We all went over it here at the house the night before the operation kicked off."

"Who else?"

"Well, you can be sure our Vietnamese counterparts clued in their key staff people. And if that's not enough for you, Major Ngoc flew to Can Tho the next day to coordinate air and arty support with M-R Four. God only knows how many had access to the plan. If it's a leak you're looking for, it could have been anywhere along the line."

"Perhaps," Steelman said, conceding nothing. "What about the specific routes? How many were in on that?"

Cameron looked at Gulliver. "If I'm not mistaken, you and Dang laid out the routes yourselves, didn't you, Jake?" he asked, almost apologetically.

"That's right," Gulliver said.

"Who else knew?" Steelman asked.

"Just Dang and myself," Gulliver said. "Of course, we did go over the route plan with the point, Sergeant Phuoc, but I seriously doubt that he let himself get starched just to divert suspicion from himself."

"I'd forgo the sarcasm if I were you," Steelman said coldly. "You're not very good at it."

Gulliver did not respond, and after a pause Steelman asked: "Now, what about this chap Dang? What do we know about him?"

"We know he's a damn good leader," Gulliver said slowly, deliberately. "Probably the best troop commander I have ever known."

"That doesn't speak highly of your standards," Steelman said. "As I understand it, good leaders do not blithely walk into ambushes. Good troop commanders do not lose every man in their command and survive to tell the tale."

When Gulliver did not rise to the bait, Steelman asked: "This Dang's a Viet Cong who rallied to the GVN, a *chieu hoi*, isn't that right?"

Gulliver nodded. "A majority of our PRUs are *hoi chanh*."

"Is it possible that he's still VC?"

"This is Vietnam. Anything's possible," Gulliver said. "But aren't you forgetting something? Captain Dang saved my life, and Lieutenant Swain's. Why would he do that if he were still VC? Charlie would rather bag two American advisers than two whole platoons of PRUs."

Swain started to say something, but stopped himself. He and the others had remained quiet, grateful that Cameron and Gulliver were serving as lightning rods, absorbing Steelman's charged ire for them all. But he grudgingly nodded agreement with Gulliver's statement. He didn't relish taking Gulliver's side against Steelman on any count, but he felt that he owed Dang that much for saving his skin.

"Perhaps," Steelman said to Gulliver. "But you have not answered my question. What do you know about him?"

Gulliver shook his head. "Not a lot. We make it a point in the PRU not to probe too deeply into a man's past."

Steelman blew up. "Sweet Jesus, man, he's your goddamn counterpart!"

Most of them knew that the chief of operations rarely used profanity. It was an eruption all the more violent for the icy control that had preceded it. But Steelman reined himself in quickly. He was back in character by the time he said, in a tone of exaggerated civility: "He must have told you *something* about himself. From what I understand, you're the only one he ever talks to."

"I don't know about that, but I guess he has told me a little."

"Enlighten us."

"I know that he was a main-force VC company commander," Gulliver said with a shrug, "and that he was born in the North to a Catholic family. The family came South during partition in '54, and he was raised in a tiny, predominantly Catholic village up in M-R One, not too far from Dong Ha. His father was the village chief. Dang told me he was schooled by the nuns. He must have done well because the church paid his way through Saigon University. I guess he did okay there, too, because he won a couple of scholarships to do graduate work abroad. First at Notre Dame in the States and then in Paris. From what I gather, it was in Paris that he got religion. He fell in love with the writings of Ho and Mao and decided to climb aboard the bandwagon of historical imperatives."

Steelman looked doubtful. "If this Dang is so brilliant, why wasn't he used as a political cadre?" he asked. "Why a common soldier—cannon fodder?"

Gulliver smiled and let the dig go by unremarked but not unregistered. "I wouldn't know about that," he said. "But my guess is that Hanoi would not trust a Catholic, even a lapsed Catholic, to preach the gospel of liberation. The Politburo is not a big fan of the One True Church."

"True," Steelman conceded. "Is that why he rallied, then? Because he had such limited opportunity for advancement?"

Gulliver smiled again. "Unlike some people, Dang doesn't suffer from that kind of driving ambition."

Steelman did not smile back. "Why did he rally, then?"

"I don't know for sure," Gulliver said, "but probably because of an incident that happened a couple of years ago."

"What was that?"

"A marine medcap team went into this village—this tiny predominantly Catholic village up in M-R One, not too far from Dong Ha—to treat the children for an epidemic of pink-eye. The local VC paid the ville a visit that night. They rounded up every kid who'd been treated and plucked out one eye. Then they gouged out both the village chief's eyes. They made him eat them before they disemboweled him."

"Good God!" George Cameron whispered. Riesz and Coughlin both made horrified faces. Swain looked merely fascinated.

"Let no one accuse our enemies of failing to appreciate the power of a dramatic gesture," Steelman said with a smile. "I would imagine that when the marines returned on their next humanitarian visit they received a decidedly cool reception."

"I would imagine," Gulliver mimicked.

"So where does that leave us? He's a Northerner, he's educated, and the communists killed his father," Steelman recapped, ticking off the highlights of Dang's life on his fingers. "Is that everything you can tell us about him?"

Gulliver nodded. "Except for what I said before: in my opinion he's the best troop leader I ever saw."

Steelman chose to show his opinion of Gulliver's opinion by ostentatiously turning to face the others. He gave each of them a stern look before saying: "Our objectives from this point, this *low* point, forward, are twofold, one a corollary to the other: to tighten in-house security and to tidy up this province in the short time remaining to us. That means no more leaks and no more mistakes. It is possible, as George suggests, that our leak may be one of the Vietnamese in the Phoenix chain of command. If that is the case, we can try to plug it by keeping everything on a strict need-to-know basis. Tell your counterpart only what he must know to do his job. Do not let anyone outside of the Embassy House get a look at the whole picture. If we narrow the number of those who have access to our plans, we narrow the field of suspects."

Steelman said to Cameron, "George, I want you to talk to the province chief. Tell him we'd like him to keep to a minimum the number of people he involves in Phoenix planning. Tell him we'd appreciate a list of the names of those people. And, George, go see Colonel Minh yourself. You do not have to go through the PSA on this one. I don't want that fool Sloane garbling the message."

"Right, Bennett," Cameron said with a grin.

Steelman turned to Coughlin. "You do the same with that other idiot, Ngoc at Field Force. And, of course, your counterpart at Special Branch, Major Do."

Coughlin also grinned. "Yes, sir."

"Oh, one more thing, Coughlin. I want that whore of yours—Miss Tuyet, is it?—out of the house by morning."

Coughlin's grin died. He reddened but said nothing.

Steelman leveled his gaze on Chuck Riesz. "We need a good deal more quality control in your department, Riesz. From now on, I want an American present at all interrogation sessions. If for some reason you can't be there yourself, get someone else from the Embassy House to sit in for you. I've ordered Saigon to ship your cadre—the PRU's big snatch—back to you. Perhaps he didn't know that the papers he carried were phony, but then again, perhaps he did. Let's find out. I don't care how you do it, but do it. Break him."

"I don't think that man can be broken, sir," Riesz said.

Steelman fixed him with a look. "*Any* man can be broken."

"Uh, yessir, that's what I always thought. But—"

"No buts. Do it. If it proves to be more than you can manage, you can send him back to us in Saigon . . . and we can send *you* home."

"Yessir."

Steelman nodded. "And let's see if we can't reduce the number of people who get to hear what a prisoner has to tell us. It might be a good idea for you to team up with someone from Special Branch rather than the Provincial Interrogation Center regulars. See if you can find someone who is qualified in interrogation procedures and who is already on our list of need-to-know Vietnamese. Someone like that number-two man on Major Do's staff . . . a Captain Bich, I believe."

Riesz nodded and jotted the name in his notebook.

Finally it was Swain's turn. "Swain, you'll have to keep Captain Dang fully advised, of course," Steelman said, "but I see no reason why individual PRUs have to know where they are going, or why, until they are actually at the mission site."

"Roger," said Swain.

"Two more things, Swain," Steelman said. "You won't have to waste time training replacements. In the interest of speed, I've decided to send you some experienced PRUs. I can siphon them off from other teams around the country."

"Number One! Thank you, sir."

"Also, as of this moment, you are no longer acting PRU adviser. You're permanent. I am relieving Captain Gulliver."

Swain's mouth actually fell open. He looked like a lousy actor registering shock. The others were struck equally dumb. Only Gulliver himself seemed unsurprised. He met Steelman's glance and returned his knowing smile.

For a brief moment Cameron forgot both his fear and his pension. In uncalculated, unthinking reflex, a holdover from his younger days, he rose to Gulliver's defense. "Just wait a minute here, Bennett. I know it was Jake's plan and all, but you can't blame him for what happened out there. We voted on that plan and okayed it. Every man here, and Sloane, and our counterparts. Besides, I'm the ranking officer in this house, and if somebody's got to take the rap, it should be me."

Gulliver held up a hand to stop him. "George—"

"Calm down, George," Steelman interrupted. "This move is not a punishment; it's a striving for continuity. By the time Captain Gulliver is well enough to resume his duties, it will be time for Swain to take over anyway." He turned to Gulliver for an endorsement. "Am I right?"

Gulliver did not answer Steelman. Instead, he turned to Cameron with an appreciative look and said, "To tell you the truth, I don't care about the reasons, George. It sounds good to me. You know as well as anyone that I've never been overly fond of this job. It sure won't break my heart to lose it."

"You see, George, it works out for everyone," Steelman said.

Cameron was sweating more profusely than ever. He was a little proud of himself for having spoken up, but mostly he was horrified at his foolishness. What could he possibly have been thinking of? He jumped at this chance to wriggle off the hook, mumbling with a relief that was painful for the others to witness, "Well, I mean, that's completely different, isn't it . . . of course it is . . . I mean, when you put it like that . . . why, any fool can see . . . my fault entirely . . . I'm sorry, Bennett."

"Don't be silly, old boy," Steelman said with a forgiving smile. "I like a man who stands up for his subordinates when he thinks they're being treated unfairly." Amusement played in the corners of his mouth.

Gulliver came to Cameron's rescue with a question. "Does this mean I can pack up and go?" he asked Steelman.

"I'm afraid not," Steelman said. "Your wound has to mend and it might as well mend here, where you can help Lieutenant Swain get—pardon the pun—oriented. I know you will want to do anything you can to assist him. Also, we in the embassy will need a little time to decide what we're going to do with you." He was watching Gulliver closely.

Gulliver nodded nonchalantly, as if the subject of his future were immaterial to him. It was unlikely that the pose fooled Steelman.

"One last item of business," Steelman said, turning back to the group. "I'll be leaving in the morning. Before I go, I would like those team members who were at the Seven Mountains planning session to undergo a technical interview. That means all of you here in this room, and Captain Dang, of course. A company technician will be coming from Saigon this afternoon. Please stay within the compound where we can find you when we need you."

There was a chorus of muffled groans as plans went up in smoke. Riesz had an interrogation in progress at the PIC and was champing at the bit to try an interesting technique once used by the Japanese Kempetai. Coughlin had to start looking for a place for Tuyet to live, a place worthy of a woman who was once an emperor's mistress. And Cameron wanted—needed—a drink.

Swain bent toward Riesz and whispered a question: "What the fuck is a technical interview?"

"That's what we call a poly—a lie-detector test," Riesz whispered back.

Then Swain groaned too. He had been planning to resume his stakeout at Mai's house.

Of them all, Cameron's need was the most pressing, and he ventured a mild objection. "Uh, Bennett, we just took a poly ten days ago. Is it really necessary to do it again so soon?"

"Yes, it is, George," Steelman said coldly. "And until the leak is found, I want everyone in this house, American and Vietnamese, to submit to the interview once a week. Is that perfectly clear?"

Cameron backed off. "Sure, Bennett. Whatever you say. Better to be safe than sorry, eh?"

"The only thing that makes me sorry is that we can't ask our provincial counterparts to do the same without insulting their Oriental dignity," Steelman said. He made a gesture of dismissal, a brushing motion with his fingers. "That's all for now, gentlemen. Lieutenant Swain, if you would care to join me, I'd be happy to outline your expanded duties for you. We can use Captain Gul . . . *your* office."

They filed out and scattered through the Embassy House. Coughlin, looking for a place to hide after he did what he had to do, challenged Riesz to a game of pool, telling him to go ahead and rack the balls, then went up to tell Tuyet she would have to move out. Cameron followed Riesz to the common room, making a beeline for the bamboo bar, having persuaded himself that a vodka, just one, couldn't hurt. Steelman and Swain went into the PRU adviser's office, *Swain*'s office.

Gulliver, feeling like a refugee, went upstairs to take his pills.

Swain settled in behind the PRU adviser's desk like a junior executive newly promoted to a corner office, tilting back his chair and putting up his feet, already making his plans for redecorating.

"This is great, Mr. Steelman; I really appreciate it," he said.

"You've earned the job, old boy," said Bennett Steelman, looking uncomfortable in the visitors' chair, straight-backed and hard, with no arm to throw his leg over. "Your first memo was bang-on with its premonition that something was rotten in Denmark. It was not in time for me to take preventive action, of course, but that wasn't your fault."

Swain shrugged modestly. "I was just reporting what the province chief told me, and my own gut feelings about what's going on around here."

"That is just what I want, old boy. Just want I need."

"Yessir. Uh, if I may ask, sir, what *are* you going to do with Gulliver? Send him back to Special Forces?"

"No. Throwing Brer Rabbit back into his briar patch is not an option. Quite frankly, and this is for your ears only, I am considering bringing charges against Captain Gulliver."

"Jeez!" Swain took his feet off the desktop and sat up straight. "You don't think he's the leak you talked about, do you? I mean, I've got no use for the man, but I can't believe he's some kind of traitor."

Steelman shook his head. "I'm not sure yet what form the charges might take; that's where I need your help, old boy. I want you to keep up the reports on Gulliver. Continue to drop them at the tailor's shop."

"Yessir. Will do."

"To maintain cover, you should actually have some clothes

made, at company expense, of course," Steelman said, smiling. "You will find that Mr. Tho is, in fact, a very fine tailor."

"Uh, yessir."

There was a long, deep pause while Steelman gave Swain a measuring look. Then he said: "I had a talk with the province chief yesterday. He seems to like you."

"Yessir. Me and Colonel Minh get along pretty good."

"He was saying he may have a few, ah, a few special jobs in mind for you."

"What kind of special jobs, sir?"

Steelman waved the question away. "He can tell you about it himself. All I'll say is that the province chief is a good friend of the United States of America, and anything you can do to help him would be noted, and appreciated."

"Uh, yessir," Swain said.

"Good, good," Steelman said, smiling. "Now then, tell me again about the ambush."

11

THE HELICOPTER, AN AIR AMERICA LOH–1 LOACH, settled on the ballfield behind the Embassy House villa, landing in a whirlwind of laterite dust, a storm of its own making. Even before the blades stopped turning, a line had formed at the door. Troops came flying from the barracks, sprinting toward the cooling machine, even the dour Nungs laughing and playing grab-ass. It was payday, and the bird bringing the man with the black box also brought the man with the black bag.

The polygraph technician climbed out and started for the villa, pulling a case fitted with rollers. The paymaster did not get out at all; he sat in the chopper door with a satchel on his lap and ticked names off a roster as he dipped into the bag and came up with a fistful of currency for each man.

Gulliver watched the scene from a chair by the window in George Cameron's office, there because he had nowhere else to go. Steelman and Swain had commandeered his office and he had been driven out of his room upstairs by the sound of Tuyet's sobbing across the hall.

"The Bag Day riot gets worse every month," he observed.

"Today is special," Cameron reminded him. "It's the payday before Tet. They know they get a bonus for Tet."

"Hide your daughters tonight, province town," Gulliver joked without mirth. "Someone's going to get fucked."

"And it just might be you," Cameron said. "Do you really think Steelman's going to let you off the hook?"

Gulliver shrugged. "I can hope."

"I've just got a bad feeling that if there's a way to screw you, Steelman will find it," Cameron said.

"You're probably right," said Gulliver. "I'm just sorry your ass had to get thrown into the blender along with mine."

"He doesn't scare me. What's he going to do, send me to Vietnam?" For the moment at least, George Cameron was telling the truth. Four vodkas, taken neat, made him invulnerable.

Gulliver stood, wincing with the effort. He had taken his pills just thirty minutes ago, but they were not doing for him what the vodka was doing for Cameron. They seemed to have lost their curative powers. Still, he had taken only the two.

"Well, I'd better go tell Dang the prevarication police have arrived," he said.

Cameron nodded morosely. "I still don't think it's right for Steelman to make us go through the box again so soon," he groused. "After twenty-five years of service the bastards are still giving me loyalty tests. They don't leave a man a shred of dignity, do they?"

"It's not like you to bad-mouth the agency, George."

Cameron shook his head. "It's not the company I joined. Besides, it's not so much the company . . . it's Steelman. It's the . . . ah, hell, I don't know. The man just gets to me. Always has. You never know what he's thinking or what he's gonna do. Something happens to me when I'm around him. I can't help it, it just . . . happens. I still can't believe I stood up there and gave a pep talk for Phoenix. That . . . that wasn't me, Jake. You know it wasn't. You know how I feel about Phoenix . . ."

Cameron's eyes teared up and his quivering chin battled for control. It was a quick, but complete, collapse, one that seemed to surprise him almost as much as it did Gulliver. He tried to hide his face behind a hand which was dotted on the back with brown liver spots.

Gulliver did not know how to help. "George . . ." he said, taking a step toward him, but Cameron shook his head quickly and waved him away. Gulliver left the office quietly, chased from yet another refuge by tears.

He went out through the kitchen, giving Chi Ba a playful goose as he passed. The moon-faced cook yelped, her 180 pounds rising an inch off the floor. She threw a lettuce leaf at him and brandished her cleaver threateningly. Laughing, Gulliver backed away, blowing her a kiss as he went. Chi Ba gave him a lecherous grin full of blackened teeth, and called his bluff: *"Gap nhau o dau cung?"* Where shall we meet, sweetie?

As soon as his wound healed, he promised in Vietnamese, he would take her to America, where they picked their rulers according to size. She would be queen and he'd be her consort and they would do nothing all day but watch color television and make love and she would bear him ten children, all boys, all strapping little princes. Chi Ba bellowed like a buffalo and came at him with the cleaver. Gulliver wrenched his side trying to get out the door before she could catch him.

The horseplay with the jolly cook had lightened his mood for a few moments, but the feeling did not last. A picture of Tuyet and Cameron, weeping on different floors for different reasons, stayed with him.

He walked toward the PRU barrack with the hitched gait of an old man, the bandage around his torso so tight he could hardly breathe, as if a boa constrictor had hold of him. The house doctor had come by that morning to change the dressing. Dr. Loi, the best man in the province town; Medium Minh's own physician.

He was guessing Dang would be in the PRU barrack, as far from the payday mob scene as he could get. Dang did not like crowds. Besides, his salary came out of Medium Minh's pocket, not out of the cowboys' saddlebag.

Gulliver lengthened stride, ignoring the twinge in his side, anxious to catch Dang alone. It was important to let Dang know the poly man was here. He did not know why he felt that it was important, only that he did. Perhaps because he thought Dang might need time to prepare himself; because he was not convinced his counterpart could pass a lie-detector test.

Gulliver had defended Dang at the meeting, had done what he could to deflect Steelman's aimless insinuations. But even as he had told Steelman what he knew about Dang's background, a voice in his head had been asking how much of it he himself believed.

For starters, Gulliver did not believe that his friend was from the North. In Vietnam, much as in America, there was a Northern prejudice against Southerners. Delta people were said to be darker-skinned, rather lazy, not altogether trustworthy. None of it was true, of course. It was largely jealousy; the Delta's rice crop was as reliable as it was bountiful, the North's iffy at best. But, prejudices aside, there were real differences, especially in accent. Southern speech was much slower, less precise, with none of the harsh, overpunctuated sound of the North. Talking with a Northerner was like being pummeled with a stiletto. With a Southerner, it was more like a slow drowning in thick syrup. And Dang's accent, his use of idiom, his awareness of local custom, all pointed to a Southern birth and upbringing.

Also, Dang displayed far too many unusual qualities ever to have been the simple Viet Cong fighter he claimed. Unlike the other PRU team leaders Gulliver had run across, Dang was educated, with a sophisticated understanding of politics and philosophy. And Dang was not preoccupied with money, or rape, or blood for the sake of blood, like so many PRUs. He could be cruel when the job required it, of course, but he didn't seem to enjoy that part of PRU work the way so many of the others did. No, Dang was not your typical PRU at all.

The strange thing was that Dang genuinely seemed to care for the war's victims, the peasants, even as he and his men brutalized them. He could order an old man's scrotum nailed to a table, then squat for hours with other old men, chewing betel and talking of crops and of how the middlemen cheated them when it was time to ship their rice to market. He could put a bullet through the temple of an undisciplined soldier, then swab a child's fevered brow while reassuring its worried parents. He could cut off a prisoner's finger during a field interrogation, then give a helping hand to a schoolteacher having trouble with lesson plans. He could expertly plant a mine where it would do the most damage, then carry home the boy who accidentally stepped on it, helping the mother ready her son for burial, hauling up pails of canal water to wash down the corpse.

Gulliver had seen his counterpart do all those things, and more. Things which, on the surface, seemed beyond the possibilities inherent in such a finely honed instrument of apocalypse.

But Dang's many contradictions did not satisfy the many questions Gulliver had about his friend, did not explain the many odd happenings, of which the ambush was only the latest.

How, for instance, had Dang survived the ambush when no one else in his team managed to? Why had he been out of radio contact with Dog Pound in the critical moments just prior to, during, and after the ambush? And how had he gotten through the VC's cordon to come to his and Swain's rescue? Dang was good, but was he *that* good? Was anyone? Dang's glib answers to such questions had been too convenient to be convincing.

And what about routine PRU operations? Why was it that whenever Special Branch identified and targeted an important VCI cadre, something invariably went wrong, while there was seldom a hitch when the target was low-level, and no hitch at all when it was not a VCI but one of Medium Minh's "specials"?

Aside from the one cadre who, thanks to the old man, they had picked up in the Swamp of the Spirits, Phoenix had not bagged itself a communist above the rank-and-file level in the seven months he and Dang had been assigned to the province. And as it turned out, even their lone success had boomeranged. Their snatch had fed them poisoned candy. Trick or fucking treat.

Gulliver had had his fun with his counterpart, with all the jokes about how once a VC always a VC, but his bantering had grown less jocular as the coincidences piled up. Never a particularly playful man, Dang would usually ignore him . . . or give him one of those looks Westerners insisted upon calling inscrutable . . . or say very seriously, "You are wrong, Sandman. I am not a communist. Communism is a bad system. Bad for the people." Such solemn pronouncements had done little to ease Gulliver's mind. Who else but the VC gave a rat's ass about *the people*?

As much as it galled him to admit it, Gulliver knew that Steelman's concern was justified. But he refused to entertain the suggestion that Dang was behind it. He told himself that it was coincidence and nothing more. He believed it. He had to believe it. What else could he do? Dang was the only real friend he had in this place. A friend who had saved his life.

The barrack was empty of troops and Gulliver found Dang right where he thought he would, sitting cross-legged on his bunk oiling an AK–47, wearing nothing but a sarong pulled up between his legs and tucked in at the waist to make a kind of loincloth. Sitting that way, dressed that way, with his flat, broad face and longish black hair, the PRU team leader looked like a Cheyenne warrior preparing for battle.

Dang stopped what he was doing and watched his adviser approach. He waited for Gulliver to get close before saying in English: "The eagle shits today."

Gulliver laughed and nodded. It was an old Regular Army expression for payday. He wondered where Dang had picked it up; probably from the Americans for whom he'd run Kit Carson Scouts before coming to the province.

"The eagle didn't come alone," Gulliver said. "The poly man came with him. They want us in the common room. They're going to ask us about the ambush." He watched Dang's face for signs of panic. It was as serene as a novitiate's.

Dang reassembled the weapon in a time that would have won the competition at Bragg, then stripped off the sarong and put on black pajamas and tire sandals. "I am ready," he said at last, both his face and his voice still worry-free.

As they walked toward the villa, Dang slowed his pace to match Gulliver's cautious steps. Neither man spoke until they were halfway to the main house and Gulliver suddenly asked: "Dang, do you consider soldiering to be an art?"

"Yes."

"So do I."

After a few more yards Gulliver asked: "Do you consider us friends? Good friends?"

"Yes."

"So do I."

Several steps later Gulliver asked: "Do you suppose the one has anything to do with the other?"

Dang gave it some thought. If he considered Gulliver's questions odd, he gave no indication. At last he nodded and said: "Madriaga said that art is a bridge of matter between spirit and spirit. A soldier's art is the bridge that joins our spirits. That is what I think."

"So do I," said Gulliver, wondering who in hell Madriaga was. For all his questions about Dang's background, there was no doubting that a Western liberal-arts education was part of it.

Then Dang asked a question. "Tell me, Sandman: why do you not hate Vietnamese people like the other Americans?"

Gulliver looked surprised. "What's to hate? I admire the Vietnamese. They're the most resilient people I've ever seen. When you consider all they've been through in the last thirty or so years, and how they've managed to retain their humor and generosity . . . But I don't think I'm alone in feeling that way. Do you honestly believe Americans hate the Vietnamese?"

"Most Americans do not like us. Even those who pretend that they do, like your Mr. Sloane. In their hearts, they do not think we are worth dying for."

"Is anything worth dying for?"

"Yes," Dang said with a quiet conviction.

They made the rest of the walk in silence. It was not the longest conversation they had ever had, but it was the most intimate.

The technical interviewer from Saigon, whose name was Seiple, was still setting up the box in Coughlin's office, the closest one to the common room, where the Embassy House team members were gathered.

At the pool table, Coughlin and Riesz continued their game of nine-ball. They had been at it for most of the afternoon. In a corner, Swain and Steelman continued the private conversation they had started in Gulliver's office. And at the bamboo bar, George Cameron defiantly continued to drink, the back of his sweat-soaked shirt absorbing the disapproving looks Steelman sent his way.

The latecomers, Gulliver and Dang, took seats at the poker table and watched the others.

A few minutes later, Seiple poked his head into the room and announced: "I am ready for them now, Mr. Steelman. Who is to be first?"

All eyes turned to Steelman. After a deliberate pause he said: "Gulliver."

Gulliver slowly got to his feet and followed Seiple back to the interview room.

Seiple was a fussy middle-aged man who wore a Princeton class ring and Earth shoes. He motioned for Gulliver to sit, and began fooling with knobs at his console. With his slight build, fat-lensed spectacles, and bantam-rooster air, he could have been Chuck Riesz's older brother. Gulliver thought there must be an underground laboratory at Langley where earnest true believers were produced as uniformly and predictably as pistons on a Detroit production line.

Gulliver thought he knew most of the interviewers on the embassy house circuit, but he did not know Seiple. He tried to break the ice. "You must be new in-country. I don't think I've seen you around before."

"No, I am not new," Seiple said officiously. "But it is true that I do not do monthly rounds. I only do special jobs for Mr. Steelman."

"Oh," said Gulliver.

Seiple stopped fussing with the machine and picked up a notepad and a pen. "Since you are, or certainly should be, fully familiar with interview procedure by now," he said, "I should not have to remind you that all of my questions are to be answered with a simple yes or no."

Gulliver nodded. The technical interviewer's speech, his inflections and locutions, were much the same as Steelman's, Gulliver noticed: formal, stilted, almost British, with very little slang and few contractions. Gulliver wondered if it was the residue of an Ivy League background both men shared, or merely imitation on Seiple's part.

"Are you comfortable?" Seiple asked. Gulliver nodded.

"Are you ready to begin the preexamination phase of the interview?"

When Gulliver nodded again, Seiple said, "Fine. We shall begin."

Is your name Jonathan Gulliver? Yes.

Were you born on January 2, 1938? Yes.

Were you born in Fayetteville, North Carolina? Yes, uh, no, uh, Hope Mills really, just outside Fayetteville.

Answer yes or no, please. Sorry; yes.

Are you currently on active-duty status with the armed forces of the United States? Yes.

Do you now know, or have you ever known, an official of a foreign country? Yes.

Do you now know, or have you ever known, an official of a communist country? No.

Do you now know, or have you ever known, an intelligence officer of a foreign country? Yes.

Do you now know, or have you ever known, an intelligence officer of a communist country? No.

Were you recently a participant in combat with hostile forces operating in the Seven Mountains region of Tinh Bien district, Chau Doc province, Republic of Vietnam? Yes.

Did you participate in a military operation bearing the code name Dog Catcher? Yes.

Were you privy to the operational plans for Dog Catcher? Yes.

Did you discuss the plans for Operation Dog Catcher with any person or persons outside the immediate planning council? No.

Do you have reason to suspect that Operation Dog Catcher was compromised because of an unauthorized person or persons gaining access to the plan? I don't know.

Yes or no, please. No.

If Operation Dog Catcher *was* compromised, have you any thoughts as to who might have been involved? No.

Have you answered all my questions truthfully? Yes.

"You may relax for a moment," Seiple said, putting down his pen. "As soon as I connect you to the apparatus, we will resume the interview."

Seiple was a man absorbed in his work. He saw the humans involved, both subject and interviewer, as nothing more than appendages of the hardware—flawed but necessary handmaidens to technology. He could not seem to keep his eyes, or hands, off the box. He gave it fondling looks and little love pats, caressing it as conscientiously as he would a new bride. He readjusted the vents on the air-conditioner so that the box, or "apparatus," as he called it, would be more comfortable.

The console and plotters took up most of Coughlin's desktop.

There was a panel of switches and three stylus pens that were poised over the graph paper like needles over phonograph records. From the console snaked three cables which connected the unit to an equal number of sensory devices, and it was to these devices that Seiple plugged Gulliver.

He had Gulliver turn his chair around and face the door, then went to work on him like a death-row warder preparing a condemned prisoner for the electric chair. He fastened a tube made of corrugated rubber around Gulliver's chest and snapped the ends together in back. The tube would monitor any changes in breathing. To record pulse and blood pressure, he wrapped an inflatable cuff around Gulliver's arm. The last item was a handheld instrument fitted with electrode sensors to measure changes in perspiration.

When Seiple finished trussing his subject, he returned to the console and began playing with his dials and switches. The arm cuff ballooned, and Gulliver was suddenly conscious of his pulse, as metronomic, as monotonous, as a ceremonial drum.

"Are you relatively comfortable?" Seiple asked the back of Gulliver's head.

"Relatively."

"Take a few seconds to relax," Seiple said. And a few seconds later: "All right, let us begin."

Seiple started through the questions again, going even more slowly this time, asking them of the back of Gulliver's head while Gulliver gave his answers to the door. Behind him, Gulliver could hear rustling noises: Seiple popping up and down to check graphs . . . the thin scratching of pens on paper.

When he reached the end of the list, Seiple said, "If you please, I would like to go through them one more time."

They went through the list again. The interviewer asked the same questions, the subject gave the same answers. When they finished, Seiple fiddled at the console and Gulliver's cuff deflated. He started to turn around, but Seiple's voice stopped him: "Please maintain your position, Captain. We are not quite finished."

When Gulliver settled back, Seiple asked: "What were you thinking when you answered the question about whether you had discussed Dog Catcher with anyone outside the Embassy House?"

"Nothing really. What was there to think about?"

"Do correct me if I'm wrong," Seiple said testily, "but I believe that the standard operating procedure is for me to ask the questions and for you to answer them."

"Sorry. I wasn't thinking about anything in particular."

"I see," Seiple said, jotting in his notebook. "And what were you thinking about when you answered the question about whether the operation might have been compromised?"

"Nothing in particular."

"Come now, Captain. You had to be thinking about *something*."

"Only that I couldn't give a straight yes-or-no answer to the question. That I honestly didn't know if it had been compromised or not."

There was the sound of note-taking. "And what were you thinking when you answered the question about who, if anyone, might have been responsible for compromising Dog Catcher?"

"I don't remember."

"Please try to remember. It's important."

"If I was thinking anything, it was that I couldn't very well answer that question if I couldn't answer the one before it. I mean, if I don't know whether or not the operation was compromised in the first place, how can I speculate as to who might or might not have compromised it?"

Seiple said, "Hmmm . . . well, I guess we will just have to go through them again. You seem to be having difficulty with one or two."

The arm cuff was reinflated and they crawled through the questions again. This time Gulliver was acutely conscious of his heartbeat, which seemed out of control, and his hands felt clammy. When they got to the questions in which Seiple had shown a special interest, Gulliver thought he could hear the pens scratching frantically, like animals at the door of a cage.

When they came to the end, Gulliver heard the notepad being slapped shut behind him. He was about to turn around when Seiple said: "One final question, if you please, Captain. Are you acquainted with a Vietnamese actress named Nhu Quynh, more commonly known by her stage name, Quynh Nhu?"

Gulliver felt his face flush and his pulse quicken. The pens went scratch, scratch, scratch. He turned around slowly. "How in the hell do you know—?"

"Yes or no, please."

"But what does this have to do with anything?"

"Yes or no, please."

"Yes, goddammit!"

Seiple nodded. "Thank you, Captain Gulliver," he said in a pleasant voice. "I believe that terminates the interview."

* * *

Gulliver's interview had taken nearly an hour; Dang was back in half that. Gulliver studied his counterpart's face for signs of anxiety and found none.

"How did it go?" he asked as they watched Cameron get to his feet and walk unsteadily toward the interview room.

Dang shrugged. "The same as always."

Gulliver was aware of an undeniable feeling of relief, but not of certainty. It was difficult to beat the machine, but not impossible. If anyone had the necessary temperament and control to do it, it was Dang.

Never one to hang around the villa if he had any choice in the matter, Dang tapped Gulliver on the arm in a gesture of farewell and started back to the PRU barrack.

Feeling tired, Gulliver climbed the stairs to his room. He stopped at Coughlin's door and rapped lightly. There was no answer, no disconsolate weeping behind the door. Tuyet had checked out of the Embassy House. At management's request. It was too bad, Gulliver thought. While he had never approved of the policy that allowed women to live in, Tuyet had been one of the better ones, an old-fashioned gentlewoman.

He napped for two hours and woke with pain. He took two pills, cheating on the time by only four minutes. They eased his pain but did not help his restlessness. He went back down to the common room to look for something to read and saw that George Cameron was still in with Seiple.

Gulliver was browsing at the bookshelf, scanning titles in a futile hunt for something he had not already read, when Coughlin blew up: "Son of a fucking bitch! We'll be here all fucking night at this fucking rate! What the fuck is going on in there?"

Coughlin's patience had run out. He had been pacing the common room for more than three hours, unable to go comfort his mistress because he had not yet been through the box, unable to use the dead time to catch up on his work because Seiple was using his office. Already on edge because of the business with Tuyet, the delay had pushed him over.

The bookshelf was in a corner of the room, not far from where Swain and Steelman were sitting. Gulliver saw both men turn to look at the frothing Coughlin, then saw Swain glance at his watch.

"Jeez!" Swain said. "He *has* been in there a long time. There must be a problem. Do you think he's lying?"

"He's not lying," Steelman said in disgust, his nose in the air, his nostrils pinched. "He's drunk."

* * *

In the morning, Sally Teacher was up early. She bathed, packed her things, and went down to breakfast, where she found George Cameron sitting alone in the dining room. At her place at the table was a large bouquet of flowers of mixed variety, prettily arranged in a reed basket.

She held them to her nose and sniffed, then probed the basket for a card. There was none.

"Where did these come from?" she asked.

Cameron grinned. "Steelman, I assume. They were already here when I came down. Sure wish I'd thought of it first."

Sally smelled them again and set them aside. "Did he happen to call?" she asked. "I need to know the plan."

"About ten minutes ago," said Cameron. "He said he'd meet you at the airfield in an hour. He's having breakfast with Colonel Sloane."

Cameron rang a small brass bell and a few seconds later Chi Ba came waddling in to take Sally's order.

"Sorry we all abandoned you yesterday," Cameron said.

"Oh, I had a wonderful day," Sally said brightly. "Some people I met at the Hoa Hao dinner invited me to go sailing on the Bassac. My host and hostess from the night before, in fact; Dr. Loan and his wife. Very sweet people. We packed a picnic and had a marvelous time." She was about to ask how his day had gone, but caught herself just in time, remembering the scheduled meeting; she had no way of knowing what was said at the meeting, but, knowing Bennett Steelman, she could imagine.

Cameron confirmed it in the next breath. "Sounds nice; wish I'd been there," he said wistfully. Then he muttered: "Wish I'd been anywhere but here."

After Sally had finished her breakfast of ham and eggs, Cameron sent one servant up to get her bags and another out to find her driver. They said good-bye on the veranda and he seemed honestly sorry to see her go.

When she arrived at the airfield, the Beech Bonanza was already gunning its engines and Bennett Steelman was tapping his foot at the bottom of the gangplank, looking fidgety and anxious to be under way. Sensing his urgency, Sally made sure that her suitcase and overnight case made the transfer from the Bronco to the plane, and hurried aboard. It was not until she had strapped herself in and the plane was beginning to taxi up the strip that she realized she had left her basket of flowers on the rear seat of the car.

"The flowers were beautiful," she said across the aisle, hoping that Steelman would not ask where they were.

He looked up from the report he was reading. "Flowers?" he asked, his confusion plain.

"Yes. The flowers . . . the basket," Sally said uncertainly, beginning to grow a little confused herself.

"Sorry, old girl, but I don't know what you're talking about." He went back to his report.

The Beech taxied to the end of the tarmac, turned, and started its takeoff run. As they whizzed past the terminal, nothing more than a Quonset hut with a windsock on the roof, Sally caught a fleeting glimpse of Captain Gulliver leaning against the front of the building.

12

BENNETT STEELMAN'S VISIT to the province town ended on the day before the Tet holidays began. He and Sally Teacher left for Saigon early that morning. What was to become known as the Trung Affair began late that night.

It began a little before midnight with a telephone call from Captain Bich at Special Branch headquarters. He needed a PRU force to make an immediate arrest. Five men should do; no real trouble was anticipated.

As the adviser to Special Branch, Bill Coughlin took the call. He relayed Bich's request to Cameron, who relayed it to Swain, who relayed it to Dang, who mounted a squad from among those PRUs who were not out on the town running through their Tet bonuses.

Rousted from their bunks, the PRUs dressed, grabbed M–16s, and drowsily loaded onto a waiting deuce-and-a-half rigged up with full canvas. Once aboard, they handed around a camouflage stick, painting up. The truck was passed through the compound gate by a yawning Nung sentry at 12:01 A.M.; the first minute of the first day of Canh Tuat, the Year of the Dog.

Swain rode along up front with Dang and the driver. His presence was not required on such routine missions, but this was the first call the PRUs had taken since he'd become their permanent adviser. He wouldn't have missed it for the world.

Normally the province town was buttoned up for the night at this late hour, but not in these first moments of a brand-new year. The *pop-pop-pop* of firecrackers echoed through its neighborhoods, and the odors of incense and black powder came together to clog the air with an eccentric perfume.

That afternoon, in a ceremony called Tat Nien, or Year's End, the townspeople had offered their sacrifices to deceased relatives, inviting them back to enjoy the holidays with the living. Now, in a ritual called Giao Thua, or New Year's Eve, additional offerings were made to the spirits, on open-air altars. From lush villa gardens and grimy back alleys alike came the ghostly flicker and sweet smell of perfumed candles.

The truck carefully made its way through streets full of people. Buddhist families on their way to the pagodas walked hand-in-hand, carrying new buds broken off recently purchased Tet plants. Those who had already been to the pagoda plucked more buds and placed them on top of special columns outside their houses, to bring the family luck in the coming year. Those of the Hoa Hao sect, who did not consider pagodas a necessary prop for effective prayer, went through their own simpler Tet rituals at home.

The truck stopped at the provincial compound to pick up Captain Bich. He gave the driver directions in Vietnamese and the truck continued its journey through the celebrating town.

At first glance, Captain Bich appeared to be a clone of his superior, Major Do. He was ferret thin and intense, and he affected the same pencil-thin mustache. The similarities stopped there. Bich could not duplicate Major Do's mind. He was not a truly stupid man, the way Major Ngoc of the Field Force was a truly stupid man, but neither was he blessed with Major Do's subtle combination of intellect, acumen, patience, cynicism, and paranoia. He was not, like Major Do, the perfect policeman.

Speaking English for Swain's benefit, Bich briefed Dang as the truck crawled toward the edges of the province town. Acting on a tip from a highly placed VCI penetration, Special Branch agents had been keeping an isolated Bassac River boat landing under surveillance for the past two weeks. Four times during those two weeks a woman, who had since been identified as a local seamstress, had been observed using a small sampan to transport weapons. The woman had not been apprehended because it was hoped that she would lead Special Branch to other VC in the chain. On each of the four occasions the same sequence transpired. The woman was seen to transfer weapons bundled in oilcloth—AK-47s, rocket-propelled grenades, light mortars, and machine guns—from the sampan to an enclosed cyclo, a Lambretta. She would then drive to a suburb of the province town. It was assumed she took measures against being followed, since the tailing agents lost her each time. About two hours later, they would pick up her trail again as she left the suburb via the main highway leading back to the capital. They would tail her to her house, which was only a few blocks from Special Branch headquarters, and find the back of the Lambretta empty.

"We're going to arrest her now?" Swain asked when Bich was finished.

"Yes."

"Where is she?"

Bich shook his head. "My people lost her again. But if she follows the pattern, we will pick her up on the highway when she starts back to the capital."

"How come you're picking her up instead of maintaining surveillance?" Swain asked.

"Because tonight she did not come upriver alone," Bich said. "There was another person with her. It could be someone important."

Dang had not spoken at all. He seemed to be dozing. His eyes were closed and his chin rested on his chest as he sat squeezed between Bich and the driver. The truck's long bench seat could easily have accommodated four adults had they all been Vietnamese, but Swain took up as much space as Bich and Dang together.

There was little traffic once the truck left behind the tin-roofed shanties that rimmed the capital and turned toward the Bassac. They rolled past still rice fields, the flooded paddies winking like gems in the moonlight, as if they, too, celebrated the new spring. No one spoke for another five or six kilometers, until Swain saw a galaxy of lights up ahead.

"Hey, I know this place!" he said. "It's Senh Tien!"

"Yes, Senh Tien," Bich confirmed. "It is where the woman goes to deliver the weapons."

As they drew nearer the suburb, Bich leaned close to the windshield and peered up the road, then ordered the driver to pull in behind an unmarked police car parked on the shoulder of the highway. Two Special Branch police, often called White Rats by Americans to distinguish them from common cops, White Mice, stood by the car. Both were dressed in the ubiquitous telltale Special Branch uniform of white shirt, dark slacks, pointy-toed shoes and, in total disregard of the fact that it was the dead of night, dark glasses. One of them was speaking animatedly into a hand-held radio.

When they got out of the truck, Dang said something to the five PRUs in back, who disembarked and took up positions in a drainage ditch along the side of the road. With their black pajamas and painted faces they were almost invisible.

Then he spoke to the truck driver, who nodded, started his motor, and made a U-turn. When he'd gone two hundred yards back toward the province town he pulled over, cut the engine, and doused the lights.

The policeman with the radio called something to Bich. His voice was high-pitched, full of excitement. Swain asked Dang what was going on.

"The Lambretta is coming now," Dang said. "It has just passed our first observation post. There are two passengers inside."

The White Rats went to the trunk of their car and pulled out two long metal objects studded with spring-loaded spikes. One man slid behind the wheel to move the car farther off the shoulder while the other set out the traps, one in each lane, the steel spikes pointed at Senh Tien. Even in the moonlight they could not be seen from more than a few feet away.

Dang motioned for Swain to move off the macadam, to hide himself. Swain was halfway across the road when Dang called gently: "I think this side would be safer for you, *Trung Uy*. If there is resistance and our men have to shoot, over there you would be in the direct line of fire."

Swain cursed. Jeez! How fucking dumb! "Uh, yeah, right, thanks." He joined the others in the ditch, grateful for the darkness which hid his red face.

Two minutes later a bouncing ball of light broke away from the illuminated string on the horizon, disengaging from the glare of Senh Tien, moving their way. Two minutes after that they could hear the high whine of a cyclo, coming fast.

Bich's men switched on the spotlight when the cyclo was less than five yards from the trap, aiming it directly into the plastic windshield. The Lambretta wobbled slightly, but hit the steel stakes at speed. Within the space of a second, first the single front tire, then both back tires blew out. *Pop! Pop-Pop!* The Lambretta fishtailed across the highway, made two 360-degree spins, and flipped over on its side.

The PRUs scrambled out of the ditch and approached the wreck with caution, weapons at the shoulder. First a bloody hand, then a dirty arm, and finally a rumpled head poked up through the Lambretta's side door, which now opened skyward.

It was an older woman, about fifty, dazed and in shock. Two PRUs helped her climb out, then fished up a young woman who looked to be no more than eighteen. She, too, seemed to be suffering from mild shock. But aside from minor cuts and abrasions, neither woman appeared to be seriously hurt.

One of the Special Branch agents pointed his flashlight down the road and signaled, and the waiting deuce-and-a-half started up and came toward them. While the PRUs dragged their prisoners to the truck, Captain Bich checked the back of the Lambretta. It was empty.

Bich, Dang, and Swain made the trip back to the province town in the police car, following close behind the truck. Not only was it more comfortable, it let them keep an eye on the back of the truck. With PRUs riding shotgun it was not likely that the women would attempt an escape, but Bich wanted to be sure that the watchdogs did not mistreat the prisoners. That was his department.

Bich got on the radio and asked to be patched through to the Provincial Interrogation Center. When he was connected, a long conversation followed, of which Swain understood exactly one word: Riesz.

Then Bich handed Swain the handset and said, "Mr. Riesz is coming on. He would like to speak to you."

Swain hit the transmit button. "Swain here; over."

"Harry, Chuck Riesz. Listen, Harry, just how big a deal is this arrest you've got?"

Swain looked at Bich, who shrugged. "We don't know yet," he said. "We probably won't know until we've had a chance to question the suspects."

"Yeah. Well, look, the situation is this: I'm in up to my ass over here. Half the PIC staff is on leave for Tet. On top of that, the VC cadre who set us up on the ambush was shipped back down to us this afternoon and Saigon wants me to work on him around the clock till he opens up. I just don't have time for sideshows, Harry. Steelman's watching me on this one."

"I read you loud and clear," Swain said sympathetically, remembering Steelman's anger.

"I knew you'd understand. Uh, look, Harry, I know you've already put in a long night and I hate to ask, but Steelman was serious about having someone from the Embassy House in on interrogations. Do you think you could do these *mamasans* for me? Captain Bich has agreed to honcho the session. All you'd have to do is be there."

Swain was already nodding. "Hey, no sweat. Number One. I'd be glad to help out."

"Great! One other thing, Harry. The center's going to be a zoo while we're working on this cadre. It might be a good idea if you were to take your prisoners over to DG and E at the Embassy House and work on them there."

"DG and E? What's that?"

Riesz laughed. "Delta Gas and Electric. That's what the house comedians call the interrogation shed."

"I didn't even know we had one," Swain said.

"We got one all right," Riesz said. "Dang can show you where it is. Speaking of Dang, you might want to ask him to sit in. He's the best interrogator we have; after myself, of course."

Swain looked at Dang, who nodded. "Okay, Chuck. That's what we'll do then."

"Great! Thanks, Harry. I owe you one; over and out."

It was just after two o'clock when they pulled into the Embassy House compound. Bich dismissed his White Rats while Dang's PRUs herded the prisoners to a large shed sided with sheets of stamped metal that read, over and over, row upon row, "Budweiser." It was only then that Swain remembered the innocuous building as the one Gulliver had passed without comment during the familiarization tour of the compound on his first day in-province.

The PRUs emerged from the shed without the two VC women. Dang tapped two men to stand guard outside the door and sent the other three back to bed.

When Swain followed Dang and Bich inside, he saw by the light of a solitary bulb that the prisoners had been secured. The older woman was strapped into a sturdy high-backed chair made of wood and bolted to the floor. Restraining belts were buckled around her wrists, ankles, midriff, and forehead. The younger woman was strapped to a gurney, her legs elevated and spread wide, her knees hooked over stirrups. The table looked like the kind found in a gynecologist's office or a hospital delivery room. Both women were naked.

Swain tore his eyes away from the girl's yawning crotch and looked around. The room was a twenty-foot square. Panels of soundproofing material covered the walls and ceiling. The floor was concrete and slightly beveled, sloping to a drain, a fist-sized hole in the floor. Besides the two contraptions occupied by the prisoners, there was a table with four chairs and, along one wall, a long workbench. The bench held half a dozen field telephones and battery packs, a wooden box, and a coiled high-pressure hose which fed into the wall. There were no windows, no air-conditioners, no fans. The air was close and heavy and tinged with a medicinal smell of disinfectant.

A strange noise made Swain turn his attention back to the young woman. Her eyes were closed and she was crying and talking to herself in a barely coherent, moaning singsong. It was a sound more animal than human, one that went beyond tears, beyond common terror.

Even twisted by fear, her face was pretty. Swain examined her body. She was a bit thin and sinewy, with small, shallow, dark-tipped breasts and clearly defined stomach muscles that roller-coastered each time she sobbed. There were only a few straggly wisps of pubic hair around her *mons veneris,* giving her mound the look of an old *papasan*'s chin. The positioning of her legs in the stirrup cups pulled the lips of her high-riding vagina slightly apart and Swain could see a flash of tucked and folded pink. The beaver shot, the very notion of such exposed helplessness, started a crawling stir in his groin.

He glanced at the older woman and the stirring stopped. Breasts like empty wineskins drooped halfway to her lap. They were wrinkled and slack like her face. She had a surprisingly big bush for a gook; the thick mat crept like a runaway vine to her navel. She was calm and her eyes switched between Bich and Dang, sowing their hatred equally.

Bich touched Swain's arm. "*Trung Uy,* you may leave now if you wish," he said. "I can tell Mr. Riesz you stayed."

Swain was confused. "Leave? Why should I want to leave?"

Bich shrugged. "Things may become . . . difficult."

Swain had a feeling MACV Directive 525–36 and the Arabic method were about to go out the window on this one. He tossed Bich a grin and said, "Hey, no sweat, Cap. If *difficult* works, *difficult* is fine with me."

"Ahh, you understand, then," Bich said with approval. "I had to be certain. Good. We will start with the older one."

"Why her?" Swain asked. "If it was me, I'd go with the bimbo, the young one. She looks ready to pop now."

Bich smiled again. "By working on the older woman we *are* working on the girl," he said. "On this." He tapped the side of his head with a finger.

Bich nodded at Dang and they approached the old woman's chair. Swain noticed that the young girl's moaning soliloquy had stopped. Her eyes were wide and watching. She had only to turn her head slightly for a clear view of her friend.

Dang squatted in front of the older woman and asked in a gentle voice: *"Ba ten gi?"*

Even Swain understood the question. What is your name? The woman did not seem to. She stared back with a blank face and did not answer.

Bich went to the bench and rummaged in the wooden box. He returned pulling on a pair of black leather gloves. When he was back beside Dang he smiled and nodded, and Dang asked again in the same soft voice: *"Ba ten gi?"*

Bich waited five seconds. When there was no response, he punched the woman in the face, breaking her nose. Swain heard the cartilage crack and saw the spray of blood. It spattered Dang's face, spotting him like a case of measles. He did not flinch or duck; just repeated his question: *"Ba ten gi?"*

Bich waited another five seconds and punched the woman in the mouth. She spit out pieces of enamel. Behind them, the girl on the gurney had started talking to herself again.

"Ba ten gi?" No response.

Bich looked at Dang. "Electricity?" he asked in English.

"Wet her down first," Dang replied.

Dang stood and moved aside while Bich went back to the bench and uncoiled the hose. He dragged it across the room by the nozzle and said to Swain: "*Trung Uy,* would you be so kind as to start the water for me, please? Turn it to full force, please."

Swain found a wheel next to where the connection went through the wall and turned it. The water came in a hissing stream, eight inches in diameter. It struck the woman full in the face, flattening her against the chair back, distorting her features, making her look like a test pilot pulling G's in a power dive. She vanished in a plume of spray as Bich worked the jet up and down her body.

After a minute Bich drew a finger across his throat, and Swain turned off the water.

All up and down her front, the woman's skin looked red and riled. She looked as if she had contracted a heat rash or a bad dose of poison oak. Dang squatted back down in front of her. *"Ba ten gi?"* No response.

Bich pulled the hose back to the bench. He returned with two field phones and two battery packs. Swain could see that the wires were tipped with metal alligator clips.

While Captain Bich was attaching clips to the woman's nipples, Dang unbuckled her ankle restraints, spread her legs apart, and restrapped them. He moved away and Bich stuck his head between her legs and attached a clip to her labia. Then he spread the labia with the thumb and forefinger of one hand and felt for her clitoris with his other index finger. When he found it, he fastened the last clip there.

Bich stepped back and grasped the crank on one of the phones, motioning with his head for Dang to take the other.

Dang shook his head and nodded at Swain. Bich smiled and asked: "*Trung Uy,* would you care to assist?"

"Roger that!" Swain grabbed the other handle and, on a signal from Bich, they both cranked. The woman stiffened and screamed.

After a half-dozen revolutions Bich stopped, so Swain stopped too. Dang waited until the woman stopped twitching before he asked: *"Ba ten gi?"*

She was breathing hard, in famished gulps, and her eyes were not quite in focus. She was dripping wet and blood still leaked from her skewed nose and ruined mouth. But she did not answer Dang's question.

Dang stood and looked down at her. Then Swain heard him say very softly, almost to himself: "Very good, sister. Very good." Swain could have sworn he heard pride in Dang's voice.

Bich went to the door, opened it a crack, and called out: *"Ha si! Mau!"* One of the guards materialized instantly. Bich spoke in rapid Vietnamese and the PRU nodded and vanished.

"What do we do now?" Swain asked.

"Now we talk to the girl," Bich said.

The girl, still moaning softly with her eyes closed, did not hear Bich approach. When he touched her breast, giving it a squeeze, her eyes flew open and she screamed. Bich laughed. He put both hands over her breasts, leaned over, and asked in a mocking, scornful tone: *"Co ten gi?"*

Swain would have wagered a year's pay that the terrified girl would break as easily as a mishandled egg. He was amazed when she refused to answer the harmless question. She twisted her head around to look at her compatriot, drawing strength; then she set her chin and said nothing.

Almost lackadaisically, Bich backhanded her across the face, once, twice, then asked again in a rather bored voice: *"Co ten gi?"* No response.

Swain shook his head in disgust, but Bich did not seem unduly concerned. He laughed, moved away from the gurney, and took a seat at the table where Dang had already parked.

"What's next?" Swain asked anxiously, afraid they might be thinking of giving up.

"We wait," Bich said.

Swain didn't understand. Wait for what? But he shrugged and sat down too. The minutes ticked by in silence. Swain's eyes kept coming back to the girl on the gurney, to the pink envelope between her legs.

Captain Bich noticed and smiled. "*Trung Uy,* if you want her you can have her," he said.

Swain shrugged. "It would help pass the time."

Bich spoke Vietnamese to Dang and both men got to their feet and moved toward the door. "You have fifteen minutes," Bich said as they left.

Swain needed less than half that.

He locked the door, untied his black pajama bottoms and let them drop, then took off the jock he wore underneath. He was walking toward the gurney, massaging his penis with one hand and his testicles with the other, when the older woman began to curse him in Vietnamese. Grinning, he made a detour over. He stood in front of her, semierect, milking himself.

"Hey, *mamasan,* you want some of this? Yeah, I bet you do. You've never seen anything like this, have you, bitch? You're used to them tiny gook peckers." He wagged it under her nose, brushed it along her tightly clamped lips. The woman strained against the headstrap, trying to turn her face away.

Swain laughed. "Don't sweat it, *mamasan,*" he said. "You ain't got nuthin' to worry about. You're too ugly to fuck."

Still stroking himself, letting his penis lead him like a water witch, he waddled back to the gurney, where the girl lay quietly with her eyes closed, no longer moaning. Swain positioned himself between her raised legs and, after a bit of fumbling, gained entry. She did not move or make a sound. She did not open her eyes. He was finished in ninety seconds.

When the knock came, Swain opened the door to an unholy racket, the squeal of a bagpipe played by a lunatic. Bich and Dang came in, each carrying a cardboard box, followed by the PRU, who had a leash in one hand. At the end of the leash was a very angry young pig.

Swain backed away. "What the hell . . ."

They brushed past Swain and set the boxes on the bench. Bich gave an order and the PRU tethered the pig to a support and left. Both women watched with perplexed, darting eyes.

"Jeez! What's the pig for?" Swain asked Bich.

"A demonstration," Bich said. Then he ignored Swain and became all business. He went to the bench, reached into one of the boxes with both hands, and came out with a green snake, two inches in diameter and three feet long. He carried it to the gurney, one hand back by the tail, the other hand about nine inches from the head. The front part swayed in the air.

The girl began to scream even before Bich reached her. He positioned himself between her legs, much as Swain had done only minutes before, and lowered the reptile. The snake, feeling the heat coming from the girl's vagina, straightened out above Bich's fist, straining to reach the warm burrow.

One touch was all it took. The girl, her eyes wild and flecks of spittle flying from her lips, issued one piercing scream and began to babble. Bich smiled, put the snake back in the box, and began his interrogation.

Dang translated for Swain. "She is from M-R Three, from Tay Ninh. The weapons come into Tay Ninh from a supply depot at Snoul, in Cambodia. From there they are sent to where they are most needed. She was sent with the shipment on this trip to check on the distribution system, to see if the weapons are reaching the hands they were meant to reach."

"So whose hands did they reach?" Swain asked.

"That is what Captain Bich is asking now," Dang said.

The girl said something in an apologetic tone and Bich spoke sharply. She shook her head. Bich hit her in the face with a gloved fist and pointed to the snake's box. The girl began to whine.

"She says she does not know who he is," Dang said. "She knows him only as Comrade Trung. He knew the password, and the other woman, who is from this province, confirmed that he was the right man."

"Trung?" Swain's eyebrows shot up, then went flat with suspicion. "And he lives in Senh Tien?"

"Yes."

"What's this Trung look like?" Swain asked with growing excitement.

Dang asked Bich, who asked the girl, who answered. Dang shrugged. "She could be describing anyone," he said to Swain. "Slight, short, between forty and forty-five years of age."

"Anyone, my ass!" Swain said, thoroughly excited now. "I know this guy, Dang! I know him! Ask her where he lives."

Bich, who had been listening to Swain, asked. The girl answered, shaking her head. Bich hit her again. "She says she does not know where he lives, *Trung Uy*," Bich said. "She says that this is her first visit to our province and she did not know where she was. She says to ask the other one."

"Ask her if she saw the Senh Tien police station," Swain said. He turned to Dang. "The Trung I know lives four houses down from the police station, on the same side of the street. It's a two-story house with fancy bars on the windows. It's the only house on the block that doesn't have a shop on the ground floor."

Bich asked, the girl answered, shaking her head. Bich hit her again. "She does not remember a police station."

"Damn!" Swain said, pounding a hamlike fist into his palm. The significance of what he was onto had not escaped him. A seductive scenario was playing itself out in his head. If Trung were to be put away, Mai would be without a husband. She would no longer be *Ba* Mai; she would be *Co* Mai. Miss Mai.

"Let's ask the old bitch," he suggested.

Bich nodded and asked the woman a long question. He got no response. Instead of hitting her, he crossed to the workbench, untied the pig's leash and, tugging with both hands, skidded the frightened animal across the floor. He handed the leash to Dang and returned to the bench. He reached into the other box and came up with a short-handled sledgehammer, an accordion-style bellows, and a straight razor.

Both women were watching Bich's every move with morbid fascination, looking for clues as to what might happen. So was Swain, who felt as though he were a kid at a magic show, watching a maestro work an audience.

Swain could hardly believe what he witnessed next.

Bich took the hammer, raised it overhead, and brought it down in a mighty blow, striking the pig squarely between the eyes. The animal dropped with a sharp squeal. It lay stunned, its eyes wide and glassed, its sides heaving. While Dang held the pig still, Captain Bich picked up its corkscrew tail with one hand and the bellows with the other. He stuck the barrel of the bellows as far as it would go into the pig's rectum. Then, standing up and using his foot, he started to pump.

The pig began to inflate like a dirigible. It got larger and larger, improbably large, almost comically so, like some hapless Saturday-morning cartoon character. An animal which a moment ago had been the size of a small dog had grown to the size of a very large dog. The abdominal wall was stretched so taut that its outer layer of skin had turned transparent, and Swain could see a blue-and-red network of veins.

Captain Bich took up the razor and tested its edge with a theatrical thumb. He glanced over to see how the woman was reacting and then smiled, satisfied. Her mouth hung open and her eyes bugged.

Very slowly, making sure that the woman was following his every move, Captain Bich held the razor poised over the pig's distended belly for a long, dramatic moment. Then, in one quick, smooth motion, he ran the blade the length of the bulging sac.

It was like popping a balloon. The mass of entrails blew out of the hot cavity in an explosion of gas and goo, landing with a wet plop in a tidy, steaming package at the prisoner's feet. The woman screamed and tried to jerk away, only to be brought up short by her bonds. She gagged.

"Jeez," Swain breathed, nearly gagging himself. A putrid stink filled the room. The pig, still very much alive, jerked spasmodically, its cloven feet scrabbling against the concrete floor.

Working quickly, Bich and Dang untied the prisoners and had them trade places, strapping the girl to the chair, the woman to the gurney. When the woman had been secured and her legs were up in the stirrups, Bich retrieved the bellows and moved to the end of the gurney, positioning himself between her legs, like a lover.

It went much the same as it had gone with the young one. Captain Bich did not have to carry his threat through to the end. He had inserted the barrel of the bellows no more than an inch or two into the woman's anus when she let out a great howl and began to tell them what they wanted to know.

The woman did not know much. Her struggle group employed a cut-out system at all levels, with each cell member knowing only the person immediately below and above, and then only by a code name, a *nom de guerre*.

But she knew enough, and once she started, she talked freely, almost eagerly, letting Dang lead her. Captain Bich seemed to lose interest when she turned cooperative; it was the inducement phase of the process he enjoyed. He left the rest of it to Dang and went outside for a cigarette.

In turn, Dang let his new adviser steer the session. Swain put the questions to Dang, who put them to the prisoner and then translated her answers. She confirmed all of Swain's anxious suppositions. Every trip had been the same, she told them. She would travel to the Tay Ninh sector to pick up the weapons and bring them back to the Delta, back to a Comrade Trung in Senh Tien. She did not know what he did with them.

Then, according to Dang's interpretation, she went on to describe Comrade Trung's house in almost the same words Swain had used to describe it to Dang—four houses down from the police station; two floors, with bars on the windows; the only house on the block without a shop on the ground floor.

It was all the proof Swain needed. He called in Captain Bich and proudly told him what they had learned. Bich agreed that Comrade Trung should be picked up at once.

Then Bich issued a rash of orders. The *Trung Uy* was to go to the PRU barrack and remount the arrest team. Dang was to give the two prisoners an injection of morphine. While it was true that the drug would ease their various pains, Bich had not suddenly turned altruistic; it would also muddle their minds. There was no time to transfer them to the PIC, and Bich did not want them putting their heads together to work up a pat story to use when the interrogation was resumed. Bich himself went off to find a telephone, to check in with Special Branch headquarters.

In all the fuss, Dang was left alone with the prisoners. No one was left to see him tend to them. With each, first the girl and then the woman, he went through an identical ritual. From under his pajama tunic he drew up the chain, the one he wore on PRU missions. He uncapped the syringe of morphine and administered the injection. Then he opened the tin dangling beside the syringe, took out a capsule and placed it between the teeth, and pushed down on the top of the head with one hand while pressing up on the chin with the other.

He was as gentle about it as he could be. It pained him greatly, but he could not allow them to be questioned further about Comrade Trung or to clarify the identification and thus defuse the opportune time bomb the *Trung Uy* had unwittingly handed him. These brave women had no way of knowing it, of course, but he was proud of them. They had done their duty.

And as he held their mouths closed, he dipped his head and softly touched his lips to theirs, kissing each good-bye. He could taste a salty, slightly bitter taste, a subtle blend of sweat and fear and almonds.

They returned to Senh Tien in the same deuce-and-a-half with the same PRU team riding in back, and parked in front of the Senh Tien police substation, less than half a block from Nguyen Khac Trung's front door.

Captain Bich of Special Branch HQ, the deputy chief of police in the province and the right-hand man to the powerful Major Do, did not deign to check in with his country cousins of the Senh Tien police substation. Leaving the *Trung Uy* with the truck at Swain's own suggestion, Captains Bich and Dang marched their PRUs straight to Comrade Trung's front door and kicked it in.

For any Vietnamese family, the first visitor of a new year is of utmost importance, a sign of whether the year is to be a good one or a bad one. If the first Tet visitor is rich, the family will prosper; if a holy man, the family will enjoy a year of spirituality and peace. Most people planned ahead and invited a lucky person to be the first to *dap dat,* to cross the hearth. The Trung family's first visitors in the Year of the Dog were not invited, and they were more than a harbinger of bad luck; they brought utter and complete calamity.

Fifteen minutes after they went in, the PRUs came back through the smashed door, pushing before them a middle-aged man wearing only a thin nightshirt. He was bleeding from the mouth and had a badly discolored eye. They loaded him into the back of the truck and drove away. It was on the dot of four A.M.

Nguyen Khac Trung was dead before dawn.

They had not meant to kill him, of course. It was only that they were angry; angry because the search of the Trung home had failed to turn up the weapons, angry because when they returned to the Embassy House interrogation shed they found the two VC women dead.

Captain Bich, who fancied himself something of an expert in such matters, found the cyanide burns on their tongues. At first he couldn't imagine where they had hidden the capsules or how they had managed to get them into their mouths, then reluctantly concluded that the pills had been inside the oral cavity all along. Not one of them had thought to check there. They all felt like fools and, understandably, they had taken out their anger and frustration on the prisoner at hand. They were so angry they beat him to death.

None of the three considered the night a total disaster, however, because before he died Nguyen Khac Trung confessed.

The prisoner had tearfully maintained his innocence at first, and mere beating and the sight of the women's bodies had not been enough to break him down. But other methods had done the trick. Within an hour he had admitted being both a communist and a gun runner. He had confessed to the first when Captain Bich used the field phones on his genitals, to the second when Dang cut two joints off the pinkie finger of his left hand. Dang had been careful to ascertain first that Trung was right-handed. A small but important detail, one that reflected Dang's experience in these matters: Trung had to be able to sign the confession that Captain Bich so kindly wrote out for him.

It was later, when they were working on the kidneys in an effort to persuade him to identify the person to whom he had passed on the weapons, that Nguyen Khac Trung had coughed once, twice, and passed out, just when he seemed ready to give them a name. Lieutenant Swain had been so frustrated that he swung his massive fist and hit Trung on the side of the head, just above the ear; a prodigious blow with all of his weight behind it, one that caved in Trung's skull like an eggshell.

They had loaded the three bodies into a jeep and ordered one of the PRUs to deliver them to the morgue at the province town military hospital. Then Bich, Dang, and Swain, having put in a full and exhausting day's work, went to bed.

A little after sunrise Dr. Loan reported to the military hospital, tired and a little grumpy over having drawn morning duty on the first day of Tet. He had been up late celebrating the advent of the new year, and he wanted to be home with his wife to greet the flood of holiday visitors which would flow through his house later in the day.

He donned his smock, had a quick cup of tea, and, hoping to get it over with as quickly as possible, trooped down to the basement morgue to see if anything had come in during the night. The morgue orderly promptly told him there were three unidentified bodies, dumped only minutes ago by the PRU.

Dr. Loan had his own profitable practice, but there was a shortage of physicians all over the country and, like many others, he had been drafted to donate a number of hours each week to the war effort. He did not begrudge the time, but he considered the signing of death certificates on Nguyen Vans, the Vietnamese equivalent of John Does, a demeaning chore and beneath his dignity. So it was with distaste that he pulled the sheet from the first of the three bodies and started, by force of habit, with the lower extremities, his practiced eye slowly inching its way up the naked male corpse that lay facedown on the slab.

Loan was not unfamiliar with mutilated bodies—there was a war on, after all, and this was a military hospital. Nor was he unused to Phoenix program casualties, which he had to assume these were if they had been brought in by the PRU. But neither was he completely inured. His lip curled when he saw the deep vermilion bruises in the lumbar region, above the kidneys. He felt revulsion when he saw that two joints of one finger were missing. He cursed aloud when he spied the mushy indentation in the cranium, just above and slightly to the fore of the ear. But it was not until he turned the body over and looked into the dead man's battered face that he let out a gasp of genuine shock.

"What is this?" he bellowed.

The startled morgue orderly glanced over in surprise. "Just another dead communist, sir," he said with a shrug.

"Don't be ridiculous," Dr. Loan thundered, his face packed with blood. "Come and look. I know this man, and so do you. He works here in the hospital. It is Nguyen Khac Trung."

The orderly came over, looked, and saw that the doctor was right. It was Mr. Trung, who ran the admissions office upstairs. The orderly shook his head sadly. "Who would have suspected that our Mr. Trung was a communist?" he asked in a tone that suggested that the ways of God and man were indeed mysterious.

"Shut up, you fool. Trung was no communist. He was Hoa Hao."

Dr. Loan took the orderly by the back of the collar and shoved him toward the door. "Get me the province chief on the telephone," he commanded. "Those animals of his have gone too far this time."

Book Two
Razor

13

UNLIKE THE SUMMER MONSOONS, which could come in a wink and be gone as quick, the storm that followed the killing of Nguyen Khac Trung gathered slowly, in layers. Meek clouds of protest turned dark and lowering, building to thunderheads which fed upon themselves, then broke, creating a flood that undermined not only the Tet holiday, normally a time of dry tranquillity, but also the very foundations of provincial life.

The initial demonstration, two days after Trung's death, was spontaneous, a visceral reaction of an outraged populace. Although many more would later claim to have been there, only two hundred people took part, mostly Hoa Hao who got the news through the market grapevine, in violent harangues from atop upended cooking pots, in sad whispers over noodles and sweetened tea.

The next day more than nine hundred took to the streets, many sympathetic mainstream Buddhists among them. This was a marginally more organized affair, hastily thrown together by local sectarian leaders scrambling to catch up with the mood of their followers, and egged on by the Widow Trung herself.

By week's end the hundreds had become thousands. As word spread, the Hoa Hao faithful continued to pour into the province town from hamlets and villages all across the Delta.

The public outcry took provincial officials, Vietnamese and American, by surprise, but so long as the demonstrations remained manageable, no one was overly concerned.

The first marches were peaceful. People carried signs reading "Abolish Phung Hoang," and papier-mâché caricatures of a phoenix bird with President Thieu's face and talons that dripped blood. But aside from tying up traffic along the main street and around the entrances to the provincial, CORDS, and Embassy House compounds, there was no real inconvenience.

Only when the crowds topped the five-thousand mark, with no sign of abating, did the province chief grow uneasy. Colonel Minh ordered Major Do to salt the crowd with Special Branch agents armed with cameras, to take photographs of the ringleaders. Major Do's White Rats pretended to be *bao chi,* journalists, fooling no one. They stuck out like clowns in their white shirts, dark glasses, pegged pants, and pointy-toed shoes.

The Hoa Hao leadership pointedly kept its distance from the hub of the protest, hoping to foster the impression that it was the will of the people and not its proselytizing that filled the streets. Major Do, who had many informers inside the Social Democratic party, knew better, of course. But his knowing better, and saying so, did not dissuade the Hoa Hao from sticking to their hastily limned fiction.

Leading the demonstrations, out in front of the mass of citizens, were students; firebrands from the Hoa Hao University and Can Tho University and even a few from Saigon University, a caldron of political activism. And in front of the students marched the Widow Trung, her three offspring in tow, draped in mourning white and carrying a placard reading: "Despicable Phoenix Murderers: Return to my orphaned children the body of their martyred father."

An undisguised Jake Gulliver, in Levi's and an N.C. State Wolfpack T-shirt, monitored the demonstrations for a nervous George Cameron. Day after day he bobbed in the procession's wake, his head a white sail above the tide, watching tempers grow worse. At the end of each day he would report to his P officer, who would sigh and sweat and head for the bamboo bar. Cameron was right to worry. The escalation was as inevitable as it was predictable: students taunted police, who targeted students for the draft, who grabbed cameras and notepads from police, who arrested students, who stoned police.

When the rowdiness became too much for Major Do's police to contain, Medium Minh fed Major Ngoc's Field Force into the fray. Brief but bloody skirmishes coursed through the streets and alleys of the province town. Major Ngoc's troops, hysterical peacocks in their powder-blue berets and matching scarves, ran from one gang of rock-throwing troublemakers to the next, clearing streets one by one, using truncheons and tear gas.

And standing by just out of sight, but not out of mind, was Medium Minh's reserve force: a battalion of the ARVN Fourth Infantry, which had been hastily moved into the province and conspicuously bivouacked on the outskirts of town, along both sides of the Senh Tien Highway.

Given Colonel Minh's ham-fisted tactics, the quick slide into chaos did not surprise Gulliver. What did surprise him, late in that first week, was to see the town's most famous personality marching alongside the Widow Trung at the head of the parade—Quynh Nhu and Nguyen Thi Mai, hand-in-hand in a dramatic show of solidarity. Two stunningly beautiful women, the celebrity of long standing and the province town's newest star. It made for a striking picture.

Gulliver was in for yet another surprise the very next day, when he stood at the back of a large crowd and watched his mistress, in makeup and costume and accompanied by a band of pickup musicians, perform in the small park across from the sandbagged gate of the provincial headquarters compound. A playlet in one act, a graceful pantomime with an awkward title: *The Cruel Murder of a Decent Man by an Evil Bird*. A brief but brilliant bit of impromptu theater depicting the arrest, torture, and death of Nguyen Khac Trung in graphic, and amazingly accurate, detail.

After her performance in the park she half-expected him to come to the alley that night, and come he did. And he came angry; as a superior, not a lover.

She was just finishing her bath when he knocked, and she came to the door wrapped in a towel. Accustomed to his sudden comings and goings, she was surprised that he used the front door. He brushed by her without speaking, as stone-faced as a piece of Cham sculpture, bolted the door behind him, and went to the window to check the alley.

Then he turned and faced her. "It was stupid, Nhu. Why did you do it?" he asked, his face half in shadow. He took a step toward her and into the light of the lamp. He had on a uniform. She did not ask him why; he often came in disguise. Besides, she had other things on her mind; she could see the anger in his eyes and in the set of his mouth.

She pulled the towel she had been using to dry her hair down around her bare shoulders, suddenly chilled despite the cloying heat. "The students asked me to perform. It stoked the people's anger. It was useful," she reasoned.

"Fuck the students. They are pawns to be used, like the Hoa Hao. And we have comrades in the crowd whose job it is to stoke the people's anger. It was stupid."

Nhu was surprised by his profanity, his vehemence. "What harm did it do?"

"Did you not see the police in the audience? Did you not see Major Do's men with their expensive Japanese cameras and their notebooks and their American pencils plated with gold?"

Nhu shrugged. "I never see individuals in the audience when I am onstage."

"They were there, a dozen of them," he said. "At times I think that if all their people went home the demonstrations would be half as large as they are now. And if all our people went home too, there would be no one in the streets at all."

It was almost a joke, and so unlike him. Perhaps he was not as angry with her as he seemed. She ventured a tentative smile, meant to disarm, and said, "I still do not see what harm there was in what I did."

Another mistake. The coldness came back into his voice, chilling her more. "Do not be dense," he said. "What you did will focus the attention of the police on you, and you do not live a life that can afford such attention. It means you are no longer just a popular chanteuse in their eyes, the lovely Quynh Nhu, pride of the province. Now you are a provocateur, someone to be watched."

"But half the town's population have taken part in the demonstrations," she argued. "They cannot keep watch on half the population."

"Half the population did not know precisely how Nguyen Khac Trung died," he snapped. "Half the population did not stand up in public, in front of Special Branch's spies, to show them how much they know. I must congratulate you. Though brief, your performance was quite thorough. You put into it everything I made the mistake of telling you. I especially enjoyed the part where you cut off Trung's little finger, joint by joint."

She had not thought of that. It had been stupid of her. She felt a twinge of fear, but it was pushed out by an anger of her own. How dare he scold her as if she were a child?

"Many people know that Trung died under interrogation," she said, bristling. "The doctor who examined him, who took the matter to the authorities, was Hoa Hao, a lay leader. He told his party colleagues that Trung had been tortured, that the body had been mutilated. Why else do you think the people are so upset?"

It was a true but feeble argument and he did not even consider it. "I will not debate with you. There will be no more. You will keep off the streets. Do you understand?"

Nhu bowed her head, her short-lived uprising over. "Yes, of course."

"Good," he said in a more gentle voice. He put a finger under her chin and raised her face, then kissed her lightly on the tip of the nose. "I just do not want anything bad to happen to you," he said. "I do not want trouble for you."

Nhu, her surrender complete, rested her forehead on his chest. "And you?" she asked quietly. "Has there been trouble for you?"

"Not yet, but soon, I think," he said with a stoic shrug. "Colonel Minh will bluster, then threaten, then promise. He will do nothing for as long as he can. But the louder the people shout, the sooner he will be forced to do something."

"What will he do?" Nhu asked with vague alarm, leaning back so she could see his face when he answered.

"I don't doubt that the Hoa Hao are genuinely upset over Trung," he said calmly, "but even now they will be thinking of how to turn his death to their advantage, how to use it to force concessions from the government. Minh's soldiers will keep them in check for a while, but they will be like hungry tigers chased from a kill, and sooner or later he will have to throw them a few pieces of meat to keep them away from his own throat. I could be one of those pieces."

"Like my brother," she said with bitterness.

"Yes, like your brother."

"Then you cannot let him throw you to the tigers," she declared. "You must not allow it to happen."

He made a clucking sound. "But that is what we want to happen. The Hoa Hao are our unknowing allies in this thing. If the authorities are forced to make concessions to the Hoa Hao, the people will see their weakness. The Saigon clique and the Phoenix program will be discredited."

"Then you must get away before it happens," she said firmly.

"Yes," he agreed. "If it is possible."

Nhu was quiet, the thought that it might not be possible working in her mind.

"But it has not yet come to that," he said. "For the moment, the province chief is still more concerned about the ambush on Nui Giai Mountain. And in that, his displeasure is more with our mutual friend."

Nhu's eyes turned soft. "I have not yet thanked you for saving him for me," she said. "I know how difficult it is for you. How you are torn between your duty and your feelings for me . . . and for him."

"Yes, it is difficult for me to share you with another," he acknowledged matter-of-factly, with no trace of self-pity.

"Do not forget that it was you who forced me into his arms, into his bed," Nhu said archly. "I did not want to do it but you said that it would help the cause, that it would help you."

"I know," he said softly.

"As long as you remember that."

"It is not the sharing of your body that is difficult; it is the sharing of your love."

Nhu's aggressiveness disappeared. "I did not expect to love him; I did not want to love him," she said weakly. "It just . . . happened."

"I know," he said again, still speaking in a soft voice. "But it has created a problem. Colonel Minh is not the only one who is angry about what happened on the mountain. Comrade Hoa Binh does not understand how the American was able to escape. He is angry that the ambush did not work. He is angry with you for being so slow to carry out his orders. So he has told me to do it myself, to kill the One Who Comes at Night."

Nhu gasped. She grabbed him by the arm and looked deep into his eyes. "What are you going to do? What did you say?"

He shrugged. "What could I say? I agreed."

"But—"

"I held him off for the moment," he interrupted. "I told him that this business with the Hoa Hao over Trung was moving too quickly and becoming too important to let anything put it in jeopardy, that I would do the job when I could. He was not happy, but he agreed. He is pleased with the new developments in the province. He promoted me to the rank of colonel."

"But it does not solve the problem; it merely postpones it," Nhu said. "You have not said what you are going to do."

"I will decide when I must."

Nhu just stared at him, saying nothing, and he used the pause to announce: "I must go now."

Nhu nodded reluctantly and, without a word, returned to her toilet; he always made her go in there when he left, so that she could not see him leave. When she came out he would be gone, and the front door would still be bolted.

But when she closed the toilet door he did not go into the bedroom . . . to the wardrobe and the trick wall that hid the stairs to the roof. He left the way he had come, by the front door, like an honest man. It was risky but he wanted to check the alley again, to see if the police already watched her.

It was late and the alley was quiet and dark, lit only by the dying fires and the lanterns of those few refugees who found it too hot to sleep. He quietly shut Nhu's door behind him and started away quickly, too quickly, stumbling over a figure stretched out on a strip of cardboard. He whispered an apology. The figure stirred and whispered back: *"Trung Si."*

Anxious to pass through the alley's gauntlet and already upbraiding himself for his incaution in not taking his normal escape route, he took a few more steps before it sank in that *he* was the *Trung Si,* the sergeant, and that the roused figure was calling to him. *"Hsst! Trung Si! Hsst!"*

He spun and sidestepped in one flashing motion, his hand darting like a striking krait to the pistol at his belt while his screaming brain fed it data: MAN. SITTING UP. RIGHT HAND EXTENDED. RIGHT HAND . . . empty.

He reholstered the pistol and relaxed, taking a moment to register and evaluate the details. The man was long-haired and dirty. He wore a tattered ARVN uniform, a fatigue blouse and unhemmed shorts fashioned from the trousers. One leg, the right one, was missing and a wooden crutch lay next to him on the ground. The stump, a bleached, dead-looking thing, stuck out from the leg of the shorts. It was covered with a flap of skin pulled over and tucked back and sloppily sewed. Behind him, on straw mats against the whitewashed alley wall, lay a snoring woman and two sleeping children.

"What do you want?"

The man put on an insincere face, a beggar's face, and wheedled: "A few dong only, *Trung Si.* A few dong with which to feed my family. A few dong to buy some soup and rice for my hungry children."

He dug into the pocket of his army fatigues and gave the cripple a few wadded piaster notes.

The man smiled, showing bad teeth, and bowed his head, a jerky, bobbing motion. *"Cam on, Trung Si, cam on,"* he gushed. "I can return your generosity only with some advice: do not let yourself be wounded; do not become crippled like me. They will throw you away like a soiled battle dressing. You'll be left on your own, left to starve, your sacrifice forgotten."

"I know."

The beggar watched his benefactor go, staring after him. Then he swiveled around to face the woman, who was now sitting up. "Did you get a good look at his face?" he asked.

"The light is bad," she whined. "I told you the light is bad here. But would you listen to me? No! I told you—"

"It doesn't matter; *I* got a good look," he said quickly, cutting her off, cursing fate for being stuck with this ugly harridan, grateful that he wasn't really married to her. From beneath the cardboard mat he pulled a notebook and a pencil plated with gold and began to scribble.

Colonel Minh was pulling out all the stops for the Widow Trung. The province chief's smooth, doughy face was a picture of devastation, the greasy smile and its flash of gold tooth gone, replaced by the sorrowful but bravely determined look of a responsible official doing his disagreeable duty.

"My dear *Ba* Mai," Minh said soulfully. "I am authorized to offer you the republic's condolences for your tragic loss. And, of course, I extend my deepest personal sympathies as well."

Gulliver faked a cough behind a covering hand, hiding a smile. There was nothing amusing about the death of Nguyen Khac Trung, but he couldn't help it. The lack of art in the province chief's performance was awesome, almost art itself.

Colonel Minh had given up his own oversize desk chair to Nguyen Thi Mai, insisting she take it. The province chief sat on one of the folding metal chairs he'd had his orderly bring in. Gulliver thought he could hear the metal groaning, its inadequate tubular legs buckling under the load.

The province chief's office was as stuffed as his chair, surfeit with flesh. There were nine people in Madame Trung's delegation, and five representing the provincial authorities: Minh, Sloane, Do, Cameron, and Gulliver, who had been asked to join the party because Cameron's Vietnamese was adequate but less than fluent, and Sloane's was less than nonexistent. The two groups sat opposite each other, facing off like teams of rival athletes. The petite Mai, almost lost behind Minh's big desk, her prodigious chest shielded from view, was off to the side and in the middle, like a hometown referee.

"Thank you, Colonel," she said coolly, no gratitude in her voice. "Others, too, have expressed a desire to pay their final respects. That is why I am here today, to ask that you release his body into my care. We . . . I . . . have decided he is to be put on display so that his many friends can say farewell."

Minh's eyes, lost in their caves of fat, did not panic. The most powerful man in the province made a small gesture of helplessness. "I cannot do that. The body is evidence and my investigation into the tragic circumstances of your husband's death is continuing. Surely you want to know what happened?"

"I already know what happened!" Mai said, abandoning all polite pretense. "Phoenix tortured him until he died!"

"That is a lie!" Minh shouted, his jowls shaking.

"It is the truth!" she hissed. "Dr. Loan saw the body! Ask him yourself!" She had jumped up from the chair, chest heaving, her breasts jiggling like Minh's chins inside the bodice of her *ao dai*. The eyes of every man in the room, even those of the priests, were helplessly fixed on them. When she realized it, she flushed and sat down abruptly.

Just as abruptly, Minh changed tack. He spread his arms in placation and smiled, finally showing his golden tooth, a ray of sun peeping from behind storm clouds. "Madame Trung, please," he implored. "Let us not shout; we shall accomplish nothing with shouts. Each of us wants something of the other. You want justice for your dead husband. I want an end to the civil unrest in my province. Let us try to work together so that both of us may get what we want."

After a silence, disturbed only by Gulliver's whispered translation for Sloane, Mai nodded grudgingly.

The tooth gleamed again. "Good. Now. I do not deny that the venerable Dr. Loan saw what he saw," Minh said, making a sitting bow in the direction of the venerable Dr. Loan. "I do not even deny that Nguyen Khac Trung's body was mutilated, horribly mutilated. But I *do* deny that this unspeakable thing happened while he was in the custody of the police."

"Then where did it happen, Colonel Minh?" asked a male voice, a quiet but resonant voice full of calm authority.

Gulliver scanned the opposing players and quickly found the source: the man who had been introduced as Bui Dinh, the Hoa Hao monk from Long Xuyen province town in An Giang.

Gulliver did not know the man, but he certainly knew a good deal about him; they all did by now. Bui Dinh had swept into town four days earlier, and within twenty-four hours of his arrival Phoenix officials had asked for, and received, a complete dossier on him from Saigon—a report, Gulliver had noticed, prepared and sent by S. Teacher of the United States embassy.

Dinh was one of the most powerful bonzes in the Hoa Hao, a

man who had helped steer the sect's religious and political course since its birth in 1939, and who at one time or another, often at the same time, had been both a help and a hindrance to the emperor, the French, the Japanese, the Viet Minh, the Americans, and every sitting government along the way. It was Dinh who had persuaded Huynh Phu So, the "Living Buddha," to accept arms from the Japanese to fight the French in the hope of winning independence for the Hoa Hao. And when Japan was in retreat, it was Dinh who had urged taking arms from the French to use against the Viet Minh when the Hoa Hao's land-grabbing ambitions came into conflict with those of the communists, and who then turned around and ordered the Hoa Hao army to shoot at both sides. In those waning days of World War II, it was Dinh who had set up what was in effect a Hoa Hao state in the Delta, collecting taxes and running home villages in a feudal manner. It was Dinh who had led the losing fight against the new national army—the ARVN—of President Ngo Dinh Diem. And it was Dinh who had organized the Hoa Hao's Social Democratic party in 1952 and who urged the defection to Saigon after the overthrow of the hated Diem. And through it all, he'd made no secret of his goal: independence for the Hoa Hao provinces.

Gulliver had been watching Dinh, fascinated. The monk was old, seventy or seventy-five, with a scored face and a scraggly white shock of chin whiskers, like Ho Chi Minh. He was thinner than Ho had been, as thin as Gandhi after one of his fasts, but his was not the thinness of the ascetic, of the holy man, Gulliver thought as he studied the man's eyes, which were flecked and feverish and belied the controlled voice; it was the lean-and-hungry look of the fanatic.

Dinh was one of two people in the Widow Trung's party who were not locals. The other was Nguyen Loc, president of the students' union at Saigon University, twenty-two years old, organizer of the students in the streets. While Bui Dinh was the oldest person in the room and Loc the youngest, they had much in common. Nguyen Loc had come to town the same day as Bui Dinh, and his dossier was nearly as thick. His name had been referred to Saigon for a background run and the CIA had bucked the job to its Vietnamese clone and counterpart, the Central Intelligence Organization. The CIO's response, translated and coded, had tied up the Embassy House's telex for nearly an hour.

Dinh and Loc had one last thing in common: since their arrival, Colonels Minh and Sloane had invariably referred to them as "outside agitators" in their daily sitreps to Saigon.

Medium Minh, too, had been staring in fascination at Bui

Dinh, as if he were gazing upon the Devil himself. The priest repeated his question: "Where did it happen, Colonel?"

"Ah. Yes. We are still not sure, of course, but we think that the body may have been disfigured after it was delivered to the hospital."

"At the *hospital*?" Dr. Loan interrupted, his tone one of incredulity. "By whom?"

Colonel Minh shrugged. "By some communist who wanted to cause trouble for the government."

"Ridiculous!" the doctor said with a snort.

"It is not ridiculous at all," Medium Minh replied with a condescending smile. "If the hospital staff can harbor one communist, why is it ridiculous to suppose that it could also harbor others?"

That was too much for Mai. She came to her feet again and shook her fist at the province chief. "My husband was not a communist!"

Minh shrugged again and gave her a pitying smile. "He signed a full confession," he said gently, helpless in the face of incontrovertible evidence.

"More lies! More of your filthy—"

Bui Dinh left his chair and rounded the desk, sprightly in his movements in spite of his advanced years. He took Mai by the shoulders and gently pushed her back into her seat, murmuring comfort: "Please, my child. Do not let him upset you. Sit. Let me deal with these slanderous falsehoods."

He turned to Minh and asked: "May I be permitted to see this so-called confession?"

"Of course," Minh said. "Major Do . . . if you please."

The chief of police dipped into his briefcase and pulled out two stapled sheets. He handed them to the province chief, who labored to his feet and gave them to the priest, saying, "This is only a photocopy, of course, but I have the original if you want to see it."

Dinh glanced over the pages, then set them on Minh's desk for Mai to see. He did not seem concerned. "This is nothing," he said with contempt. "It could have been prepared after his death."

"It is signed," Minh said.

"Signatures can be forged."

"Yes, they can," Minh agreed. "But this one was not. It is quite genuine. And a handwriting analysis would prove it."

"It would prove nothing," Bui Dinh said.

"And what of the thumbprint next to the signature?" the province chief asked with a smile. "Can it also be forged?"

The priest shrugged. "The thumb of a dead man makes the same mark as that of one who is alive."

"He was very much alive at the time," Minh said wearily, tired of fencing with this meddlesome monk.

Bui Dinh merely smiled and said: "Perhaps so, Colonel. But anyone can be persuaded to sign anything if the methods of persuasion are inventive enough."

What little was left of the province chief's patience evaporated. "Trung was not tortured," he flared. "My men do not torture prisoners."

"Then how did he die?" Bui Dinh asked softly.

The province chief had been waiting. "How did he die?" he echoed, looking amazed. "But I thought your complaint was about the unfortunate marks on the body. I assumed that you knew the cause of death. He killed himself, of course."

Minh sat back, his face crafty and complacent, savoring his triumph, waiting for their exclamations of disbelief. But the Hoa Hao had been stunned into momentary silence. So Minh went on: "Cyanide. A capsule of some sort. He must have had it in his mouth all the time. If my men are to be criticized for anything, it is for their failure to conduct a thorough search of the prisoner. Inexcusable."

Gulliver was as speechless as the others. His knowledge of what happened the night Trung died was still sketchy, but it was enough to tell him the province chief was lying. Minh's audacity was as boundless as his waistline, Gulliver thought with wonder. He had even managed to salvage something useful from the deaths of the two Viet Cong women.

Gulliver checked the faces around him. Major Do's lips were pursed under the thin mustache, his eyes unreadable. He was unable to get a good look at Cameron's face, but it was clear that the P officer's Vietnamese was good enough to pick up thc gist of Minh's statement. Cameron was leaning forward in his chair, hands clasped and forearms resting on his thighs, staring fixedly at the floor. He was perspiring, of course.

Gulliver felt a tug at his sleeve; Sloane signaling for an interpretation. He gave it to him and the amiable PSA sat back nodding as if a light had been turned on in a dark room, relieved and content now that the cause of Trung's death had been cleared up once and for all. It was a question that had been bothering him.

The Hoa Hao had finally found their tongues. A buzz filled the room as they turned to one another and began gabbling among themselves. Only Nguyen Thi Mai and Bui Dinh remained silent;

they were staring at the province chief with unconcealed loathing.

The voice of Dr. Loan was the first to break out of the chattering pack. "I must refute your diagnosis, Colonel," he announced with the confident authority of his profession. "I found no evidence of cyanide poisoning in my examination."

Minh shrugged. "I am not surprised, Doctor," he said. "Did you check for it?"

"I . . . No, of course not. There was no need. The cause of death was plain to see. He was beaten to death. The evidence was anywhere one cared to look. The crushed cranium, the burn marks on the genitalia . . . uh . . . his finger . . ."

"All put there after the fact," Minh said with a smile.

Dinh came to the doctor's rescue. "Colonel Minh, if a man being questioned by the police is going to take his own life, why would he wait until *after* he confessed to do it?"

Minh, nonplussed, held up pudgy hands. Having put forth a falsehood of massive proportion, he was immune to logic. "I haven't the slightest idea," he said.

In an attempt to recover a little of the face he'd lost, Dr. Loan spoke up again. "Colonel, I would like to perform an autopsy," he announced.

"You are most welcome if you like," Minh said with a shrug, "but another autopsy would be useless at this point; the affected organs have already told us their sad tale and have been removed."

"*Another* autopsy?"

"Certainly," said Minh. "How do you think we determined the cause of death?"

Dr. Loan paled, his shame completed. The authorities had thought to do what he should have done. Gamely he tried to bluster. "Who performed this autopsy?" he demanded to know.

"Dr. Le Van Loi. Would you like a copy of his report?"

Game, set, and match. Gulliver could see the conflicting emotions dance across Loan's face, a *pas de deux* of suspicion and defeat. Loan knew that Loi was Minh's personal physician and that he served as the Embassy House doctor on the side. He also knew that Dr. Loi was perhaps the most distinguished medical man in the city, unassailable, beyond professional reproach. "No. That is quite all right," Loan said weakly.

The Widow Trung, who had been quiet during the routing of Dr. Loan, now said: "If you have your autopsy report, then you should have no further use for my husband's body in your so-called investigation. May I have it, please?"

Gulliver knew what Minh's answer would be; so did Major Do, and Cameron, and Sloane. The question had come up during the strategy session they'd conducted before this meeting. It hadn't been difficult to guess what the Hoa Hao demands might be; the banners in the street proclaimed them loudly enough.

Minh hesitated, pretending to give her request careful thought, then said, "Yes, of course. You can take delivery this very afternoon, at the hospital."

Mai struck again while he was in a generous mood. "Will you also issue me a permit for a funeral procession?"

Instead of answering her right away, Minh turned to Bui Dinh with a quizzical look. "I am not Hoa Hao, of course, but it was my impression that your faith does not favor elaborate public funerals," he said.

Dinh nodded. "That is quite correct, Colonel," he said. "But we think a traditional Buddhist ceremony is appropriate under the circumstances. So many people, *thousands* of people, not only Hoa Hao but those of other faiths, have taken this courageous widow into their hearts. How can we cheat them of the opportunity to honor her, and to honor the memory of her husband?"

Again Gulliver faked a cough, grinning behind his hand, impressed with the way Dinh had played his trump, casting the issue in terms of the faceless, unpredictable crowd, evoking the one thing Minh truly feared in all this, the specter of the incensed mob. The province chief had a worthy opponent in this gaunt monk.

And again the province chief appeared lost in thought. Major Do, too, was playing his part to perfection, Gulliver saw. Do was frowning at Minh, implacably opposed to the idea.

In truth, Medium Minh had anticipated this request too, and had already come to the conclusion that to deny it would be to court even more public resentment. A funeral permit was one of the planned concessions. There were more—if the Hoa Hao could find them. Gulliver watched the old monk patiently awaiting the province chief's answer, pulling absentmindedly at his wild whiskers, and thought that if anyone could find them, Bui Dinh would.

"You must understand that it is my duty to keep the peace, no matter how," Minh said at last. "Will those of you in this room guarantee that there will be no disturbances, no emotional excesses to threaten the peace?"

The local Hoa Hao looked to Dinh, an open acknowledgment that he was their spokesman, their guide. He shook his head and said: "You must understand, Colonel, that we in this room do not control the people. We can guarantee nothing."

Before Minh's face could fully darken, Dinh smiled and added: "But of course we will do all we can to see that there is no disorderliness. A funeral is a spiritual rite, a holy thing, neither the time nor the place for anger or hatred."

Minh let go a small sigh. "Good," he said. He looked at Nguyen Loc. "Mr. Loc, can you keep the, ah, the *enthusiasm* of the students in check?"

"Yes, yes," Loc said in a weary, scornful voice, with all the impatience and arrogance of his youth.

"Good," Minh said. "I will issue the necessary permit." He got up and waddled to his desk. He opened a drawer, took out a form, and filled it out, his signature a final flourish.

It was going just as Minh had planned, Gulliver thought as he watched the province chief hand Mai the permit with a ponderous, grunting bow. The Widow Trung had her funeral and Medium Minh had his promise of peace in the streets. All that remained was Minh's little surprise, his crowning touch.

On cue, as if suddenly inspired, Minh clapped his hands and turned to Mai, grinning hugely, his tooth almost blinding her. "My dear *Ba* Mai, I have a fine idea!" he said excitedly. "On behalf of the provincial government I will donate fifty thousand piasters to help pay the cost of the funeral. And I will give you another fifty thousand from my own pocket!"

"Wh-Why would you do that?" Mai said, bewildered.

Minh, still grinning, said: "Why, to fertilize the spirit of peaceful cooperation that has been planted here today, of course. And to show that we in the government are not callous and unfeeling, that we do not have claws that drip blood. Oh yes, ha ha, I have seen the posters in the street, ha ha." He waggled a fat finger of good-natured admonishment at her.

Mai, confused, looked to Bui Dinh for a signal, to see whether she should accept.

The priest held up a cautionary hand as he stared at the province chief with a new appreciation; the unexpected public-relations maneuver had caught him off guard.

Finally he said: "It is a generous offer, Colonel; too generous. But it is not fair to you. Why should you pay for Nguyen Khac Trung's funeral? Would it not, instead, be better to make the three men responsible for his death pay? It seems the least they could do."

Gulliver stiffened as the words sank in, drowning hopes that the meeting would end well. He saw like signs of alarm in the others. Cameron's face was red and splotchy. Major Do was frowning again, genuinely this time. And the bright light of Minh's tooth had gone out as quickly as it had come on.

Even Sloane sensed that something was wrong. He tugged at Gulliver's sleeve for a translation. Gulliver shook him off irritably, keeping his eyes on Minh.

"The th-three men?" Minh stammered.

Bui Dinh smiled faintly and nodded. "Yes. The three who interrogated Nguyen Khac Trung at the CIA's villa, the place you call Embassy House if I am not mistaken."

"You are mistaken," Minh said coldly. "About a good many things."

"I humbly agree," the monk said, no trace of either humbleness or agreement in his voice. "But this is not one of them."

"I don't know what you're talking about," Minh snapped. "Which three men? Who are they? What are their names?"

"You know who they are. And we know who they are. And we know that they are responsible."

"I told you before, no one is responsible for Trung's death but Trung himself," Minh said. "He committed suicide."

"We cannot and do not accept that, Colonel," Dinh said matter-of-factly. "Even if it were true, Nguyen Khac Trung would not have taken his own life unless the pain of torture was so great that he could no longer bear it. Either way, the men who interrogated him at the CIA villa are responsible for this death."

"*I* say who is responsible, not you. *I* say, not you," Minh ranted, his composure shattered, the spittle flying.

The attack of nerves told Gulliver that the province chief did not know whether the Hoa Hao really had the names or were bluffing. Gulliver didn't know either. This monk was a cagey bastard.

The object of Gulliver's grudging admiration did not respond to Minh's outburst. He stood waiting, a picture of unruffled serenity, while the province chief made a visible effort to regain control of himself. The rest of the Hoa Hao were watching with satisfaction, especially Dr. Loan.

Minh took a few deep breaths, his barrel chest heaving like the prow of a ship in heavy seas, then said: "As I told Madame Trung, the investigation is continuing. It is still to be determined who, if anyone, is to be held responsible . . . for dereliction of duty. I would agree that it is inexcusable for anyone to let a prisoner take his life. And if it so happens that someone is responsible . . . for dereliction of duty . . . then I assure you that the guilty party shall be punished."

Dinh smiled. "And what of the American officer? Will he be punished along with the two Vietnamese . . . for dereliction of duty?"

Gulliver's diaphragm seemed to slam shut. Oh Jesus! They knew! They knew about Swain! How did they know? Beside him he heard Cameron gasp, could almost hear him sweat.

Gulliver closed his eyes, just for a second. But when he opened them, he saw that he might have underestimated Colonel Duong Van "Medium" Minh. The province chief had not risen to the priest's bait. He just shrugged, shook his head, and said: "You are talking in riddles again."

Bui Dinh started to say something more but Colonel Minh barked: "No! I will speak now. I will say the things I should have said in the beginning. I was trying to be considerate of *Ba* Mai's feelings, but now you force me to be frank. You talk of responsibility, of punishing people. Why should people be punished for doing their duty, for arresting and questioning an enemy of the republic? Nguyen Khac Trung was a communist. The Phoenix program is made to eliminate communists. Phoenix has done its duty in the case of Nguyen Khac Trung and I, for one, am satisfied. If the Hoa Hao people are decent citizens, then they too are against the communists. They too should be satisfied. And it is the duty of you here, their leaders, to make them satisfied. Do not insult my intelligence! Do not try to tell me that you have no influence with the people in the streets! I am the authority in this province. I have the soldiers to enforce that authority. And I am warning you! I am telling you that I want the troublemakers off my streets! *Now! Today!*"

The silence that closed in behind Colonel Minh's final shouted words was deep and lasting. The air-conditioner's whirring racket did not affect it. Nor did Gulliver's hushed voice as he whispered a translation for Colonel Sloane. It was broken at last not by Bui Dinh, as everyone expected, but by Sloane, who heard Gulliver's translation out, then loudly exclaimed: "Hear, hear."

Only then did Bui Dinh have his say. "You've been frank, now I shall be frank," he said quietly. "My friends here have known Nguyen Khac Trung for many years. They know he was not a communist. He was Hoa Hao, and the Hoa Hao are against the communists. We believe that Nguyen Khac Trung was wrongfully arrested, that he was tortured, and that he died as a result of this torture. We are not alone in our belief. The people also believe these things, as you have seen for yourself, as you will continue to see—"

"Do not threaten me, priest," Minh said, his own threat evident in the low growl of his voice.

Nguyen Loc said, "Let him finish."

"I threaten no one," said the monk. "I only state facts. And the facts are that this is a Hoa Hao province and people are angry. The Hoa Hao leadership did not start the protests, but it is true that we may be able to stop them. We might be willing to try . . . if we were properly motivated to do so."

"And what would it take to motivate you?" Minh asked sarcastically.

Bui Dinh held up a finger. "The government must admit that it made a mistake in arresting Nguyen Khac Trung and clear his name." He held up another finger. "Those directly responsible for his death must be punished." A third finger went up. "*Ba* Mai and her family must be compensated for their loss of livelihood . . ."

When Dinh paused, Minh smiled, shook his head, and said, "Out of the question."

Dinh smiled back and said, "I am not finished, Colonel." He held up a fourth and final finger. "The Phoenix program in this province must be immediately abolished and replaced by a system in which the Hoa Hao are partly responsible for policing themselves."

Minh laughed aloud this time. "In other words, a total abrogation of GVN authority in the province."

"Not at all," Dinh said. "Major Do will still be chief of the Special Branch. You will still be the province chief."

Colonel Minh stopped smiling. "What impudence! Do you take me for a fool?" he said, his voice rising. "He who has police power has complete power! He who controls the police controls the province!"

"No!" shouted Nguyen Loc. "He who has the backing of the people controls the province! You have the power on paper. We have the power in the streets—"

Bui Dinh cut in quickly, smoothly, the voice of reason. "We do not want to control the police. We simply would like to see the formation of a committee made up of Hoa Hao which would work with the police. You can even appoint its members if you wish."

"How very generous of you," the province chief said with a sneer. "And what exactly would this committee do?"

"It would review all Phung Hoang arrest orders. No Hoa Hao could be arrested without the knowledge and consent of the committee."

"These are your demands?"

"Not demands, Colonel. Just what it would take to induce us to use our influence to stop the demonstrations."

"Get out," Minh said calmly. "All of you. Get out of my office now. This meeting is finished. We have nothing more to discuss."

Bui Dinh looked at the others and nodded. They got to their feet.

"If the demonstrations continue, they will be broken up; by whatever means are necessary," Minh said in postscript to his dismissal. "If there is blood, it will be on your hands. And remember this: it will be Hoa Hao blood."

The Hoa Hao delegation filed out in silence. Bui Dinh, Nguyen Loc, and Nguyen Thi Mai were the last to leave. On her way out, Mai stopped in front of the province chief and held up a sheet of paper, the funeral permit Minh had signed. She kept her eyes on his as she slowly and deliberately tore it in half, then into quarters, and then eighths. She held out both arms, her hands only inches from Minh's round face, and let the pieces fall. They fluttered to the floor like flakes of spring snow, a sign that winter was not yet over.

14

"KNOW WHAT AN OPTIMIST IS, Major?" Gulliver asked as he put one long, narrow box of finger cards on the floor beside his chair and reached for another. "A pessimist without much experience."

Major Do smiled.

They sat facing each other across the police chief's mussed desk, going through the files, looking for the magic formula that would turn Nguyen Khac Trung into a communist.

They had been at it all afternoon and Major Do's office, usually compulsively tidy, was now strewn with dirty teacups and butt-filled ashtrays. The stale smell of cigarettes long since smoked lingered in the room. They had had to close the windows to shut out the chants of the demonstrators outside.

"It's hopeless," Gulliver said. "Why are we doing this?"

Major Do, puffing calmly on a foul-smelling Gauloise set in an elegant ivory holder, did not answer. He made a rule of never responding to rhetorical questions.

"And why us?" Gulliver insisted. "Why did we get singled out to conduct this charade of an investigation?"

Deciding that this was a real question, Do gave a Gallic shrug and said: "Because it was a Special Branch/PRU arrest. Because I am the chief of Special Branch and you are the PRU adviser. Because you speak Vietnamese. Because our colonels, my Colonel Minh and your Colonel Sloane, want to dilute the responsibility. Because this way if things go wrong they can always say our detective work was bad, that we gave them bad information."

"Know what a pessimist is, Major?" Gulliver asked with a grin. "A cynic without much experience."

Major Do smiled again. "Let us just say that I have few illusions left. But you are wrong. I am not a cynic."

"And I'm not the PRU adviser," Gulliver said.

"*Au contraire*. I heard you were reappointed to the post just this morning. My congratulations," Major Do said wryly.

Gulliver gave him a disgusted look and nodded. "Cameron wants to keep Swain off the streets and out of sight."

"Well I, for one, am happy to have you back," Do said. "Besides, we can't ask the *Trung Uy* to investigate himself."

"I've been thinking that if it wasn't for the *Trung Uy* we might not have anything to investigate," Gulliver said.

"If . . . " Do said with another philosophical shrug. "If I had not been born Vietnamese and you American. If neither of us had become soldiers. If men did not settle their arguments by going to war. If. . . ."

Gulliver could see that although they spoke English, a language the major was not supposed to know, Do was feeling very French today. He grinned. "I know, I know . . . and if a frog had wings he wouldn't bump his ass when he jumped."

Do thought about it, got it, and laughed.

Their orders were to find something, *anything* that would link Nguyen Khac Trung to the communists; something besides a suspect confession and the accusations of two women who were no longer in a position to repeat the charges. They had gone through the old interrogation reports, checking to see if his name had ever been mentioned by other detainees, and now they sifted finger cards to see if anyone had ever brought charges against him. There was nothing in the alphabetical sequence, but they had pushed ahead anyway, checking all the cards, in case one had been misfiled.

Colonel Minh had been emphatic as to what he expected of his investigators. "The Hoa Hao's strategy is anchored on the premise that Trung was not a communist and should never have been arrested," he'd told them. "If we can prove that he was a VC, their argument crumbles like dry rice paper. They will look like fools. Especially that mad monk from An Giang."

For Major Do, the investigation was merely a matter of doing his job. For Captain Gulliver, the province chief had made clear, it was a do-or-die proposition: find something to pin on Trung or be cashiered. This was Gulliver's opportunity to redeem himself for the disaster of Nui Giai Mountain, Minh had told him with a conspiratorial grin. "Bring me proof that Trung was a communist and all is forgiven. Fail me and there will be no more chances for you. You will be finished in my province."

Gulliver couldn't have cared less about that; nothing would suit him more. He was interested in finding out what had happened to Trung for his own reasons. Something about this case smelled, and he wanted to know what it was.

The Mad Monk. It was a good name for the priest even if it did come from Minh, Gulliver thought as he thumbed through another box of finger cards. Medium Minh and Mad Monk Dinh. He stood the two men side by side in his mind, comparing. The province chief fared badly.

For some reason, Gulliver was reminded of the time Minh had visited a PRU op in progress after hearing on his C-and-C ship radio that they had cornered a Viet Cong village chief. The villagers had told them that during the day the VC cadre lived in an underground bunker in the nearby forest while the government's village chief ran things. At night, Saigon's man went home and locked his door while his communist counterpart came in from the cold to take his place.

Minh had been waiting for them in the village when they brought in their man. The cadre was about fifty, the same age as Minh, but it was all they had in common. The prisoner was thin and well-muscled, and bore the stigmata of a lifetime's worth of wounds and diseases. He was missing half of one ear and one eye was covered with a film the color of buttermilk.

Minh, playing to the gallery of villagers, had tried to humiliate the man, slapping him with an open hand the way he would a disobedient woman, spitting in his face. The VC took it unflinchingly, saliva dripping off his calm face, his good eye fixed on the province chief with contempt.

Gulliver had been impressed. And so, apparently, had the villagers. Like silent judges they had looked from the cadre, scarred and emaciated, dignified and defiant, his proud face a diary of a lifetime of sacrifice . . . to their province chief, obese and reeking of hair oil and after-shave, his puffy face revealing a lifetime of gluttony and corruption. Without a word, first one villager, then another and another, had turned and walked away, leaving Minh without an audience, alone with his victim in the market square. And in that moment Gulliver knew, really knew for the first time and without doubt, that the war was lost.

"Well, that is the end of it," Major Do said with a sigh as he pushed his last box of cards away. He looked across the table at Gulliver. "Have you found anything, *Dai Uy*?"

Gulliver hurried through the last of his own cards and shook his head. He leaned back wearily in his chair and said, "It seems our Mr. Trung is just what the Mad Monk says he is: a model of respectability."

Major Do stuck another Gauloise into his holder and lit it, sending up a blue cloud and the harsh smell of rough-cut tobacco. Then he too leaned back. "Let us summarize. What do we know?"

Gulliver thought a moment. "Well, we know that Bich got a tip the VC were running weapons into the province by boat. We know that his White Ra . . . er, Special Branch agents ran a surveillance and confirmed it. We know Bich called in the PRU and they arrested two women who were interrogated until they confessed, and who then bit the bullet . . . literally. We know that before they allegedly killed themselves they implicated Nguyen Khac Trung of Senh Tien as an accomplice—"

"They implicated *Comrade* Trung of Senh Tien," corrected Major Do.

"What's the difference? According to Dang, one of the VC women described Nguyen Khac Trung's house perfectly."

"Only after a bit of prompting from the *Trung Uy*," Major Do said. "But go on."

"All right, Trung was arrested and taken to the Embassy House, where he was interrogated. He confessed to being part of the Viet Cong infrastructure and to being a conduit for VC weapons. He also revealed that he'd been with the Viet Minh in the war against the French. He signed a full confession, written out for him by Bich. He had complained of chest pains off and on throughout the session, and died without warning, clutching his heart. That was the cause of death, not suicide as the province chief told the Hoa Hao. . . . By the way, why do you suppose Minh made up that story?"

Do smiled. "Suicide is so much more dramatic than heart failure, don't you agree? Besides, heart failure can result from torture, whereas suicide is always seen as conclusive proof of a guilty conscience."

"You are a cynic, Major," Gulliver said.

"According to our people's statements, of course, Trung was not tortured," Do said. "So where does that leave us?"

"It leaves us with our people's statements and Trung's confession in one hand, and Trung's clean sheet in the other hand," Gulliver said with a shrug. "Trung's got no record of antigovernment activity and no record of ever having served with the Viet Minh. By all accounts, he was a loyal husband, a doting father, and a top official in the Hoa Hao political party. A regular pillar of the province."

"That is not entirely accurate," Major Do said. "Trung was only a minor functionary in the SDP, little more than a clerk. In their effort to create a martyr, the Hoa Hao are inflating his importance."

"Well, you've got to give them credit," Gulliver said. "They've done a pretty good job of it so far."

"Yes, they have," Major Do agreed. "So what would you suggest we do now?"

Gulliver made a sour face. Do already had his people out questioning Trung's neighbors and coworkers at the hospital. "I guess all that's left for you and me is to sit down with our boys and go over their statements line by line," he said. He paused, then added, "There's no doubt in my mind that they tortured Trung until he died. All that stuff Minh was saying about Trung's body being mutilated after it was delivered to the hospital is bullshit."

Major Do was tilted back in his chair, his boots propped on the desk, combing his thin mustache with a three-by-five card as he watched Gulliver with a pensive look.

"*Dai Uy,* are you quite sure that you want to be right?" he asked in a quiet voice. "That you really want to find all you are looking for?"

"What do you mean?"

Major Do continued to comb out his mustache with the card while he searched for the right words. "Captain Dang is your counterpart and your good friend," he said at last. "The *Trung Uy,* Lieutenant Swain, is an American and a brother Army officer. You even have much in common with Captain Bich."

"Bich?" Gulliver snorted. "What could I possibly have in common with that little weasel?"

Major Do smiled. "You both serve the same master."

Gulliver was confused. "The same master? What mas . . ." he began, then realized what Do was telling him.

Do nodded. "Your little . . . weasel, is it? . . . is an agent of the U.S. Central Intelligence Agency."

Gulliver whistled. "Does Cameron know?" he asked.

"No one knows but me. And Bich's CIA case officer, of course."

"Who is none other than Bennett Steelman himself, I'll bet!"

Major Do applauded. "Excellent! Yes, it is Mr. Steelman himself."

Gulliver groaned. "I should've known." It all made more sense now. Why Bich was the delivery boy for Minh's "specials." Why George Cameron had stubbornly refused to question the hit orders or forward Gulliver's memos of protest to Saigon. The hapless P officer obviously had instructions from Steelman to cooperate with Bich and Minh, to ask no questions.

"How did you find out?" Gulliver asked.

Major Do laughed. "*Dai Uy,* how can you ask? Am I not the chief of the notorious National Police Special Branch in this province? Do I not see all, know all, just like your CIA? Ask the common people, they will tell you."

"Okay, I can see *you* aren't going to tell me," Gulliver said. "But I still don't know what you mean. Why wouldn't I want to know what really happened to Trung? What do Bich and the others have to do with it? Dang's the only one I give a damn about, but if he's lying we've got to know it. Whatever Colonel Minh eventually decides to do with what we find, he should at least base his decision on the facts."

"Hmm, yes, the facts, a noble thought," Major Do murmured. "Let me put it to you this way: Colonel Minh is in a delicate position with this Hoa Hao business. As is your CIA."

Do stopped as if he had explained something. Gulliver was losing patience with the major's oblique references; the time Do had spent with Interpol had added a European penchant for seeing conspiracy everywhere to the already considerable Vietnamese love of intrigue. He couldn't see what the man was driving at. He shrugged. "I can see the obvious, Major."

"Look a bit further," Major Do said gently. "Try to see beyond the obvious."

"Goddammit," Gulliver said with irritation. "I'm just a country boy from North Carolina. If you have something to say, then say it. I'm too fucking tired to play games."

Major Do laughed. "I too am a country boy, *Dai Uy*. So I will tell you, one country boy to another. It would be best for everyone involved if we were to find only that which the province chief wants found. The Hoa Hao are angry now and the province chief will probably have to make some concessions to them before the trouble goes away. However, so long as there is a possibility that Trung was working for the communists, the Hoa Hao position is not strong, they cannot ask for too much."

"But . . ." Gulliver said, knowing Do was not finished.

"But . . . if we submit a report that says Trung was not a communist and that he died as a result of Phoenix torture, it puts a burden on our superiors. What are they to do? If they reveal the truth, the people will be even more angry and will demand public retribution. If they suppress the truth and the Hoa Hao gets its hands on our report, the result will be much the same, only worse. And we have already seen evidence that the Hoa Hao has a good intelligence network."

Major Do stopped to suck on his stinking cigarette and Gulliver said, "Okay. I understand all that, but what does it have to do with our three blind mice: Dang, Swain, and Bich?"

Major Do smiled. "Colonel Minh is the province chief and a personal friend of President Thieu. Colonel Sloane is PSA, the most important American official in the province. If the Hoa Hao demand retribution, who do you think will pay?"

"The little people? The three blind mice?"

Do shrugged. "Perhaps all three. But more likely just your friend Dang. Swain is American. Will the American Army let one of its officers be tried in a Vietnamese court? Bich is Steelman's agent. Will the CIA let one of its men testify? But Dang is a former VC who does dirty work. He's expendable. Others will pay too. My government and yours. The people of America know little about Phoenix. A scandal would change all of that. Your newspapers will sermonize. Your Congress will threaten to cut aid. Your CIA will come under fire. And for forcing the issue, you and I will also pay. With our careers."

"So why doesn't the government just tell the Hoa Hao to go piss up a rope?" Gulliver asked.

"Piss up a rope? This is English?"

Gulliver grinned. "Another way to say 'go fuck yourself.'"

"Ahh, yes?" Major Do beamed. Then he grew serious again. "We cannot tell them to . . . to piss up a rope because we cannot afford a complete break with the Hoa Hao," he said. "They are a small minority in Vietnam, but a majority in this province and others. We need them. Why do you think the ARVN does not garrison large numbers of troops here? Because they are not needed. The VC find it hard to play the fish in the sea of people here. The Hoa Hao have disliked the communists since the Viet Minh murdered their prophet. It is vital that they go on disliking them. Your employer must think so too; the CIA gives them bribe money to cooperate with the government."

Gulliver knew that what the major said was true. Chances for true accommodation between the Hoa Hao and the communists had been dashed in 1947 when the Viet Minh murdered Huynh Phu So. The "Living Buddha" had gone to a conciliation meeting at the invitation of the communists, only to be arrested, tried on charges of treason and rebellion, and executed. His body had been quartered, the pieces buried in separate places so that he could not be resurrected in spirit or actuality; many of those who did not believe Huynh Phu So to be the incarnation of Buddha *did* think he was a sorcerer. The murder so inflamed the Hoa Hao faithful that they joined forces with the French, who armed some twenty thousand Hoa Hao soldiers. These days there were a few places—notably Chau Thanh district over in An Giang province—where the Hoa Hao and the VC lived quietly side by side, but they were the exception, not the rule.

"Major Do, are you suggesting that we not conduct a real investigation? That we just give Minh what he wants? Because if you are, you can . . ."

"Go piss up a rope?" the major asked with a delighted laugh. "Excellent!" He shook his head. "No, *Dai Uy,* I do not suggest that we look only for what Colonel Minh wants us to find. I suggest that we look for the truth. I am a policeman. I must *know* things. If we are to work together, I had to be certain you also are the kind of man who must know things. We will make a good team, I think. We will come to know things together. We can decide what we will do with the truth once we know it."

Gulliver thought about it a moment, then nodded. "Sounds fair enough; you're on," he said. "Where do we start?"

"I know Captain Bich the way a father knows his prodigal son," the major said. "I will question him. You can question your people, Captain Dang and Lieutenant Swain."

"All right," Gulliver agreed, getting to his feet.

Major Do stood too. "I've been so busy with the trouble in the streets," he said, nodding toward the window. "Perhaps you can do me the favor of checking this out." He was holding up the three-by-five card he had been using to comb his mustache.

"What's that?" Gulliver asked. "It looks like a finger card."

"It is," said Do.

"Whose?"

"Comrade Trung's, I think. Comrade Trung of Senh Tien."

"What! Nguyen Khac Trung? You found it? When? Where?" Gulliver babbled with excitement.

Major Do smiled. "I found it in the first five minutes, in the file, under the name of Trung," he said calmly. "But it does not belong to Nguyen Khac Trung. It belongs to a man named Nguyen *Van* Trung, who also lives in Senh Tien."

"What? Jesus Christ! They got the wrong man!"

Do held up a hand of restraint. "Perhaps, perhaps not," he said. "We must not jump to conclusions, *Dai Uy*. Will you check it out?"

"You bet your ass I'll check it out!"

"Bet my ass?" Major Do shook his head in bewilderment. "Frogs with wings . . . weasels . . . urinating up ropes . . . wagering with your buttocks . . . blind mice. I think your Colonel Sloane is quite correct, *Dai Uy*. I do not know English."

Gulliver found Swain on the ballfield behind the villa, running pass patterns. One of the PRUs was at quarterback and a lame yellow dog was playing defense. The PRU lofted a pass, a wobbly end-over-end Joe Kapp spiral. The dog, barking with excitement, hobbled after the receiver for a few yards, then turned and rushed the passer.

Swain spotted Gulliver and broke toward him, faking and cutting, showing off. "Hey, Cap! What's up?" he called as he made a nice grab right in front of Gulliver.

"Hate to break up the Sugar Bowl, Swain, but I'd like to talk to you inside if you have a few minutes."

"No sweat, Cap." Swain threw a tight spiral back to the PRU and yelled. "You wait! Me come back, chop-chop. You wait! Understand? You wait!"

The PRU dropped the pass. "Okay, no sweat. Numbah One. Me wait," he yelled back. He retrieved the ball and fired a pass at the dog, missing badly. The two Americans started walking toward the villa.

"I should have taught the dog how to throw instead of the gook," Swain said. "The dog's better." Then his face lit up and he asked: "Hey, Cap, what do you call a gook with no dog?"

"I give up, Swain. What?"

"A vegetarian."

"Only the North Vietnamese eat dog, Swain," Gulliver said. "And then only black dogs."

Swain, laughing heartily at his own joke, did not hear him. When he had caught his breath, he asked: "What do you call a gook with two dogs?"

Gulliver shook his head wearily.

"A rancher." They had to stop a moment while Swain bent over and beat on his thighs, howling.

They used the back door, taking the shortcut through the kitchen to get to Gulliver's office. It was Gulliver's office again. Cameron had relieved Swain and Dang of all duties and had put both under loose house arrest pending the outcome of the investigation. It had been done more to keep them off the volatile streets of the province town than as punishment, but since the veteran Sergeant Phuoc and his years of experience were still up on the mountain, Gulliver not only was PRU adviser again, but acting team leader as well.

Swain scooted the visitors' chair up to the edge of the desk and sat with his thick legs bowed over the sides, just as he had done that first day. It put him directly under the fan. "I was gonna get this office air-conditioned but I never got the chance," he said with a grin. "It was only mine for a day."

The big man was loose and easy; he didn't seem to have a care in the world. So Gulliver showed him a matching grin and said: "I wouldn't worry about it, Swain. From what I hear, *all* the buildings at Fort Leavenworth are air-conditioned . . . even the federal penitentiary."

It seemed to have the desired effect. The smile vanished from Swain's face. "Leavenworth? What the fuck you talkin' about, Cap?"

"That is where the Army sends its murderers," Gulliver said with a shrug.

"Murderers? Jeez! Who murdered anybody?"

"You did, Swain. You and Bich and Dang. You murdered Nguyen Khac Trung."

"I don't know what you're talkin' about, Cap, I really don't," he said calmly. "Nobody was murdered. That gook had a bum ticker and it gave out on him when he saw that we had him cold, that's all. He might have scared himself to death, but nobody murdered anybody."

"Which one of you cut off his finger?" Gulliver asked quietly.

Swain stared back with a flat, blank face and did not answer.

"My guess is Dang," Gulliver went on. "He does love his K-bar. Always keeps it nice and sharp."

A nerve jumped in Swain's face, but he kept silent.

Gulliver said: "And I'd guess it was Bich who played Ma Bell with Trung's nuts, who hooked him up to the field phone. Bich just strikes me as the type who'd get his own rocks off by playing with someone else's."

Swain's face had gone grim. "As long as you're playing games, Cap, what about me?" he said. "Didn't I get to have any fun?"

"Sure you did, Swain," Gulliver said amiably. "You had the most fun of anybody. You got to bash in his skull. You got to be the one to put him away for keeps."

A flitting shadow, a brief flash of panic, came and went behind Swain's eyes. He tried to smile but he could tell that it wasn't coming out right. Gulliver had hit it right on the nose. Did he know or was he guessing? The fucker really wants to nail me, Swain thought in disbelief. Over a gook.

Harry Swain was not immune to fear, but neither was he overly familiar with it. Having been afraid so few times in his life, he did not have much experience in handling it. He reacted instinctively now, and his instinct was to bluff. He tensed the muscles in his bull-like neck and said menacingly: "You got nothing on me, Cap, and if I were you I wouldn't be trying to find something that isn't there. You're messing with the wrong guy. You'd just as soon try to slip a rubber on a bobcat as fuck with me."

"You got me shaking in my boots, Swain," Gulliver said in a bored voice.

"If you're not, maybe you should be. I've got friends in the company. Powerful friends. I've got more protection than Fort Fuckin' Knox."

Gulliver laughed and said scornfully: "Protection? The spooks don't give a flying fuck about you, Swain. Why should they? You're not even on the payroll, much less on the old-boy network. And after this latest escapade you're nothing but an embarrassment to them; dirt to be swept under a rug."

Gulliver's shot in the dark hit a nerve. The day before he was restricted to the compound, Swain had gone to leave a message for Steelman at the tailor's, only to find the shop locked and dark, closed for the holidays. He had tried a backup drop, but when he checked back hours later the message had not been picked up. And when he had used the Embassy House's Diamond Net to reach Steelman, he had gotten the runaround. The duty officer manning the sixth-floor situation room at the embassy had told him to hang on, then, after a long wait, that Mr. Steelman could not be found. Swain had known the man was lying.

"The case against you is pretty strong," Gulliver said.

"*Case?* What case?" Swain said with a rising voice. "You got no case against me!"

Gulliver shrugged. "There may be a few holes in it, but it's definitely a case; the best we've got, anyway," he said. "Somebody has to go down for this, and you're the easiest to nail. It was you who delivered the fatal blow and it was you who fingered Trung in the first place. So it looks like it's you who's gonna be left holding the bag."

"I didn't deliver any goddamn blow, fatal or otherwise! And those two commie broads fingered him, not me! They said their contact was Comrade Trung, from Senh Tien. I just made the connection, that's all."

"Ah yes, the connection," Gulliver said. "That's puzzled me, Swain. Just how did you happen to know Comrade Trung?"

"I didn't know him, I just knew of him," Swain said with an overly casual shrug. "I ran into his wife over at the gook compound. I gave her a ride to Palm Springs, to USAID. We got to talking and she told me about her husband, this guy Trung, and about how they lived in this place called Senh Tien."

Even though most of what he said was true, Swain knew he sounded like a liar. He rushed ahead: "That's what made the connection for me. I mean, jeez! How many Trungs can there be in a little dump like Senh Tien?"

"Oh, at least two," Gulliver said quietly.

"Two?"

Gulliver held up the card. "This is a finger card on a Nguyen *Van* Trung. Nguyen *Van* Trung lives in Senh Tien too. Nguyen *Van* Trung has a record of NLF sympathies. Close, but no cigar, Swain. You snatched and snuffed the wrong man."

Swain felt suddenly dizzy. He blinked to clear the sweat from his eyes and he tugged at the neck of his LSU sweatshirt to get some air. At last he said: "I never snuffed nobody. Ask Bich and Dang. They were there. They'll tell you."

"Sure they will," Gulliver said softly. "But what will they tell me? That *they* tortured and murdered the wrong man, not you? Come on, Harry. You know how *gooks* are. *Gooks* stick together. Think a couple of *gooks* are going to take the fall for you just because you're such a friend of the Vietnamese people?"

Swain's glowering silence was an answer in itself and Gulliver smiled, pleased with the way things were going. He took a moment to tot up the score.

He had taken an educated guess as to who'd done what to Trung, based on what he knew about each of the interrogators, and Swain's reaction said he had guessed right—Gulliver 1, Swain 0.

But Swain had admitted nothing, and as long as all three of them stuck by their stories, there was not much that could be done—Gulliver 1, Swain 1.

Also, Swain had talked of CIA protection with all the confidence of a man who had a promise in his pocket. It had to be Steelman he was counting on, but Gulliver knew from experience that Razor would be nowhere to be found when the chips were down, and he knew from Swain's worried look that he had succeeded in shaking the big man's faith—Gulliver 2, Swain 1.

Swain scraped back his chair and stood. He stared down at Gulliver and said in an uncharacteristically quiet voice: "I don't have to take this shit. Not from you. Not from the *Sandman*. You wanna talk about murder? Let's talk about how many gooks you've greased. You wanna talk about Dang and his K-bar? Let's talk about how many throats you've cut. Did you check their ID before you put 'em to sleep? You wanna talk murder, do it with somebody else. I don't wanna hear it, you sanctimonious cocksucker." Swain turned and walked out of the office, heading for the radio room to try Saigon again.

Gulliver just sat there, feeling ambushed. Indeed. Who was he to talk of murder? How many had the Sandman killed?

He didn't know, couldn't remember. The killing was bad enough in and of itself, but not being able to remember how many there had been somehow seemed the greater sin. And how many innocents, how many Nguyen Khac Trungs, had been among the Sandman's victims? He didn't know that either.

He tried to tell himself that it was not the same, that it had been different for the Sandman. That had been war, the targets legitimate, enemies who had committed crimes. He saw a pair of black eyes, large and liquid in the gloom, and his head filled with a drumming ran-tan, the sound of rain on a tin roof. He felt the quivering body under his hand and heard a last soft sigh. What crime had *he* committed? What crime had any of them committed? That was just one more thing Gulliver did not know. Razor, keeper of the secrets, hadn't said. The Sandman, half-stoned on pills, hadn't asked.

Swain's questions had been tough but fair, and right on target—Gulliver 2, Swain 2. The tie-breaker also went to Swain. Gulliver had to give him half a point for knowing the word "sanctimonious," and another half for using it in context. Final score: Gulliver 2, Swain 3.

He sent a houseboy to fetch Dang, an act of deliberate disrespect, thinking that by treating Dang like a servant by using a servant to summon him, he might set the tone.

If Dang was bothered he did not show it. He was in the doorway five minutes later, and when beckoned to enter, sat down and looked at Gulliver calmly, waiting.

Gulliver waited too, not speaking, letting the seconds tick by, staring back with unfriendly eyes, trying, without success, to make Dang fidget.

"Tell me about it," he said at last.

"It is all in the statement I gave to Mr. Cameron."

Gulliver opened a desk drawer and pulled out a copy of Dang's statement, using a thumb and forefinger to hold it by a corner, as if it were contaminated. He tossed it onto the desk. "This? This is a pile of shit, Dang."

"It is what happened."

"Trung was not tortured or abused . . . he confessed of his own free will, without coercion . . . he died of heart failure," Gulliver said derisively, waving a hand at the report. "There are no North Vietnamese soldiers in South Vietnam . . . American B–52s do not bomb Cambodia or Laos . . . Santa Claus lives at the North Pole . . . know the truth and it shall set you free."

"You do not believe my report," Dang said. It was not a question.

Gulliver was silent a moment, then said: "Let's start with those women. How come you didn't find the cyanide caps they allegedly hid in their mouths?"

Dang shrugged. "No one thought to look in their mouths."

"I've seen you do a body search, Dang," Gulliver said softly. "I've seen you stick your finger up a two-month-old baby's cunt. But I never saw you make a mistake like that."

Dang shrugged again. "I did not do the search. My PRUs stripped them; I assumed they conducted a thorough search."

"That's something else I've never seen you do before, Dang . . . *assume,*" Gulliver said.

When Dang did not respond, he asked: "Do you realize the damage you've done? You could not have helped the VC any more if you were still one of them."

Again Dang answered only with a maddening silence, and Gulliver remembered once when he had jokingly accused Dang of still working for the VC, and Dang had said, utterly serious, "If I were, the best thing I could do for them is what I am doing now, working for Phung Hoang as a PRU, alienating the masses, making them fear and hate the government."

"Stand up," Gulliver said.

Dang stood.

"Let me have your K-bar."

Dang paused, then reached back under the pajama tunic for the knife he wore in the sheath strapped just above the tailbone at the small of his back. Holding it by the blade, he handed it to Gulliver handle-first, and sat back down.

Gulliver set a pencil on the desk in front of him. Using his little finger, he measured off half an inch from the tip of the eraser, the distance from the end of the fingernail to the first joint, set the blade across the pencil, and pressed down hard. Dang's K-bar was honed to razor sharpness and the pencil—a No. Two—

was not very thick, but it still took all his strength to cut through it.

He looked up at Dang and said: "You know, I've seen you do it on field interrogations, maybe three or four times, but I never realized how difficult it really would be. You always made it look so easy."

Dang just looked back at him, his black eyes like two drill bits, and said nothing.

Gulliver used his finger to measure off another section, an inch this time, the distance between the first and second joints. As before, he had to use every bit of his strength to cut through the center core of lead, the bone of the pencil.

He cleared away a space, and plunged the K-bar into the desktop. He looked up at Dang. Their eyes seemed to meet at a point midway across the distance separating them, directly above the still-quivering knife.

15

GULLIVER LEANED on the horn until the front gate swung open, then gunned the Bronco out of the compound, showering the Nung sentry with dust and scattering the small knot of sign-carrying demonstrators who milled just outside.

He made for the Senh Tien Highway, using side roads to skirt any disturbances that might be going on in the middle of town, driving fast, his knuckles white on the wheel, his stomach still full of acid from the argument with Dang. It had not been a real argument, of course. It took two to have a real argument, and Dang had not been even that cooperative. The tactics that had gotten a rise from Swain had not worked with Dang. It had been foolish of him to think they might.

Not once had Dang lost his temper or raised his voice. He had looked Gulliver straight in the face, straight in the soul, and lied. It had been their first real falling-out in seven months of daily contact, seven months of living in one another's pocket, and Gulliver was as wounded by it as if it had been a lovers' quarrel. Hedging and evasiveness were out of character for Dang; along with courage and competence, it was honesty that Gulliver most admired in his counterpart. It hurt to think Dang would lie to him. Oddly, it seemed to have hurt Dang, too. When there had been nothing left to say, he had put a hand on Gulliver's shoulder and said, "I am sorry, Sandman. I am truly sorry I cannot help you."

Thinking of the remorse in Dang's voice, Gulliver found himself looking for excuses. He must have had a good reason, beyond the obvious one of wanting to save his skin, Gulliver told himself, applying a tourniquet to his injured feelings.

The road was dense with traffic and Gulliver reined back on the Bronco. He was passing the string of connected paddies that separated the capital and Senh Tien, a cool glimpse of green between hot pustules of sooty sprawl. Cars, cyclos, and motorbikes rushed up and down the highway like charged atoms, darting into and out of dicey, life-threatening situations with manic energy, with the national jumpiness that seemed to afflict everything these days. Road etiquette, or the lack of it, was just one more symptom of a country at the edge of a nervous breakdown.

Gulliver concentrated on his driving. This was no time to run down a local and add another grievance to the town's list. He kept away from the shoulder and its clutter of water buffalo, papaya and mango stalls, children, and mollusk-hatted women with heavy loads on their bambook carrying poles.

A truck with Fourth ARVN Division markings stenciled on its bumper passed him with a whoosh. It was full of soldiers, one of whom was perched unsteadily at the tailgate, holding tight to a canvas-strut with one hand and his penis with the other. Droplets of windblown urine sprayed the Bronco's windshield and Gulliver saw the other troops in the truck falling about in paroxysms of laughter.

The truck turned in half a mile later, and Gulliver saw the sprawling camp of the province chief's reserve battalion. The troops were no doubt enjoying the unexpected assignment, Gulliver thought uncharitably. Even if the demonstrations got totally out of hand and they were put to work, they would be up against unarmed civilians rather than Viet Cong or North Vietnamese regulars. Even the Fourth ARVN could handle that.

When he reached Senh Tien he stopped at a soup stand and got directions to the address on the finger card. Ten minutes later he found it down a dirt lane so narrow he could barely squeeze the Bronco through, a dusty strip of shabby shops and dilapidated houses fashioned from wood and tin, clear across town from the police station and the Nguyen Khac Trung house.

Sitting out front was a large wheeled cart piled high with housewares—crockery, cooking pots, sleep mats, stools, and tables. A single stuffed chair was precariously planted on the slope of goods and a thin middle-aged woman wearing a white tunic and black pajama trousers sat in it like a queen on a jeweled throne. From her perch she directed a small army of children who were unloading things and carrying them into the house.

Gulliver stopped next to the cart and rolled down the window. "Good afternoon, sister. Can you please tell me who lives here?"

If the woman was startled to find herself confronted by a strange-looking American who spoke Vietnamese, she gave no sign of it. Her eyes narrowed suspiciously. "I do," she said.

"Excuse my intrusion, but I am looking for a friend of mine. His name is Nguyen Van Trung. I was told that he lives here."

"You were told wrong," she said truculently. "I live here. I have paid the landlord rent in advance. It's mine."

"Then Nguyen Van Trung does not live here?"

"Yes," she said, and Gulliver knew that she meant yes he does not live here. His one weakness in the language was his habit of posing negative questions.

"Did Nguyen Van Trung ever live here?"

"Yes, but he is gone. It's mine now. I've paid."

"Can you tell me when Mr. Trung left?"

The woman shrugged and said, "Last week sometime. It was on the first day of the holiday, I think. In the morning."

"Do you know where he went?"

"No. No one knows. He left without telling any of his neighbors. He left without paying last month's rent. Mr. Tai, the landlord, was very angry. He is a Chinese man, you know, and he likes prompt payment. After a week's time passed and Mr. Trung did not come back, Mr. Tai said I could have this house. It is a much better house than the other one he rented to me, on the corner over there . . ." She stopped to bellow at one of her laborers. "*Men dat oi!* Be careful with that, you clumsy child!"

"One last question and I'll leave you in peace. Can you tell me anything about Mr. Trung? How he makes his living. If he has a family. Who his friends are."

The woman gave him a sly smile. "I thought he was your friend." But before Gulliver could come up with something, she went on: "He was very quiet and kept to himself. He had no family and no friends. No one on the street knew him well. That is all I can tell you."

"Thank you, sister. You've been of great assistance."

There wasn't room to turn the Bronco around so Gulliver backed it the length of the lane. He made it without hitting anyone and headed back to the highway.

He had not gotten much from the woman—perhaps Major Do's White Rats would learn more when they canvassed the rest of the neighborhood—but what little she had given him was significant: Nguyen Van Trung had left in a hurry, only a few hours after Nguyen Khac Trung was picked up. It would appear that someone had warned Comrade Trung in time for him to use the arrest to screen his escape.

Gulliver had left the suburb and was well down the road when he suddenly slowed, made a U-turn, and headed back toward Senh Tien. He had no address for the house he wanted, but it wasn't hard to find. He found the police station and counted: four doors down, a two-story house with bars on the windows and no shop on the ground floor. He parked, went to the door, and knocked.

People had been calling all day to pay their respects, and Nguyen Thi Mai herself came to the door with a sad smile ready, expecting someone roughly her own height, her eyes set on a normal plane. They bounced off Gulliver's chest, went round as wheels, and scanned up. She issued a soft, breathless "Aiiee!" and swayed, her hands flying to her face.

Outrage quickly displaced the moment of panicky fear at finding a tall American on her doorstep. "Who are you? What do you want here?" she asked rudely.

"I'm Captain Gulliver. We met at Colonel Minh's office the other day. I'd like to talk to you."

"Go away!" she said sharply. "How dare you come to this house! How dare you come when I am receiving mourners!"

"I come as a mourner."

"*Oi!* Such blasphemy!"

"*Ba* Mai, please. I understand how you feel, but I am not your enemy," Gulliver said quietly. "Please believe me when I say that I want justice for your husband as much as you do. I think he was innocent."

His words stopped her just as she was about to shut the door in his face. She looked at him through a foot-wide crack and asked uncertainly, "You do?"

"Yes, I do. May I come in?"

"I . . . y-yes, please." She opened the door wide and backed off a step, bowing slightly as if admitting an honored elder. She was confused but Gulliver could see that her attitude was already undergoing a change.

She ushered him into a typical middle-class living room, an inharmonious mix of the old and the new: hot fluorescent lights overhead, cool French tiles on the floor; tables with inlaid mother-of-pearl; antique Chinese benches, decorative but uncomfortable, set along the walls under prints of birds; an open-reel tape deck and a small TV set bought on the black market.

Even the cooling system was a compromise between past and present, East and West—a wooden ceiling fan working in tandem with a cheap oscillator fan with rubber blades.

Gulliver saw that the Widow Trung was not alone. A dozen men and women in mourning clothes filled the room, sitting on folding chairs and a sofa padded with square, block cushions. Their soft chatter faltered and stopped when he came in. Two of the men stood abruptly, their faces as full of surprise at seeing him as Nguyen Thi Mai's had been a moment before: the student hotspur Nguyen Loc, and the Mad Monk Bui Dinh.

Before Mai could say anything, Bui Dinh had already made a recovery. Smiling, he offered his hand in Western greeting, and said in perfect English, "Ah, Captain Gulliver, I believe. It is good to see you again."

Gulliver returned the sentiment in Vietnamese, noting that Nguyen Loc was studiously avoiding greeting him in any language. The others merely looked on in curiosity.

"Please sit down," Mai said. "Would you like tea?"

"Yes, thank you," Gulliver said as they all took seats. To refuse would have been an insult.

Mai went off to fetch the tea and Gulliver turned to the monk and said in Vietnamese: "Your English is excellent. I am ashamed that my Vietnamese is not worthy of it."

"Your facility with our language is not only worthy but also impressive," Dinh said in his own tongue, friendly but wary, unsure of why Gulliver had come. "So few Americans speak our language. I myself also speak French, Japanese, and Chinese. I have always believed that languages are important."

"Yes, I too have always believed this. But tell me, why is it that you have learned only the languages of your historical adversaries?" Gulliver asked.

Dinh laughed in appreciation. "A common language is not necessary between friends, Captain; friends can communicate with their eyes, their hearts, their souls. But not knowing the language of one's enemies can prove fatal."

"I would like to think that a common language between enemies helps them to settle their differences peaceably," Gulliver said.

The monk nodded. "There is an ancient saying that the great wall between East and West is not the Wall of China, but rather the wall of misunderstanding."

"So I've heard," Gulliver said. "It is unfortunate that such a wall divided Colonel Minh's office on the occasion of our first meeting."

"Ah, yes, a most regrettable affair," the monk agreed.

Gulliver looked at Nguyen Loc, who had yet to say a word. Loc had been listening with a sour expression, a collage of hostility, distaste, and boredom. He doesn't seem to like the Mad Monk any more than he does me, Gulliver thought. Probably thinks Bui Dinh is nothing but a doddering dinosaur, ancient history, a necessary bedfellow only because it was a Hoa Hao show they were engaged in. The arrogance of youth could be as shortsighted as it was boundless.

Gulliver looked around the room and noticed that the Tet decorations had come down. The hope for a benign new year was already a cruel joke for the Trung family. The only flowers and candles in the room were on an altar in a corner. He got up and walked over to it.

It was no traditional Tet altar prepared for long-dead ancestors, but one commemorating a more recent wound. It was draped with mourning crepe, and with photographs of the late Nguyen Khac Trung. He was a gentle-looking man, bespectacled and middle-aged, thin and stooped, meek and harmless. Such an unlikely spark for the passionate fires sweeping the province town's streets. There were three bowls of rice set out on the altar, and three cups of tea, to nourish the dead's soul.

The old monk had come up behind him and Gulliver turned and asked, "Would it be all right if I paid my respects to the deceased?"

"Of course. Come with me."

Bui Dinh led the way into a bedroom, pushing through a door made of shredded plastic strips, then left Gulliver alone. Nguyen Khac Trung lay on a narrow bed under mosquito netting. Gulliver could see that the body had been prepared in the traditional Buddhist fashion rather than in the simpler Hoa Hao style; to better impress visitors, no doubt. The family had washed him down with a scented lotion and dressed him in his best clothes, a cheap suit. The face of the dead was usually covered with a white piece of paper or a white handkerchief as a symbolic barrier between the living and the dead, and to help shield visitors from too great an emotional shock, but in this case it was not. The widow wanted visitors to be shocked, Gulliver guessed; wanted them to see her dead husband's battered face; wanted them to see the government's crime for themselves.

Trung's mouth was propped open so visitors could drop in grains of rice or gold coins, and a bunch of ripe bananas had been placed on his stomach to distract the Devil, to keep the Evil One from devouring his intestines. His fingernails and toenails had been cut, the clippings put into small packets and attached to the limb from which they came, an indication that the *cai tang* ceremony would be performed later. It was a rare practice, employed only by families plagued by trouble. In three years, Trung's body would be exhumed and the bones transferred from the wooden coffin to an earthenware box. A geomancer would direct the family to another, more auspicious site for reburial, and the nail parings would help him sort the bones so that he could arrange them in the proper order.

Gulliver stared into Trung's waxy face for a long time, then turned away.

When he returned to the sitting room he found that the visitors were gone. Only Bui Dinh and Nguyen Loc were left, and Gulliver suspected that they had shooed the others away to clear the deck for business.

Mai brought in the tea and served them. She was wearing a simple white *ao dai* and when she sat she gracefully pulled the back panel up and around into her lap. Her hair was also pulled back, to the nape, and rolled into a bun in the style of mature women. Nguyen Thi Mai was a lovely woman, Gulliver thought, not for the first time; as beautiful as his Nhu. He could still see the two of them marching side by side at the head of the demonstration, like mythical heroines.

As if she had read his mind, the Widow Trung said: "You must be Quynh Nhu's American friend."

Gulliver was surprised. "She mentioned me?"

Mai smiled. "No. But one hears things. Nhu is our most famous citizen, so it should come as no surprise that she is also the most gossiped about."

Gulliver remembered Seiple and his box, his *apparatus*. Even the cowboys couldn't be expected to miss what's common knowledge in the streets, he thought.

He said to Mai: "There are so many Americans; how did you know it was me?"

"It is said that Quynh Nhu's friend is more Vietnamese than American," Mai answered.

"It's certainly true that you seem to share our fondness for circumlocution," Dinh cut in with a wry smile, tugging at his whiskers. "So I will be more American than Vietnamese and put it to you directly: Why are you here, Captain Gulliver?"

"To see if we might work together," Gulliver said. "I am investigating the death of Nguyen Khac Trung and I'm starting with the premise that Mr. Trung was not a communist, that he was innocent."

"Ah yes, the American way," Bui Dinh said in a mocking tone. "The accused is innocent until proven guilty."

"That's right."

"How very commendable!" the monk said. "I've always been a great admirer of your Constitution and your Bill of Rights. What you say makes me all the more ashamed for thinking that perhaps Colonel Minh sent you here to spy on us, to see what you can learn about what we know."

"Colonel Minh did not send me; I have come on my own," Gulliver said. "If he knew I was here he would be angry."

"You are very brave," Dinh crooned.

He doesn't believe me, Gulliver thought, a little angry himself. The bonze's droll sarcasm, masquerading as exquisite Oriental politeness, goaded him into playing a trump card. He turned to Mai and said: "Madame Trung, I have reason to think your husband may have been mistaken for another man from Senh Tien, a man named Nguyen Van Trung. I believe the wrong Trung was arrested."

"I knew it! I knew it was something like that!" Nguyen Loc exclaimed, jumping to his feet, fire in his eyes. "I said as much! Did I not say as much?"

The others ignored Loc's pyrotechnics. Dinh was staring at Gulliver with an indefinable expression, while Nguyen Thi Mai looked stunned. "Wh-why do you tell us this?" she asked, as amazed at his honesty as at his news.

"I told you; I want to see justice done as much as you," Gulliver answered.

Finally Bui Dinh asked, "Tell me, Captain; this Nguyen Van Trung, is he a communist?"

"I don't know," Gulliver said truthfully. "He is listed in the police files as a possible suspect, but the accusation against him was not substantial enough to warrant his arrest at the time."

"Then arrest him now; question him," Dinh suggested.

"I don't know where he is. He disappeared the same day Nguyen Khac Trung was arrested."

"There is the proof of his guilt," exclaimed Nguyen Loc, "and of Nguyen Khac Trung's innocence!"

The ancient monk paid his young co-conspirator no mind. "Did the province chief know of this man, this second Trung, when we met with him at his headquarters?" he asked Gulliver.

"He still doesn't know. I found out only this morning."

"What do you think he will do when you tell him?"

Gulliver shook his head. "I don't know," he said. He did not voice his fear: that Colonel Minh would do nothing, that it would change nothing. "Until we find this other Trung, we have nothing but a vague suspicion," he added. "And there is still the matter of the signed confession. As long as he has that and nothing else, the province chief will undoubtedly be satisfied that the arrest was justified."

"A confession obtained through torture," Dinh said. "If there was a confession at all."

Gulliver shrugged and said nothing.

"Is there anything more you can tell us, Captain?"

Gulliver shook his head again. "Only that I will do my best with the investigation," he said. "And so will Major Do."

"Major Do? Major Do of Special Branch?" The monk's tone was unabashedly skeptical.

"Yes. I know you won't believe it, but Major Do is a good man, a fair man. It was he who found Nguyen Van Trung's name in the records."

Gulliver got up to go. "I must be getting back. Madame Trung, I thank you for your hospitality. You have been very kind."

The old monk shook his hand again, but more warmly this time, and even Loc gave him a curt bow of good-bye. Nguyen Thi Mai showed him to the door.

"What you have told us will be of great help," she said. "Thank you for coming."

"Thank you for hearing me out," he said.

"You are so different from that other one," she said, a note of wonder in her voice. "I can understand now how Quynh Nhu could have an American for a . . . a friend."

"Thank you, but I'm not sure I know what you mean. What other one?"

"There is another American, who follows me home, who stops me in the street like a prostitute and makes indecent proposals. He is very rude, very frightening."

Gulliver's stomach clenched. *"I ran into his wife over at the gook compound. That's what made the connection for me. I mean, Jeez! How many Trungs can there be in a little dump like Senh Tien?"*

"What is this American's name?" Gulliver asked.

"I don't remember," Mai said. "He told me his name, but I don't remember. I don't want to remember."

"What does he look like?"

"A giant," she said. "With hairy eyebrows. Like a forest monkey."

Harry Swain sat brooding at the bamboo bar, drowning his

sorrows in San Miguel beer. The end stool, the one nearest to the stairs, was his now, a private perch. With little else to do with his time, he spent the better part of his days there; a man could spit-shine only so many boots, clean only so many weapons.

Swain had much to brood about, many sorrows to drown. He had not laid eyes on Mai since the day before they picked up Trung. There she was, unencumbered and ripe for picking, and here he was, confined to the Embassy House. It was for his own good, Cameron said. Just until tempers cooled, Cameron said. Meanwhile, some gook was probably already putting his gook moves on Mai. It wasn't fair.

Almost as troubling was the silence from Saigon. Unable to get to the message drop, he had tried repeatedly to reach his "Chinaman," his company sponsor, on the scrambler phone, only to hear that Mr. Steelman was out of town . . . Mr. Steelman was in a meeting . . . Mr. Steelman was busy. Cameron, who called in a daily sitrep, didn't seem to have any trouble in getting the chief of operations on the phone. It wasn't fair.

Swain was puzzled and frustrated, but he wasn't worried. If he hadn't known better, Steelman's odd silence might have led him to think that he and the others were being set up to take the fall for Trung's death, the way Gulliver had tried to make him believe. But Sloane and Minh were standing by the official story, and Saigon was standing by Sloane and Minh. Trung was a confessed communist who died of a heart attack during a routine questioning and was taken to the hospital, where his body was mutilated by someone out to embarrass the provincial authorities; probably that Hoa Hao doctor, Loan, who claimed to have discovered the marks on the body.

No sweat, Swain reassured himself. As long as he, Dang, and Bich stuck to the story they had agreed upon, everything would be Number One. And he was pretty sure he could count on Dang and Bich; they had just as much to lose as he did.

He finished his beer with a long swallow and was trying to decide whether to have another or take a stab at reaching Steelman again when he glanced into the mirror behind the bar and saw one of the PRUs come into the common room. It was one of the new people, one of the replacements Steelman had sent them. He spun around on the stool to tell the man he was not supposed to be in here, that PRU troops were not allowed in the main house, when the man said excitedly: "*Trung Uy*, come quick! Big fight! Big fight!"

"Fight? Where?"

"In barrack! Come quick!"

"Jeez!" Swain hopped off the stool and yelled, "Follow me!" He led the way through the dining room and kitchen and out the back door. When they were outside, both men started to run.

He heard it long before he got to the barrack—shouts, curses, crashing sounds . . . then a long piercing scream quickly followed by one loud cracking sound, then another . . . gunshots.

He threw open the screen door and dropped into a crouch, prepared for anything . . . only to find that he had stepped into a dead silence.

Swain looked around in confusion, and saw a stop-action frame from a movie, a barroom-brawl scene. Bunks and lockers were overturned and a score of men were frozen in place among the debris. He saw men on the floor, bleeding. He saw others in a frieze of hand-to-hand combat, one with his hands around the throat of another, one with a fist raised and cocked. One PRU was moving, writhing on the floor, a K-bar stuck into his thigh. Next to him was a man with half a head; the other half had been shot away. At the center of it all was Captain Dang, a pistol in his hand.

"Jeez!" Swain breathed.

Dang started to speak in a slow, hard, compelling voice. Swain could not understand what Dang was saying, but the tone made him pay attention anyway. It was a short, sharp speech, and when it was over the PRUs came back to life. The man with his fist raised dropped his arm. The man who had been choking his comrade let go and got to his feet. One PRU tore a strip from a bedsheet and put a tourniquet on the knifing victim's leg. Another man threw the rest of the ripped sheet over the dead man. Yet another dashed out of the barrack, heading for the villa. The rest of them began to straighten up the place.

"Jeez, Dang; what the hell's goin' on?" Swain asked.

"I have sent a man to call for an ambulance."

Swain made a sweeping motion with his arm. "I mean this. What the fuck happened?"

Dang shrugged. "You cannot keep men like these—men of action—locked up," he said. "It has been little more than a week and already they are like caged animals. An explosion was inevitable."

"But why did you shoot that guy?"

"He went after that one with the K-bar," Dang said, pointing to the man with the knife wound. "I fired into the ceiling and told him to stop. When he did not, I shot him."

"Jeez!" Swain looked around the barrack. The PRUs were

righting bunks and lockers, and some were helping others put dressings on their injuries. "What started it?" Swain asked.

Dang shrugged again. "I do not know," he said. "It was an argument between one of our people and one of the new men. Our people are mostly from the *nambo*, the southern area; the new men are mostly from the coastal strip north of Danang. It was a mistake to mix them."

The screen door banged open and George Cameron and Bill Coughlin came flying in. Coughlin was carrying an Uzi at the ready and even the peace-loving Cameron was armed, a Browning in his hand. They looked around. Cameron, his face pink and flushed, said in an awed voice: "We . . . we heard shots. What's going on here?"

Swain shook his head. "Dang was here from the start and he can tell you about it better than I could," he said. "I'd better go make sure that ambulance is on the way."

Swain was halfway to the villa when an ambulance from the military hospital roared across the compound and pulled up in front of the PRU barrack. Two orderlies jumped out of the back and went inside, carrying a stretcher.

Swain started back to the barrack, then changed his mind and turned for the villa. He went to the radio room, placed a call to Saigon, and asked for Bennett Steelman.

"Who should I say is calling, sir?" asked the situation-room duty officer.

"Cameron," said Swain. "George Cameron from M-R Four. And please hurry; it's important."

There was a pause. "I'll need your password for my logbook, Mr. Cameron."

"Oh, well, uh, I'm not actually Cameron. This is Swain. Harry Swain. I'm, uh, just placing the call for Mr. Cameron. To save him a little time."

There was another pause, longer than the first. Then the duty officer said, "I'm sorry, but Mr. Steelman is not in the embassy."

16

IN ALL HIS YEARS as an intelligence officer, Bennett Steelman had never confused the facts with the truth. One could know the facts; one seldom knew the truth. For that alone, he valued the facts over the truth.

From the facts one could always fashion *a* truth, if not *the* truth. And when he did accidentally trip over *the* truth it was because he had paid attention to the facts; getting them, getting them right, getting them in order. Facts were the currency of his calling, and he would not play fast and loose with them. He would lie, of course, but that had to do with truth, not facts. He did not lie to himself. He faced facts. And the fact he faced now was this: replacing Gulliver with Swain had been the second biggest mistake of his career.

Not that he was having second thoughts about Gulliver; only about Swain. Steelman gave credit where it was due; for all his faults, the Sandman would never have been so careless as to let Nguyen Khac Trung be killed without first checking him out.

Steelman sighed and put down the decoded cable he had just finished reading—Gulliver's investigation report. He would have to read through it again, but later, not now. He didn't have the stomach for it now. Two of the tale's heroes, Swain and Bich—*his* boys—lay at the bottom of his belly like lumps of raw dough, indigestible reminders that Bennett Steelman could make mistakes.

First the Vuong Affair, and now the matter of Nguyen Khac Trung. The feeling of *déjà vu* was stronger than ever, an eerie tingle. It was inevitable, he told himself. The two cases contained striking parallels. Both had to do with Vietnamese civilians killed in circumstances that raised as many questions as they answered. Both happened during a cycle of unexplained mission failures. Both involved U.S. Army "trigger" men. Both had the common factor of Jake Gulliver lurking in the shadow of the main event. And both threatened to do terminal damage to the career of Bennett Steelman IV.

The Vuong Affair had already done its damage, of course. His error in that one, he had long since decided, had been to trust those Army clowns to get rid of Vuong instead of having a company specialist do it. But there had been a reason: he had not wanted Saigon to know about it. The real mistake had been in letting the Sandman overhear him issue the hit order.

Steelman recalled his talk with Sally Teacher. Now, there was a prime example of the difference between the facts and the truth. He had given Sally most of the facts of the Vuong Affair: Vuong had been his agent; had been infiltrated into the B–40 Detachment to report on what the Berets were up to; had been taken out on a phony operation, shot in the back of the head, and dumped in Nha Trang harbor. But Steelman had not given her the truth. For that, all the facts were necessary, and he had omitted a few. The Green Berets had, *in fact,* told the truth, right down the line. Nguyen Tu Vuong had, *in fact,* been a Hanoi agent, and when Steelman had seen the evidence, he had, *in fact,* given the authorization to terminate. Were it not for that team member's confessional letter home, and the Sandman's own angst-ridden compulsion to purge imagined sins, nothing more would have come of it.

But those were just two minor links in a long, looping chain of error and miscalculation. Recruiting Vuong in the first place had been the initial link, of course; the kill order and the cover-up just the last and most serious. Fact: Bennett Steelman had panicked, and in his panic had taken what looked to be the best way out—taking Vuong out. At the time, it seemed a way to keep his superiors from learning that his recruit was a double agent, a way to keep spots off a spotless record.

And once word of Vuong's death had leaked, he'd had no recourse but to deny any knowledge of it, to leave Sculler and the green beanies holding the bag. For while the inadvertent recruitment of a double agent was not necessarily fatal to a man's career, ordering up an execution without clearance was.

He should have known better than to overreact like that. There had been no real need to have Vuong terminated. Double agents were an unfortunate but not an uncommon occupational hazard, especially when one took into account the relentless pressure from Langley to recruit, recruit, recruit. Tainted agents were as much a fact of modern warfare as were civilian casualties. They were what happened when you set quotas to be filled. The United States Army was not the only organization with a body count.

Steelman knew now that the wise thing would have been simply to inform Saigon that Vuong was a double and recommend that he be thoroughly squeezed, then terminated with extreme prejudice. Nguyen Tu Vuong's fate would have been unchanged; he would still be at the bottom of Nha Trang harbor in a body bag weighted with rocks. But Bennett Steelman's fate would have been different. He would still be on the company's fast track rather than parked off on a siding.

But he knew his real sin had been one of pride. For all his candor when it came to self-analysis, he could not bring himself publicly to admit error, to let anyone think he was only human. He was better than the others. They might recruit double agents, but not Bennett Steelman. Bennett Steelman had to be perfect, flawless.

It had been that way with him since his earliest days with the company, since Yale; but identifying one's demons did not necessarily mean one knew how to go about slaying them. He had tried, and failed. It all stemmed from another fact: Bennett Steelman had acquired his patrician style, he had not been born to it. For all his easy urbanity and lazy sophistication, for all of his aristocratic tics, he had not exactly been what his old agency prefects would have called "a true gentleman."

For one thing, no true gentleman let himself be seen to work very hard at anything, and ever since high school Bennett Steelman had been as conspicuously industrious as a beaver on amphetamines. He had worked hard in school, graduating at the top of his class, the finest student Brattleboro, Vermont, had ever produced. And he had worked hard at helping his handyman father take care of the summer homes of the rich, doing what needed doing, from painting gazebos to patching stone fences to getting in firewood. He also had worked hard at learning the ways of the summer people. He had set up the wickets for their croquet games, shagged their tennis balls, brushed down their horses, all in exchange for a closer look at them. And his hard work had paid off; it won him a scholarship to Yale and a first thin coat of social polish.

It had been much the same at New Haven. He had been a brilliant student, again graduating with honors, and, even more gratifying, he had gained admittance to Skull and Bones. He had made the most of it, cultivating the more privileged boys, aping their manners and mannerisms. None of them ever suspected he was at Yale on scholarship, or that his torrid tales of trysts with a former burlesque queen were flights of fancy, hatched on the long walk back from Beinecke Library, where he spent his evenings hidden away in cloistered nooks, studying.

His friends at Yale never knew, but the men who ran the Central Intelligence Agency did. And while they acknowledged his brilliance, dutifully promoting him to the next rung on the ladder when his time came up, they did not take him under their wings, or home for dinner, the way they did the bright young men being groomed for "big things." Few of these bright young men were as bright as young Bennett Steelman, but they were the scions of old friends and company colleagues and, as such, they all had something young Bennett Steelman did not: a birthright membership in the Central Intelligence Agency's old-boy network.

The roots of the old-boy network went as deep as 1947, when the CIA was first formed to fight the cold war, perhaps even farther back than that, to the hot-war days of World War II, to Army Military Intelligence and the OSS, the Office of Strategic Services, from whence came the company's founding fathers. When the CIA recruited Bennett Steelman in the mid-1950s, it was still operating under the legacy of that Old Guard. Men like William "Wild Bill" Donovan, Allen Dulles, William Sloane Coffin, Desmond FitzGerald, William Sullivan, William Bundy—the "gentlemen who did exciting things in the war."

They were also the men who nursed the company along in its toddler years and who had raised the child in their own highly refined images, men of impressive academic and social credentials, as fully respectable as the best people over at State, as the best people anywhere. The top agency officials of that era went to Andover or Exeter or Choate or Groton or Hotchkiss, matriculated with honors from Harvard or Yale or Princeton, served as officers in the First World War and with Military Intelligence or the OSS in the Second. They dressed conservatively, right up to the prep-school tie, knew all the best people, and were never at a loss as to which fork to use when there was more than one to choose from. They did not put family photographs on their desks, but pictures of their dogs or snapshots of themselves receiving a Best of Show award at Madison Square Garden. They set a tone and a standard for the nascent agency, and they decreed that recruits be as close to being younger versions of themselves as possible.

Steelman could not and would not deny that the company's *éminences grises* belonged to a special race, but he also knew he was not one of them. Ambassador Elliston Cave—Groton, Yale, and a former deputy director of the CIA—was one of them. Station chief Tom Scott—Choate, Harvard, the Harvard Russian Center—was one of them. Even poor besotted George Cameron—Boston Latin School, Harvard—was one of them, although Cameron had been derailed by coming to Vietnam too early and staying too late. For that matter, even the Vietnam station's most recent addition, Sally Teacher—the Madeira School, the Sorbonne, Georgetown—was one of them.

But Bennett Steelman was not one of them. He dressed the way they dressed, talked the way they talked, thought the way they thought; but he was not one of them. He had even taken their prejudices as his own, disdaining what they disdained, so he understood why he wasn't one of them. He even approved, so complete was his psychic assimilation. But it galled him nonetheless.

For Steelman there were no triumphs like Skull and Bones at Langley. He found himself relegated to the second tier, a level invariably made up of men who had just missed World War II and were in graduate school when recruited by the company. It was from this pool of bright young students, most of them specializing in the East European countries, that the CIA had plucked Bennett Steelman. And when the offer came, he had not hesitated. It was a time when anticommunism and the Cold War Crusade were still palatable on American college campuses, and the agency had no trouble getting the people it wanted.

"We had intelligent, committed young people," Steelman was fond of telling his younger agents, usually in the course of lamenting the precipitous drop in company standards. "The people who are now buying guns for the Black Panthers would have been helping us organize an underground in Albania back in those days."

Steelman was genuinely distressed at how drastically the quality had fallen off. By the mid-1960s, academia had turned on the CIA. To the brighter students, the CIA was a bogeyman who was suppressing nationalist aspirations around the globe. The traditional Harvard-Yale-Princeton recruiting base was gone and the new blood was coming from among the second-rate, but anticommunist, students at the University of Virginia or the Boston College Law School. These days, he thought with a trained curl of the lip, they were coming out of Ohio State.

In a way, he should have derived a certain satisfaction from the decline in standards; he was now a "true gentleman" when compared to the new proletariat, as good as the best of them now that the Old Guard was largely dead or retired. But he did not. He had nothing but contempt for most of the new people. Besides, the changes in the cast had done little to improve his own prospects.

He was thirty-seven years old and did not have a station of his own. After fifteen years with the company he was still off on a side track, a clandestine services officer of the DDP—coming under the Deputy Director, Plans—rather than an analyst of the DDI—Deputy Director, Intelligence. And it was to the DDI officers that most of the chief-of-station postings were going these days.

It hadn't always been that way. When he had first joined the company, and later, when he volunteered for the DDP, field agents were not held in the low esteem they were today. Until the early 1960s, the clandestine services were as good a path to the top as any other. Many of the field agents were former "Oh So-So," OSS men who had done bold things during the war, like parachute behind the Nazi lines to link up with Tito's Yugoslav partisan bands. They were cultivated, well-educated, physically daring men, and when the CIA got a promising new agent it did not dissuade him from going into operations if that was where his natural inclinations led him.

Bennett Steelman's natural inclinations pointed him more toward the drawing room than the gymnasium—he'd never been the physically courageous, athletic type—but clandestine services had appealed to him for a number of reasons. For one thing, there was a certain mental toughness to the operations officers that was lacking in the more squeamish analysts. It was that special sort of button-down, Brooks Brothers, L. L. Bean *machismo* that would soon infect Ivy League cold warriors like the Kennedys, the Bundys, Rostow, and McNamara. The ops officers of the DDP took a perverse pride in seeing the world as it was—from the trenches, not from ivory towers—and in knowing that they were capable of doing whatever had to be done.

Bennett Steelman was that kind of cold-eyed intelligence officer. There were no photographs of children or dogs in his office.

He had neither. Instead, on the wall behind his desk was a blown-up cartoon showing a Viet Cong soldier loading a spear into the trunk of an elephant while another VC soldier got ready to bash the elephant's testicles with a hammer.

But another, equally compelling reason for going with the DDP was that he had seen the favored few, those with old-boy sponsorship, being networked into the DDI, and thought the deck might be less stacked in the clandestine services, that there would be more room for maneuver and advancement.

He had been wrong. There had been no way to anticipate the agency's philosophical turn of the mid-sixties, one that saw the more promising people being channeled into analysis while the second-raters were shoveled into operations and used to do the company's dirty work. Behind the shift was an abiding faith in the new technology, a belief that the field agent would soon be rendered obsolete by electronic intelligence gathering. Only the analysts, who would be needed to collate and interpret the data, would survive. As with the Air Force and its dream of pilotless planes, the idea had proved to be premature at best, but that realization had not come in time to do Bennett Steelman much good. He was already in Vietnam, out in the provinces and far from the corridor career jockeying going on at Langley, when the company began to shift the emphasis away from DDP operations. By the time he twigged to what was happening, his experience and proven competence in the field were such that his request for transfer was rejected out of hand. Once again he had found himself stuck in the second tier through no fault of his own.

One reason that Steelman, who never let himself get too close to anyone, had taken such a special interest in Sally Teacher—aside from the obvious one, of course—was her ambition to work on the covert side of the fence. With her connections, evidenced by her very presence in Vietnam, she could easily have wangled a good starting spot in the DDI. He suspected that her primary motive for wanting operations was much the same as his had been years ago: that because of CIA prejudice—a lack of social credentials in his case, simple gender in hers—she would find the sledding easier in the DDP.

But Sally was the exception that proved the rule. Most of the young comers knew the score. Only a couple of days ago, Steelman had overheard a station analyst, one of the so-called "clean" agents, refer to the field operatives as "necessary scum." He had given the man a tongue-lashing, and might have done worse than that had he not agreed.

For the fact was that far too many of his field people were indeed necessary scum, limited-duration contract agents rather than career intelligence officers like himself. They were castoffs from unsavory, violent worlds—former city cops lured to Vietnam by the promise of fatter paychecks; retired military men who could not face going home when their tours were over; active-duty types, SEALS and Green Berets, assigned to the agency without a say in the matter, although few seemed to mind working for the "spooks" once they sampled the comforts of the embassy houses. They were the people who had made a joke of quality control; they were the infectious carriers of decline and decay, the unsightly rash that had covered the Central Intelligence Agency like jungle rot.

Steelman was just starting his second Vietnam tour when they began to show up in significant numbers, the result of a madcap hiring binge. It was 1965–66, a watershed period when the communists were threatening to cut South Vietnam in two, and the Johnson administration's decision to accelerate the American presence caught the CIA out of step, in the process of shifting away from covert operations. The agency, finding itself short of suddenly needed field hands, rushed to build the network of provincial embassy houses and to hire the necessary scum to set up and advise Phoenix. Steelman had watched with growing alarm and distress from his post in Nha Trang, never dreaming that within a couple of years he would be ringmaster of that particular circus.

He should have been content with the promotion to chief of operations, because he had not been particularly happy in Nha Trang, where, as Razor, he had done the company's dirtiest job and had kept its blackest secret. But he was not content. Because of the Vuong Affair, he knew that this promotion was the last. Besides, running a small band of assassins had been relatively straightforward and simple work, a breeze compared to trying to pull the company's chestnuts out of Phoenix's fire without burning his fingers.

The thought took him full circle, back to the fact still waiting to be faced: the Trung Affair. And back to a question still waiting to be answered: how was he going to handle it?

The flap over Trung couldn't have come at a worse time. He had big deals cooking. On March 10, only two weeks away, Cambodia's Prince Sihanouk would be deposed in a coup while on a visit to Paris and replaced by a group of generals led by Lon Nol. To coordinate support for the coup, Steelman had agents in the border town of Tinh Binh, the command post of bandit leader Son Ngoc Thanh and his CIA-backed Khmer Krom army. With a neutral Sihanouk out of the way, Cambodia could become a full partner in the war; allied forces could at last go in and clean out the sanctuaries. In fact, an invasion was set for May 1. Steelman had been working around the clock to collate, evaluate, and update pre-op intel being collected by his agent nets on both sides of the border. The Director and the President didn't want any surprises waiting for the lads.

With such entrées in the oven, the last thing Bennett Steelman, master chef, needed was a pot boiling over in the Delta because a couple of his apprentice cooks had turned the heat too high under a side dish like Trung. Yet in a single morning, from a single insignificant province, he had three reports, all saying something very different, yet all very much the same: all contained the ingredients for disaster.

There was Gulliver's report, unauthorized and unasked-for, sent without George Cameron's signature of approval. It was full of rumor and smoke, sound and fury, a compost of unsubstantiated speculation and reckless accusation, charging Swain, Bich, and Dang with torturing a guiltless man to death.

Then there was the province senior adviser's official report, prepared by Sloane and cosigned by Colonel Minh for emphasis. It concluded that Trung had been a VCI cadre—a signed confession was attached—and that he had died of a heart attack during routine questioning.

And finally there was the short but interesting report submitted by the agent he had assigned to watch the actress's house. This last one had nothing to do with the Trung Affair as far as Steelman could see, but in some indefinable way it was the most troubling of the three. A man in an ARVN uniform had been seen leaving the woman's apartment. It had been too dark to use the trick camera, but the agent had gotten a good look at the man's face. The agent had run through the picture file of suspected VCI cadre without finding a match. He then was shown photographs of key Phoenix program personnel, and quickly identified Quynh Nhu's visitor as Captain Dang.

Steelman could not say what Dang's visit to the alley might mean. He knew Dang was not the Embassy House leak. That puzzle, and the related mission failures, was already solved to his satisfaction. It was Gulliver. It had to be Gulliver. Young Riesz had been right—the cadre had been too tough to break—but Steelman did not need confirmation. He had the tailor's tapes. With his pillow talk the Sandman was, albeit unknowingly, feeding information to the actress, who passed it on to her VC comrades. The only reason he hadn't already moved against

Gulliver was that he knew his evidence had to be indisputable. After the Vuong Affair, his superiors were well aware of the enmity he felt for Captain Gulliver. If he were going to put the Sandman out of commission once and for all, he had to avoid any suggestion of a personal vendetta.

But how did Dang fit in? Could he be one of Quynh Nhu's comrades? Perhaps the mysterious contact Tho the tailor had heard? No; that didn't make sense. Why would Dang need her? He had access to the same intel Gulliver did. Also, Dang had entered and exited through the front door, and according to the tailor that had not been the modus operandi of her meets with her nocturnal visitor. Maybe Dang had merely been on an errand for Gulliver. Or maybe he was sleeping with the woman too. Everyone else seemed to be. Then why the bogus uniform? It was all very odd, Steelman thought; very odd indeed.

It might be odd, but unlike the matter of Trung, it was something he could look into right now. He punched a button on his intercom. "Eva, are you at your desk?"

The secretary's voice came back tinny and cheery. "I'm right here, Mr. Steelman."

"Check with Records and bring me what we have on a PRU captain named Dang working out of George Cameron's province house. And I want it ASAP."

"Yes, sir; right away."

It would take her ten minutes to chase down Dang's file, he estimated. As long as he had to wait, he told himself with a sigh, he should probably be mapping out an approach to the more pressing problem of Trung. It was hard to know where to begin; it always was when the facts were in dispute. He sat unmoving for a moment, then reached into a desk drawer for a pencil and sheet of paper, and began to doodle. He drew two boxes, numbered them, and in box number one jotted: "C.Y.A."

Cover your ass. An inelegant bit of popular terminology, Steelman thought, but a wonderfully descriptive one. He would have to be careful with this Trung business; his career could not absorb another close call.

But while the ruckus over Trung had great potential for harm, it also provided a great opportunity. Ambassador Cave and President Thieu had been briefed on the situation in the Delta and were concerned. They counted on the company to keep the lid on. If he could clean up the mess without any further escalation, Bennett Steelman would be back on the fast track, the Vuong damage undone. It would be both tricky and simple: if things worked out he had to be in position to take credit; if they didn't, he had to be able to lay off the blame.

In the second box he put down: "Sloane." He had decided to accept the PSA's report as the official statement of the facts.

Steelman's instincts told him that Gulliver's report, as long on guesswork and short on evidence as it was, might well be closer to the truth than Sloane's. He knew from experience that the Sandman had his own instincts and that they could be remarkably prescient in such matters. But Steelman would not pursue the notion, no matter how entertaining or enlightening it might prove to be. He was not interested in the truth. The fact was that he simply could not accept a scenario in which three company employees under his aegis wrongfully arrest a Vietnamese citizen and then torture him until he expires. The CIA did not need that kind of publicity at a time when it was disengaging from Phoenix because of that very sort of thing. Bennett Steelman IV did not need it either. He would ignore Gulliver's findings. Sloane and Minh had put their official seal of approval on a far more sanitary version of events. If there was any fallout later, let it fall on them.

At the same time, he thought he should probably send a man to the Delta to go through the motions of fact-finding, just to cover himself. It would show that he'd left no stone unturned in his pursuit of the truth. And the man he picked for the job would be one more buffer between himself and any unforeseen consequences. As though unbidden, independent of any conscious input from the brain, his fingers took up the pencil, drew a third box, and labeled it: "Teacher."

Only when the name was down did his brain seem to catch up with his hand. Well, why not? She was smart, she spoke the language, she knew their beliefs, and she had met many of the local leaders. He had promised her a play of her own; why not this one? If it went bad Langley wouldn't go too hard on her; after all, she was a woman and inexperienced. And if it went well, as he fully expected, it would be quite a coup for her. Sally would be grateful to him. Perhaps even *very* grateful.

He was thinking about how he was going to sell the idea to Scott when his secretary buzzed. "Mr. Steelman? I'm sorry, sir, but we don't seem to have any background material on anyone called Dang."

"That's quite impossible, old girl," Steelman said with great patience. "The man used to be a Viet Cong officer. At the very least there will be a debriefing file from when he came over to our side. It was a couple of years ago, I think. You can get the exact date by checking with Payroll."

"I checked with Payroll, sir. He's not on their books."

Steelman started to say something tart, then remembered the extra money Dang got for doing Minh's "specials" and the accounting trick that kept it from being traced back to the station. Dang's salary went straight to the province chief, who tacked on a bonus before passing it along. Steelman said: "Hmm, how odd. But the fact remains, he is a company contract employee. There must be something on him."

"Well, there are Mr. Seiple's charts from the technical interviews, and Mr. Cameron's performance-evaluation reports, of course. But that's all, sir. I looked everywhere."

"Then I suggest you look some more, old girl," Steelman said, his patience showing cracks. "There's a file. Find it."

"Y-yes, sir."

"And call my CIO counterpart and see what they have on him," Steelman added. The company's sister agency would have something. Thanks to CIA largess, the Central Intelligence Organization had the most modern mainframe computers, and an army of IBM technicians to advise them on their use.

Half an hour later a slender manila folder was on his desk. Steelman flipped it open and began to read. It didn't take long; there wasn't much. What there was came mostly from the Military Security Service which ran Chieu Hoi, the "open-arms" program which enticed communist soldiers to defect. The only personal background was contained in a summary of the interrogation sessions Dang had undergone when he first rallied to the government. It was the same skeletal story Gulliver had told—of fleeing south in 1954; of church schooling; of college in Saigon, America, and France; of his father's death at the hands of the Viet Cong.

All Dang had brought with him were his personal weapons, an M–16 he'd taken off a dead American, and a Chinese sidearm. That and the name and location of his unit. But when allied troops swept the area, they found nothing but cold campfires. As *hoi chanh* went, Dang had been pretty much of a bust.

Steelman picked up the next sheet and scanned the brief list of Dang's subsequent duty posts. His first job for his new government had been running Kit Carson Scouts for a U.S. infantry unit working near the Cambodian border. Steelman was just thinking that the assignment made good sense—it was the same area of operations Dang had worked as a Viet Cong troop commander, so he knew the AO better than anyone else—when he saw something that set off a bell, a carillon, in his head: the name of the district town where Dang and his scouts had been bivouacked. It was the same district town that had served as a forward operations base for the B–40 Detachment. Steelman quickly checked the dates. They matched. Dang had been on the border when things started to go bad with the B–40 agent net. He had been there at the time of the Vuong Affair.

Steelman leaned back and closed his eyes, the familiar eerie tingle spreading through him like a cramp. Coincidence? Perhaps. Probably. The disasters had ceased once Vuong had been removed. Then why this tingling feeling?

He looked back at the name he had written in the third box, doubt nagging him. Maybe he should look into the Trung thing himself. No! With the Cambodian show coming up he did not have time. Teacher could handle it. All she had to do was what he would tell her to do: go down to the Delta for two or three days to make it look good, sweet-talk the Hoa Hao, then rubber-stamp Sloane's report. The more he thought about it, the more convinced he became that the smart move would be to delegate the Trung Affair. Sally could tackle the job with a clear head, with no ghosts to get in her way.

As for him, he had to get a grip on his imagination and stop letting this obsession with Vuong-Trung parallels spook him to the point of phobia. He had been unnerved ever since learning of Trung's death, when his first thought had been to check on Gulliver's whereabouts during the hours Trung was in custody. According to his man in the alley, Gulliver had spent that night with his VC girlfriend. But instead of putting his mind at ease, that fact had only reinforced Steelman's sense of foreboding. As with the Vuong Affair, the Sandman was off at the edge of things, lurking in nearby shadows, there but not there. It was yet one more parallel.

Steelman knew his paranoia for what it was, but he did not dismiss it just because he recognized it. Paranoia could be healthy. If someone was out to get you, the paranoid was least likely to be caught by surprise. Besides, there *was* an unbroken line if one wanted to play connect-the-dots. Trung was fingered by the two Viet Cong women . . . who were arrested by Bich . . . who learned of their illegal operations from Tho the tailor . . . who got it from Quynh Nhu the actress . . . who was Gulliver's mistress. It did connect up, and surely that meant something, even if there was no discernible pattern when the dots were joined.

The antidote to confusion was decisiveness, so Steelman made a decision: he would send Sally down to the Delta. Maybe she would bring him back a key. There had to be one; if only because he needed one so badly. For in spite of the myriad possibilities, he had nothing that could be elevated to the status of fact. All he had now was coincidence, and Bennett Steelman did not believe in coincidence any more than he did in the truth.

17

A Beech, the same plane that had ferried Sally Teacher to the Delta on her first visit, was gassed and waiting for her at the Air America terminal. Both engines were revving, the chocks had been kicked out, and the pilot, looking down from the cockpit through Terry-and-the-Pirates sunglasses, was giving her the thumbs-up sign.

The air of urgency was infectious. She quickly boarded, helped up by her traveling companion, Duc Hoang, President Thieu's top political troubleshooter. When their luggage was aboard, the plane taxied quickly to the end of the runway. A moment later they were airborne.

The rushed departure was in keeping with the pace of the rest of the day. Sally was still in something of a daze. It had all happened so fast. One minute she'd been in her office plugging away at the daily station report and the next minute in a company plane banking south, crossing the Mekong River where it made a fat turn and began to fracture and splay in preparation for its web-footed kick at the sea.

Or so it had seemed. Actually, she'd had an hour to go home and pack and, before that, two hours of briefings in the COS's office; just her, Scott, Steelman, and Hoang. Ambassador Cave had been invited but hadn't shown up. The ambassador was trying to put as much distance between the State Department and the Hoa Hao problem as he could, Sally thought. As far as he was concerned, it was a mess of the CIA's making and the CIA could clean it up. He didn't want to know.

Doc Lap Palace was also looking to the company to make things right, but President Thieu did want to know—he *had* to know—and he had sent Duc Hoang along to make sure that the repair job met his specifications. Sally looked across at Hoang and found him looking back at her, an appreciative look in his eyes. A *Playboy* magazine was in his lap, open to the centerfold, and he glanced down at it, then back up at Sally.

Hoang was a handsome young man about her own age. He had a reputation as something of a roué. He had been educated in the States where he was said to have majored in bacchanals, but Sally had also heard that despite the rake image, he was a capable and savvy politician. She also knew President Thieu trusted him without reservation. Duc Hoang was not only the president's political counselor but also his nephew.

Hoang had been more of an observer than a participant at the strategy session, saying only that he wanted one thing understood from the beginning: under no circumstances would his uncle agree to dismantle the Phoenix program, not even in a single province. Scott and Steelman had showered him with swift assurances.

Scott, too, had been less than voluble, content to let Steelman emcee the show. Steelman had acted as though it was his right, not a privilege, taking charge with a surefooted confidence. He had started by giving them the background of the Trung Affair, reading aloud from the report prepared by Sloane and endorsed by Colonel Minh, and had concluded with a recommendation that both the embassy and the palace tough it out and concede nothing. Both governments should stick to the position that no crime had been committed by Phoenix program personnel.

Then he had offered a few more specific suggestions. The official line should be firm: Trung was a confessed enemy of the state, a communist, and while his death was unfortunate and regrettable, there was no evidence to back Hoa Hao claims of foul play. But the line should also be understanding: the authorities would conduct a thorough investigation into the affair, because there was no place for brutality in Phoenix. And it should leave the Hoa Hao with a vague hope and an even vaguer promise: if firm evidence of brutality were found, the guilty party would, of course, be severely punished.

Both Hoang and Scott had agreed to the recommendations, but Hoang had asked: "What if this approach does not work, Mr. Steelman? What if the demonstrations continue?"

"Then we give them someone to lynch," Steelman had said with a shrug. "This chap Dang, I think. He's an ex-communist, and he's the most expendable."

That was how they had left it; they would meet again to reassess the situation in two or three days, when Sally got back from the Delta.

Hoang was still appraising her with a connoisseur's eye, Sally saw. It made her uncomfortable. Maybe the form-fitting safari suit hadn't been such a wise choice.

"Will you be going with me to talk to the Hoa Hao, Mr. Hoang?" she asked.

Hoang gave her a glistening white smile, showing off a mouthful of caps, a souvenir of his time in the States. "All my American friends call me Duke, like John Wayne," he said. "But to answer your question: no. I have dealt with the Hoa Hao before and I am afraid they do not like me very much. My presence would only incite them. Besides, it is often useful to use an intermediary in these things—you Americans in this case. Then if there is a misunderstanding, we can blame you."

He laughed when he said this and Sally laughed with him, but she did not think it all that funny. "Then why are you tagging along?" she asked.

"I must confer with the province chief, to make sure he knows the president's wishes in this matter. Colonel Minh is an old friend of the family, you know." Hoang dazzled Sally with his dental work again and added: "Of course, the real reason is that it allows me to spend time alone with a lovely woman, a beautiful American spy."

Sally squirmed. "Um, well, this spy had better get going on her homework if she expects to keep on spying," she said, fumbling at the clasp of her briefcase.

Hoang laughed and said, "When I was at school, at Pitt, I used to cram for finals too."

Sally gave him a shallow smile and dug out her notes, leaving him alone with Miss February, Playmate of the month.

As she leafed through the material, Sally felt a sense of excitement, tempered with a twinge of apprehension. This assignment was a chance to show her stuff, to show them she was tough enough for Vietnam after all, and for that she was glad. At the same time, the job was a delicate one, calling more for experience than toughness, and despite her work on religious minorities, she was rather surprised they trusted her with it. But maybe that was the point, she thought with sudden suspicion. Maybe they expected her to fail, counted on her to fail. Then they could say, "You see, we told you so," and, with a clear conscience, leave her to do woman's work for the remainder of her tour, nothing more than an overpaid secretary who did the daily station report and typed up crib notes for the boss.

Compliment or curse, this assignment made her nervous. She had not felt this nervous since her fifth-grade school play, she thought—and regretted the comparison as soon as she made it. She saw herself standing alone and paralyzed on the stage, her simple lines as unutterable as Urdu, so many vanished wisps of smoke. Her tear ducts had voided first, then her bladder, the fluids flowing at both ends until a teacher came to snatch her to safety, away from the waves of silence and sniggering that had washed up from the seats below.

She cringed at the memory and admonished herself: enough nonsense; get to work. She skimmed through the files she had hastily thrown together that morning, her extensive notes on the Hoa Hao and the profiles of Bui Dinh and Nguyen Loc, the two men who, according to Sloane's report, were orchestrating the protests.

Nguyen Loc was the model of the leftist student leader, born into an upper-middle-class mandarin family, schooled in a French *lycée,* in revolt against his bourgeois background; he just as easily could have been a product of Berkeley or the Sorbonne.

Bui Dinh was another matter. Although the Hoa Hao had never found a true successor to Huynh Phu So, had instead become an allied band of factions, Dinh was as close to being the Living Buddha's heir as anyone. When So was killed, the spiritual leadership of the sect was assumed by his elderly and ailing mother, but her adviser—her high priest—was the monk Bui Dinh, and when she died he was there to fill in. Political leadership had been divided among the heads of the various factions, but there, too, Dinh appeared to be first among equals.

Sally was not sure—no one was—just when Bui Dinh had come into the picture, but he was there early, at So's side during that first year of the new religion. One story was that Dinh had been the protégé of the prophet's first teacher, Tra Son, and that the older bonze, knowing he was dying, had passed the tutelage of Huynh Phu So on to the younger monk. All Sally knew was that he had been around for as long as anyone could remember.

She had first come across his name years ago, in one of her Eastern religion courses at the Sorbonne, and here she was on her way to meet him. A little awed at the prospect, Sally did not know what to expect, but she had no doubt that the Hoa Hao objectives in the Trung Affair had little to do with Nguyen Khac

Trung himself. Bui Dinh would be looking to wrest more autonomy from Saigon. Using Trung's death to go after Phoenix was proof in itself; the Phoenix program was the government's most pervasive means of control. The Hoa Hao were too few in number—estimates ranged between one and two million—to realistically expect to gain the degree of independence they wanted, but if past was indeed prologue, the sect's history, and Bui Dinh's, told Sally they would never stop trying.

The pilot turned around in his seat and called down the aisle: "Buckle up, folks. We'll be on the ground in sixty seconds."

Sally put away her notes and saw Hoang do likewise with his randy daydreams, stuffing his *Playboy* into a monogrammed attaché case. A moment later the Beech touched down.

As they rolled toward the camouflage-painted Quonset hut that served as the terminal, Sally put her face close to the window and saw a Ford Bronco off to the side. Standing next to it was George Cameron, a smile of greeting already on his face.

Behind Cameron, a wink of white came from the shadows in the lee of the terminal building. Sally could make out that it was a man with white hair, squatting Vietnamese style in the shade, his back against the corrugated tin side of the Quonset hut. When he stood and stepped out into the fiery sunlight, blinking like a startled owl, she saw that it was Captain Gulliver.

"Sorry we're crowded, but when I laid on transportation I wasn't counting on there being this many of us," Cameron apologized as a QC waved the Bronco out through the aerodrome gate. "It wasn't until the last minute that I remembered we'd have to pass right through the funeral. So I asked Jake along to ride shotgun, just in case there's trouble."

"We're fine, George; really," Sally said. "As I recall, it's a fairly short ride to the villa."

Hoang stirred and asked: "Are you *expecting* trouble, Mr. Cameron?"

Cameron, squeezed between Sally and Hoang in the back seat, found room enough to shrug. "We don't really know, but our people inside the students' union say something's up."

Sally sat behind Gulliver, who was up front next to the driver. A bizarre-looking shotgun with a short flange-tipped barrel was planted between his feet. He had not spoken since she had gotten off the plane, not even to say hello. He faced the front, his eyes hidden behind mirror-lensed sunglasses.

Cameron chattered on, something about the meeting later that afternoon. He seemed to have aged since Sally last saw him. His color was that of a fever victim, and the tremor in his hands had grown noticeably worse. He was dripping sweat. Sally was feeling rather clammy herself; the Bronco's cooling system was broken and the windows were down.

Gulliver seemed the same to Sally, unchanged by recent events. He still resembled a piece of cracked, badly tanned leather. He had on sandals, Levi's, and a sleeveless sweatshirt emblazoned with an N.C. State wolf jauntily dressed in a red-and-white sweater with a blocked letter S. She could see the line of corded muscle running down his arms.

They heard the funeral before they saw it, a clangor of trumpets and drums and strings and reeds and screechy voices. A few streets farther on, the Bronco's passage was blocked by a human wall.

"Jesus Christ almighty," Cameron muttered. "I knew there would be a crowd but it's worse than I thought. We'll have to backtrack and try to find a way around it."

Duc Hoang was staring out at the throng with loathing and fear. "A good idea, Mr. Cameron," he said in a slightly shaky voice.

"Oh no, do we really have to?" Sally said, disappointed. "I've read about Vietnamese funerals but I've never actually seen one. Couldn't we get out and watch for a while? It looks fascinating."

Cameron shook his head. "I'm afraid hanging around here wouldn't be too smart, Sally," he said. "The townspeople know these Broncos. We're not too popular these days—today of all days. Just look at them. They're already starting to give us the evil eye."

Gulliver abruptly moved the duckbill shotgun to one side and opened the glove compartment. He took out a Browning 9mm pistol and tucked it into his waistband, hiding the butt under his sweatshirt, and said: "I'll stay with her if she wants to watch."

Cameron opened his mouth to protest but before he could get it out Sally said: "Why, thank you, Captain. That's very kind of you."

Gulliver turned around in his seat and looked at Hoang. "How about you, sir?" he asked. "Would you like to come?"

"Me? Oh, no, no," Hoang said quickly. "I have to talk to Saigon before our meeting. The palace is waiting for my call. It is important, very important."

Sally could not see Gulliver's eyes through the mirrored glasses, so she couldn't tell if they were laughing. Gulliver just nodded, then got out and opened Sally's door. He did not offer her a hand.

As the driver backed the Bronco out of the cul-de-sac, Cameron stuck his head out the window and called in a voice that got smaller and smaller: "Jake, be careful. Take good care of her. Sally, you do what Jake tells you. Okay? Okay?"

They stood on the perimeter of the crowd, conscious of being stared at. Some of the looks were hostile, some merely curious. Then Gulliver said, "Right. Let's go. Stay close," and strode off without looking back to see if she followed.

He led her across a crowded street and through a narrow alley, across another crowded street and down another alley, until at last they came out onto the mobbed main street, just in time to see the funeral's lead elements heave into view.

From the size of the procession and the number of people lining the curbs, it was obvious that the Widow Trung had not found it necessary, the way some did, to hire extra mourners to show that her husband had been held in high regard. It seemed to Sally as if every last one of the province town's 100,000 people was in the streets. Perhaps more, she thought, given the influx of out-of-town visitors. The funeral of Nguyen Khac Trung had become an object of pilgrimage.

Monks, both Hoa Hao and mainline Mahayana Buddhists in their brown and gray robes, led the long procession, some of them borne along in hammocks like ancient pharaohs, a sign of their exalted status. Behind the priests came a group of old women marching in rank across the width of the street, carrying a long ribbon of white cloth, the sign of mourning. And beside them, banner carriers held up proclamations of the deceased's virtues for all to read.

Next came an altar, also held aloft, holding photographs of the dead man, and peanut-oil lamps and flowers and incense burners and candlesticks. And following that, pallets laden with offerings: a whole roasted pig, cakes, gelatined fruits, urns of rice wine. Nguyen Khac Trung would not go hungry on his journey to heaven.

Sally was about to make the observation that it looked like a Roman circus when she saw the hearse and changed her mind; Gulliver might think she was being flip. The motorized hearse was not the usual plain black Vietnamese wagon but the kind used in Chinese funerals, ten feet high and covered with brightly painted dragons. Strolling alongside it were a dozen musicians who played a caterwauling tune that sounded like fingernails being drawn across a chalkboard. Nothing in her studies had prepared Sally for the mind-numbing noise, the explosion of color, the bittersweet aroma of food, flowers, incense, and body odor.

Gulliver bent over to yell into her ear, the same as a whisper in all the noise: "Trung."

Sally nodded. "He's wrapped in cloth strips and a white silk shroud," she said. "They usually wedge the body in with reeds and papers to keep it in place while it decomposes. The Vietnamese don't do much embalming." Gulliver straightened up and gave her a surprised look.

Sally didn't see it; she was staring, fascinated, at the cortege. Walking behind the festooned hearse was a contingent of people wearing loosely wrapped white turbans and tattered mourning garb made of low-grade white gauze which looked like it might fall off at any moment. They stumbled along behind the hearse like drunks, holding on to one another and leaning on stout bamboo rods to stay upright. They cried and shouted laments for the dead, loudly detailing his many virtues and accomplishments, and crying: "Why? O why have you left us?" Their voices, a chorus of pain, joined with the cacophonous, soulful dirge of the orchestra to dot Sally's bare arms with goosebumps.

Gulliver leaned down to put his mouth to her ear again. "That's the widow and other relatives and close friends," he said. "The torn dress and groping walk are supposed to show how overcome with grief they are."

"I know," Sally said, her eyes on the widow. The woman was as precariously dressed as the others, but she was not carrying on in the same deranged fashion. She was grim-faced but dry-eyed. Sally had just decided that it was the most beautiful face she'd ever seen when the weaving cluster of people rearranged itself to reveal one even lovelier. "Good God," Sally said. "Look at that beauty."

Gulliver followed her pointing finger with his eyes and sucked in sharply. After a pause he exhaled slowly and said: "Her name is Quynh Nhu. She's a Cai Luong actress." Then, as though anxious to change the subject, he said, "The dignified elderly gentleman behind her is Bui Dinh. He's the one you'll be dealing with."

The hearse was directly in front of them now and Sally dutifully studied Bui Dinh, a living footnote stepping from the bottom of a textbook page. But she could not concentrate; her eyes were drawn back to the actress, and she saw that Quynh Nhu was staring at Gulliver. As the cortege passed and moved on, Quynh Nhu turned again to look, straight at Sally this time.

"That actress was looking at us. Do you know her?" Sally asked Gulliver.

Gulliver shrugged. "I've seen her perform."

"Is she as talented as she is gorgeous?"

"Yes."

They stood at the curb for nearly an hour watching the procession unfurl. After the relatives and close friends came casual acquaintances, silent in comparison, exchanging quiet reminiscences of the deceased. Then, walking with the convoy of cyclos carrying flowers, came the hordes—merchants and peasants, young and old, Hoa Hao and Buddhist and Catholic, the hundreds who had not even heard of Nguyen Khac Trung a month ago but who now wanted to be a small part of his life, of his death. They sang and chanted and scattered petals and golden votive papers, symbolic money for Nguyen Khac Trung to spend in heaven's fine shops.

Behind them, last but loudest, marched several hundred more people. They too sang and chanted and carried banners, but the messages were political rather than spiritual. These were students, from universities as far away as Can Tho and Saigon, and out in front of them, waving a flag stamped with a reversed swastika—a Buddhist symbol long before the rise and fall of the Third Reich—marched a slight, animated young man who was clearly their leader.

"That's Nguyen Loc, isn't it?" Sally asked Gulliver, sure of the answer.

"Yep. Young Harry Hotspur himself," Gulliver said. "You can always tell where he is by the crowd around him. Look."

Sally looked and saw a school of Special Branch agents swimming around Loc like pilot fish. They were not bothering to mask their surveillance. They stuck cameras in Loc's face and talked urgently into hand-held radios. Nguyen Loc ignored them. He marched along backwards, pumping his standard like a drum major's baton, leading his followers in a rousing chant: *"Down with Phoenix! . . . Down with Phoenix! . . ."*

Gulliver took Sally's arm and said, "It wouldn't take much for this to turn nasty. We'd better go."

Reluctantly Sally let him lead her away, and when they were on a quieter street, said, "That was wonderful, Captain; thank you. How long will it take us to get to the cemetery?"

"We're not going to the cemetery. And you might as well call me Jake."

Sally looked at him archly. "What do you mean we're not going to the cemetery?"

"Just what I said. We're not going. I have to get you to the Embassy House."

"I want to see the funeral, Captain," Sally said firmly.

"Cameron will be getting worried."

"Please . . . Jake."

His eyes, neither blue nor gray but some indescribable hybrid color, were on her face. Then they drifted, dilating like a camera's aperture. Sally was suddenly aware that her perspiration-soaked shirt was plastered to her body and that she was not wearing a brassiere. She was about to blush, but Gulliver beat her to it.

"What the hell," he said in a husky voice. "If that's what you want, I guess we've got time. Wait here a minute." He walked off and was back a minute later with a motorized cyclo.

They made the trip to the cemetery in awkward silence, holding on tightly in the turns in a futile effort to keep from being jostled together in the cramped seat. Sally could feel his thigh, hard as a marble statue's, against hers.

They took side streets, avoiding the roads that had been blocked off to accommodate the procession, finally pulling up to the cemetery's rear gate. The crowd was thick, and to make sure of a return ride, Gulliver promised their driver triple the fare if he would wait for them. Then he and Sally began inching their way through the press of mourners, trying to get as close to the grave as they could, homing on the sound of wailing and crying.

They made it to the gravesite just as the coffin was being lowered, in time to see the relatives of Nguyen Khac Trung struggling with the casket handlers, trying to prevent them from burying their loved one. Nguyen Thi Mai, her mask of reserve finally jettisoned, was right in the thick of it, sobbing and hammering her fists against the chest of an attendant. It was all part of the ritual, Sally knew; a show of Mai's unwillingness to accept the death of her husband.

When a semblance of order had been restored, Sally saw a boy of about twelve toss a handful of dirt into the grave and step back, his chin trembling but his eyes manfully dry. That would be Trung's eldest son. Then the monk, Bui Dinh, threw a handful of dirt into the grave and went to give his respects to both the boy and his mother. The remaining relatives did the same, and the mass of onlookers began to move away from the hole that had swallowed their hero, giving his family and special friends a rare moment of privacy in what had been a long and most public day.

Gulliver was guiding Sally away from the grave when an old woman stuck her gnarled face close to his, then backed away and shouted: "I know you! You work for the killers! I know you!" She turned to those nearest to her and repeated loudly, "I know this American. He works for the killers!"

"You cannot know me, sister. I have never been to the Cau Mau

Peninsula," Gulliver said, taking a guess at the accent, keeping an eye on the meaner-looking men as people began to crowd close.

"Ha!" the old woman cackled. "You Americans do not know everything? I left the Cau Mau when I was a young girl, many years ago. Now I sell noodles just outside your walled fort. I have seen you many, many times. You live at the house where Nguyen Khac Trung was murdered. Oh yes, I know you!"

"Just keep cool and keep walking," Gulliver whispered to Sally. He turned to the old woman and said calmly, "We have come to pay our respects to Nguyen Khac Trung, sister; same as you."

"Ha! You have come to gloat!" She turned to her audience and crowed: "He comes to gloat! He comes to gloat! He has put Nguyen Khac Trung in the grave and he comes to gloat!"

The crowd around them, grown larger and more hostile, closed the circle, blocking the path. Gulliver kept his face calm, as if nothing were wrong, and said in English to Sally: "If anything starts, stay out of it. Get back to the cyclo and get the hell out of here. Understand?"

"Y-yes."

The murmur of the crowd grew louder and a few individual voices, shrill and fevered, could be heard above the rumbling hum.

"Killer!"

"Foreign devil!"

"Get him!"

Several of the men who had carried signs in the funeral procession looked ready for action; they were gripping their placard sticks like bats and sneaking sidelong glances at one another, waiting for someone to make the first move. Several others had begun to work their way around the circle, which was now unbroken and several people deep, trying to get into position behind Gulliver.

Sally moved closer to Gulliver, almost molding herself to his side, and felt his left arm slip protectively around her waist. She glanced at his face and almost stepped back; it looked like a skull mask, as shiny and hard as yellowed bone. Only his eyes moved, tracking the circling men.

One of the men to their front took a step toward them and Sally felt Gulliver's body tense—a wave she could feel ripple along her own side—and saw his right hand inching for the pistol in his waistband. He was just reaching under his sweatshirt when a booming voice cut through the crowd's angry muttering: "Enough! Enough of this!"

The crowd parted and Bui Dinh, his face furious and his spidery goatee quivering, stepped into the circle. "What is happening here?" he demanded to know.

No one spoke and the monk scanned faces, searching for a ringleader. "Do you people know who I am?" he asked of no one in particular. Heads bobbed up and down.

"Then answer my question. What is going on here?"

A man spoke up, his voice uncertain. "This American is one of the men who killed our martyr."

Bui Dinh gave the man a scathing look and said, "I know this man, and you do him a great injustice. He did not kill Nguyen Khac Trung. He is a friend of Nguyen Khac Trung, whom you also insult with your hysterical accusations."

"But—"

"Quiet, idiot! Get out of his way! Go home, all of you!"

They could not comply fast enough. Many of those at the edge of the circle had already slunk away and now the others almost trampled one another in a rush to follow suit.

Gulliver watched them scatter, then said: "There go some very surprised people. Thank you."

Bui Dinh smiled and, with a glance at Sally, replied in English, "I too am surprised, Captain Gulliver. I would not have thought you so foolish as to come here today."

"It's my fault," Sally said in Vietnamese. "I wanted to see the ceremony and I asked Captain Gulliver to bring me."

"It is a day full of surprises," Dinh said to Gulliver. "Who is this pretty child who speaks our language so well?"

Gulliver, who was staring at Sally, wondered. He had not known that she spoke Vietnamese. "Uh, this is Miss Teacher of the United States embassy in Saigon. Sally, may I present the venerable Bui Dinh of An Giang province?"

Instinctively Sally started to stick out her hand, then quickly pulled it back and gave the bonze an abbreviated bow. He returned it with one of his own, a bemused nod.

"Miss Teacher has come from Saigon specifically to meet you," Gulliver said, "but I'm sure she didn't expect to do so under these circumstances." When he saw the puzzled look on the monk's face, Gulliver added: "She will be representing the United States government in the talks concerning Nguyen Khac Trung."

If Bui Dinh was surprised that the Americans would send a woman to represent them, he did not show it. Aside from a slight widening of the eyes, he made no visible reaction to Gulliver's news.

"Ah, then we shall be seeing each other again tomorrow morning," Bui Dinh said to Sally with another truncated bow. "A meeting has been scheduled for ten o'clock at the home of Nguyen Thi Mai. Now I must return to her; she is suffering much distress. I will look forward to our next meeting, Miss Teacher."

They said good-bye and Dinh started back to the grave, moving slowly and cautiously up the grassy slope, leaning on his mourner's walking stick as though he really needed it.

"What a perfectly marvelous old man," Sally said as she and Gulliver walked back to where their cyclo waited. "I like him!"

"I like him too," Gulliver said, "but I don't trust him. And you'd better not either. If you start thinking of him as an old man, or as some kind of grandfather figure, he's going to eat you for breakfast tomorrow."

"Why, thank you for the vote of confidence, Captain," she said, smiling sweetly.

He smiled back and was about to say something, when a figure jumped out at them from behind a nearby tree. It was the old woman. She glared at them for a moment, wagged a bony finger at Gulliver, and took off running, her skinny elbows and knees pumping, cackling to herself.

The cyclo driver, humming contentedly, already assured of a profitable day, was taking his time on the return trip, slowly threading his way through the homebound funeralgoers. Sally, exhilarated but feeling drained, slumped in her corner of the open cab, savoring the prospect of a hot bath before the Embassy House meeting. She needed a nice long soak.

The thought of the meeting depressed her. "Wouldn't it be nice if the problem could have been buried with the man?" she asked with a sigh, more of herself than of Gulliver.

Gulliver smiled at her, showing straight white teeth, which looked even whiter because of the ocherous cast of his skin. When he smiled he seemed almost human, Sally thought, not at all the professional killer.

The way to the Embassy House took them back through the center of town. The streets were not as crowded as they had been, but they were still full of people. The cyclo was just picking up speed on the wide main street, a block from where Sally and Gulliver had watched the funeral procession, when a billowy white cloud came rolling down the boulevard at them like the forward wall of an avalanche.

"GAS! TURN HERE!" Gulliver yelled in English. The driver missed the turn and continued on a collision course with the ghostly fog. He was slack-jawed with paralysis, incapable of heeding Gulliver's barked command even if he'd understood it.

Gulliver yelled again, in Vietnamese this time: "NGUNG LAI!" Stop! The driver reacted instinctively, and the cyclo fishtailed to a halt.

Gulliver pulled Sally out roughly and herded her toward the mouth of a narrow alley in the middle of the block. The cloud was thirty yards away now and people were running out of it toward them, materializing like ghouls, coughing and clawing at their eyes. Right behind them came a squad of soldiers in blue berets, matching blue scarves, and black gas masks: National Police Field Force—Major Ngoc's Mod Squad.

As he hustled her toward the alley, Gulliver's fingers dug into Sally's upper arm like the teeth of an animal trap. She struggled against his grip, trying to get free, lodging an outraged complaint: "Let go of me! You're hurting my . . . !"

Out of the corner of her eye she saw the soldiers drop to one knee, level their rifles, and fire in volley. Four of the running figures fell. The troops fired a second time and two more people fell. Just before Gulliver dragged her around the corner and into the alley, she saw their cyclo driver running toward them. She was looking right into the man's terrified face, barely ten yards away, when his head seemed to swell to twice its normal size and fly apart in a pink spume, like a melon dropped on a sidewalk. All Sally could think of was that they had to go back, that the driver was being cheated; they had not paid him his fare.

She was sobbing and shaking when they came out the other side of the alley into a connecting street. Gulliver had an arm around her shoulders and was crooning: "Take it easy now. Easy now. It's all right."

"They shot them. They shot those people. Our driver . . ."

He kept on gentling her, stroking her hair. "I know, I know. Easy now. It's all right. Just hang on to me. We'll be all right. I'll get you out of here."

They were in a wide but short street, only a block long, with nothing moving on it. Both sidewalks were lined with the familiar two-story pastel buildings, apartments over street-level shops that sold everything from tripe to plastic shoes. Most of the shops were closed and shuttered. The funeral had closed down the town as effectively as a national holiday.

Gulliver paused, unsure of which way to go. The sounds of the riot were all around them, ricocheting off buildings like an echo off a canyon's walls. They could hear shouts and screams and more gunshots, but it was impossible to say where the noise was coming from or which of the streets at the ends of the block would lead them to safety.

A moment later it no longer mattered. Twin rivers of humanity sluiced into the short street from both directions, with Major Ngoc's Field Force police in hot pursuit. These troops were more sensibly outfitted than their blue-bereted brothers; they wore helmets fitted with plastic face-guards and carried truncheons instead of M–16s.

It wasn't until they met in the middle of the block that the two herds of stampeding people realized they were boxed in, trapped. When they did, their panic burst its seams. Some turned and tried to dash back through the cordon of soldiers, only to be clubbed down. Some spied the alley that Sally and Gulliver had used. They made for it *en masse*, stacking up at the narrow entrance and clogging it. Then that escape hatch, too, closed; more soldiers were coming up the alley from the other end. From every direction people were being pushed into the middle of the block by converging lines of club-swinging police, fused into one writhing, howling ball. They fought each other now, trying to punch a way out of the smothering press, trampling the young and the old and the infirm.

The screaming was dreadful, a soundtrack of hell that numbed Sally's senses. All she could feel were Gulliver's arms, as tight as a cooper's stays as he pinned her against the wall of a shop. Peering around him, Sally could see four policemen beating a student, their clubs rising and falling, rising and falling in syncopated rhythm. The young man lay at their booted feet, rag-bodied and unmoving, a doll that had lost its stuffing. The policemen continued to beat him long after he was dead.

A few yards away another policeman was clubbing a boy of about ten. The unconscious boy looked as if he were sleeping. He lay curled in a ball, his skinny knees pulled up to his chest, his palms pressed together to make a pillow between his cheek and the pavement. The child's mother pushed out of the crowd with a shriek and fell across her prostrate son, trying to shield him, but the policeman's arm continued up and down like a piston. The woman raised her arm to cushion the blows and Sally heard the crisp, clean sound of breaking bone.

Then the painful, yet comforting pressure of Gulliver's body was suddenly gone. Sally heard him bellow like a wounded animal as he threw her aside and rushed the soldier. He aimed a savage kick between the policeman's legs from behind. The soldier dropped his club and grabbed his genitals, staggering and turning. Gulliver's fingers, bunched like talons, jabbed the man's throat, going in just under the plastic face-guard. The soldier sprawled alongside the boy, as unconscious as his young victim.

Gulliver rolled the bleeding mother away and bent over the child. He checked for a pulse, then began to administer mouth-to-mouth resuscitation.

The four nearby policemen had seen Gulliver's attack on their comrade and they left off beating the student and came to help. "He's American!" Sally yelled at them in Vietnamese, thinking it would matter somehow, that the mere fact of U.S. citizenship was a passport to inviolability. By the time she realized differently, the lead man was only a step away from Gulliver, his truncheon raised. She yelled again, in English: "Jake, behind you!"

Her warning proved unnecessary. Gulliver's arms whipped around viciously, swinging the downed policeman's truncheon as though it was a Louisville Slugger. It caught the attacker across the knees, shattering both caps, and he dropped with a scream. A second man swung, and Gulliver, coming to his feet, got his club up in time to parry. Sally saw the impact knock the club from Gulliver's grip, saw his empty hand rise and fall like a broadsword in a flat chop that landed where the neck joined the shoulder. The second man dropped his club. Gulliver's hand blurred again, splintering the policeman's Lucite face-guard into his nose.

Sally screamed as the two remaining, undamaged men swung their clubs at Gulliver. One vicious swipe grazed the side of his head; the other struck him flush on the bicep. Sally saw Gulliver, his head bleeding, fall and roll away, only to come up on one knee a few yards away just out of their reach, both arms extended. His stalkers stopped in mid-step, stunned to find themselves looking down the bore of the Browning. In concert, they dropped their billies and fled.

Sally ran to him. His face had lost its amber tint; it had gone the same chalky color as his hair and eyes, making him look more than ever like an albino. She hooked her hands in his armpits, trying to help him stand. He brushed her off and scrambled on all fours back to the boy and his mother, who sat spraddle-legged in the street, rocking her son, already singing a lament. Gulliver snatched the child from her, laid him out flat, and resumed mouth-to-mouth resuscitation.

A few seconds later he paused and said, "Sally, get over here and hold his nostrils closed. My other arm's numb where that bastard hit me."

She knelt and pinched the child's nose while Gulliver tried to blow life back into the small motionless body. She kept her head up and her eyes straight, unable to look at the boy's waxy pallor. She saw that the street was nearly empty, and remembered being vaguely aware that even as Gulliver had fought off his attackers, the townspeople were doing much the same. They had rushed the police lines and broken through, to scatter, the club-crazy troops giving chase.

Gulliver labored over the child for five minutes before there was a stir, then a piercing cry.

"Oi!" The mother grabbed Gulliver's hand and started to knead it. He pulled it away and said: "He will live, sister, but he must get to a hospital. You too; your arm is broken."

Just then a cyclo careened around a corner and rocketed up the street toward them. Gulliver jumped squarely into its path, drawing the Browning and pointing it at the driver. The front sight danced at the end of his arm, even though he held the pistol with both hands. The cyclo screeched to a stop and Gulliver ordered the driver to load the mother and child and take them to the hospital.

By the time the cyclo was out of sight, Gulliver's hands were shaking so badly that he dropped the pistol. He got down on his hands and knees to retrieve it . . . and stayed there, too weak to stand by himself. Sally helped him up, and this time he did not object.

Sally was alarmed at Gulliver's condition. His ear was badly torn where the policeman's club had sideswiped it. The lower portion of the lobe dangled by a thin strip of skin. If the blow had been flush, Sally realized, it would have caved in his skull. She forced herself to look at it, fighting back nausea, and said, "We have to get you to a hospital."

"It's not serious," he said, breathing harshly. With a wince he hiked up his shirt and she saw a large bloodstain, soaking a bandage around his middle.

"Oh dear God," Sally said, feeling helpless, not knowing what to do. "The soldiers have gone. We can get out now. I'll take you to the hospital."

Gulliver shook his head. "They'll be too busy for the likes of me. I've just reopened my stitches. A needle and thread and a new dressing and I'll be okay."

"But—"

"I'll be okay," he said again. "I know a place we can go and clean up. A friend's house, not far from here. C'mon."

Gulliver led her down the street, going slowly but not leaning on her. She held on to his arm and thought: This is what a battlefield must look like. The block was a mess. Shop windows were broken, the goods scattered in the street along with more personal debris: pieces of torn clothing, shoes, banners, musical instruments. She even saw a set of dentures lying in the street, open in a hideous grin.

And, of course, there were the bodies. Sally saw three in all, awkward and still, trousers soiled where bladders and bowels had voided. They all looked to be young men, students, selected targets. Half a dozen wounded were also still about, sitting on curbs in shock or propped against walls, cradling their injuries, crying silently to themselves.

Gulliver, too, was surveying the carnage, cursing under his breath. He suddenly changed course and began going up and down the street, stopping at each of the casualties, making sure the dead were dead, checking on the injured. He kept one hand pressed to the tear in his side, but blood oozed through his fingers. Sally could see he was getting woozy and at last she insisted they go somewhere where he could be cared for. He gave in, too weak to argue.

Stopping every twenty-five yards or so to rest, Gulliver took her through the alley back to the main street, up three blocks and down another long alley that was crowded with food carts and refugees. There were more riot victims there, laid out on sleeping mats, being tended to. It was clear that the violence had not been limited to the block where Sally and Gulliver had been trapped; it seemed to have swept through the whole of the city center.

They carefully picked their way through the cries and whimperings until they came to a door at the far end of the alley. Gulliver leaned against it for a second to catch his breath, then knocked. Sally was surprised when the actress, Quynh Nhu, answered.

Quynh Nhu seemed no less surprised. She gasped, then exclaimed in a melodious voice: "*Anh* Jake!"

The actress took a step toward Gulliver, then noticed the dangling earlobe and the bloodstained hand at his side and drew back in horror. "*Troi oi!*" she cried. "Quick! Come inside! Dr. Loan is here." She took one of his arms, Sally the other, and together they helped him in.

There were two other people already in the front room. One was Dr. Loan, Sally's host of two weeks before. He had a roll of gauze in one hand and a roll of adhesive tape in the other and was leaning over a young man whose face was smeared with dried blood.

"Doctor, we have another injured man here," Quynh Nhu called. Dr. Loan turned, saw Sally, and started to smile with surprise and recognition. Then he saw Gulliver, whom he also recognized from the meeting in Colonel Minh's office. He gave Quynh Nhu a questioning look, and she volunteered, somewhat defensively Sally thought: "He is a friend."

Working quickly, Loan finished bandaging the young man's head, then dug into his medical bag for a curved needle and a spool of surgical thread and started on Gulliver. He cut away Gulliver's shirt, cleaned and closed the rip in his side, and put on a fresh bandage. Then he went to work on the ear.

Sally watched the doctor tend to Gulliver while Quynh Nhu went into the back of the house and returned with a wet cloth. It was only when the actress had washed off the young man's bloody face that Sally saw who it was: the same young man who'd marched at the head of the students in the funeral procession—Nguyen Loc.

Quynh Nhu had also brought back a small packet of pills. When she finished with Loc she came over to Gulliver's chair and slipped a few of the pills into his mouth.

"What are those?" Dr. Loan asked as he finished taping Gulliver's ear.

"Painkillers," Gulliver answered.

The doctor took the packet from the actress and examined its contents. One knowing eyebrow shifted. "Tell me, Captain, do you take these, ah . . . *painkillers* . . . often?"

Gulliver shrugged and winced and muttered in English, "As often as I need to, Doc . . . as often as I need to."

Quynh Nhu retrieved the packet and changed the subject, saying: "Your friend is quite beautiful, *Anh* Jake. She is the ideal American woman, is she not, with her light hair and big breasts? Who is she? The wife you neglected to mention?"

Gulliver chuckled. "No. And if you don't believe me, you can ask her yourself. She speaks Vietnamese."

"Troi oi!" Nhu flushed and turned to Sally. "I am sorry. I did not mean to be rude. Please accept my apology."

Sally was blushing too. "I heard only a compliment," she said diplomatically. "My name is Sally Teacher. I work in the American embassy in Saigon. Captain Gulliver and I are merely professional acquaintances. We hardly know each other."

"I saw you earlier, in the street," Nhu said. "I thought you were very beautiful."

"I saw you too," said Sally. "And I thought *you* were very beautiful."

Gulliver laughed and said to Loan: "They are both very beautiful, but maybe you should sew their mouths shut before they drown each other with compliments."

Dr. Loan smiled hesitantly, unsure of Occidental humor, further confused when Gulliver abruptly turned serious to ask: "Is Loc badly hurt?"

Loan looked at Loc, who slumped on the settee with his eyes closed. "No. A minor concussion and a cut on the head is all," he said. "It bled freely but did no real damage. He was very fortunate. They tried to kill him."

"Do you believe that?"

"Yes," Loan said emphatically.

"It's the truth," said Nhu. "That is how it began. The Field Force soldiers came in two trucks. They went straight for Nguyen Loc and began to beat him. If the other students had not distracted them by throwing stones, they would have killed him. He managed to get away in the confusion."

"I see," said Gulliver. "So they took their frustration out on the other students."

Loan nodded. "Yes. Many more trucks full of policemen came. They were like wild beasts. They attacked everyone, not just students. There are rumors that they used guns, that they shot some people."

"It is not a rumor, it is a fact," Sally said with a shudder, remembering how the driver's head had swelled and exploded. "We saw it."

Gulliver, obviously more peppy since Nhu had given him the pills, looked over Dr. Loan's shoulder at Loc and asked, "How did he happen to end up here?"

"I found him on the street and brought him here," Loan said. "I knew Quynh Nhu lived nearby."

When Gulliver looked puzzled, Loan elaborated: "*Co* Nhu has become a friend in recent weeks; ever since she began to help us in our cause."

Gulliver nodded and looked back at Loc. "Are you sure he's all right? He looks unconscious."

"A slight case of shock," said Dr. Loan. "He wanted to go back into the streets. He kept insisting that a leader's place was at the head of his followers."

"Yes, I can just hear him," Gulliver said bitterly. "I'm sure he is enjoying himself despite the discomfort; or maybe because of it. When one is his age and has a righteous cause, it all seems so important, so romantic. What are a few bumps on the head? What are a few bodies in the street?"

"Do not make fun," Nhu admonished. "People have died."

"Would they have died if Loc had kept the students off the streets, as he promised Colonel Minh he would? It was supposed to be a funeral, not a political rally."

"All promises were canceled when Minh rejected the Hoa Hao demands," Loan said heatedly. "You were at that meeting, Captain. You know the way it ended."

At the mention of a meeting, Sally caught Gulliver's eye.

"We must go," he said, standing gingerly, testing his side. He gave Loan a nod. "It feels fine; you do good work."

Loan just glanced at the pill packet in Nhu's hand and grunted.

Gulliver said, "Send me your bill. And make it large; I plan to pass it on to Major Ngoc."

Dr. Loan smiled grimly, then said: "Come, I will walk you to the street. My driver can take you to your villa. I must stay with young Loc."

Sally and Gulliver said their thanks and good-byes. As they left, Sally told Nhu: "I hope we meet again. I would very much like to see you perform. I've never seen the Cai Luong."

"Then you must come as my guest," Nhu said. Then, rather wistfully, she added, "When this terrible trouble is over."

Dr. Loan's car was an ancient, roomy Citroën saloon, the kind that brought to mind a 1930s gangland getaway car, with sweeping fender skirts, long running boards, and a hole in the grille for emergency crank starts. Sally and Gulliver melted into the luxurious upholstery of the wide back seat, suddenly and utterly exhausted.

Dusk was coming on and the streets of the province town were empty and quiet now. They made the trip without talking, each alone with his own thoughts, tucked into corners that seemed miles apart after the tight squeeze of a cyclo.

The Citroën was stopped at the Embassy House gate, being cleared by the Nung sentry, when a figure materialized from the evening shadows, coming from among the soup stands that plied their wares just outside the compound wall. A wrinkled face, gap-toothed and betel-gummed, loomed at the window, and as the chauffeur drove through the gate, his passengers heard a demented cackle drifting after them: "I know you! Oh yes, I know you! Ha!"

18

THE EMBASSY HOUSE, as isolated as an offshore lighthouse behind its walls and wire, did not know exactly what had gone on in town beyond a report that shots had been heard, but the Nung garrison, taking no chances, was at battle stations.

The tower searchlights came on one by one as the Citroën pulled up to the villa to drop its passengers. Gulliver could see extra gunners in the blockhouses and troops at the firing posts as he led Sally up the steps and past a detail of Nungs who were stacking sandbags on the porch. He took her through the common room, past the bar where Swain sat drinking away another idle day, and straight in to see Cameron, wanting to put the man's mind at ease—only to find that he and Sally had been the least of the P officer's worries.

All Cameron said when he saw them in his doorway was: "Oh, Jake, Sally, you're back." Then, more in afterthought than curiosity, he inquired: "What happened to your ear?"

"We had a little trouble," Gulliver said.

"Who hasn't?" Cameron groaned. "I've spent the last two hours on the Diamond Net holding Saigon's hand. That goddamn Steelman keeps demanding to know what's going on, and I keep telling him I can't find out if I'm stuck in the radio room. The man needs a saliva test." He winced and looked anxiously at Sally, immediately regretting the indiscretion.

"So? Did you find out?" Gulliver asked.

"Coughlin and Riesz got on the phones and fed me bits and pieces. It seems Ngoc's boys went berserk and tore into the students when they wouldn't disperse. Ngoc himself gave the order. It was pretty bad out there."

"We know. We had box seats," Gulliver said, noticing Cameron's eyes drift to the drawer where he kept his bottle. He knew Cameron was torn between need and fear of what Sally Teacher might report back to Steelman.

Cameron sighed and said: "Luckily for us it was Ngoc's people and not Do's. We're not responsible for Field Force. CORDS and MACV can go to the wall for this one."

"It's all part of the Trung problem, and that makes it our problem," Gulliver reminded him. "Have the Hoa Hao been heard from yet?"

The P officer let out another long sigh. "Only hourly. That Mad Monk character you find so colorful has been camped out on Minh's doorstep at provincial HQ. I'm sure we'll hear all about it at the meeting."

"When is the meeting?" Sally asked, her voice still a little shaky. "Do I have time to take a bath?"

"We won't start until the province chief can get here," Cameron said. "We were planning to hold it in his office but Mr. Hoang insists that we have it here. The way things are, he's not too keen to make a thunder-run through the streets. It'll be another hour at least. Go ahead and take your bath."

"I will. I need it," said Sally. "By the way, where *is* Mr. Hoang?"

"In the radio room consulting with the palace," Cameron said. "Stirring up more trouble for me, no doubt."

As he and Sally left, Gulliver saw Cameron reach for the desk drawer.

An hour later they were back for the meeting, Sally fresh and clean and smelling of rosewater, Gulliver still filthy and smelling of freshly dried sweat. He had thrown on a clean T-shirt, but that was all he'd had time for. While Sally had been soaking in her tub, he had been helping Dang break up another fight in the PRU barrack, the second in as many weeks. This one had not been nearly as bad as the first and they had put it down quickly, before it could really get going, but it still disturbed him. It had been three weeks since the ambush on Nui Giai Mountain, and almost that long since the PRU had last been out on any pretext; the men were going stir crazy, becoming as unpredictable as tigers in a trap—and as dangerous.

The distemper among the PRUs merely reflected the temper of

the Embassy House as a whole, Gulliver thought; the temper of the whole town, for that matter. Everyone was on edge. And for good reason. It had been one goddamn thing after another: the leak that told the VC when and where to pop their ambush; the suspicious deaths of the two VC women; the mishandling of the Trung arrest; the leak that gave the Hoa Hao the names of Trung's interrogators.

Gulliver even thought he saw a connection—a tenuous one, perhaps, but a connection all the same—between the ambush and Trung's death. The viciousness that Dang and Swain had shown in their interrogation was no doubt at least partly due to the lingering frustration over the ambush and the loss of twenty good men.

Gulliver looked around the room and counted heads. He got six including his own: Sally, Cameron, Hoang, Sloane, and Minh. Majors Ngoc and Do were supposed to have been there but were not. Major Do was still at his desk at Special Branch; at last report the town was quiet, and he wanted to keep it that way. Major Ngoc was in hiding.

The one positive note in the whole mess, Gulliver told himself as he watched Minh shoehorn his improbable bulk into Cameron's chair, was that when Cameron had restricted Dang and the rest of the PRUs to barracks, he had effectively put a moratorium on Medium Minh's "specials." The province chief's business had to be suffering.

For the moment, Minh did not seem unduly concerned. He used one fat fist to gavel the meeting to order, then turned his sparkling smile on the president's nephew. "Mr. Duc Hoang he work for president, so he go first," he said, establishing a langauge for the rest of the meeting by using English to begin it. It put him at a slight disadvantage, but it made things easier for Colonel Sloane, and the province chief was relying on his counterpart to join him in showing the palace a united front.

Hoang stood. "I bring you the president's greetings," he said. "I also bring his instructions. I can be brief, because they are simple."

Both Duc Hoang's English and his smile were better than the province chief's, thanks to the University of Pittsburgh and to Dr. Morris Saperstein, DDS, of suburban Upper St. Clair. He showed them Dr. Saperstein's fine work once more before going on: "The president does not want to have to send in the Army to keep the peace. He trusts you local officials to find a solution to the trouble here. In doing so, you will have to work from two premises. One: the government does not want to upset the working relationship it enjoys with the Hoa Hao, so we know that some compromise will be inevitable. Two: tampering with Phung Hoang cannot be part of that compromise. It is not an option. We realize that Phoenix is not popular with many of the people, but it is our most effective means of combating the communists' subversive political apparatus; what you American friends call the Viet Cong infrastructure. If we were to dismantle Phung Hoang here, troublemakers in the other provinces would quickly agitate for the same thing. The president cannot and will not permit this to happen. Do you all understand?"

Heads bobbed. Duc Hoang said, "Excellent! That is all I have to tell you," and sat down.

"Thank you, Mr. Hoang," Minh oozed. "Now we hear Miss Teacher of the American embassy."

Sally said: "My embassy agrees with Mr. Hoang. While we must do everything possible to avoid a split between the Hoa Hao and President Thieu's government, we must not tamper with Phoenix." She looked at Minh. "But in all frankness, Colonel, I must say that what happened today won't make reconciliation any easier."

Minh smiled at her. "A most unfortunate incident," he admitted, "but not one of our making. Major Ngoc do right thing. He tell students to go home. They do not do this."

"It was a police riot, Colonel," Sally said, her voice rising. "A vicious attack by Major Ngoc's men. I know. I was there."

Minh's smile vanished. "The streets do not belong to Hoa Hao," he said. "They belong to me."

"They won't be yours long if you let people like Ngoc run amok," Sally said coolly. Gulliver, sitting only a few feet from her, saw the green eyes glitter, as if dozens of tiny explosions were going off in them.

Cameron the peacemaker jumped in. "Uh, Sally, just how does the embassy suggest we proceed?"

She took a deep breath, nodded, and said, "We recommend that the government make whatever minor concessions it must and simply wait for the protest to fall of its own unbalanced weight. And it will, because the facts are on our side. Trung was working for the communists. His arrest and interrogation were perfectly justified under Phoenix program guidelines."

"Whoa now; wait just a minute," Gulliver said quietly, looking at her in surprise. "How can you say that in light of my report?"

Sally looked back at him, confused. "What report?"

"The report I sent Steelman. My investigation report."

Sally looked even further confused. "I'm afraid I don't know what you're talking about, Captain. The only report I've seen is the one submitted by Colonel Sloane here."

Cameron broke in. "Jake's report went up the same day," he said with an apologetic glance at Sloane. "I, uh, couldn't approve it because I couldn't verify its conclusions, but I told him to go ahead and send it anyway. I, uh, thought that Bennett would want to hear all points of view."

The PSA and the province chief exchanged a quick glance, then gave Cameron and Gulliver malevolent looks. This was the first they had heard of a conflicting report.

"So what was in this report?" Sally asked.

"I looked into the Hoa Hao allegations and found cause to doubt Nguyen Khac Trung's guilt," Gulliver said patiently, as if explaining arithmetic to a child, still unsure whether she really didn't know of his report or was merely pretending that she didn't. "I uncovered the existence of another man named Trung from Senh Tien, a man with communist connections. It was this man who received the illegal arms shipment."

"If that's so, then how did Nguyen Khac Trung come into it?" Sally asked.

"A case of mistaken identity. It seems Lieutenant Swain was bird-dogging Trung's wife, and he—"

"Nonsense!" Colonel Minh interrupted brusquely. "Our job now is to stop demonstrations, not to worry if Nguyen Khac Trung was VC. He was VC. He confess."

Gulliver looked at Minh with undisguised loathing. "That confession was procured by torture."

"He confess," Minh repeated. He smiled at Sally. "If CIA has report by Captain Gulliver and report by Colonel Sloane, and if your Mr. Steelman has seen both, does that not mean he has decided which one is proper and correct?"

Before Sally could respond, Gulliver was up and shouting at Minh. "How the hell would Steelman know? For that matter, how the hell would you know? Have you talked to anybody? Have you gotten off your fat ass and gone out into those streets you claim to own—"

"Captain Gulliver!" The always affable Sloane was on his feet, his face red with uncharacteristic anger. "How dare you talk to Colonel Minh that way? I won't have it! You are under arrest as of this moment. Go to your room!"

Gulliver laughed bitterly. "Gee, Dad, you mean without supper?"

The president's nephew held up both hands and said in a

soothing voice, "Gentlemen, gentlemen, please." He smiled at Gulliver and said, "Captain, please sit down."

Gulliver did not budge. His fists were clenched and he was leaning forward on the balls of his feet, eyeing the two colonels as if he could not decide which of them to assault first.

"Captain, please," Hoang cooed again.

Gulliver waited a beat, then took a deep breath and sat, looking disgusted.

Hoang turned to Sloane. "I am told by Colonel Minh that Captain Gulliver has been under a great deal of stress, with the ambush and his wounding and all. Please make allowances."

Sloane harrumphed. "We've all been under a great deal of stress, Mr. Hoang. That's no excuse for rank insubord—"

Hoang was holding up his hand again. "Please. Colonel Minh also tells me that we need Captain Gulliver."

Sloane looked skeptical. "Need him? How?"

Hoang turned to Gulliver. "The Hoa Hao have told Colonel Minh that after what happened today they will not meet with him or any member of his staff. They will speak only to you."

"Me?"

"Yes. You and Miss Teacher. The monk, Bui Dinh, asked for you by name. He says you can bring Miss Teacher or not, as you choose, but it must be you." Hoang paused, then asked, "Do you know why he would make such a request?"

Gulliver hesitated, then said, "No," with extra emphasis, to make up for the pause.

"Could it be that he has somehow learned of your, ah, your sympathy for Nguyen Khac Trung?" Hoang asked, watching Gulliver closely.

"That would seem unlikely," Gulliver said carefully.

Sally said: "Well, considering that your feelings are in conflict with the official point of view, Captain, I have to insist on going to that meeting with you. You can't go alone. And before either of us can go, we'll have to agree on a line. We can't have me saying one thing while you say another." She paused, then asked, "Do you really think Trung was innocent?"

"Yes."

"Does that mean you're guilty?"

"Am *I* guilty?"

"The PRU then," said Sally. "Is the PRU guilty?"

"Guilty of what?"

"Of murdering an innocent man."

"You should know; Phoenix is the CIA's baby."

"Please answer my question."

Gulliver sighed wearily and said: "The PRU is guilty of murdering many innocent men."

Sally looked at Minh. "Is that true, Colonel?"

The province chief shook his head, setting his multiple chins aquiver. "Of course not. But it is true that people are afraid of PRU, because of the hard way it deals with VC. I tell people: if you have complaint, bring it to me and I fix. But people sometimes afraid, afraid of PRU." Minh said this with regret, looking accusingly at Gulliver. "I tell people only VC have reason to fear PRU, but they are still afraid to complain. I tell people Phung Hoang is there to protect them and they need not fear."

"The PRU is only a small cog in Phoenix," said Colonel Sloane. "There is a difference between Phoenix and the PRU."

"Yeah," said Gulliver. "*We* get our hands dirty."

Minh graced Sally with a gold-capped smile. "I will tell you a story. Many weeks ago my PRU, under Captain Dang, catch a VC. Captain Dang and Captain Bich, the same who interrogate Trung, question this VC for three days. This VC is a true VC, very tough, very hard-core. He say nothing. He deny he VC. On fourth day, the PRU ambush another VC criminal gang and take another prisoner. This man admit he VC and identify the first prisoner as VC too. Now both VC are in POW camp. I tell you this to show you we ask hard questions, yes, but we do not torture prisoners. If we torture first man we can find out he VC on first day, not fourth day. We do not torture them. We do not murder them. I am very sorry this man Trung die, but he have bad heart. Nguyen Khac Trung was VC. No doubt of it. Even so, we sorry he die. We offer to pay for his funeral, because is sad, so sad. You see? Even though he VC, we offer to pay. We are not barbarians."

Sally listened with pursed lips, like someone sitting still for an unctuous sales pitch merely out of politeness. When he finished, she asked: "What about this other Trung Captain Gulliver mentioned? Has he been questioned?"

"There is no other Trung," Minh said flatly.

"His name is Nguyen Van Trung," said Gulliver. "Major Do found a finger card on him in the files and asked me to check it out. I went to Senh Tien and found that he'd skipped town just hours after Nguyen Khac Trung was arrested. According to neighbors, he was a mystery man, a loner with no visible means of support. It's all in the report I cabled to the embassy."

"Do you have any leads, any idea where he might be now?" Sally asked.

Gulliver shook his head. "No. And the chances of finding him aren't too good, either; nobody's looking."

"We do not waste time looking for ghosts," said Minh.

Sally ignored him and asked Gulliver, "Do you still have the Special Branch card on this man?"

"Roger. I'll get it for you. I'll bring you a carbon of my report while I'm at it. Be back in a second."

Gulliver gave Minh a grin as he left. He went down the hall to his office, reached under his desk for the key taped there, and opened his file cabinet. It took him less than ten seconds to determine that both the finger card and the copy of his report were gone.

He examined the lock and saw no evidence of a forced entry. He locked the drawer, taped the key in a new hiding place—behind the file cabinet—and sat down to think.

As far as he was aware, the only other person who knew where he kept the key was Dang, but that did not mean much. The Embassy House was full of intelligence professionals and it wouldn't have taken any one of them more than a couple of minutes to find that key; he had only hidden it in the first place to discourage the household staff from indulging their curiosity. As puzzling as *who* was *why*. Surely not to remove evidence. A replica of the finger card was on file at Special Branch, and his biggest problem with his investigation report had not been in keeping its contents a secret but in getting someone—anyone—to read it and take it seriously.

He went back to Cameron's office and announced: "They're gone. Someone's pinched both the report and the card."

This time it was Minh who grinned. "Maybe another ghost, eh?" he said. "Or maybe there was no card."

"There was," Cameron said quickly. "Jake showed it to me when he brought in his report."

"Who could have taken them, Captain?" Sally asked.

Gulliver shook his head. "I don't know."

"Why would they do it?"

"I don't know that, either."

"Enough silliness," Minh said with finality.

"I agree," said Hoang. "The position of the government, mine and yours, Captain Gulliver, has been determined: Nguyen Khac Trung was a confessed communist. The important thing now is to confront the Hoa Hao with unity. Unless you can give me your word of honor that you will represent the GVN's position and not your own, I cannot allow you to meet with the Hoa Hao tomorrow. That means no meeting, and no meeting means further bloodshed. Are you prepared to shoulder that responsibility?"

Gulliver glared at Hoang but did not say anything, and Sally

Teacher used the silence to ask: "George, do you have today's casualty count?"

"Seven dead and I don't know how many wounded," Cameron said. "We haven't gotten a final tally yet."

Gulliver shot Sally Teacher a venomous look but it was purely reflex; he did not really see her. Instead he saw a boy lying in the street, curled in a ball, his skinny knees pulled up to his chest, his palms pressed together to make a pillow between his cheek and the pavement. Then the child's face changed and Gulliver was looking into black eyes, large and liquid in the gloom, and his head filled with a drumming ran-tan, the sound of rain on a roof. "Okay," he said weakly.

"You'll go?" asked Duc Hoang. "You'll meet with the Hoa Hao?"

"Yes."

"On the terms that Miss Teacher and I set out?"

"How many goddamn times do I have to say it? Yes! Now, if you'll excuse me, I need a bath." He got up and slowly walked out of the office.

He climbed the stairs to his room and ran a tub, peeling away sweat-stiff clothes and kicking them into a corner. When he was clean, he toweled off, took two pain pills, and wrapped on a sarong. Then he stretched out on his bunk with one arm thrown over his eyes, the drumming sound still in his ears. The noise was real to him, real enough to prevent him from hearing the knock on his door.

It was not sound but movement, sensed rather than seen, that made him shift his arm. He saw the door crack open, saw a vertical slice of Sally Teacher's face in it. "Come in," he called, sitting up and swinging his feet to the floor.

She stood uncertainly just inside the door, embarrassed. He was not wearing anything under the sarong and his genitals flopped from side to side under the batik as he came into the living area and motioned for her to sit.

"I didn't mean to disturb you," she said, taking the uncomfortable straight-backed chair. "Were you asleep?"

"No."

"I . . . I just thought we should get our story straight for tomorrow," she said. "You didn't seem terribly happy when you left the meeting."

"Maybe it's because I *wasn't* terribly happy."

Sally shook her head. "You honestly believe that he was innocent, don't you?"

"I know he was."

"But he confessed."

"They tortured him," Gulliver said. "They beat him, they zapped his nuts with electricity, they hacked off his pinkie finger. You bet he confessed."

"But there's no proof of anything like—"

"Look, proof or no proof, I know what I know. Okay?"

She was quiet for a moment, then said, "I just wondered why something like this would get to you. I mean, from what Bennett Steelman told me about . . . I mean, with your, uh, your background and all . . ." She faltered to a halt.

Gulliver was watching her with cold eyes. "So Steelman told you about the Sandman, did he? And now you can't figure it out. You're asking yourself what's the problem, what's the big deal here? What's one more dead dink to someone like the Sandman? A killer. A *specialist*. Is that it, Miss Teacher? Is that what's bothering you?"

Sally stared down at her lap, then raised defiant eyes and said: "All right, then. Yes, Captain Gulliver, that's what's bothering me."

Gulliver nodded. "Fine. As long as we understand each other."

She made a helpless gesture. "I'm trying to understand, Jake, really I am, but it's hard. The man I heard described, this . . . this Sandman creature, doesn't seem related to the man I was with today. I mean, the way you helped that little boy, the way you took care of those people . . . the way you took care of . . . of me. The man Bennett Steelman described would not have done those things. He wouldn't care if Trung were innocent."

Gulliver was scowling at her. "Steelman doesn't know a goddamn thing about the Sandman and neither do you," he said. His face suddenly softened. "Hell, I don't know what it is. There's just something about the way he died that sticks in my craw. He hadn't harmed anyone. He hadn't done anything, except to get in Swain's way. Is that anything to die for? You're damn right it matters if he was innocent."

"Even if he was, innocent people die every day in this country," she said. "You've seen enough of it to know that."

"Maybe that's it. Maybe it's because I've seen enough of it. Maybe it's because I've *done* enough of it."

"I didn't mean to imply . . ."

Gulliver closed his eyes and shook his head. "I can see him there in that room, frightened and confused and in pain, sitting in his own waste. He wants to please them; he wants to give them whatever they want so they'll stop hurting him. But he doesn't *know* what they want. He can't figure it out in time to save himself. He doesn't know he's there only because he was on Horny Harry's mind, because his name was on the tip of Horny Harry's tongue."

"Jake . . ."

"Then, finally, there comes a point when he knows, knows they've gone too far to stop, that they'll go on and on until they kill him. But he still doesn't know why. He doesn't know he's got to die because his wife made the mistake of catching Swain's eye. He doesn't know he's got to die because his wife has a great pair of tits."

"Jake . . ."

"I know how it was for him because I've been in there a hundred times with a hundred Nguyen Khac Trungs. I know that tight, dark, breathless room that stinks of piss and shit and fear. Where there's no hope. Where there's no God. I've spent the last seven years of my life in that fucking room."

There was a silence, broken only by the squealing of the wobbly ceiling fan and the scratchy sound of a gecko chasing bugs across a wall, until Sally said: "You did a humanitarian thing today. You saved a child's life."

Gulliver snorted. "He'll thank me for it when he's old enough to be drafted and sent to the Iron Triangle. Or maybe he'll join the Field Force and get a nifty blue beret and a club. Ngoc should be a general by then."

"It was a fine thing you did; don't make light of it," she said.

When he didn't respond, she asked: "How's your side?"

Gulliver grinned. "Loan's a good doctor. But he went to the Torquemada School of Medicine; this bandage is cutting me in half."

"Turn around and I'll loosen it for you."

He turned, and Sally got up and unhooked the clasps and started to unwrap him like a nervous Egyptologist unwinding a mummy, standing close, her breasts lightly brushing his bare back, her arms snaking around him as she passed the loose end of the dressing from hand to hand. Her cheek was an inch away from the skein of muscles running over his back and shoulders and she thought she could hear the hum of an electric current passing through them. She let a hand drift and felt a pulsing tingle, as if she'd touched a live model-train track.

When it was time to uncover the wound itself, she placed both hands on his waist and turned him, so she could see what she was doing. As she did, she felt something rake her across the abdomen and looked down to discover he had an erection. She jumped back in shock and confusion, glaring at him. His face was stiff with embarrassment. "I . . . I'm sorry," he said.

There was something in his voice, his face, a touching, stricken quality that undid her. Without conscious decision, her body reacted to it, mutinying, taking command from a mind still shell-shocked. She let the bandage unravel and fall in a loose coil around her feet, where it lay like a gauze serpent. She put one hand flat on his stomach and ran it slowly up his chest while she fumbled with his sarong with the other. As he leaned down to kiss her, his odd-colored face grew large as a moon, filling her senses.

He undressed her with unsteady hands and, bodies fused, they stumbled in a graceless dance to his Spartan bunk. He eased her down, then reached up to drop the mosquito net. It fell around them like the sides of a box trap, leaving them in a tight musk-filled space. A cell. A perfumed garden.

The wild screak of bedsprings was lost in the noise of Harry Swain returning to his room two doors down, his booming voice raised in drunken song:

To the tables down at Mory's, to the place where Louis dwells,
To the dear old Temple Bar we love so well,
Sing the Whiffenpoofs assembled with their glasses raised on high,
And the magic of their singing casts its spell.
Yes, the magic of their singing of the songs we love so well,
"Shall I wasting," and "Marvourneen," and the rest;
We will serenade our Louis while life and voice shall last,
Then we'll pass and be forgotten with the rest.
We're poor little lambs who have lost our way: Baa! Baa! Baa!
We're little black sheep who have gone astray: Baa! Baa! Baa!
Gentlemen songsters off on a spree, Damned from here to eternity;
God have mercy on such as we: Baa! Baa! Baa!

Gulliver awoke sometime in the early-morning hours and found Sally gone. The lingering scent of rosewater was all that convinced him it had not been an erotic dream.

He was a little disappointed that she had gone back to her room, but he understood her concern about appearances. Unlike him, she had a career to consider. It didn't matter. Nothing could spoil his feeling of fullness. He felt whole, complete, connected. For the first time in a long time, he felt like an American. He drifted back into sleep, thinking of . . . home.

When he awoke again it was light. He showered, did a slipshod job of rewrapping his side, got dressed, and went whistling down to breakfast.

Sally was not in the dining room, so he ate by himself at one end of the table while Cameron and Swain sat without speaking at the opposite end, both nursing hangovers.

He did not see her until it was time to leave for the Widow Trung's. He was already in the back seat of the Bronco when she came down the villa steps and climbed in front with the driver. She threw a businesslike "Good morning" over her shoulder and busied herself with some papers. They made the long ride to Senh Tien without conversation.

19

BUI DINH PRAYED before his simple altar, nothing more than a wooden table covered with a red cloth inscribed with the four characters: *Bao Son Ky Huong*. A good scent from a strange mountain.

His mind wandered, back to the strange mountain in the That Son range of An Giang province, and to a memory of the One born on its slope. Huynh Phu So. The Living Buddha. The Good Scent. It seemed like yesterday that they had traveled the hamlets together, converting hundreds in a single day, sometimes thousands—all who felt the good scent blow over them. The Divine Boy and the then-humble monk who gave him occasional words of advice. "It is I who need advice now," he said aloud. "Tell me what to do."

This first, morning prayer session was for the Buddha. The next prayers would be for the Reign of the Enlightened King. After that would come prayers for the ancestors and then the living faithful. Bui Dinh was accustomed to doing his four daily prayer sessions at the sacred Hoa Hao shrine in Tan Chau village, near Long Xuyen province town, but today he found himself on his knees in a widow's bedroom, the same room where Nguyen Khac Trung had rested in life and in death. It was somehow fitting that it should be so, he thought.

And yet he was uneasy at his prayers, unable to avoid a feeling of guilt and unworthiness. His head should be filled with Buddha now, not with worldly thoughts. "But there are so many important decisions to be made," he said aloud in feeble apology, "and so little time in which to make them. Do I keep the protests going, as young Nguyen Loc advises, or do I make a deal with provincial authorities now, today, before things get out of hand again, as they did yesterday? And if I make a deal, what kind of deal?" Candles flickered, incense swirled, but Buddha did not answer.

After more than thirty years of involvement in sectarian politics, Bui Dinh was no dreamy mystic, as Huynh Phu So had been. He was a pragmatic man who had survived as long as he had by anticipating his enemies. He had a good idea of what Colonel Minh's emissaries would say to him this morning. They would shower him with flattery and threats. They would appeal to his sense of national loyalty, fully aware he possessed none, and then brandish their army at him if he did not give in. In the end they would offer him a few crumbs so that he could save face, but nothing nourishing. Saigon would never agree to dissolve Phung Hoang in the province; he knew that.

He also knew that the path he and his colleagues walked was narrow and treacherous, one seeded with mines that could explode in their faces at the slightest misstep. The Hoa Hao could maintain the pressure, hoping to force more concessions from the government, but such an action could backfire. Even though he would come in for harsh criticism from the American government and the American newspapers, President Thieu might be tempted to use the continuing disturbances as an excuse to send in the ARVN and tame the pesky Hoa Hao once and for all. The Hoa Hao were strong, but not strong enough to take on the full might of the government. Neither could they convincingly threaten to swing their support to the communists, not after what the communists had done to their prophet. Besides, the last thing the Hoa Hao needed was to trade one totalitarian regime for another.

Then how were the faithful to be shown that their chosen leaders were strong and not toothless old men, paper tigers? The party had gambled a great deal when it decided to force the issue of Trung's murder. People had died. The leadership had to come away with enough to justify the losses.

Bui Dinh looked at the bed where Nguyen Khac Trung had lain in state and made a promise: "You will have justice, my brother. You will be avenged. I swear this."

And even as he spoke the words, the embryo of an idea came to him. He was watching it grow, smiling and stroking his sparse whiskers, when Nguyen Loc stuck his head in the door and announced: "The Americans are here."

There were a dozen people in the Widow Trung's sitting room, and Sally recognized several faces from the dinner at Dr. Loan's. The doctor himself was there, as were the senator and the old bonze who guided the local church. And Bui Dinh, of course, whom Sally had met just the day before.

She also knew Nguyen Loc from the day before but had to be introduced since he did not recall the encounter. He had a fat bandage around his head and he wore it like a decoration.

Bui Dinh led her over to their hostess, the lovely woman from the funeral. Nguyen Thi Mai's perfect oval face was just as strikingly beautiful up close, Sally thought.

"*Ba* Mai," Dinh said, "I want you to meet *Co* Teacher of the United States government."

Nguyen Thi Mai smiled shyly and said, "I am pleased to meet your acquaintance. Please to excuse my bad English."

The priest quashed a smile and said, "Your English is fine, child, but Miss Teacher speaks Vietnamese."

"Ahhh!" Mai beamed. "You honor me and my home with your presence. Please sit and I will bring tea and cakes."

Bui Dinh put Sally and Gulliver side by side on the sofa with the square cushions. A dozen wooden chairs had been set up in a semicircle facing the couch, and Dinh took the chair in the center, directly opposite the Americans. Taking their cue from him, the others sat down too, arranging themselves on either side. They sat in silence, smiling and nodding at Sally and Gulliver for no apparent reason.

A moment later, Mai came out of the kitchen at the head of a small parade of wives carrying lacquered trays holding cups of hot tea and rice cakes. They served according to a strict protocol: Sally first, then Gulliver, then Bui Dinh, then the visiting student leader Loc, then the ancient bonze, then the other monks and the representatives of the Hoa Hao party. When everyone had been served, the wives returned to the kitchen while Mai sat next to Sally on the couch with her hands folded in her lap. They were the only women left in the room.

They ate off their laps and smiled at one another. The seating arrangement gave the gathering an awkward formality, and another half-hour of sporadic and strained small talk did little to dispel it. It came as a relief to everyone when Bui Dinh set his cup on the floor beside his chair and said: "Now then, Captain. May I assume that you speak for the provincial authorities?"

Before Sally could say anything, Gulliver said, "Yes."

"Then please proceed," said the priest.

Gulliver nodded. "All right, here it is. Your demands, or recommendations if you will, were relayed to Saigon. They were considered and rejected. There will be no change in the Phung Hoang program in this or any province. If the marches do not end, the Army will be used to break them up. President Thieu has been patient and understanding so long only because of his deep respect for the Hoa Hao, but demonstrations give the communists a propaganda bonus that Saigon can ill afford, and his tolerance is beginning to wear thin." He stopped and crossed his arms on his chest, apparently finished.

Sally looked at him with surprise. His delivery had been without inflection, his voice detached, his tone friendly but firm. Sally was impressed that he could be so professional in stating a position he personally opposed.

Bui Dinh seemed to be less impressed. "Bluntly spoken, Captain," he said with a small unreadable smile. "But does Saigon expect us simply to forgive and forget, to cover the truth with dirt, to leave justice to rot in a hole alongside our brother Nguyen Khac Trung?"

"Saigon expects you to meet your obligations as citizens of the republic and to maintain the peace," Gulliver said.

With flushed face, young Nguyen Loc leapt to his feet, clearly about to launch into one of his diatribes. The monk sat him down with a stern look and, turning back to Gulliver, asked with a cluck: "Do you bring us nothing as balm for our wounds, Captain? Nothing at all?"

"Of course there is something," said Gulliver. "The GVN is aware of the financial hardship to the family of the late Mr. Trung and has generously agreed to assist *Ba* Mai and her children with the sum of one million piasters."

A murmur went around the semicircle. A million piasters was a substantial sum, almost ten thousand American dollars at the official rate of exchange.

"Also," Gulliver was saying, "the provincial authorities have agreed to promptly notify the Hoa Hao party when one of its members is detained for any reason. There can be no prior notification, of course, but such arrests will be reported to you within twenty-four hours."

Dinh was shaking his head long before Gulliver finished. "Not enough," he said.

Sally broke in. "Excuse me, but there are two additional concessions that I was able to verify only this morning," she said with a glance at Gulliver. "The United States government will double the subsidy it now provides to the Hoa Hao party, the Social Democrats . . . and Major Nguyen Van Ngoc, the man who was responsible for yesterday's disgraceful violence, will be removed as provincial commander of the National Police Field Force."

Another buzz went around the room and Sally said, "What is more, I am authorized to tell you that the new Field Force commander will be a senior officer from An Giang province, an officer of the Hoa Hao faith." The murmuring grew louder and Sally saw some smiles. She glanced at Gulliver again and saw that he was not smiling. He was staring at her.

Bui Dinh was watching her too, a thoughtful look on his face. He fiddled with his goatee for a moment before he said: "Ahhh, now you have given us something to think about. But I think we must confer in private." He made a sweeping gesture with his hand and added in apology, "I would give you another room to wait in, but as you can see, it is a very small house. Would you mind waiting outside for a few minutes?"

"Certainly," Sally said with a confident smile. She came to her feet and started for the front door. Gulliver, looking a little bewildered, was slower to rise. He gave the assembly a brief bow and followed her out. Once they were outside, he said. "All right. When did all this happen?"

"As I said, this morning. Hoang and I got on the radio with Saigon and cleared it. We thought it might turn the tide if he didn't go for the first package."

"Don't you think you might have let me in on it?"

"I didn't want to say anything in front of the driver."

"The driver is a Nung, Sally," he said evenly. "Nungs speak no known language."

She bit her lip and smiled at him. "You're angry."

After a moment he smiled too and said, "Not much. To tell the truth, I'm relieved to know that you were working this morning. When I didn't see you at breakfast I thought maybe you were avoiding me."

"Maybe I was," she said, not looking at him.

"Oh." He had stopped smiling. "Why?"

She shrugged. "This is an extremely critical time in my professional life, Jake. I can't handle a romance right now."

"Don't you think you're about twelve hours too late?" he asked quietly. "That was more than a one-night stand, Sally. I've had enough of those to know the difference."

"Last night was last night. Today is today."

"How very fucking profound," he said.

Sally did not say anything for a moment, then asked: "What about the actress?"

Gulliver's eyes widened. "Nhu? What about her?"

"Are you in love with her?"

"Why would you ask that?"

"She's in love with you."

"What makes you think so?"

"Oh, come on," Sally said. "I saw how she looked at you, the way she touched you when she thought no one was watching. She might as well have had a sign pinned over her heart. Are you going to try to tell me that you and she aren't lovers?"

Gulliver, honestly startled by Sally's observation, and wondering if what she had said about Nhu loving him could be true, did not answer.

To Sally, his silence was an answer. "I thought so," she said.

"No. You're wrong about love," he said finally. "It's not that way with Nhu and me. It's . . . it's just not that way."

"It's not that way with you and me either," Sally said. "Last night was something that happened at the end of a very long and very strange day. We hardly know each other."

Gulliver shook his head slowly and said. "You're wrong, Sally. I know you as well as I know any woman; as well as I know anyone."

Sally watched his face as he said it, and had to believe him. "That is one of the saddest things I've ever heard," she said.

He shrugged and watched the street, unused to intimate disclosures, obviously embarrassed. The door opened behind them and Nguyen Khac Trung's oldest son, the new man of the family, poked his head out and said, "You may come in now."

Gulliver knew it was trouble when he saw Nguyen Loc's face. Vietnam's version of the Angry Young Man was smiling.

The soulful look on Bui Dinh's scored face confirmed the premonition, as did his opening words. When everyone had been seated, the old monk put his palms together and said, "I want you both to understand that what I have to say now causes me great pain."

Gulliver and Sally exchanged a quick glance of alarm but said nothing.

Bui Dinh went on: "The things you offer us will go far toward healing the wounds of the past few weeks. If it were up to me alone, or even to those of us in this room, it might even be enough. But our people are angry. They have told us, in word and deed, that they demand more. It will take a very dramatic gesture by the government to appease them."

The priest paused and Sally Teacher asked warily, "What kind of dramatic gesture?"

Dinh smiled sadly. "Let me say first that we try to be responsible people. We understand the government's position. We realize that the government cannot abolish Phung Hoang, no matter what mistakes it makes, no matter what evil is done in its name. And so, we withdraw the demand."

Gulliver felt no sense of elation or victory, not even relief. The Mad Monk had another shoe to drop. "What kind of dramatic gesture?" he asked, echoing Sally's suspicion as well as her words.

"In good time, Captain," Dinh said. "Please allow me to finish what I have to say."

"I'm sorry; go ahead."

"We also know how difficult it would be for you to bring the guilty men to trial. A public trial would put Phung Hoang itself on trial. It would give the whole world a good look at Phung Hoang and the world might easily come to the conclusion that in trying to save itself from the cruel communist beast, our small democracy had spawned a terrible beast of its own."

"What kind of dramatic gesture?"

Dinh sighed. "We have only one demand, but it is final and not subject to negotiation." He paused, then said: "The men who caused the death of Nguyen Khac Trung, including the American officer, must be executed for their crime."

Now that it was out in the open, a stir went up around the room and the assembled Hoa Hao nodded their approval.

Gulliver was incredulous. *"What?"*

Sally was confused. "But . . . but you just said that you understood why there couldn't be a trial," she said.

The monk wagged a finger at her. "I did not say that there should be a trial first," he said. "We know that if justice is to be done, it will have to be done outside the usual channels," he said.

"Execution without a trial? But that's murder!" said Sally.

"No!" shouted Nguyen Loc. "That is justice! What they did to Nguyen Khac Trung—*that* is murder!"

Bui Dinh said, "A life for a life. It is fair."

"I don't have my abacus with me, but it sounds more like three lives for one," Gulliver said sarcastically. "That does not sound like justice; it sounds like vengeance."

The priest showed emotion for the first time. "You dare speak of numbers?" he asked angrily, pointing a shaky finger at Gulliver. "Add to Nguyen Khac Trung the seven lives lost yesterday. That makes eight. I ask only three in return."

"Then you ask too much, old one," Gulliver said softly.

"Perhaps so, but I will take no less."

Sally said, "Bui Dinh, please. I beg you to reconsider."

The priest shook his head sadly. "I am sorry, my child. It must be done," he said.

Sally turned to Nguyen Thi Mai for support. "*Ba* Trung, please talk to him. If anyone in this room has been wronged, it's you. Tell him that this is not the way to atone."

Mai, who had not taken part in the discussion, shook her head. "I am sorry," she said in a soft voice, "but this is a matter for men to decide. This is something that goes beyond the death of my husband, beyond the life of one man. It must be left to our leaders to say what's to be done."

Bui Dinh smiled at the widow, nodding his approval. "To show that we understand how difficult it is, and that there is a matter of face involved for the government," he said to Sally, "we will not insist that it be a public execution. It can be a tragic accident if you wish."

"But what good would that do you?" Sally asked. "Where is the dramatic gesture for the people in that?"

"Oh, it's there all right," Gulliver answered for Dinh, his voice bitter. "It would be public without being public. The Hoa Hao rank and file will be told what will happen in advance, then watch it happen just the way they were told. They would know then that their bonze must be a strong man indeed to demand and obtain the lives of a Special Branch captain, a PRU captain, and an American Army lieutenant. And the venerable Bui Dinh here will be the undisputed leader of a unified Hoa Hao. The monk who made Saigon crawl; the man who forced the Phoenix bird to devour its own fledglings."

Dinh turned to Sally with a ghost of a smile and a shake of the head. "The good captain is obviously too distraught to think clearly, so I will speak to you," he said. "What we ask must be done within two weeks' time. And as a sign of our good faith, there will be no further demonstrations while we await your response. For the next two weeks, Colonel Minh can have his city back."

"B-but you're talking about three human beings," Sally said.

"In light of what they did to our brother, I could argue that these three men are not human beings," Dinh said gently as he leaned forward a little in his chair, his flecked eyes boring into Sally's. "But I am not so cruel and opportunistic as Captain Gulliver makes me out to be. If the demonstrations continue and if the Army is brought in to put them down, more lives will be lost, will they not? Women and children will be killed. Are the lives of three evil men worth that?"

"I—"

Gulliver interrupted. "We don't even know that these men are guilty of anything."

"*You* certainly think they are," Dinh announced.

Gulliver made a face. "How would you know what I think?"

"Because you have told me yourself, Captain," the monk said, reaching inside his robe and pulling out Gulliver's investigation report and the Special Branch card on Nguyen Van Trung.

The look on Gulliver's face was testament to the success of Bui Dinh's surprise. "Wh-where did you get those?" Gulliver stammered.

"A friend of Nguyen Thi Mai's brought them to us."

"Which friend?"

"A new friend. A good friend."

"Who?" Gulliver demanded.

"Quynh Nhu." Bui Dinh smiled, his coup complete.

Gulliver just stared at the monk for a moment. Then he gave his head a shake, as if that would be enough to clear it. There was a sudden aching just below his sternum, as if he had been kicked there.

"Where did she get them?" he asked in a whisper.

"That I do not know. Perhaps you could ask her yourself. I have been told that you know her quite well."

"I'm not so sure," Gulliver said in a hollow voice, more to himself than to Dinh.

The priest gave a little sigh of understanding, then got back to business. "You have our terms."

When it was clear that Gulliver would not, or could not, speak, Sally said: "Neither of us has the authority to make a response to them. We will have to consult with our superiors. You must give us time."

"Yes, yes, of course," Bui Dinh cooed. "You do not have to give us your decision in words. In fact, it would be best for us both if you do not; that way no one can say that they heard us ask, and no one can say that they heard anyone from the government consent. We would rather have your answer in deeds. Besides, we will know soon enough whether there is to be peace or more bloodshed—by the stroke of midnight, two weeks from this day."

Gulliver stood abruptly. "Let's get out of here," he said to Sally in English, holding out a hand to her.

"Let's," Sally said in a grim voice, taking his hand and letting him help her up. They left quickly, without the usual elaborate Oriental good-byes, not even pausing long enough to thank the Widow Trung for the tea and cakes.

The return drive differed from the ride out only in that they sat together in back this time. She reached over to take his hand once, but there was not much more conversation than before. He did not respond when she said, "Jake, I'm really sorry about Nhu." And she did not respond when he asked, "Do you still think he's a perfectly wonderful old man?"

20

THE SAIGON RIVER SPARKLED in the midday sun, reflecting noon's brilliance like a handful of spilled diamonds. Little explosions of light popped like flashbulbs off the water and off the tin roofs of shanties along the bank. Fragile sampans rocked gently in the wakes of the massive freighters and oil tankers that churned upriver for the port of Saigon or downriver to the open sea. Buffalo and children wisely moved into the shade of banana fronds. From the air it was an idyllic world, unmenaced and unmenacing.

The illusion of pastoral peace quickly vanished as the Beech made its approach into Tan Son Nhut airport—Dodge City—flying through a gritty barrage of smog over slums and refugee camps and military compounds, corkscrewing in to discourage ground fire from the edges of the field, finally lighting among birds of prey—helicopter gunships nesting in camouflaged revetments; rocket-taloned F–4 Phantoms ready on the runways.

The three passengers—Gulliver, Sally Teacher, and Duc Hoang—had passed the flight like strangers on a commuter train, sitting as far apart as the cramped cabin would allow, studiously ignoring one another. Their sovereign states of separateness landed with them. Gulliver was the last one off the plane and no one waited for him.

Doc Lap Palace had a black Mercedes limousine standing by for Hoang at the Air America office and he did not bother to say good-bye before ordering himself whisked away. Bennett Steelman had sent a modest Ford Pinto, along with the station duty officer, an earnest young agent who put Sally's suitcase in the trunk and solicitously rushed around to open the door for her, leaving Gulliver's duffel bag sitting on the tarmac.

With a sigh, Gulliver shouldered the bag and was humping it toward the car when the duty officer slammed the trunk and said apologetically: "Uh, sorry, sir, but I'm only authorized to transport Miss Teacher. Mr. Steelman's orders. He said to tell you to be at the embassy at sixteen hundred hours." As the Pinto pulled away, leaving Gulliver feeling all alone in the middle of the busiest airport in the world, he saw Sally Teacher turn and look back at him through the rear window.

He bummed a lift from the pilot as far as the civilian passenger terminal, where he transferred to a blue-and-yellow taxi for the long ride into the city. "Duc Hotel," he told the driver.

The cab went out the main gate, past the sign that never failed to make Gulliver smile—"THE NOBLE SACRIFICE OF ALLIED SOLDIERS WILL NEVER BE FORGOTTEN"—and took its place in the creep of traffic along Plantation Road. They went past tattoo parlors, uniform shops, bars, and massage parlors with names like "Golden Palms" and "Magic Fingers." As Gulliver watched the whores eating lunch and gossiping at the noodle stands, still hours away from the evening rush, his mind inevitably turned to women. Two women. Sally and Nhu.

He had not been able to get Sally alone since they had returned from Senh Tien. She had been all business when they got back to the villa, rounding up the triumvirate—Minh, Sloane, and Cameron—to brief them on the Hoa Hao's impossible demand, then locking herself in the radio room to chat with Steelman on the scrambler phone. Gulliver didn't know how specific she had been, but it obviously had been enough to upset Steelman; he had ordered her and Gulliver to Saigon.

Gulliver had tried one last time to see her before going to bed, knocking on her door a little after midnight. She had either been asleep or had elected to ignore it. He suspected the latter.

He had not had any more luck with Nhu. While Sally was busy playing case officer, he'd slipped off to verify Nhu's treachery. She had not been at home. He had returned to the alley three times before giving up, his questions unanswered. Why had she done it? Where had she gotten his report?

He was hurt and surprised that Nhu had . . . *what*? Betrayed him? Was he entitled to feel betrayed after plumbing Sally Teacher? And how could he honestly claim surprise? Having infiltrated her bed, perhaps even her heart, Gulliver had no illusions about penetrating Nhu's mind. He had seen her play a dozen different roles on that private stage of hers at the end of the alley, from Nurturing Mother to Shameless Harlot, and he still couldn't distinguish between Quynh Nhu the woman and Quynh Nhu the actress. She remained for him, then as now, a circle within a circle, a wheel within a wheel . . . Everything and Nothing.

It had been eight months since he was last in Saigon. He had not missed it. They were in the city center now, colonial Saigon, and Gulliver could see that having lost her youth to the war, the Pearl of the Orient continued to age badly. The traffic was thick as ever, a supercharged, horn-honking riot of cars, trucks, bicycles, cyclos, and scooters. Exhaust haze, which had already suffocated most of the tamarind trees, hung over everything, and the once stately ministry buildings were shabbily dressed in combat gear—sandbags and barbed wire.

The Duc, halfway between the U.S. embassy and Doc Lap Palace, was also wrapped in wire, and hard-eyed Nungs rather than doormen manned the sandbagged entrance. It was not the average hotel's idea of enticing decor and cheery staff, but then the Duc was not the average hotel. It was the CIA hostel for transients, for visiting field agents and new staffers awaiting permanent housing. Gulliver signed in, sent his bag up with a sixty-year-old room "boy," and headed for the bar.

Despite the pretty Vietnamese hostesses in *ao dais,* the bar was thoroughly American, dark and cold and loud. When his eyes adjusted to the gloom, Gulliver found the source of all the roisterous laughter—a crowded corner table; contract agents, by the look of them; drunk at noon.

Gulliver looked again and saw that he knew one of them, a public-safety adviser from II Corps who operated a string of whorehouses in Pleiku to supplement his income. Gulliver saw the adviser, whose name was Shipley, glance his way and give a start of recognition. But there was no friendly wave, no comradely call to come over and join them. Gulliver was neither offended nor surprised; he had once given Shipley a savage beating.

It was an ugly story with no heroes, one that began two years back with Shipley's call for a specialist to eliminate a top VC cadre. The request had been approved by the province chief and everything seemed to be in order. It was channeled to Razor, who approved it and sent in his best, the Sandman. To the Sandman it was just another mission, to be filed and forgotten, until three months later, when Gulliver got an invitation to go boozing from Master Sergeant G. D. "Dog and Carrot Salad" Jaynes, his team sergeant from those happy days in CIDG, and so nicknamed for his culinary specialty.

Gulliver, in one of his black depressions, had been so glad to hear the Dog's voice that he decided to defy Razor's edict against fraternizing with old Special Forces buddies. He took Jaynes to his favorite opium den and they had gone through half a dozen pipes each and a case of beer, as well as their common repertoire of war stories, when Jaynes had said with a slur: "The guys at Group tell me you're workin' for the spooks full-time these days. Don't gimme no fuckin' innocent looks. I been with a SOG team myself for the past seven months, workin' out of Pleiku."

"That right?" Gulliver said noncommittally.

Jaynes laughed. "C'mon, Lieuten . . . oops, it's Cap'n now, ain't it? I ain't lookin' for no details. I don't wanna know what you do for them, and I ain't gonna tell you what I do for them. I'm just tryin' to find out if you ever get over to Pleiku?"

"Every once in a while. Just in-and-out stuff."

"Wish I'd known. I'd have taken you to one of Shipley's Shacks and got your ashes hauled for you. He's got one place stocked with nothing but Yard girls, and I remember how you like that dark stuff . . . that Moi Meat." He laughed again.

"Shipley's Shacks?"

"Yeah. There's this guy Shipley on the mission team who runs a few *boom-boom* joints on the side. He used to be a vice cop in D.C. so he knows the trade. He's a real slimeball, but his girls give an honest bang for the buck."

"Does Vann know?" Gulliver asked, referring to John Paul Vann, the senior U.S. official in II Corps. "I'm surprised he would let something like that go on in his domain."

Jaynes shrugged. "I don't think so. And I know he don't know about some of the really bad shit Shipley pulls."

"Like what?"

"Oh, just little shit . . . like murder."

Gulliver felt his heart skip. "Murder?"

Jaynes nodded. "Couple of months ago Shipley sends in this intel report on some honcho VC cadre, recommending that the guy be blown away, terminated with *extreeeme* prejudice. And damn if the spooks in Saigon don't buy his fairy tale. Next thing you know they send in a button man . . . and bingo."

"*Fairy tale?* What fairy tale?"

Jaynes made a long-suffering face, one that summed up twenty years of having to explain the obvious to officers. "It was a setup. That dink wasn't no commie; he was pure capitalist; a regular Chamber of Commerce *on-tray-pree-noor*. But he filed for the Big Bankruptcy Court in the Sky when he fucked up and opened a rival house on Ol' Slimeball Shipley's turf. Ol' Slimeball don't much like competition."

Gulliver was suddenly sober. "Dog, you sure about this?"

"Sure I'm sure. I heard him laughing about it with the *mama-san* who manages the business for him. There won't be any new houses opening in Pleiku anytime soon. Ol' Slimeball's got the market all to himself."

Gulliver stewed for the rest of the evening, feeling more soiled than usual. It was bad enough to be used against legitimate targets, real enemies, but not like this. This was more than even the Sandman should have to take. He was at the chopper pad at sunup the next morning. He hopped a ride to Pleiku, went to the provincial compound, and caught Shipley alone in the shower tent. He broke his nose, his jaw, both arms and both legs, and was back in Nha Trang for noon chow. The whole time he was working Shipley over, he was picturing Razor.

Now he took a stool at the end of the bar, as far from the corner table as he could get, but he could still see them in the mirror. He saw Shipley tell the others something in a conspiratorial whisper and thought he heard the word "Sandman." The sounds of high hilarity died, and he saw their faces turn his way. He chugged his beer and left quickly, before he could be tempted to give in to the rising urge to stomp Shipley all over again.

In his room, he switched off the air-conditioner, opened a window, and unpacked. He called room service and ordered a *croque monsieur* and a Ba Muoi Ba. When they came, he killed the sandwich in four bites and the beer in one long pull. He stripped, showered, and stretched out naked on the bed. He had intended to nap but he spent the next two hours reliving his night with Sally Teacher instead.

At three-thirty he put on a shirt with a collar and his one pair of civvy trousers that hadn't been designed by Levi Strauss, and went down to catch the CIA shuttle bus to the embassy.

The United States embassy took up a full block of Thong Nhut Street, a massive white box as substantial as America's commitment to South Vietnam. It was six stories high and set back from the street, surrounded by a ten-foot-high wall; an alabaster fortress with a concrete rocket shield for a facade and rows of shatterproof plastic porthole windows. It looked isolated and out-of-place in a colonial-era neighborhood that was otherwise distinguished by a sleazy Gallic charm.

Gulliver was halfway across the lobby, making for the elevators, when the marine guard, a teenage lance corporal, came out of his kiosk to intercept him. "Uh, sir, I'll have to see your pass before you can go up."

Gulliver had been issued a State Department I.D. card when he was attached to the spooks, but he refused to carry it. He pulled out his old MACV identification card instead.

"Sorry, Captain, but this card has expired," the young marine said. "Who do you wish to see, sir?"

"Steelman. Fifth floor. And it's 'whom,' not 'who.'"

"Uh, yessir. If you'll stand by, sir." The boy consulted his list of embassy extensions, dialed Steelman's office, and confirmed Gulliver's appointment with the secretary. "They'll be sending an escort officer for you, sir," he told Gulliver.

Gulliver's escort turned out to be the duty officer, the same young spook who had left him stranded at the Air America compound. Gulliver ignored the man's smile and proffered hand and walked ahead to the elevator. The agent followed him in, punched the button for the sixth floor rather than the fifth, and explained in cathedral tones: "They're waiting for you in Mr. Scott's office."

Gulliver was cleared with the sixth-floor marine guard, led past the situation room, where someone was yelling into a transmitter in an effort to be heard over the racket coming from the incinerators on the roof, and turned over to a pair of secretaries who flanked the chief of station's office door like marble lionesses outside a public library. One of them, the homelier of the two, ushered him into Scott's office.

Gulliver could tell that Sally had already delivered the Hoa Hao's bad news. There was an air of impending disaster in the room. It was as though he had stumbled into a theater in the middle of the deathbed scene.

The first person he saw was the one he was looking for. Sally was sitting on the sofa in a summer dress that showed off her fine long legs, looking cool and lovely in spite of the crisis atmosphere. Duc Hoang was there too, standing by a window, looking out moodily. He had changed safari suits, but still looked the same as he had that morning—peeved. And, of course, Steelman was there, sitting next to Sally in his usual floppy sprawl.

There were two men Gulliver did not know. One was tall and silver-haired and dressed in seersucker, the other short and bald and dressed in gabardine. The short man sat behind a large oak desk which was bare except for a manila folder.

Without getting up, Steelman said, "Ah, Gulliver, there you

are, old boy. I don't believe you've met Wyatt Howe, our DCM, or Tom Scott, our chief of station. Gentlemen . . . Captain Gulliver."

Howe, the deputy chief of mission, accepted Gulliver's hand with diplomatic reluctance, not quite sure what to make of someone so unconventional-looking. Scott shook hands from his chair, making Gulliver lean across the wide desk.

When Gulliver was seated, the station chief nodded at Steelman and said, "It's your show, Bennett."

Steelman straightened and gave him a cool smile. "Thank you, sir," he said with such expertise that no one, least of all Scott, could tell if he was being sarcastic or not.

He paused a beat before continuing in a grave voice: "I believe we all are familiar with the background of this case. And, of course, Miss Teacher has already given us the bottom line from the meeting she and Captain Gulliver had yesterday with the Hoa Hao. What we'd like this afternoon is a verbatim account of that meeting." He turned to Sally. "Why don't you go ahead, Sally. I'm sure Captain Gulliver will jump in if he thinks you're leaving anything out."

Sally began with the province team's strategy session at the Embassy House and took them straight through the meeting with the Hoa Hao leaders, with only an occasional reference to her notes. It was a concise but complete briefing. As far as Gulliver could tell, she omitted only two things: his clash with Colonel Minh and the Hoa Hao's source for his report.

When she finished there was a somber silence. Hoang was still looking out the porthole. Howe and Scott were looking at each other. Steelman was looking at Gulliver. "Well, old boy, did she leave anything out?" he asked.

"Miss Teacher seems blessed with total recall."

"Good." Steelman looked around the room. "Does anyone have any questions for Miss Teacher before I proceed?"

"No, but I've got one for Captain Gulliver," Scott said. "This purloined report of yours, contending that this Trung fellow is innocent . . . why in God's name did you write it? And why would you keep such a document in your files?"

"I wrote it because I believed it to be true," Gulliver said calmly. "And it's standard operating procedure to keep a file copy of all reports forwarded to this office."

"To *this* office? Nonsense. We never received anything like that . . ." The station chief did what he always did when he was confused; he turned to Steelman. ". . . I mean, did we, Bennett?"

Steelman nodded. "Yes, sir. I did get such a report from the captain."

"Oh. Uh, why don't I know about it?" Scott asked. It was not a demand for an explanation; he was merely curious.

"It came in without the province intelligence officer's approval and it contradicted the official findings of the PSA without a shred of hard evidence in support," Steelman said with a shrug. "I didn't think it was anything that warranted a moment of your valuable time."

"Oh. Yes. Of course. Thank you," Scott mumbled. "Carry on, carry on."

Steelman looked at Gulliver for a few long seconds, then asked in a quiet voice, "Captain, how did the Hoa Hao come to possess classified materials that were in your keeping?"

Gulliver caught Sally's quick glance of regret and gave her a little shrug that said she had tried. "I was told that they got them from a local woman," he said. "An actress with the regional popular theater."

"And how did she get them?"

"I don't know."

"I see. Do you, ah, *know* this woman, Captain?"

"Yes, I do."

"What is her name?"

"Quynh Nhu."

"And what is the nature of your relationship?"

"We're friends . . . good friends."

"I see."

Steelman paused again, and this time the silence was noisy. Gulliver could hear the pennies dropping all over the room. He looked at Sally and saw that she was biting her lip, distressed for him.

Steelman pursed thin lips and pushed an unruly shock of hair away from his eyes, which never left Gulliver. At last he asked: "Did you give the materials to this woman?"

Gulliver glared at him and said: "No. I did not."

"I see."

There was another silence, one that dragged on until the chief of station broke it by clearing his throat and asking: "Captain, could this Bui Dinh fellow be bluffing?"

"He could be," Gulliver said with a shrug, "but I don't think so. He's a rough old cob and something of a fanatic, I think; the kind who wouldn't hesitate to cut off his nose to spite his face."

Scott looked at Sally and she nodded her agreement. "I'm afraid Captain Gulliver's right. It was my . . . our feeling that the whole notion of summary justice was Dinh's to begin with, not the will of the people as he'd have us believe."

Scott nodded. "We suspected as much. Well. Thank you for the briefing, Miss Teacher." He looked at Steelman. "Bennett, do you have anything more for either Miss Teacher or Captain Gulliver?"

"Yes, I do," Steelman said. "I think we should pursue a bit further the question of how a copy of Captain Gulliver's report found its way into the hands of this actress person."

Scott nodded. "Go ahead."

"Thank you, sir," Steelman said with a thin smile. He looked at Gulliver. "Where did you keep the materials?"

"In a locked file cabinet in my office at the Embassy House," Gulliver said.

Steelman nodded. "Is it possible, Captain, that whoever is leaking information about Phoenix program operations might also be responsible for this latest breach of security?"

Deputy Ambassador Howe looked sharply at the chief of station. "What leak? There's a leak? Does the ambassador know about this?"

"Uh, well . . ." Scott looked at Steelman.

"A minor internal problem, sir," Steelman said smoothly, a reassuring smile on his face. "We expect to have it cleared up in no time at all."

"Well, I certainly hope so," Howe harrumphed.

When Steelman turned back to Gulliver, the smile was gone. "Does this actress have access to the province house, Captain?"

"No. She's never set foot inside the Embassy House."

"Is she acquainted with any other member of the province team; anyone besides yourself?"

It was not until Steelman put the question into words that Gulliver realized he had probably known all along how Nhu had gotten the things from his file cabinet. Dang had given them to her. Dang was the only other person she knew with access to the material. He hesitated, then lied. "Not that I'm aware."

"Is she acquainted with your Vietnamese counterpart, Captain Dang?"

Gulliver paused again. Did Steelman know, or was he just fishing? It didn't matter, he decided. He did not know Dang's motives, or Nhu's, but he knew Steelman's. He repeated: "Not that I'm aware."

Steelman just looked at Gulliver for a moment, then said abruptly: "That will be all for the time being, Captain. I'd like you to remain in Saigon for a few days, in case we need you. I'll be getting back to you. You too, Sally. Now, if you would be kind enough to escort Captain Gulliver out."

Gulliver and Sally got to their feet and left the office without good-byes. As they passed the situation room, Gulliver could hear the agent still shouting into the radio, trying to be heard over the noise from the roof—a chopper landing on the rooftop pad this time.

Neither of them spoke until they reached the elevator. Sally punched the call button and said, "Jake, I'm sorry the thing about Nhu had to come up."

Gulliver shrugged. "Thanks for trying, anyway." He nodded back down the corridor toward Scott's office. "What will they do about the Hoa Hao's terms?"

"I don't know," Sally said. "They're not including me in the decision-making process. They've put me on hold too."

"If we're both on hold, maybe we should hold together," he said with a thin smile. "Can I buy you a cup of coffee or something?"

"Oh, I . . . I'm sorry, Jake, but I really don't have time," she said. "The COS wants me to put everything I remember of the meeting down on paper."

"Oh. Sure. I understand." The elevator arrived. Gulliver stepped in and said, "Well, I'll be seeing you around maybe."

She stepped in with him, an apologetic look on her face. "I've got to stay with you to the lobby. It's the rules."

"I thought I was supposed to be working for this bunch," Gulliver said. "Do they think I'm going to steal something?"

She shrugged helplessly and repeated, "It's the rules."

They rode the rest of the way down in awkward silence. When they reached the lobby, Sally got out with him. She put a hand on his arm and said, "They're having a party tonight at Number Forty-seven. I don't think anyone would mind if you came. Just tell them I invited you."

"You can't mean the One Forty-seven Club," Gulliver said with a look of mock horror. "That dive is the original den of iniquity."

"No, Number Forty-seven Phan Thanh Gian Street. It's a residence shared by a group of the younger embassy officers," Sally said. "The villa is something of an institution. It's been passed down from one generation of fun-loving bachelors to the next, and some of their parties have become legends. They've got CBC, Saigon's hottest rock band, playing tonight. It should be fun."

To Gulliver it sounded anything but fun. Parties and hot bands were for young people, and he could not remember having ever been young. "Are you going?" he asked.

"I might drop in for a while."

Gulliver seemed to be thinking it over. "Maybe we could go together," he suggested.

"Oh, I don't know when I'll be through here," she said quickly. "If you want to go, it would probably be better if you went without me."

Gulliver just looked at her. After a moment he asked, "Who else will be there?"

"Oh, I don't know. The usual embassy crowd, I guess."

"Is Steelman going?"

"Why, uh, yes, I think he is. He's the one who told me about it."

"Then thanks but no thanks." He turned his back on her and walked off. It was rude of him, he knew, but it gave him a perverse pleasure all the same. He was tired of being odd man out, the one left standing foolish and alone with egg on his face. It was time someone else took a turn.

Gulliver tried making an evening of it, going round to all the old haunts, hoping one of them might take his mind off things he did not want to think about now. He did not want to think about Dang. Or Nhu. He did not want to think about Sally Teacher.

He tried the Dragon Bar off Le Loi Boulevard first. Then Mimi's Flamboyant on Nguyen Hue. Mistakes. The loud music and stale smell of tobacco and beer only reminded him of parties, of Sally surrounded by a randy ring of admirers; fun-loving bachelors.

His final stop, the One Forty-seven Club on Vo Thanh Street, was the biggest mistake of all. He had one beer and left.

He walked slowly along Vo Thanh, rummaging through his mind for something else to think about. He came to a corner and spotted a street sign and told himself it would have to do.

Vo Thanh Street . . . named for General Vo Thanh . . . national hero . . . eighteenth century . . . fought for the Nguyen dynasty in the war against the Tay Son dynasty . . . held out for two years against superior army at Qui Nhon, waiting for reinforcements that never came . . . offered to surrender if the Tay Son general would spare his troops . . . put on his dress uniform and circled his men around a stake in the middle of the fort . . . told them he would die rather than let the enemy see his face . . . ignited the gunpowder beneath the stake with his own hand.

The exercise did not work. He could not help thinking that maybe he had ignited gunpowder under his chances with Sally with his own hand, by rejecting her invitation. Maybe the invitation, as indirect as it was, had been her way of telling him that she wanted to pick up where they had left off. Maybe he was on her mind the same way she was on his. Maybe he was a hopeless asshole.

He walked, saying no to the whores who called out to him from the shadows and from the backs of Hondas where they rode behind their pimps. He was debating whether to go back to the Duc and to bed or to taxi out to Cholon, the Chinese section, to see if he could find a decent opium parlor, when he heard music and laughter and a gay tinkle of glasses. He had come into Lam Son Square, and on the other side—across from the old opera house, now the National Assembly—the Continental Palace Hotel was lit up like a luxury liner on a dark sea.

White-jacketed waiters moved around the terrace—the Continental Shelf—serving drinks and making certain that beggars and free-lance whores kept to the sidewalk, admitting only those with dates or those who had "leased" territorial rights. The Shelf was *the* meeting place in Saigon, the place where the foreign community invariably began its evening or ended it. Gulliver decided to end his there with a nightcap.

He was crossing Tu Do Street, homing in on the sounds of merriment, being pulled toward the absence of loneliness like a sailor to a siren's song, when he saw Sally. She sat at a table along the edge of the Shelf, facing the street. She was with someone, a man, and even though the man's back was to him, Gulliver knew who it was. No one else sat in quite that way, with one leg flopped loosely over the arm of the chair.

Gulliver stopped dead in the middle of the street. He saw Steelman giving an order to a waiter, saw Sally looking around idly. He was close enough to see her face change when she spotted him. A cyclo swerved around him and rocketed up Tu Do, trailing blue smoke and curses. Several more cars and trucks roared by with blaring horns before Gulliver snapped out of his trance. He turned around and headed for the Duc.

When he was back in his room he telephoned down for a bottle of Pernod, a pitcher of water, and a bucket of ice. A few minutes later there was a knock, but instead of a waiter it was Sally Teacher.

They stared at each other until she said, "Aren't you going to ask me in?"

Gulliver did not move. He stood blocking the door, his arm across the portal like a drop gate at a border crossing. "What do you want?" he asked in a cold voice.

"It's rather clear, isn't it?"

He shook his head. "Lady, there's not a goddamn thing you say or do that's clear to me."

"All right, then. You. I want you."

"You don't know what you want," he said.

She ducked under his arm and into the room. He had wheeled around to ask her to leave when a meek voice behind him said, "Excuse, sir, you want two glass with drink?" Gulliver spun to find an ancient waiter in the door, tray in hand.

"Yes, we will need one more glass," Sally said. Gulliver turned again to glare at her.

"Yes, miss," said the waiter. Gulliver wheeled again to countermand her order, only to find that the old man had set down the tray and was scurrying back to catch the elevator.

Gulliver felt dizzy and foolish, like a child's spinning top.

He closed the door and turned once more. She was sitting on the bed, staring boldly at him.

"What about your party?" he asked.

"I decided not to go."

"But you might miss a legend in the making."

"It can become a legend without me," she said.

"What about your date?"

"He wasn't my date. He simply offered me a ride to the party and we decided to stop and have a drink first."

"What did you tell him?"

"I told him I changed my mind. I told him good night."

She was wearing the same thin summer dress she'd had on at the embassy. It followed the lines of her body, falling to just above the knees, cut low in front to reveal a puckered cleavage. Gulliver felt hot, short of breath. He was tempted to turn the air-conditioner back on.

"I thought you didn't have time for this sort of thing," he said.

"I've decided to make the time," she said calmly.

"Have you now?" he said. "What changed your mind?"

"The sight of you standing in the middle of the street with cars whizzing all around you," Sally said, venturing a little smile. "I realized I didn't want you squashed flat. I also figured I'd probably never see you again if I didn't do something. So I did something. Here I am."

"Why would it matter if you ever saw me again or not?"

"You touched me the other night, Jake, and I don't mean just with your hands. There was love there." She smiled and shook her head. "Why do you flinch at the word? There's a lot of love in you, just waiting to be released. Don't look at me like that. There is."

Gulliver did not say anything, so she went on. "I have a theory about you, Captain Gulliver. I think you've convinced yourself that love is impossible in a place like this, that it can't exist where there's so much cruelty and suffering."

When he still didn't say anything, she said, "My theory has two parts. Want to hear the second?"

He shrugged. "It's your couch, Doctor."

"All right," she said. "I think that because you don't love yourself, you've convinced yourself no one else could love you. So you've kept the love you have in you corked up; for such a long time that you can't recognize it's there."

"I recognize bullshit when I hear it," Gulliver said.

"It's not bullshit, Jake. You think that the Sandman is so terrible a person he doesn't deserve love."

Gulliver said nothing, just gave her a baleful look.

"And I'll admit that one reason I was reluctant to get involved with you was this Sandman business," she said. "I told myself that if even half of the things I'd heard were true . . . well, I couldn't possibly love a man like that."

"It's *all* true, Sally," Gulliver said quietly. "I'm your worst nightmare. I'm the fucking bogeyman."

Sally got off the bed and stood facing him, but did not move closer. She shook her head. "Once, perhaps, but not now. I've seen the love in you. You gave it to that boy you saved, and to those people you tried to help. And you gave it to me. I can still feel the way it flowed out of you. You filled me up with it, Jake. You can't fake something like that."

"I'm the Sandman, remember?" he said harshly. "Man of a thousand faces. The chameleon killer. Master of camouflage."

Sally shook her head again. "You just might be the most transparent man I know. Even this self-destructive crusade of yours to find the truth about Trung's death is an expression of love. I'm afraid your compassion is showing, Captain. And isn't compassion just another form of loving?"

Gulliver sighed. "Look, Sally, why don't you knock off the armchair psychoanalysis and just tell me what you want from me?"

"I want you to make love to me again, the way you did the other night," she said, unbuttoning her dress. "I want you to show me I'm right."

Sally slid the dress up over her head. She reached back to unbuckle her brassiere, then tugged off paisley panties. She moved deliberately, as calculating as a veteran stripper, her eyes on his, monitoring the effect she was having on him.

But once she was undressed, her almost mocking confidence seemed to evaporate in an instant, leaving her as suddenly hesitant as a virgin bride. Her lip trembled and her green eyes grew damp. She shook her head and took a stumbling step toward him. She put her arms around his neck, kissed him lightly, and molded her body to his, laying her cheek on his chest.

"Show me, Jake," she whispered.

He did not respond. He stood rigid and unyielding, his arms straight down at his sides, staring over the top of her head at the opposite wall.

Gulliver surrendered in stages, as each of his senses reacted to her. He could still hear the catch in her voice, still taste her on his mouth. He felt her long body pressed against him, and his nose picked up the faint scent of rosewater. Slowly, as if acting on their own, his arms came up and circled her, gathering her in, gently at first, then with a ferocity that threatened to cut off her breath.

21

"GOOD MORRRNING, VIETNAM! *Rise and shine! It's oh-six-hundred hours, Wednesday, March eleventh, and you are listening to AFVN radio, serving the American forces from the Delta to the DMZ! I'm Specialist Fifth Class John Dotson and I'll be bringing you music guaranteed to open your eyes and jump-start your heart—the Doors, Joplin, Hendrix, the Stones—but first, the latest news headlines from the wires of the Associated Press and United Press International . . . the Cambodian capital of Phnom Penh spent a quiet night following yesterday's takeover by senior military . . .*"

Gulliver, lying in Sally Teacher's big bamboo bed in her villa on Nguyen Du Street, lit the first cigarette of the day and listened to the news. When it was over, he reached across a still-sleeping Sally to turn off the radio. There had been no mention of trouble in the Delta. The Mad Monk was keeping his promise.

Or so he assumed; it was hard to tell. The Saigon press corps, which usually swarmed to potential scandal like flies to feces, had ignored the Trung Affair to now. As far as he knew, the American media were unaware that there even was such a thing as the Trung Affair. A half-dozen street marches in an insignificant provincial capital had not caused enough of a stir in Saigon to lure them away from the Continental Shelf or the rooftop bar of the Caravelle Hotel.

Gulliver had considered leaking the details of the Trung case to the press, but he had dismissed the notion as soon as it came to him. The reporters would only do what they always did—go straight to the "official" sources—and he feared that people like George Cameron and Major Do would end up as fall guys. The press could do its dirty job without his help.

So why didn't they? At the moment they were busy with Cambodia. Before that they had been busy with something else, although Gulliver could not say what. Ever since his transfer to the Phoenix program, he had lost touch with the other war, with the Big Picture. His war, his world, had shrunk to a narrow strip, bounded by the Embassy House and Medium Minh's headquarters, by canals and hostile hamlets, and peopled not by soldiers but by spies and politicians, by mercenaries and victims. Gulliver had been isolated enough as a soldier, even as the peripatetic Sandman, but if he had had a jailer's view then, he now had that of an inmate.

He watched Sally sleep. She lay on her back with a damp sheet bunched at her hips, arms above her head, her flattened breasts spilling down the sides of her rib cage, as round and white as unleavened loaves. She was covered with a beaded dew of sweat that made her shine like an oiled concubine, and she breathed in quick, short gulps, her lungs laboring to process the soggy air. It was the hottest and most oppressive time of the year, a time of transition between dry and rainy seasons, a time when storms seldom broke into cooling rain.

Gulliver didn't mind. It was the dawn of their seventh day together, and they had spent the time like honeymooners, in a dreamy round robin of sex, sightseeing, lunch, sex, a stop at the embassy for a quick call to Cameron, more sightseeing, dinner, more sex. For all the heat, it had been the best week of Gulliver's seven years in Indochina . . . the best week of his life.

He wriggled down and nursed at one sprawled breast. When she did not move, he stuck a finger into her deeply recessed navel and tickled. When that elicited no response he put the finger in his mouth to wet it, then gently eased it into her. When her eyes popped open, he said: "Let's go to the beach."

"Wha . . . wha . . . ?" Sally gargled.

"Let's go to the beach," Gulliver repeated, his finger still inside her, exploring, stirring her juices.

"Wha . . . timzit?"

"Zero-six-hundred. Time to lock 'n' load and attack the day."

"Six? Gawd! Lemmelone." She reached down and pushed his hand away, then rolled over and gave him her back.

Gulliver snuggled up to her, nibbling on her earlobe, poking his erection between her sticky thighs, and scooting up to take her from behind. She was already well lubricated and he had no trouble gaining entry. She groaned, in irritation rather than arousal, and tried to move away, but his arms were like ropes, holding her close. After a few moments, he no longer needed bonds. Sally's moaning changed in pitch and intensity as she pumped back at him, finally growing so noisy he had to clamp a hand over her mouth so she would not rouse the household staff.

When they were done, she rolled over and shook her head. "I can't go to the beach today," she explained. "I'm checking into a rest home today."

Gulliver laughed. "You can rest tomorrow."

"Where do you get the energy in this heat? And why won't you let me turn on the A/C? I swear, Jake, I'm melting away."

He grinned, palmed one of her outsize breasts, and said, "Not so's you'd notice."

"Be serious, dammit," she said, slapping his hand away. "The beach is out; Vung Tau's an hour and a half from Saigon. What if the embassy calls? Besides, I'm not officially on leave. I should be spending this down time at my desk."

"Negative," said Gulliver. "Officially, you're running the Trung case and, officially, you're on hold. Don't argue; I heard the order."

"A swim would be nice," she said, wavering. Then: "No. I've got a feeling they're going to call us today."

"C'mon, just a couple of hours," Gulliver argued. "We'd have to be back by midafternoon anyway. The Vung Tau Highway isn't secure after dusk."

"No beach," Sally said firmly. Then her face lit up with inspiration. "But we can still have a swim . . . let's have lunch at Le Cercle Sportif."

"I love you for your brains, not your body. You're on!"

They showered *à deux* with a minimum of slap-and-tickle, content with soaping each other and one wet kiss, then went out for breakfast on the garden veranda.

Sally's French colonial villa on Nguyen Du Street, less than two blocks from the Cathedral Roundabout, was too grand for such a junior officer, but the station had had a problem housing her. No apartments had been available when she'd come in-country, and they would not let her share a billet with a female FSO from State for security reasons, so they had given her the villa on a temporary basis. Officially, it belonged to Steelman's predecessor, who, officially, was in Washington on sick leave. Unofficially, Sally had told Jake, the former chief of operations had suffered a severe nervous breakdown and was not expected to return. In the meantime, Sally was enjoying his house, his furniture, his liquor cabinet, and his servants. There were a few advantages to being a woman in a man's world.

Chi Ba, the cook, served them coffee from Ban Me Thuot, dark and thick, and fresh papaya, eggs and bacon. Sally's Chi Ba could have been the twin sister of the Embassy House's Chi Ba. She was round and jolly and wholly approving of the fact that her missy had finally found a man to share her bed. She fluttered around them like a wide-bodied moth, giggling and sneaking appraising glances at Gulliver until Sally cleared her throat pointedly and said: *"Cam on, chi ba."* Thank you. "Yes, missy." Chi Ba giggled once more and left them alone.

"We can't pitch up at the Cercle before ten o'clock, so what do you want to do until then?" Gulliver asked.

"I don't care, as long as it doesn't involve walking in the heat," Sally said. "As long as it doesn't involve moving at all. I'm bushed."

"Well, let's see," Gulliver mused. "We've done the An Quang and Xa Loi pagodas, the zoo, and the botanical gardens. What have we missed?"

"Sleep," said Sally.

"I've got it!" he said, snapping his fingers. "If you're worried about not doing any work, let's go to work. Let's sit in the coffee shops and listen to the gossip; see if anyone's talking about the Trung case. You can play spy."

"Sit? Did you say sit?" Sally asked with beatific smile. "I love *you* for your brains, not your body. You're on."

They finished breakfast and, holding hands, walked the few blocks to Givral's, which occupied a corner across from the Continental Palace Hotel. Givral's, along with Brodard's down the street, was one of the stations in a network known as Radio Catinat, rumor mills masquerading as coffee shops along the Rue Catinat, the old French name for Tu Do Street. Each morning and afternoon the shops filled with Vietnamese students, professors, local journalists, and bureaucrats who made up Saigon's political grapevine. They exchanged gossip, started rumors, and plotted small intrigues. Once in a while, one could even overhear something useful, something true.

They had a second breakfast, croissants and more coffee, and eavesdropped. There was nothing about Trung; all talk was of Cambodia. The prevalent theory seemed to be that the CIA had engineered the coup. That was not surprising. Ever since the overthrow of Diem in 1963, a bit of mischief in which the CIA had indeed been up to its armpits, Saigonese had believed that all coups everywhere were the CIA's handiwork.

They stayed an hour before moving on to Brodard's, where they heard much the same. They had another pot of coffee and stayed another hour, then made their way to Le Cercle Sportif.

The French sporting club of colonial days took up several acres along Hong Thap Tu Street, strung across the back of the presidential palace grounds. When Jake and Sally got there at midmorning, there was already a good crowd on hand. It was the usual crowd but it was not business as usual. The old French *colons* did not silently nurse opium hangovers; the rich Chinese merchants did not make deals over pots of tea; the Vietnamese bureaucrats and military officers did not compare ideas on how to spirit foreign currency out of the country; and the contingent of privileged Vietnamese youths in skimpy bathing suits did not debate the merits of Sartre and Freud and their other Occidental gurus in bored, misinformed voices. As with Radio Catinat, all the talk this morning was of the developments in Cambodia.

Gulliver and Sally changed and swam awhile, then sat poolside with Bloody Marys. Sally in a wet bikini—little more than two Band-Aids and a cork, Gulliver joked—turned heads, including his. They were thinking about ordering lunch when a waiter approached the table. "Mademoiselle Teee-Chair? You are wanted on the telephone."

Sally went inside to take it and when she came back she was in street clothes. "It was the embassy," she told Gulliver. "Steelman wants us. I told you they'd call today."

"I've got a feeling the party's over," Gulliver said with a groan. He changed and they walked back to Sally's villa, picked up her motor-pool Pinto, and drove the short distance to the embassy. They went straight up to Bennett Steelman's office on the fifth floor.

Unlike the previous meeting, Thomas Scott, the chief of station, was not there. Neither was Wyatt Howe or Duc Hoang. Tom Patton, the agency base chief from Can Tho, was. So was George Cameron.

"Long time no see, George," Gulliver said with a smile. "I can't say I've missed you." Cameron just nodded. The P officer looked sober and nervous.

Steelman seemed to be in an uncharacteristically good mood. A detailed map of Phnom Penh was lying faceup on his desk, along with a notepad turned facedown. "Good news out of Nompers, eh, old girl?" he asked Sally with a broad smile.

The nickname for Cambodia's capital was an affectation Steelman had copied from the Brits. There was a whole list of them. Saigon was "Saggers," Hong Kong "Honkers," Bangkok "Bankers," Singapore "Sinkers." It was the sort of terminal cuteness that had helped lose the English an empire, thought Gulliver.

"Oh, I don't know," Sally said wistfully. "I rather liked poor old Snooky."

Steelman snorted. "Prince Sihanouk was a royal pain," he said firmly. "We are well rid of his highness."

Gulliver glanced at the map again. It was covered with circles drawn in red grease pencil and scattered notes, and he wondered if Radio Catinat might not be right about agency involvement. It would not be the first time. Steelman noticed his interest and casually but pointedly folded the map. He rolled his chair over to his cabinet safe, stuck both the map and the notebook inside, and spun the combination lock.

He scooted back to his desk and began, "Well, then . . ." He stopped, looked at Sally, and after a thoughtful pause said, "I think it might be a good idea if you left the room now, old girl."

Sally looked confused. "Me? Leave? Why?"

"I just think it might be for the best."

"Well, I don't," she said angrily. "What in the hell is going on? Am I the case officer for this thing or not?"

"Yes, but—"

"No buts, Bennett. You cut me out now and you'll have my resignation within the hour."

Steelman hesitated, then shrugged. "All right. Have it your way." He fingered his intercom. "Eva, will you send in Sergeant Perinowski? And I'll need you as well."

The secretary came in, followed by a burly marine NCO. Steelman said, "If you would all please stand. I'm afraid I must ask you to submit to a body search. Go ahead, Sergeant. Eva, would you do the honors for Miss Teacher?"

Uncertainly, they stood. "Uh, what are you looking for, Bennett?" Cameron asked, bewildered.

"Recording devices," Steelman said.

When everyone had been frisked, Steelman said, "Thank you, Sergeant; thank you, Eva." He waited until the two of them were gone before saying: "Before I continue, I must remind you that everything you hear in this room today is classified. If you repeat anything, ever, to anyone, sanctions will be taken against you. Severe sanctions."

Steelman let that sink in, then looked at Cameron, then at Gulliver, then back at Cameron. After a portentous pause he said: "Do it."

Cameron and Gulliver exchanged a quick glance. "Do what, Bennett?" Cameron asked.

"Do what the Hoa Hao want."

Everyone looked stunned except for Patton, who had known what was coming. He looked shamefaced.

"You mean *execute* them?" Cameron croaked. "Bich and Dang and . . . S-Swain?"

Steelman leaned back in his chair and placed his feet on the desk. He pursed his lips, put his fingertips together, and spoke to the ceiling. "It will be a tragic accident," he said regretfully. "Two tragic accidents, really. Captain Bich will be found in his office at Special Branch headquarters, dead of cyanide poisoning. It can only be assumed that he took his own life. We really don't know why he did it . . . does one ever know in such cases? But there will be no mystery surrounding the unfortunate deaths of Captain Dang and Lieutenant Swain. They were killed in a communist ambush while on a routine PRU outing. Undeniably a hazardous line of work."

Cameron's hands were shaking. "Bennett, we can't do this thing," he said in a strangled voice. "It's . . . not right."

"I know it's not right, George," Steelman said quietly. "But it's necessary."

"Why? Why is it necessary?" Cameron asked.

Steelman shook his head. "Oh, come now, George," he said. "You know the answer to that as well as anyone."

He paused to explain to Sally and Gulliver: "Minh and his people have been pleading with the Hoa Hao to drop their demand . . . and have gotten nowhere. Meanwhile, Dinh is putting on the pressure while he waits for our response. There have not been any more demonstrations, but he has put out the call just in case. Our estimates are that another five to ten thousand Hoa Hao have quietly slipped into town in the past few days."

Steelman turned back to Cameron. "If their demand is not met, the province is going to explode, George, and President Thieu can't have that happen. He can't have Cronkite airing film of his troops attacking his own people. This happens to be an especially critical time. The administration has major Vietnam aid bills climbing the Hill in Washington."

"So put the men on trial and let the chips fall where they may," Sally Teacher said, speaking for the first time, her face drawn.

Steelman shook his head again. "We can't. That would be the worst-case scenario," he said. "I'm afraid the Phoenix is a nocturnal bird, old girl. It does not flourish in the light of day."

"Then Jake's been right all along," Sally said. "Those men are guilty. Trung was innocent."

Steelman shrugged. "I don't know, Sally. I really don't. And frankly, at this point I don't care. It doesn't matter."

"Nothing seems to matter to you," she said bitterly.

Steelman took his feet down and slapped his hand on the desktop. The report was like a pistol shot and Sally jumped. "Don't speak to me like that!" he shouted, his face knotted in rage. "How dare you speak to me like that! Do you think I like this? These are company people, *my* people. They got into this fix because they were good company men, doing a job, and now I have to sacrifice them because I'm a good company man, doing a job. That's what the company does for our government, Miss Teacher. We're its janitorial service. We clean out the cesspools. We unblock plugged toilets. We do the filthy jobs so that the White House can stay white, so that the Congress can sleep at night. Do you see anyone from State here? Anyone from the palace? Do you even see your own chief of station? No! Because it's down-and-dirty time . . . time for Razor. Oh, I forgot, you don't know Razor, do you, old girl? Well, that's me when it's down-and-dirty time. Ask Gulliver, he knows. Oh, yes, the Sandman knows. And when it is down-and-dirty time, it's always the same: we're counting on you, Razor . . . we know you'll do what you have to do, Razor . . . handle it, Razor. Well, Razor is handling it. Razor is doing what he has to do."

Coming from Steelman, it was a remarkable outburst. It seemed to drain him. He put both his elbows on the desk and buried his face in his hands . . . a portrait of anguish.

Gulliver, who had yet to say a word, didn't buy it. He recalled a similar portrait, a photo of President Johnson in the Oval Office, his head in his hands, supposedly agonizing over Vietnam. If Gulliver himself had peeped in the window and seen such a sight . . . maybe. But LBJ was not one to forget there was a photographer in the room. And neither was Bennett Steelman. Gulliver was not sure whom Steelman was playing to. Sally probably. Or maybe he was hoping to convince himself.

"How do you want it done?" Gulliver asked.

Steelman slowly picked his head up and gave Gulliver a grateful smile for getting down to business. "Each of them will be given a limited and, of course, different version of the Hoa Hao ultimatum," he said. "Bich will be told nothing. He will be terminated first, by Dang, who will be told that Bich is being sacrificed to appease the Hoa Hao. Dang will make it look like suicide. Likewise, Swain will be told that Dang is to be sacrificed to the Hoa Hao and that you are in on the plan. Cameron will order the three of you into the bush to pick up a high-ranking communist defector. Once you are in an appropriate spot, Swain will terminate Dang. Then you, Captain Gulliver, will terminate Swain."

After a long silence Gulliver said, "So. A replay of Nguyen Tu Vuong."

Steelman winced at the name. "It is somewhat similar to the methods employed by Colonel Sculler's people, yes," he said carefully.

"Well, the Green Berets aren't going to do your killing for you this time, Razor," Gulliver said quietly. "Not this Green Beret anyway. Get yourself another boy."

Steelman clucked. "Oh dear. Perhaps you don't like the way I've allocated the assignments. No problem. We'll simply change things around. Dang can do Swain and you can do Dang. Would that be more to your liking?"

When Gulliver did not answer, Steelman added, "Ah, that must be it. Do forgive me for being so inconsiderate. You're probably anxious to take care of Dang yourself."

"Why do you say that?" Gulliver asked.

"Because he's sleeping with Miss Nhu, your Viet Cong girlfriend, of course," Steelman said. "I would think that you'd want to avenge your honor. Most cuckolds do."

There was a silence. Everyone in the room was watching Gulliver. Gulliver watched Steelman with an empty face.

"Nothing to say, old boy?" Steelman asked. "Perhaps you didn't know that your comrade in arms was having it off with Miss Nhu. Or is it that you didn't know she was a Viet Cong?"

When Gulliver still did not react, Steelman frowned. He seemed disappointed. "No doubt about it," he said. "We have the two of them on tape, going at it hammer and tongs."

Still no response. Steelman, determined now to provoke him, said: "No doubt about her political affiliation either, I'm afraid. Her neighbor—you remember Mr. Tho, the tailor, don't you, old boy?—is the local struggle-group commander. He reports to Miss Nhu. He also reports to me. We're still not absolutely certain about Captain Dang, but we strongly suspect he's VC too. But then, it doesn't really matter, does it? Or at least it won't in a couple of days. If he is, we'll just get ourselves two birds for the price of one."

Gulliver made no sputtering protest, no strident denial. It was not that he had been shocked into speechlessness, but that he was not shocked at all. The instant the accusations left Steelman's mouth, he knew they were true. If anything surprised him it was that he was not surprised. Nor outraged. Rather than surprise or anger, he felt numb, a deadness so profound it was almost a total disinterest.

"I don't care," he said. "I'm not going to do it."

Steelman smiled. "I had a feeling you might say that." He reached into a drawer, withdrew two sets of papers, and slid them across the desk. One was an undated resignation form with Captain Gulliver's name and particulars already typed in, and the other was a set of court-martial papers charging Captain Gulliver with refusal to obey a direct order in time of war and verifying that the accused had read and understood the charges against him. "If you'd be so good as to sign one or the other for me, please," Bennett Steelman said pleasantly.

Gulliver almost laughed aloud. It was the old game from Nha Trang. He knew now that it was a bluff. Maybe he'd always known it. They would not risk a court-martial that might let out their slimy secrets. No, they'd do it in other ways, ways that would make the continuation of his military career all but impossible. A succession of bad assignments, each ending with a bad efficiency report, followed by a few passovers on the promotion lists; or maybe they'd go for the quick kill, some invented scandal complete with CIA-planted evidence to get him on a trumped-up charge of "conduct unbecoming."

Gulliver looked into Steelman's complacent smiling face, then pulled a pen from his shirt pocket and flipped to the last page of the resignation form. He filled in the date and scribbled his signature. "There you go," he said, tossing the forms back across the desk.

Steelman's face changed, going from a smug look to something resembling panic. "Don't be daft, man," he said, an almost desperate quality to his voice. "It's stupid to throw away a career for a melodramatic gesture that won't change a thing. The Hoa Hao terms will still be met."

"Meet them without me," Gulliver said. He turned to Cameron. "I guess I'll be flying back with you to pack up."

"Like hell you will," Steelman interjected. "You are not to have any contact with the other Embassy House team members under any circumstances. I'll make arrangements to have your things shipped up on the morning mail bird and delivered to your room at the Duc."

"No," Sally said. "Have Captain Gulliver's things sent to Eighty-four Nguyen Du Street. He's staying with me."

Steelman's lips tightened and he gave her a contemptuous

look. "You disappoint me, old girl," he said in a quiet, cold voice. "You can give my secretary the sordid particulars when you leave."

"I'll do it when *I* leave," said Gulliver, standing. "And that's now." He walked over to shake hands with Patton, then with Cameron. He put a hand on the P officer's shoulder and said: "Good-bye, George. Don't let the bastards get you down." Then, with a final, rather enigmatic glance at Sally Teacher, he showed himself out, in violation of station rules.

When Sally saw the darkened villa, she assumed he wasn't home. Even so, she called his name as she came up the veranda steps, and when there was no reply muttered, "Damn." She was about to turn on a light when a voice came from the shadows: "Leave it off."

She jumped and spun around, then exhaled with relief and asked: "What are you doing sitting in the dark?"

"Trying to picture myself as a civilian."

There was just enough light filtering in from the street to make him out. He looked unfamiliar in his fatigue uniform, bloused paratrooper boots, and beret; a total stranger. Sally had never seen him in uniform before, had almost forgotten he was a soldier. He was drinking beer. She could see the wink of the bottle as he brought it up to his mouth.

"Are you drunk?" she asked.

"Not yet."

Sally sat in a rattan chair across from him. "Well, I'm afraid the decision stands," she said, thinking he would want to know. "Steelman ordered Cameron to take your place in his little scheme."

"Then Steelman's in for another surprise," Gulliver said quietly. "He won't do it."

"Poor old George didn't look happy about it," she said, "but he didn't say he wouldn't do it."

"He won't."

She changed the subject. "How long does it take to . . . I mean, when will you be going home?"

He laughed, a choking sound. "Home," he said, mouthing the word with suspicion, like a child trying a new vegetable.

"I don't even know where your home is," Sally said in an attempt to lighten the atmosphere. The room's air was broody and sullen, like the season's own, full of storm clouds that refused to throw rain and cool things off. "Where is home?"

"Any place where I don't stand out in a crowd, I guess," he said.

There was a long silence. Then Sally said quietly, "All right, Jake. What's eating you? Is it because you expected me to resign too?"

After another pause he said, "I don't expect anything of anyone anymore."

"That's it, isn't it? You expected me to quit too."

"I'm just puzzled by your priorities, that's all," he said. "You were ready enough to quit when you thought you were being taken off the case."

"So. You're disappointed in me, too."

She thought she saw a shrug in the shadows.

"I hate it, Jake. I do," she said in a defensive voice. "I think it's brutal and sick and I find the whole thing as abhorrent as you do. The reason I'm so late is that I stayed to argue against it. I argued against it with all my might."

"Good for you."

"God damn you," she said softly.

"Yes. God . . . damn . . . me," he said in a weary voice, separating the words, changing them. "And God damn them."

"What you really mean is God damn *me*, don't you? 'Them' is me."

"And me," he said. "I told myself that I wasn't one of them. I thought it was enough to despise them; that as long as I despised them I wasn't one of them. But I was. All it takes is . . . not telling them to go piss up a rope."

"I know the company is doing a bad thing, but in this kind of environment . . ." Sally shook her head. "I haven't been here as long as you, but I've been here long enough to know that war makes people do bad things," she said. "And that war can subvert an institution as easily as it can an individual. God, just look at the Army. But what good would it do for me to resign? The law prevents people like us from going public. So isn't it better to stay and try to change things? Reform comes easier from the inside."

"Thank you, Robert McNamara, Clark Clifford, and McGeorge Bundy."

"You son of a bitch!" Sally said. "I worked hard to get here. Why should I throw away my career because of an animal like Swain? You were the first to call them murderers. Maybe they deserve what they're getting."

"Maybe they do," Gulliver said calmly, "but they deserve a trial first."

"Good God, Jake, I know that," she said, lowering her voice a little. "But why blame me?"

"I'm not blaming you."

"Oh yes you are. And I don't understand why. If you want to sit on your high horse and hand out blame, blame Steelman, blame the Mad Monk."

"I don't wake up in the morning next to Steelman or the Mad Monk. I didn't fall in love with Steelman or the Mad Monk."

She recoiled as if he'd slapped her. "Oh . . . Oh," she said in a surprised, hurt voice. "Th-that's not fair."

When he did not say anything, she asked: "Did you really love me?"

"Yes."

"And now?" she asked, bracing herself.

"Yes."

She exhaled a little, then asked, "But you don't *like* me anymore, do you?"

"About as well as I like myself."

"That doesn't seem to be much."

"No. Not much."

Sally stood and moved to a window. The villa's windows were all paneless and Chi Ba always left the wooden shutters open until Sally had retired for the night. Sally could smell a sweet, sticky perfume coming off the flowerbeds, and from a tree in the corner of the garden a gecko called out to her.

"So what are you going to do now?" she asked, her back to him.

"Get a seat on the Freedom Bird and fly away from this place," he said.

"I mean after that, after you're out. What are you going to do?"

Sally could not see his shrug. "I don't know," he said. "Whatever it is that civilians do, I guess."

"What would you like to do?"

"I don't know. I've always done what the Army told me to do."

"But where will you go?"

"I don't know. I've always gone where the Army told me to go."

He sounded so lost she had to fight the impulse to go to him and cradle him. "My tour will be up in about a year," she said, still with her back to him. "I'll probably be sent back to Washington. Maybe you could find something there."

He did not comment. The gecko sounded again, squawking like a throat-sore mynah bird, giving Sally goosebumps. When she turned around there were tears in her eyes. "It's been one hell of a day. I think I'll go to bed. Are you coming?"

"In a while," he said.

Still at the window, standing between the light and his face, all Sally could see was the Special Forces flash on his beret and the white T-shirt top at his throat, nothing in between, nothing of his face. She trailed a finger across his shoulders as she went past him and into the bedroom. She left the door ajar, undressed, and got into bed. She lay awake for a long time, listening for him, hearing only the occasional clink of a bottle as it hit the floor. When she finally fell asleep a couple of hours later, he still had not come to bed.

22

GEORGE CAMERON, SITTING BY HIMSELF in the gloom of the Duc Hotel bar, ordered another vodka and eavesdropped on the three young couples at the next table, indulging himself in the illusion that he was not alone.

"I don't care how much you want to go skinny-dipping," one of the men was saying to his date, an Army nurse, "you shouldn't even think about driving to Vung Tau after dark."

"What could possibly happen?" The nurse pouted. "It's a major highway, for God's sake."

"Yeah, but it changes hands at night," said a second man, who had a woman, another nurse, on his lap. "Particularly one bad stretch that runs through the Michelin rubber plantation. There was an ambush there just this week."

"Then let's skinny-dip in the river," said the woman.

There were hoots from the men. "You'd be dead of a dozen diseases before you could dry yourself off," one of them said with a laugh and a shake of the head. "Remind me never to ask for you if I get wounded and end up at Third Field."

"Oh yeah?" the woman shot back. "From what I hear about you, the most likely reason you'd show up on my ward would be because you've contracted a few diseases of your own." There was more laughter.

Cameron laughed along with them, then stopped when he found himself on the verge of weeping. He was drunk, but not drunk enough to go on hoping that companionship of his very own, in the form of Jake and Sally, might still walk through the door.

He was lonely but not resentful. It made him feel better to think that Jake and Sally were together tonight, that Jake had found someone, something, to hold on to. Just as it had made him feel better when Jake had resigned his commission. He knew how much Jake loved the Army, how much it had cost him to sign that piece of paper. But it was time to draw the line. Time for everyone to draw the line . . . the company, the country, everyone.

Cameron remembered the rush of exhilaration he had felt when Gulliver had signed the resignation form. He had been full of pride and admiration for Jake . . . and full of shame for himself. He knew that he too should have quit on the spot. But Jake Gulliver had the stuff of heroes in him . . . George Cameron did not.

Even as the impulse to join Gulliver had quickened his blood, George Cameron's mind had been on practicalities: his pension, his company insurance, his daughters' college bills, his ex-wife's alimony. They might not love him anymore, but he still loved them, and felt responsible for them. How would they get along without the money he provided? It wasn't their fault he had signed on for a second Asia tour, then a third, a fourth, a fifth, and a sixth. It wasn't their fault he had abandoned them at the same time he was letting the steam out of a promising career. It wasn't their fault that just when they were expecting him to settle down at a desk in Langley, expecting the suburban good life in Virginia, he had to go and fall under Vietnam's spell. He had given up everything for Vietnam, and this was what it had come down to. Cameron sighed and signaled the waitress for another drink.

But damn if it hadn't been worth it for a time—a long time! Cameron laughed, remembering Lou Conein's stories when he got back from Hanoi in '54, where Ed Lansdale had sent him to organize an agent net before partition closed the door on the North. How Conein had crept into the compound where the Hanoi public buses were parked and poured sugar in their gas tanks.

It was a game then, a grand game played by appealing, if aging boys, and Cameron had been one of them. He could still hear Lansdale telling him about his first "counterinsurgency" operation, when the colonel was a boy and he and his brother had been ambushed by bigger boys and pelted with snowballs. Fair enough, except the snowballs were iceballs. So the two Lansdale boys made their own iceballs, with rocks packed in the center, and counterattacked. Years later, when Cameron was in the Philippines with Lansdale during his brilliant campaign against the Huks, he once suggested burning a cache of captured Huk rice. "No," Lansdale had said with a grin. "Let's sprinkle it with broken glass and leave it for them." Sabotaged iceballs, sabotaged rice—it was all the same when you were playing the game.

Cameron remembered once, in those early Saigon days, when Lansdale sneaked away on an unauthorized trip to Phnom Penh to visit with the KGB agents assigned to the Russian embassy. Lansdale and his "enemies" had spent a wonderful day tossing back vodka and recounting all the dirty tricks they had played on one another over the years. Cameron sometimes wondered if they all couldn't have switched teams and had just as good a time.

But then Lansdale and Conein were gone and things began to change. The war got serious. The time for games was over. The time for expediency had arrived.

It had been one goddamn thing after another. Like using Air America to transport opium in exchange for intelligence and other favors from the Laotian and Thai mountain tribes who were controlled by the drug merchants. Like arranging for an American helicopter gunship to fire an "errant" missile into Vice-President Ky's Cholon command post during the Tet fighting in Saigon, a missile that killed six of Ky's most powerful lieutenants and helped President Thieu consolidate his grip on the government. Like the selling-out of Cao Giao.

More than anything, it was what the company did to Cao Giao that had caused Cameron's disenchantment to take a quantum leap; Cao Giao had been a good man and a good friend. He had been a prominent Vietnamese officer who, with CIA assistance, had helped establish the Revolutionary Development Cadre Training School. Later, he came to resent CIA dominance of the R-D program and left to become province chief in Kien Hoa, where he served until his election to the National Assembly. The outspoken, popular Cao Giao soon began to worry President Thieu, who saw him as a possible political threat and who resented both his power and his popularity. Thieu looked for a way to nail him and finally found one. Cao Giao's brother was an officer in the North Vietnamese Army and the CIA had persuaded Cao Giao to keep in touch. President Thieu used this contact to charge him with being a communist, citing the provision in the law forbidding contact with the other side. After a press campaign which spread allegations fabricated by the palace, Cao Giao was physically dragged from the Assembly and jailed. He was still there. The CIA, in its accommodation of the president, denied any knowledge of Cao Giao's contact with this brother. The company left him holding the bag.

And then, of course, there was Phoenix: the shakedowns; the reprisals; the indiscriminate violence; the "specials" for Minh; the lying about how Trung died; and now the command to bushwhack three men, three colleagues, one of them a fellow American. That was what it had come to after twenty years.

He knew that the majority of the people in the Vietnam station were good people, decent people. But where were they? Why hadn't they put a stop to it all? What had happened to his company? His life? George Cameron put his arms on the table, put his head on his arms, and cried.

The group at the next table, the three agents and their nurses, fell silent. A moment later they paid up and left.

After a while Cameron stopped crying. He dried his eyes, called his waitress over, and asked for a fifth of vodka and his bill. When they came, he paid his bill, tucked the bottle in his coat pocket, and stuck a hundred-dollar bill under the ashtray, then left quickly.

He went to the front desk and asked for the concierge. "Excuse me, do you have a map showing the road to Vung Tau?" he asked the man, an elderly Vietnamese gentleman.

"Mais oui, monsieur; j'ai une excellente carte d'ici," said the concierge, who had worked for Monsieur Otavi at the Hotel Royale for six years before coming over to the Duc and tripling his salary, and who still sometimes forgot to speak English. He fished under the counter and brought it up.

"Can you show me where the Michelin rubber plantation is?" Cameron asked, opening and spreading the map. "I think I might like to have a look at it tomorrow."

The concierge showed him. "You cannot miss it, *monsieur*. You will see many many rows of the rubber trees, all straight in a line for many many kilometers."

"Thank you. Uh, *merci*."

Cameron went out into the damp night and asked one of the security guards to bring round his motor-pool Pinto. He was already beginning to feel better. He uncapped the fifth, took a deep, burning pull, and felt better still. When the guard came with the car, Cameron handed the man a hundred-dollar bill, got in, tucked the bottle into his crotch, and drove away.

He saw no traffic, coming or going, once he was through the

city and its protective suburbs and out on the open road. He drove until he had gone many many kilometers into the many many rows of the rubber trees all straight in a line, then pulled over onto the shoulder of the highway and stopped. He cut the engine, doused the headlights, and listened. The many many rows of the rubber trees, an army on parade, made night noises—rodents, insects, bats, owls, rustlings without identifiable source. He was still miles from the shore, but he thought he could hear the soft slap of the sea. He took a long pull from the bottle and turned both the engine and the headlights back on. He switched on the radio, found the armed-forces station, and turned the volume full blast.

It was hot in the car, even with the windows down, and after a while he got out. He took off his clothes and tossed them onto the highway, then climbed up onto the roof, taking his bottle up with him. He sat cross-legged, in naked profile, sipping and sweating, but feeling fine, feeling just right.

AFVN was playing his daughters' kind of music—acid rock they called it—and it was messing with his nerves, with his moment. Cameron liked jazz, and the Big Band sound. He started to scat-sing, trying to drown out the radio. He did "Take the A-Train," then "Moonlight Serenade," then "In the Mood." The radio played a screeching song called "Purple Haze." Cameron laughed and sang even louder, duking it out.

When the first cautious shadows broke away from the rows of rubber trees, George Cameron was on his feet, standing naked atop the Pinto, swinging the vodka bottle like a baton and singing the Harvard Crimson fight song at the top of his lungs.

Jake Gulliver spent the night in the chair and woke to find himself sitting in a graveyard of empty beer bottles, dead soldiers.

He policed up the litter and went out onto the veranda. A few minutes later Sally, wrapped in a sarong, joined him. They breakfasted without bickering, without words, but the silence did not constitute a truce.

The usually effervescent Chi Ba was not flitting around the table this morning; sensing trouble, she was keeping her distance. Gulliver could see her at the front gate, holding it open to let out a small, beat-up panel truck.

When she started back into the house, Gulliver stopped her. "Chi Ba, who was that?"

"A man who came to fix the cold-air machine," she said.

"Oh," he said. "I didn't know there was anything wrong with

the cold-air machine aside from the fact that it's been turned off."

Chi Ba shrugged.

"Did you call him?"

"No."

Gulliver sat up. "Did *you*?" he asked Sally.

"N-no."

He rose abruptly and went into the house. A few minutes later he was back, carrying something, something with a tail, a section of wire. He threw it onto the table.

"What's that?" Sally asked.

"Don't they teach you anything at spook school? It's a bug. I'll give you a chance to redeem yourself; let's see if you can guess who had it installed."

"Steelman?" Sally said.

"That would be my guess."

"But why?"

Gulliver shrugged. "To find out what we're saying about his grand plan. Or maybe he's worried I might do something to gum up the works."

"Would you?"

Gulliver did not answer.

"God, just look at you," Sally said, her mouth twisting. "I can hear the wheels turning. You're wondering if there's a difference between telling me and telling that thing there." She pointed to the listening device with her chin.

He looked away. "Okay. Yes. I've been thinking about it. I spent all night thinking about it."

"What did you decide?"

He looked at her, still debating, then said: "I'm going to warn them."

Sally stared back at him for a long moment, then took a deep breath and said, "Good for you."

They sat down and resumed their breakfast. Resumed their silence.

They were on their second pot of coffee when the phone rang. They heard Chi Ba answer, then call to Sally. She went inside to take it, and when she came back her face was puffy. "Th-that was the embassy duty officer," Sally said, her voice fighting for control. "George Cameron is dead."

Gulliver closed his eyes for a second, then opened them. "How?"

Sally sat down and carefully poured herself more coffee. "A VC ambush. Late last night. On the road to Vung Tau." She brought the cup up to her mouth and poured half its contents down her front. "Damn!" she said. She wiped at the spill with a feeble hand, then stopped, hung her head straight down, and started to cry.

Gulliver did not go to her, did not comfort her. He let her bawl, watching her shaking body with a cold satisfaction. In that moment he hated her, hated all of them. He was used to hating them for those who could hate for themselves—for Colonel Sculler, for the Sandman—but now he hated them for one who could not, for George Cameron.

When she had cried herself out, she wiped her eyes with a napkin and said, "I'm sorry. I didn't mean to lose control like that."

"Don't apologize for a decent human impulse," he said, his voice cutting and cruel. "And don't worry, I won't tell Steelman."

"God, Jake, but you can be a bastard," she said.

"It's my environment," he explained. "Vietnam makes me do it. You know how the war subverts people."

Sally dabbed at her eyes again. "It doesn't make sense," she said. "What was he doing out there at that time of night? Why was he going to Vung Tau?"

He was suddenly weary of her naiveté, her linear, bulky, Western mind. "He wasn't going to Vung Tau," he shouted. "He wanted to go clean! He didn't want to leave a fucking mess!"

Sally cringed. "Wh-what mess? What are you saying?"

Gulliver shook his head and lowered his voice. "He was just another burned-out case to you spooks, a drunk. But he was old-school. He was so . . . so damn *considerate,* so worried about doing the honorable thing. I'll bet he left everything in good shape. I'll bet his desk is clean and his reports are all up-to-date. That's the old-school way. You don't leave a mess for the next guy. You don't leave a mess for those who are staying on. No mess over the insurance or the pension for the wife who left him and the daughters who despised him; no mess for the room boy at the Duc to clean up; no mess for his beloved *company*. The wonderful company that turned him into a rummy, then killed him. But he loved it. How the poor bastard loved it. He loved it like an old man who looks at his dried-up hag of a wife and sees only how beautiful, how magnificent she once was."

Sally, wide-eyed, asked again: "Wh-what are you saying?"

"I'm saying I told you so. I told you he wouldn't do it. I'm saying I didn't have a family to consider, I could quit. He couldn't. I'm saying this was the only way he could think of to get out of it."

Sally put her hands to her face. "Oh no," she breathed.

"Oh yes. His only mistake was that he was in the wrong country in the wrong century. He should have been a British officer in the Indian Army." Gulliver's face buckled. "And I should have been a fucking tobacco farmer."

Sally was crying again, her face ruined and cracked. A rage rose up in Gulliver, a cauterizing rage that seared the nerve endings and froze the blood in his heart. He stood up, reached across the table, and slapped her hard, knocking her completely out of her chair. "You can stop that useless shit right now!" he barked, spitting the words at her.

Sally sat up, holding her mouth, more stunned than hurt. She took her hand away from her face and stared in wonder at her fingers, as if she had never seen blood before. Then she looked up and saw a strange man standing over her. She stared in wonder at him, too, as if she'd never seen him before . . . an unsavory-looking character with hard, taunting eyes full of a mocking contempt, and a smile, faint and cruel.

He reached down with one hand and jerked her up off the cool tiles of the veranda floor, his fingers digging into her upper arm. He took her chin in a viselike hand and swiveled her head around, holding her ear close to his mouth. "Listen and do exactly as I tell you," he said, reaching in a pocket with his free hand. "Here's fifty piasters. I want you to go out the gate and get a cup of noodles from one of the stands. While you're out there, take a casual look around and see if the villa is being watched."

"B-but—"

"Just do it!" he said. "If Razor went to the trouble of planting a bug, then he's probably got the villa staked out too. I want you back here in sixty seconds. Now move!" He gave her a shove.

She was back in sixty seconds. "T-two men. Vietnamese. In white shirts and dark glasses."

"Good," he said. He took her by the arm again and turned her around, propelling her into the front room. "Now call the embassy and find out what's happening now that Cameron's been scratched."

She made the call, then another. When she hung up, she said: "It looks like Steelman himself is taking over. He left the embassy for Air America just about an hour ago. The pilot filed a flight plan for the Delta."

He moved toward the rear of the house, dragging Sally along with him. "What's behind the house?" he demanded. "On the other side of the wall?"

"An alley," Sally said. "If you go to the right it leads to the roundabout at the cathedral, if you go to the left it takes you toward the palace grounds."

"Okay. Now listen. If the embassy calls asking for me, tell them I'm sleeping off a drunk, tell them anything, but make them believe I'm still here. If you blow the whistle on me I'll find some way to come back here and kill you. Do you understand?"

"Y-yes." She was too frightened to protest the insult.

He let her go. Sally followed him through the kitchen and out the back door. She watched him pick up a garbage can from in front of the concrete bungalow where Chi Ba lived and position it next to the high wall that ran around the villa grounds. He hopped up onto the can, then jumped, caught the top of the wall, and pulled himself up. He lay prone on top of the wall, scanning the alley, then turned to give her a last look, and dropped from sight.

The instant he was gone Sally Teacher began to shudder, a violent trembling she could neither stop nor slow. She had no doubt that she had finally, at long last, met the infamous Sandman.

23

BENNETT STEELMAN ARRIVED EARLY that afternoon to a badly shaken Embassy House. The news of George Cameron's death had preceded him, and he found himself swamped with questions he was hard put to answer.

No, he did not know why Cameron had tried to go to Vung Tau in the first place.

No, he did not know why Cameron had started after dark.

No, he did not know why Cameron had sallied out unarmed and, as it turned out, without sufficient gasoline in the tank.

No, he did not know why the VC stripped Cameron before they shot him to death.

Yes, there was evidence that Cameron had been drinking.

Yes, it was indeed a sad, tragic business.

"Jeez. It's a shame," Swain said for the fourth time in the last half-hour. "He was a pretty good guy."

And for the fourth time in the last half-hour, Coughlin and Riesz nodded their agreement.

They sat at the poker table in the common room, holding a wake of sorts, for themselves as much as for Cameron. They felt besieged. The PRU ambush . . . the Trung Affair . . . now this. They were beginning to think the house was jinxed. Bad joss.

They had dutifully spent the last half-hour dredging up amusing or poignant anecdotes about George Cameron. None of the team members had considered him a particularly good P officer, but they all had liked him well enough, and one of the verities of Vietnam was that a violent death invariably enhanced a man's reputation. Only Bennett Steelman, despite having put on his best mourning face for the occasion, was genuinely unmoved. He was still greatly annoyed by Cameron's inexplicable behavior. The chief of operations should be in Saigon basking in the afterglow of the success in Cambodia, not in some sweaty backwater doing a dirty job he had twice tried to delegate.

Steelman gave it a few more minutes, then turned to Bill Coughlin, who was now the senior resident, and asked: "What's going on in town?"

Coughlin shook his head. "Nothing, sir," he said, "It's remarkable. One day we've got pitched battles in the streets, the next day everything's quieter than a church on Super Bowl Sunday. There hasn't been a demonstration since the day after the funeral."

Swain chimed in: "That's because when Ngoc's boys kicked ass, they put the fear of God into them."

Steelman nodded as if that explained it. Among the house staff, only Cameron and Gulliver had known about the Hoa Hao moratorium on demonstrations.

"The longer Nguyen Khac Trung is in the ground, the more time tempers will have to cool," Steelman said. "Perhaps it's all over."

"I hope so," Coughlin said. "But my counterpart doesn't think so. Major Do's agents have been picking up significant Hoa Hao in-migration in the last week. And those two outside agitators—that Mad Monk and that Loc kid—are still in town. Do thinks they're just beefing up their numbers before they take to the streets again."

"Just let 'em try," Swain said belligerently. "If Ngoc can't handle it, we'll sic the PRU on them. We'll make them think the Field Force was a bunch of Girl Scouts."

Steelman did not tell Swain that Major Ngoc's days as commander of the Field Force were numbered. So were Swain's.

The mention of the PRU reminded Riesz of Gulliver and he asked, "When is Jake coming back, sir? He's been gone a whole week now."

"He will be gone much longer than that," Steelman said. "He won't be coming back. Captain Gulliver has resigned his commission."

They looked surprised; it was turning out to be a day full of change. Swain unsuccessfully tried to quash a grin.

"Why?" Coughlin asked.

Steelman shrugged. "Who knows? Perhaps George was the last straw. You have to remember how long Gulliver's been over here, how many friends he's lost. It tends to add up."

When no one said anything, Steelman added: "That was one of the things I wanted to discuss with you. Once a man leaves the company's service, he is quarantined, kept isolated from all former associates. So if Gulliver makes any attempt to contact any of you in any way, you are not to talk to him. You are to refer the matter to me. Is that clear?"

They all nodded.

"Good," Steelman said. "I know we are all disturbed by what's happened, but life must go on. In that regard, I've decided that Coughlin will serve as provincial intelligence officer for the short time left to us. I appreciate that you would rather have had the job under happier circumstances, Bill, but you have my congratulations."

It was the first time Steelman had ever called Coughlin by his Christian name. Feeling that a show of pleasure would be inappropriate, he just dipped his head in acknowledgment.

"I'm afraid I'll have to ask you to work a double shift, Bill," Steelman said. "We just don't have time to find you a new Special Branch adviser."

"No problem," Coughlin said. "Major Do doesn't need much advising anyway."

"Good. What I can do for you is give you back your PRU. Lieutenant Swain will resume his duties as adviser, and you can put him—and them—back to work."

Coughlin nodded.

"And that brings me to the primary purpose of my visit," Steelman said. "We've been contacted by a North Vietnamese Army colonel who wants to defect, the commander of the NVA forces operating from the Fish Hook sanctuary in Cambodia."

"Jeez!" Swain said.

"Yes, a big fish," Steelman said. He turned to Coughlin. "No reflection on you, but I want to handle this one myself."

"I understand, sir," Coughlin said.

"I'll be taking Lieutenant Swain and Captain Dang along with me to pick him up. And that's all I'm at liberty to tell you. I want to keep this on a need-to-know basis."

"I understand, sir," Coughlin said again.

"Good. So if you and Riesz will excuse us . . ."

"Oh, yessir." Coughlin and Riesz got up quickly. "Uh, I was thinking maybe I should box up George's things," Coughlin said, almost apologetically. "What should I do with them?"

"I will have to let you know," Steelman said. He paused, then said in a musing voice, "Just before I cabled the tragic news to Langley this morning, I was looking through Cameron's personnel sheet. Do you know what he put down as his official home of record?"

"No, sir," Coughlin said.

"The Duc Hotel, Saigon, Republic of Vietnam. Rather sad, isn't it?"

"Yessir, it is."

Steelman waited until Coughlin and Riesz had cleared the room before turning to Swain and saying, "Before we call in Captain Dang, there is something I would like to discuss with you, Lieutenant."

"Yessir?"

"Do you remember when we talked about the possibility of your joining the company on a staff basis?"

"You bet I do! I haven't thought about anything else since."

"Then you might be interested to know that it's all set. You won't even have to wait until you're free of the service. I've arranged for you to be discharged within the week."

Harry Swain was momentarily speechless. Every part of his face seemed to be in motion at once—his mouth, his eyes and, of course, his bushy brows. When he at last found his voice he sputtered: "That's . . . that's . . . Number One, sir!"

Steelman nodded benevolently. "And do you also remember when I told you that the province chief might have a special assignment for you from time to time?"

"Yessir!" Swain said, still grinning broadly, unable to get over it.

Bennett Steelman smiled back. "Well, one of those times has come up."

Gulliver's first stop was the alley. The chances of Dang being with Nhu were remote, but it was the only starting point he could think of.

He had already been by the Embassy House, cruising past the floodlighted main gate in the taxi he'd hired in Saigon, deciding at the last second not to risk it, even though there was nothing out of the ordinary to be seen from the street. He did not know where Steelman was, or what kind of tale he had told the Embassy House crew, but instinct told him that Razor would have him arrested if he just went barging in.

He left the taxi on the street and was almost to Nhu's door when he was intercepted by the flower girl who always blushed when he spoke to her. He knew it was important because she spoke first, without prompting or preamble. "She is not here. They took her away."

"Who?" Gulliver demanded, taking her by the shoulders, unmindful of the genie who lived there. "Who took her away?"

"I don't know. The police. Someone. Four men."

"What kind of clothing were they wearing?"

"White shirts and dark trousers. And glasses, the kind that keep out the sun."

He ran back to the taxi. The driver, unfamiliar with the town, had to be given directions to the provincial compound. Gulliver had him park across the street from the gate. "I'll give you an extra thousand piasters if you'll take a message in for me," he said. The driver eagerly agreed and Gulliver bummed a pencil and sheet of paper from him.

"You are to give this to Major Do of the National Police Special Branch," Gulliver said as he scribbled out a message and signed it "He Who Pisses Up Ropes." The driver gulped and nodded, sobered by the mention of Special Branch.

Gulliver watched the driver approach the QC on sentry duty, saw the military policeman make a phone call, then wave the driver in. A few minutes later he was back with Major Do, who got in back with Gulliver and told the driver: "Drive."

"Wh-where would you like to go, sir?" the driver asked, nervous in the presence of a Special Branch officer.

"Just drive."

The car pulled away and Major Do turned to Gulliver with a smile and said in English: "I am happy to see you, *Dai Uy*. I did not know whether I would have an opportunity to bid you *au revoir*."

"If you know I'm leaving," Gulliver said, "then you must have talked with Steelman."

Major Do nodded as he screwed a Gauloise into his ivory holder and lit up. "It is always such a pleasure to talk with your Mr. Steelman," he said. "His French is quite excellent."

Up front, the driver edged his face closer to the window to keep from gagging on the blue cloud that filled the taxi.

"Did he use his excellent French to tell you why I was leaving?" Gulliver asked.

"No. Just that you had resigned. Nothing more."

"Was he speaking excellent French when he asked you to arrest Quynh Nhu?"

Major Do gave Gulliver another of his skinny sideways smiles. "It is always embarrassing, in any language, when a man does not know the things he's paid to know," he said. "I had no idea you were a . . . special friend of our famous flower. You are a man of unsuspected dimensions, *Dai Uy*."

"Where is she? What are the charges against her? What have you done to her?"

The major made a ducking motion. "Please, *Dai Uy*, one question at a time," he said. "She is at the Interrogation Center. All we have done is ask her a few questions. She is being detained under the national subversives act, but I do not expect that we will bring formal charges against her. We will probably release her in the morning."

"Then she's *not* working for the communists!" Gulliver said exultantly. "Steelman was wrong!"

"Of course she works for the communists," Major Do said, shaking his head at Gulliver's ardent naiveté. "She is one of their interzone coordinating cadres."

Gulliver blinked. "Then why don't you charge her?"

The policeman shrugged. "Quynh Nhu is perhaps the most popular citizen in the province. The people worship her. My men thought they were going to have to fight their way out of that smelly alley when they went to pick her up."

"What does her popularity have to do with anything?"

Major Do gave a heavy sigh; the inability of Americans to see and appreciate political subtleties would never cease to amaze him. "If we charged her and put her on trial, then into prison, it would do the government more harm than good," he said with great patience. "For us it would do nothing but rid us of a single cadre, but for the communists it would be a propaganda victory. For if someone like Quynh Nhu supports the NLF, what are the people to think? No, we will let her go if she promises not to engage in any more illegal activities. And if she cooperates."

Gulliver managed to look both relieved and worried. "Has she cooperated?"

Major Do made a rocking motion with his hand and said: "*Comme ci, comme ça*. Mr. Steelman and I questioned her this afternoon but she would tell us nothing. Then I spoke to her alone and she opened up a little. She seemed to trust me. My charm, no doubt."

Gulliver did not smile. "What did she tell you?"

"Quite a bit, really," Do said. "She admitted using her position with the Cai Luong to carry directives and messages among the provincial central committees of the Western Nambo Interzone, the six provinces below the Bassac River. But she claimed not to know the identities of any of the people with whom she dealt;

they used a complicated cut-out system. She also told me that the chairman of the Western Nambo Interzone is a man called Comrade Hoa Binh from Can Tho—how droll to use 'peace' as a *nom de guerre*—but that she never saw his face and never met him in the same place twice."

"Did she mention Dang?" Gulliver asked.

"She admitted knowing Captain Dang—she had no choice; we have proof of their, ah, their acquaintance on tape—but she refused to implicate him, as your Mr. Steelman would have her do. She insisted that he knew nothing of her work for the communists."

Gulliver turned his face away, looking out the window. They had circled the block and were passing the provincial compound again. "What is her relationship with Dang?"

The major shrugged. "She says they are friends. They have known each other since they were children in Ben Tre."

"Ben Tre," Gulliver said quietly, nodding to himself. "I always suspected Dang was a Southerner."

"Yes," said Do, "but the rest of his story, as told by Quynh Nhu, is close to the way he has told it. He attended Saigon University, then universities in America and France. After that we cannot track him, until he became a *hoi chanh,* when he walked into the government's open arms."

The gears turned in Gulliver's head. "Dang was the one who took me to see her perform for the first time," he said. "It was through a friend of his that I met her."

Major Do nodded. "Yes. It would appear that he arranged for her to meet you."

"But why go to all that trouble?" Gulliver asked. "If she was after intelligence on Embassy House operations, she could have gotten it from Dang easily enough."

"I don't know," Major Do said, "but I believed what she told me. She was crying and even though she is a professional actress, I am a professional policeman and I always know. Her tears were quite real."

After a pause Gulliver asked: "Did she mention me?"

"Oh, yes. Mr. Steelman specifically asked about you. She said only that like Captain Dang, you too were her friend," Do said. He lit a fresh Gauloise from the first and flipped the butt out the window. "When I was alone with her she told me that she often heard her VC friends speak of an American assassin who had killed many comrades. They knew him only by reputation. They called him the One Who Comes at Night." The policeman paused. "She said that Dang once told her you had done such work for the CIA. They called you the Sandman."

Gulliver sat slumped in the seat. The taxi was passing the provincial compound for the third time; the driver was not a man of great imagination. Neither was Gulliver at the moment. His mind felt numb, thick and slow.

"Is it true, *Dai Uy*?" Major Do asked in a soft voice. "Are you this man they call the One Who Comes at Night?"

"Funny," Gulliver whispered, more to himself than to Do, "but that's what the old man called the VC. The men who come at night. Funny."

"Are you, *Dai Uy*?"

Gulliver closed his eyes and nodded.

This time it was Major Do who was silent, until Gulliver said: "I must see Dang."

"Captain Dang is not here," Do said.

Gulliver sat up straight. "What do you mean, not here?"

"I called your Embassy House not more than an hour ago to speak with Mr. Steelman about Mademoiselle Nhu," the major said. "I spoke to Mr. Coughlin, who told me Steelman left the city late this afternoon with Dang and the *Trung Uy*."

"Where did they go?"

Do held up his hands. "I don't know."

They made another circuit in silence, and as the taxi swung by the compound for the fourth time, Gulliver asked, "Can I see Nhu?"

Do shook his head. "I'm disobeying Mr. Steelman's orders even by speaking to you."

"Please," Gulliver said. "I want to tell her good-bye."

Do was regarding him with sympathy, thinking it over. To tip the scale, Gulliver said, "It may be to your advantage."

The policeman raised a thin, skeptical eyebrow. "How?"

"Did she tell you anything about the Trung Affair?"

Do looked surprised. "*Mais non*. I did not ask her about it. Should I have?"

"Yes. And I think she'll tell me about it; I know which questions to ask."

Major Do toyed with his mustache a moment, then ordered the driver to stop; they were nearing the provincial compound gate yet again. He pulled a gold-plated pencil and a notepad from his shirt pocket, scribbled something, and tore off the sheet. He handed it to Gulliver and said: "Be at this address in one hour."

* * *

Gulliver smiled when the Nung at the Embassy House gate poked his head in the window.

"You cannot enter," the Nung said in heavily accented Vietnamese.

"I live here, remember?" Gulliver said, still smiling.

"You cannot enter," the unsmiling Nung repeated. "I have orders."

Knowing that one could not argue with a Nung, Gulliver smiled once more and gave up. He had the driver back out and drive away, then ordered him to turn off the headlights and proceed up a rutted dirt road skirting the cleared area that surrounded the compound. They stopped at a cluster of shacks nestling in the palm grove at the back of the Embassy House. Gulliver got out of the taxi, went to the first hut he came to, and pushed through the door, a woolen army blanket tacked to the header.

The PRU and his family—a wife and four small naked children—were at their evening meal, squatting around a brazier set up in the middle of the room's dirt floor. They all looked up when Gulliver came in, and gaped in amazement.

Gulliver still had on the uniform he'd been wearing when he left Saigon, the beret pulled tight as it would go, hiding his pale hair. It took a moment for the man—a squad leader named Hanh, Gulliver remembered—to recognize him.

"Oi! Dai Uy!" The PRU jumped to attention. He started to salute, then realized he had a rice bowl in one hand and his chopsticks in the other. After a moment's hesitation he went ahead and touched the chopsticks to his temple.

Gulliver returned the salute and bowed to the wife. "I'm sorry to disturb you and your family, Corporal Hanh, but I'm looking for Captain Dang," he said. "Would you know where he is?"

"He is gone," Hanh said. "A helo came and he left with the *Trung Uy* and another man; an important man from Saigon."

"Do you know where they were going?"

"No, sir." Hanh hesitated, then said, "Would you take some food with us, *Dai Uy*? It's simple fare, just rice and fish, but there is plenty."

"Thank you, but no; I don't have time," Gulliver said. He gave the PRU a long look, then asked: "Have you and the others been told not to speak to me?"

"Yes, sir," the man said, looking uncomfortable. "The *Trung Uy* gathered the men today and made a speech. He said that you are no longer one of us."

Gulliver nodded. "He spoke the truth."

Corporal Hanh looked momentarily confused; then he set his chin and announced: "You are still my captain. You will always be my captain."

Gulliver smiled, but he felt like weeping. "Thank you, Corporal Hanh," he said. "Tell me, what time do you usually go back to the barracks?"

"About this time; right after my supper."

"Do you know the sentry on the back gate?"

"Yes. The Nung called Lao. One of the better ones."

Gulliver paused, then said, "Hanh, I have to get inside the Embassy House. Will you help me?"

Hanh hesitated, glancing at his wife. Her look warned him against doing anything that would get him into trouble. He looked back at Gulliver and nodded. "Yes. What would you like me to do?"

"I need you to get the sentry away from the gate long enough for me to slip through."

"But you still have the clearing to cross," Hanh said. "I could draw him a hundred feet away from the gate and he would still see you before you got to the big house."

"We'll have to get him out of the compound altogether," Gulliver agreed. He paused a moment, thinking, then asked: "Does this man Lao have any special vices that you know of?"

Hanh smiled. "All Nungs have many vices. This man is very fond of American whiskey, the kind that is made in your province of Kentucky."

"Do you have any here?"

"No, sir. I am a good Buddhist; I do not drink alcohol," Corporal Hanh said. "Besides, who could afford it?" Then his eyes shone. "I know someone who has some whiskey. Private Cu, whose family also lives here."

"Wasn't Private Cu one of those killed on the mountain?" Gulliver asked.

"Yes, but his wife may still have it."

Gulliver dug out his wallet and took out two ten-dollar bills. "Would she sell it to you for this?" he asked, holding out the money.

Corporal Hanh took one of the bills. "This will be more than enough," he said. "I will be back soon."

Gulliver went out to tell his driver to go back and wait on the street in front of the Embassy House, then returned to the hut and waited himself, under the baleful eye of *Ba* Hanh.

Hanh was back within five minutes, bearing a smile and a half-full fifth of Seagram's. "What do we do now, *Dai Uy*?" he asked, pointedly ignoring his wife's disapproving looks.

"Go and tell the guard that you'll take his post for a minute if he'd like to come back here for a drink," Gulliver said. "As soon as he leaves, I'll go in. The men in the tower are too far away to see anything except another PRU returning to barracks after an evening meal with his family."

Hanh gave it a moment's thought, then grinned. "Yes. It will work."

It did work. Minutes later, Gulliver slipped through the back door and into the villa kitchen. Chi Ba and Chi Hai were fixing dinner. Both women looked up briefly, smiled, and went on with their work. He went down the hall, stopping to listen at each door. He almost skipped George Cameron's office, then went back and put his ear to the door. When he heard a rustle of papers, he tapped lightly.

"Come on in," a voice called; Coughlin's voice.

Gulliver swung open the door, stepped inside, and closed it behind him.

"Jake!" Coughlin, sitting behind Cameron's wooden desk, stood up quickly, a smile starting to spread across his face. Then he stopped smiling and said, "God damn, Jake. You're not supposed to be here."

"Hello, Bill," Gulliver said, smiling. "Steelman's gone, isn't he?"

"Well, yes, but . . . God damn, Jake. You're not supposed to be here."

"So you've said." Gulliver looked around the office and saw that George Cameron's things were gone. The group picture of the Harvard eight-man sculling crew of 1936. The varnished oar which had hung over it. The photograph of a smiling, much younger George Cameron standing between former ambassadors Henry Cabot Lodge and Maxwell Taylor. The photos of Cameron with other notables of other eras—General Kanh, Thich Tri Quang, Generals Do Cao Tri and Tran Van Don, President Diem. Friends and foes. "You're letting your new job get to you a little, aren't you, Bill?"

"I didn't want this job; I didn't ask for it," Coughlin said defensively. He sat back down and asked in a suspicious voice, "What are you doing here, Jake?"

"Looking for Steelman. Where did he go?"

"I couldn't tell you if I knew," Coughlin said, sounding relieved. Not knowing meant he didn't have to make choices.

"It's important, Bill."

"I don't know where they went, Jake. That's the truth. Steelman didn't tell me."

"He must have told you something."

Coughlin put a cigarette in his mouth but did not light it. He played with the lighter, doing parlor tricks with it, avoiding Gulliver's eyes. Finally he looked up. "Look, Jake, I don't know what's going on between you and Steelman, and I don't want to know. All I know is I have my orders."

Gulliver just stared at him in silence. Coughlin stared back, the unlit cigarette still in a corner of his mouth, his Irish detective's face filled with indecision. He flicked the Zippo open and closed with one hand, using only his thumb and middle finger. *Click-snap . . . Click-snap . . . Click-snap*. The only sound in the room. After a long moment he sighed heavily and said: "They took one of our maps. That's all I can tell you."

Gulliver smiled and nodded. "Thanks, Bill."

He left the office and went to the map room—a large walk-in closet just off the radio room—and started going through the files, looking for what *wasn't* there. The maps were covered with acetate and hung from wooden rods set in a stand, like wide flat strips of fresh pasta on a drying rack. The maps were numbered and broken down by province, district, village, and hamlet, with several scale gradations for each geographical area. The numbers were sequential and it took Gulliver only a couple of minutes to discover which one was missing: the map of La Plaine des Joncs.

The Plain of Reeds, Gulliver thought with a sudden sense of despair. A wild, desolate place; a perfect dumping ground. Mile after square mile of swamp and wetlands that appeared or disappeared according to the rains, there one week, submerged the next. Its only real substance was its size. They could be going anywhere.

Gulliver stepped into the radio room, sat at the console, and slowly smoked a cigarette. He needed to give his panicky feeling time to wane, and himself time to think. It was true they could be going anywhere. But they would almost certainly start off from Moc Hoa, one of the few towns at the edge of the Plain. There was a PBR base there, a Navy Riverine Force—and a small embassy-house operation with PRUs run by the Navy's SEALs. Razor could find the equipment and transport he needed there. Yes. Moc Hoa would be his line of departure.

If he was right, they would spend the night at the Moc Hoa embassy house and push off in the morning, either by helo or Navy patrol boat, depending on where and how far they were going. If he could hitch a chopper ride at first light—no pilot would fly into Moc Hoa at night—he just might catch them before they left.

If he was not right, if he went tearing off to Moc Hoa and Razor had not taken them there . . . Dang and Swain were as good as dead.

He got to his feet, ground his half-smoked cigarette out on the floor, and went down the hall to his old office. It was locked. He tried his key and it slipped in easily. Swain had not changed the lock. Sloppy, Gulliver thought as he let himself in.

Swain's things were littered about the room but Gulliver saw that his own web gear—with scabbard and K-bar—still hung on the peg behind the door. He strapped it on. He found a stub of camouflage stick in a desk drawer and stuck it into his pocket, then squatted and opened the bottom drawer of the file cabinet. He groped around in the back until he found the cellophane packet of pills he had taped there, and put those in his pocket. He took one last look around, switched off the light, and left, going out through the common room and double front door.

As he passed through the compound gate, Gulliver grinned and gave the wide-eyed Nung sentry a cheerful "Good evening."

24

THE ADDRESS MAJOR DO HAD GIVEN HIM turned out to be a Special Branch safe house beside the Bassac River. It was a modest thatch-roofed bungalow hidden behind a wall covered with bougainvillea and topped with shards of broken glass. Gulliver was let onto the grounds by a heavily armed White Rat, turned over to another gun-toting plainclothesman at the door, then was taken to a room with no windows and told to wait.

The room looked as if it were used for interrogations. It was bare of furnishings except for two chairs set facing each other three feet apart in the middle of the floor under a dangling light cord. Gulliver sat down and waited another ten minutes before Nhu was led in.

"*Anh* Jake!" She wrenched away from the two White Rats who escorted her through the door and rushed to him, burying her face in the crook of his shoulder. The two Special Branch agents gave each other leering looks and withdrew.

Nhu trembled against him and Gulliver held her close, stroking her waist-long hair, running his hand from the back of her head down to the swell of her buttocks. Through the wall of his abdomen he could feel her heart pound like that of a frightened bird. He cupped her chin with his hand and raised her face. Her dark sloe eyes were misted and tears hung from the corners like notes on a line of music from a sad libretto. Her lips were wet and puffy.

She let go of him and ducked her head. He took her hands in his and sat her down. He took the other chair and they sat facing each other, their knees touching, holding hands.

"Are you all right?" he asked.

She managed to nod while still keeping her chin tucked into her breastbone. "Major Do did not tell me you would be here," she said, her voice faint. "I did not know where he was taking me, or why. I was so frightened."

"There's nothing to be afraid of," he crooned, kneading the backs of her slender, fine-boned hands. She kept her head lowered, eyes in her lap, as if she were reluctant to let him see her face. He was suddenly afraid he might have missed a telltale mark of abuse. "Have they mistreated you?"

Nhu shook her head. "Oh, no. Major Do has been very kind, very understanding. He is a gentleman."

"Then look at me."

She shook her head.

"Nhu, why won't you look at me?"

"Because I am ashamed," she said in a child's voice, one he did not recognize from any of her roles. She still had not lifted her eyes. "You must hate me now, *Anh* Jake."

He bent over and lightly kissed the top of her head. "It is this war I hate, *Em,* not you . . . never you," he said softly, knowing even as he said it that it was true. He did not hate her. In some way he could not define, Gulliver felt closer to her than ever before.

The truth of it must have been in his voice, because she raised her tear-streaked face. "Yes," she said. "I, too, hate this war."

They looked at each other without speaking for a moment, until Gulliver said, "If you hate it, why did you join it? I had no choice. I am a soldier. But why you?"

"I had no choice either, *Anh* Jake. I am a Vietnamese."

He shook his head. "I realize no Vietnamese can escape the war," he said. "But thousands of people stay out of its bloody reach as best they can, joining neither side if they can avoid it, cooperating with both sides when necessary. I thought that was what you were doing."

"That is no escape, *Anh* Jake. My brother tried to play both sides and he died."

"I didn't know you had lost a brother in the war . . . you never told me . . . I'm sorry," Gulliver said. "But that doesn't change what I am saying. You are a woman, a famous woman. If anyone could have gotten away from it, you could. You didn't have to be a fighter in this war, Nhu . . . you chose to be."

"No! I did not choose!" she said, pulling her hands out of his, no mewling in her voice now. "My life was chosen for me, when the Americans bombed Ben Tre at Tet. In one second, a single beat of the heart, my mother and father, my three sisters, my two baby brothers—all gone. An entire hamlet gone in the wink of an eye. All but me and my older brother. Your American friends were considerate enough to wait a year before killing him too." Nhu's eyes were still damp but she was no longer crying. Her face was hard yet brittle-looking.

"*Em*, I . . . I didn't know," Gulliver said falteringly, not knowing what to say to her. "But if you feel that way about Americans, why did you go with me?"

"In the beginning . . . because they told me to," she said. "Later . . . because I wanted to." Her face softened and she took up his hand again. "I tried to hate you, *Anh* Jake. You cannot know how hard I tried. In the beginning, when you made love to me, I would close my eyes and think of bombs falling and of burning houses and the crying of children. Even now I try to make myself see these things, so I might kill this love I have for you, but I have played the part of your mistress too well . . ." Her mouth began to tremble and she stopped.

Neither of them said anything for a while; then Gulliver said: "You say you love me. Then what about Dang? Where does he fit into all of this?"

Nhu was silent a moment longer, then squeezed his hand and said, "Dang is my husband."

Gulliver felt a slow paralysis overtake him, as if the blood had thickened in his veins. His mind kept on working, but not on what she had said. Instead, he was vaguely aware of how foolish he must look. He pictured himself as a comic-book figure, with mouth dropped open and eyes popping out of their sockets.

When he did not speak, Nhu said, "We were betrothed when I was thirteen, and married when I was fifteen. We have loved each other even longer than that . . . since childhood."

Gulliver still could not speak. It was not that he could not find the words to express his feelings, but that he could not find his feelings.

"I know it is hard for you to understand," Nhu said. "It has been hard for Dang too. But I think he understands. I've told him that you and he are too much alike, that you are one and the same man, and that if I did not love you both, then I could not love him. It is true. Do I make any sense to you?"

Gulliver shook his head. The movement seemed to loosen his tongue. "No."

This time it was Nhu who was silent. She let go of his hand and began fiddling with one of the panels of her *ao dai*.

"But it was Dang who arranged for us to meet," Gulliver said. "If he is your husband, why did he do that?"

"What does it matter?" she asked. "I will never see you or him again. Major Do told me you are returning to America. And I will be going to prison, to Con Son Island."

"No, you won't. They are going to release you tomorrow."

She looked at him with disbelief. "How can that be?"

"They have their reasons," Gulliver said. "But you are right that this will probably be the last time I'll be able to talk to you, so I need for you to answer some questions for me."

Nhu shook her head.

"For *me,* Nhu, not for them."

She did not say yes, but she did not say no, so he went ahead. "Why did Dang want us to meet?"

She didn't answer. She was staring at her lap, her slim fingers picking at her clothing.

"Dang is still working for the VC, isn't he?"

When she still did not answer, Gulliver said, "It makes no difference now, Nhu. You cannot protect him with silence. They plan to kill him anyway."

That got a reaction. "No! You are trying to trick me."

"Your friend Bui Dinh wants an eye for an eye," Gulliver said quietly, "and the American who questioned you, Steelman, is going to give it to him. The three who interrogated Trung are to be killed to placate the Hoa Hao."

Nhu grabbed Gulliver's hand, squeezing hard. "You are not trying to trick me? It is true?"

Gulliver nodded. "It is true."

The color left her face. "It has happened as he said it would," she whispered. "Meat for the hungry tigers." She dug her long fingernails into the back of his hand and said in a desperate rush: "You must stop them! You must! He saved you! He did it for me because he loves me, but he also did it for you because he loves you! He saved you and now you must save him! Please, *Anh* Jake! Will you save him for me?"

"I don't know if I can," Gulliver said, telling her the truth. "I don't know if I want to." That, too, was the truth.

"Please! You must try!" She had started to cry again. It amazed him how mercurial she could be, how she could be hard as tungsten one moment, as pliant as a reed the next.

"I can't decide until I know the truth," he said. "Will you answer my questions?"

"Yes," she said meekly.

"Is Dang VC?" He knew the answer; he was testing her to see if she intended to tell the truth.

"Yes. He is a colonel of intelligence in the National Liberation Front."

"Aw Jesus," Gulliver muttered in disgust, in English. It looked as though she was indeed going to tell the truth, with a vengeance, and he was suddenly uncertain that he could cope with it. He decided to start slow, to take last things first.

He asked another question to which he already had the answer. "About Trung . . . I know it was you who gave my report to the Hoa Hao, but who gave it to you?"

"Dang."

"Was Nguyen Khac Trung innocent of the charges against him?"

"Yes. Your report was quite accurate, *Anh* Jake. It was Nguyen Van Trung, one of our comrades, who took delivery of the weapons."

"Did Dang know that Nguyen Khac Trung was innocent when he helped Bich and Swain interrogate him?"

Nhu paused, then nodded.

Gulliver closed his eyes, then opened them and asked: "Then why, Nhu? Why did he help them kill him?"

"To save our own man, of course," she said with a little shrug. "When the two prisoners revealed Comrade Trung's name, Dang became worried. But then the *Trung Uy* Swain—your Ugly American—brought up the name of Nguyen Khac Trung. Dang saw an opportunity to protect our Trung and make trouble for the government at the same time, and he seized it. Captain Bich had left the room. The *Trung Uy* spoke no Vietnamese. It was a simple thing for Dang to substitute his own translation in place of the woman's answers. All he had to do was repeat the *Trung Uy*'s own description of the house. It was simple yet brilliant. Our superiors were very impressed."

Gulliver felt nauseated. The realization that Dang had set the whole bloody mess in motion hit him like a stomach cramp. "So am I," he said at last. "He is one cold-blooded son of a bitch."

Nhu shook her head. "I have known him all my life, but he can be as much of a mystery to me as he must now seem to you," she said in a soft, sad voice. "He can be a very hard man."

"He is a lot harder than I am if he could let me sleep with you," Gulliver said, unable to keep the bitterness out of his voice. "Why did he permit it? Why did he want us to meet?"

Nhu took a deep breath and said, "So that I could kill you."

Gulliver just looked at her, then shook his head slowly, got up, and started walking across the room. When he got to a wall, he stood facing it for a moment, then turned around and came back. He sat down, and, exercising control only with a monumental effort, said quietly, "Tell me about it."

"All right. It is very complicated, but I will try." She sat primly, ankles together. Both hands were in her lap, and it was to them that she spoke.

"First of all, you must understand that my people think of you as a very dangerous man," she said. "You have killed many comrades. I do not know how or when they first heard of you, only that you became known to them as the One Who Comes at Night."

Nhu raised her head and looked directly at him. Gulliver let his eyes lock with hers for a second, then looked away and nodded.

"Several men, one after another, were given the task of identifying and . . . and eliminating the One Who Comes at Night. They all failed. Then the job was given to Dang." Nhu paused, as if she needed to gather strength before going on.

"Dang and my brother worked together," she said at last. "They collected intelligence while pretending to work for the Americans. Last year, in the spring, my brother was found out and the CIA had him murdered. The One Who Comes at Night was rumored to be in the area at the same time and it was thought that he did it. In his grief, Dang volunteered to do what all the others had failed to do, to find this man and kill him."

Gulliver was staring hard at her. "Your brother . . . where was he working?" he asked with an odd urgency.

"Along the border," Nhu said quietly. "With the soldiers who wear green hats . . . like the one you are wearing."

"Vuong," Gulliver said in a hoarse, strangling whisper. "Your brother was Nguyen Tu Vuong."

"Yes," Nhu said. "Nguyen Tu Vuong."

Again Gulliver had to get up and walk. He wandered about the room, his head reeling, tracking along the walls, wishing there was a window to look out of. Just as he neared the door one of the White Rats started to open it, to check on things. Gulliver kicked the door closed, nearly taking the man's head off, and yelled: *"Dung phien toi!"* Don't bother me!

It seemed to break the spell. He returned to Nhu and sat down. She had not moved. She sat perfectly still and straight in her chair, like a pious young girl in a church pew. He met her eyes and said slowly: "I have killed many men, Nhu, but I want you to know this: I did not kill your brother."

"I know that," she said. "Do you think I could have let you into my bed if I did not know that?"

"I . . . I just wanted to be sure you knew."

"But I did not always know it, *Anh* Jake. For a time I thought you had . . . and that was when I agreed to kill you for them."

"Jesus," he said. "Maybe you'd better tell me the rest of it."

Nhu nodded and said, "When my brother's death became a scandal, Dang went to Saigon to see what he could learn. He learned many things. I do not know how. Dang has sources of information I know nothing about."

"What did he learn?" Gulliver asked.

"That the CIA had its own name for the One Who Comes at Night—Sandman—and that you were this man. That you spoke at the sham of an inquiry and told the generals that it was a man called Razor who ordered the death of my brother."

"Did he learn who Razor was?"

"No," Nhu said with a shake of her head. "But he hoped you might tell him. He followed you to this province, using one of our people in the government to arrange his transfer here. He was hoping to gain your confidence, then kill you. That you had not killed my brother made no difference . . . you had killed others."

"But he never asked me about Razor," Gulliver said.

"It did not take him long to see what kind of man you were, that you would never tell him," Nhu said. "If he had been clumsy about it, you would have been suspicious."

"So why didn't he go ahead and kill me? He could have done it easily enough, on any number of missions."

"Because Comrade . . . because his superiors decided that it would be better if I did it." Gulliver passed a hand over his face. "They saw an opportunity to get me to work for them at last," Nhu said simply, as if it were perfectly clear. "For a long time they had tried to recruit me. They thought I could be useful—with the Cai Luong I can travel without arousing suspicion, and I mix with many important officials. Dang had asked me, but I had refused. I cared nothing about politics, only about the theater."

"What changed your mind? Ben Tre?"

"No, not even that. Ben Tre made me bitter, but I know that war is war," she said. "It was Vuong, the way they shot him in the back. Dang's superiors ordered him to tell me you had killed Vuong and to ask if I wanted revenge. Once I had killed for them, they thought they could use me any way they chose. I . . . I agreed." Nhu hesitated, then said softly, "It was not fate that brought my troupe to this town, *Anh* Jake . . . or you to my bed."

"But you didn't do it."

"Only because Dang disagreed with the plan," she said, as if it were important that he should not think too well of her. "Our superiors had no interest in my brother; all they wanted was you. But Dang wanted this Razor. So before you and I were together that first night, even as I steeled myself to kill you, he told me you had not murdered my brother. He suggested that I go ahead and play your mistress, that we work together to find out who had killed Vuong. To buy the necessary time from our superiors, I agreed to work for them."

"Well, you have done a good job for them, *Em*," Gulliver said, his mouth twisting. "They must be very happy with you."

"No, they are not happy," she said, her tone as empty of bitterness as his had been full. "When their patience ran out they told me to go ahead, to kill you. When I did not do it, they told Dang to, and when he did not do it, they tried to do it themselves. The ambush on Nui Giai Mountain was meant for you. But Dang disobeyed them again." Nhu paused a beat, then said quietly, "He saved you, *Anh* Jake. And now you must save him."

When he didn't say anything, she said: "I have betrayed you and I have no right to ask anything of you, but you must save him. I love you, *Anh* Jake, but he is my husband. He is of my people, my past. My family is gone. He is all I have left of my old, happy life."

"You don't have to explain to me, Nhu," Gulliver said. "I understand."

Nhu smiled, her first smile since she had come into the room, and nodded. "Yes, I know you do. It is a good thing you do not love me, *Anh* Jake. It makes everything easier."

He started to say something, a protest perhaps, but she leaned over and put a finger to his lips. "Be quiet. I have always known that you do not love me and I, too, understand."

"I'm not sure I understand anything anymore," Gulliver said. "God help me but I love this fucked-up country. But I know it can't love me back. I have sinned against it. It is not mine to love. It was never mine to love, just as you—Dang or no Dang—were never mine to love."

She touched his cheek and said, "You have left too much of yourself in this land for it not to be yours. I, too, will always be yours, for you have left too much of yourself with me for it to be otherwise."

He was silent.

"*Anh* Jake? You will save him for me?"

Gulliver made a grating sound that was supposed to be a laugh. "It's almost funny," he said. "I find myself willing to forgive him everything: the fact that he's my enemy . . . the lies . . . even for having you in a way I never can—but I can't forgive him for helping them murder Nguyen Khac Trung, a man I never even knew."

"Do not be so quick to judge him," Nhu said quietly. "He has done many bad things, I know, but so have you. He has done them because he loves his country. I do not know your reason. I think perhaps you are jealous of him."

"Jealous? If you think that I don't love you, how can you think I'm jealous?"

She was shaking her head. "I do not mean that. It is not my love for him that makes you jealous, because you know that you have it, too. But he has something you have not been able to find here."

"What's that?"

"A cause."

Gulliver gave a snort. "A cause? What kind of cause? Some fool's paradise like communism?"

"Any cause," said Nhu. "And he is not a true communist. He is a nationalist, a *Southern* nationalist. But that is a struggle for the future."

"After the foreigners are out, you mean," Gulliver said. "Foreigners like me."

"You are different. You are his brother."

"Bullshit!" Gulliver said hotly. "I am not his brother. I am his enemy."

"You and he are far more alike than you will admit," she said. "At times I think you were both pulled from the same womb, seconds apart, like twins."

He began a dissent, but she quickly said: "No. Let us not quarrel. It is time to say good-bye. Let us do so with an embrace, like old lovers, like old friends." Tears formed in the corners of her eyes and she showed him a brave smile. "I hope you find a cause, my *Anh* Jake. I hope you find a happy life. I hope you find a good American woman and marry her."

In spite of his mood, in spite of himself, Gulliver had to smile. "Now, who would want a slightly damaged former soldier with no home, no marketable skills, and no prospects?" he said.

"What about the red-haired one you brought to my house? She was very beautiful and very nice and there was something, an enchantment, between you. It made me jealous to see you with her. But also I was happy for you, too. I thought that with such a woman you might find what you need—someone, something, to believe in."

He shrugged and looked away. "It doesn't look like it's going to work out. Nothing ever works out," he said. But he did not want her to think he was indulging in self-pity, so he tried to make a joke of it. He gave her a grin, shrugged, and said, "What's a man to do?"

Nhu cocked her head and put on a serene face, a sage's face. "Everything . . . and Nothing," she intoned solemnly. "You must always remember that nothing is what it seems, that there are circles within circles, wheels within—"

With a bellow that was half a laugh, half a cry, he grabbed her, snatched her out of her chair, and twirled her.

They were still hugging each other when the door swung open. It was Major Do. "*Dai Uy,* I am sorry, but you must say good-bye now. I must return to my headquarters at once."

The police chief seemed uncharacteristically flustered. "What is it?" Gulliver asked. "What's happened?"

"It's Bich. They just found him at his house. It seems he has taken his own life. Please, you must say good-bye now." Major Do disappeared from the doorway, leaving in his place the two White Rats.

Gulliver, still holding Nhu, looked down at her. "It's started," he said quietly.

With a little sob, she pulled his face down to hers and kissed him. It was a deep, heartbreaking kiss and she packed everything she was feeling into it: regret, terror, sadness, and love. When she broke off, she stepped back, looked into his eyes, and whispered: "*Anh* Jake. Save him."

25

GULLIVER ATE A LATE SUPPER of pills and stale canteen water, then fed the mosquito population. His blackened face, hands, and forearms were puffy with bites and he felt drained, as if he'd lost a gallon of blood. The camouflage paint had not deterred the insects in the slightest, had only been the frosting on their cake.

He lay in the tall grass along the edge of the airfield, midway between the helicopter revetments and the long line of Quonset huts where the married VNAF pilots lived. The junior pilots of the Vietnam Air Force did not live much better than the infantry.

He poked up his head every ten minutes or so for a look, keeping watch on the second Quonset hut from the end, and on the Popular Force soldier who was supposed to be guarding the helicopters. The sentry, stretched out on a stack of sandbags no more than twenty yards away, had been asleep for almost an hour. The light in the Quonset hut had gone out on the dot of midnight, some forty minutes ago.

The second hut from the end was the home of a Lieutenant Canh. For Gulliver's purposes, any pilot would have done, but there was an undeniable satisfaction, a certain symmetry, in enlisting the services of his *friend,* the pilot who had flown the medevac mission on Operation Dog Catcher. A quick call to the VNAF Flight Operations Center had been all he had needed to get the man's name and address.

Gulliver spent the next three hours there in his night blind, lying on his back, longing for a smoke, letting the mosquitoes feast. He topped up his high as needed. The pills were working fine. They held the urge to sleep at bay and let his amplified ears monitor the snoring of the guard even as his jazzed brain raced with random thoughts—of Sally, and Nhu, and Cameron, and Dang; of his own uncertain future.

At four o'clock he went to work. The guard, still sound asleep, was easy. Gulliver just walked up to him and knocked him out, using the butt of the man's own rifle. He used his K-bar to cut away enough of the sentry's shirt to make a gag and used a combination of clothing strips and the man's belt to make a truss. Then he laid him on the ground and stacked sandbags on top of him, leaving just enough space around the nose for him to breathe.

He crossed a drainage ditch and the road that fronted the row of huts and tried the front door. It was surprising how often the Sandman had found doors unlocked. Not this time. He walked around the hut and tried the back door. Locked. He tried each of the eight windows—two in front, two in back, and the two on each side—all locked, even the window with the air-conditioner bolted in. Lieutenant Canh was a careful man.

Gulliver took a moment to think. There would be no roof access; the only hole was where the stovepipe poked through, and the curving side wall made quiet climbing impossible. He would have to tunnel—Americans usually put floors in their Quonsets; the Viets rarely did.

He went back to the window with the air-conditioner and peered in. There was some moonlight coming into the room, and in a corner a candle flickered. It was enough for Gulliver to see that it was the main front room and that it was empty.

The air-conditioning unit was working and making enough of a racket to render Gulliver's stealth more a holdover from habit than a necessity. He knelt to inspect the ground below the air-conditioning unit and, as expected, found it soft and muddy from the steady drip of the condenser. Gulliver grinned in the darkness, unsheathed his K-bar, and began to dig.

The corrugated siding was only a half-inch thick and was sunk less than a foot into the ground. Gulliver spent fifteen minutes clearing away enough dirt to get his head under, ten more minutes making the hole large enough to squeeze through, and was in.

Gulliver spent a moment getting his bearings. A plywood partition with two doors cut into it divided the house. The room he was in took up about two-thirds of the hut's total length and seemed to be a combination living room and dining room. It was sparsely furnished with a sofa, two chairs, and a table for meals. The candle in the corner was set on a small Buddhist altar, and hanging on the wall above it was a velvet painting of Christ. Lieutenant Canh was a very careful man.

Gulliver picked a door—a shower curtain cut into long strips—and stepped through. It was a small bedroom crammed with three cots. In each was a sleeping child. He backed out and went into the other bedroom. Lieutenant Canh and his wife lay side by side on a large slat bed. *Ba* Canh was curled into a ball. Her husband slept on his back. Both were wearing the *ao ba ba,* the sleeping pajamas made of light cotton. Directly above the bed hung a framed photograph of Air Marshal Nguyen Cao Ky, the patron saint of the Vietnamese Air Force.

Gulliver took out his knife and set the edge just under the man's Adam's apple, then reached down and put a hand over the pilot's mouth.

Lieutenant Canh's eyes popped open and he tried to sit up and speak at the same time. Gulliver applied pressure on the blade, shook his head, and breathed a soft "Shhhh." The woman stirred but did not wake.

Canh sized up his situation in an instant. His eyes bugged in terror but he managed a slow, careful nod. Maintaining a light but constant pressure on the K-bar, Gulliver took his other hand away from the man's mouth and grabbed a handful of greasy hair. He slowly eased the pilot out of bed and backed him from the bedroom. They went out through the front door.

Gulliver took his prisoner across the road to where he'd left the guard. The guard was still out, snug under his quilt of sandbags. Gulliver stepped away from Canh and squatted to pick up the sentry's rifle. The pilot stood stock-still for a long moment; then his knees buckled and he sat down hard. He stared at his legs as if they had betrayed him.

"It's just a reaction to tension," Gulliver explained in a soft voice, speaking English. "Very common."

The man squinted up at Gulliver, trying to make him out behind the camouflage, getting no help from the stray cloud that drifted across the moon. "Wh-who are you?" he stammered. "Wh-what do you want with me?"

"My name is Gulliver, and I want that chopper ride you promised me . . . *friend*."

* * *

They spent the remaining hour of darkness in Lieutenant Canh's ship and took off at the first streak of light. There was no problem about clearance; when Gulliver had Canh radio the tower, they both were surprised to learn that it was not manned at that hour.

The flight to Moc Hoa took forty minutes. They made the trip with the radio switched off and Gulliver had the pilot make his approach from straight upriver and put down on the helo pad inside the spook-house compound.

Before the main rotor stopped spinning, two tiger-suited Nungs were at the door with Uzis at the ready and a jeep was coming fast from the direction of the team house. Gulliver and Lieutenant Canh were standing beside the ship when the jeep skidded up to them and braked in a cloud of dust.

The man who jumped out was six and a half feet tall and weighed close to 250 pounds. He had a short-barreled shotgun in one giant hand. It looked as if he had dressed in a hurry. His heavily muscled upper body was bare and he was barefoot. He wore only the bottom half of a pair of black pajamas and a "do rag"—a nylon stocking—on his head. The early sun seemed to bounce off his black skin.

He looked at Gulliver in his camouflage paint, then at Canh in his sleeping pajamas, then back at Gulliver, peering more closely this time. Then he grinned and said: "You're too early, Massa Jake. The minstrel show ain't till next week."

Gulliver grinned back through his blackface and said: "You're quite a picture yourself, Lester."

The giant laughed. "Hey, you know how it is when a man don't get enough beauty sleep."

Gulliver laughed too, and hooked a thumb toward Canh. "Meet Lieutenant Canh of the Vietnamese Air Force." Then he turned to the bewildered pilot and said, "This is Lieutenant Monroe of the United States Navy."

Monroe motioned for the Nungs to lower their weapons and clear out. They both saluted and trotted off, in step.

Gulliver said: "Canh here is missing breakfast with his lovely wife. You mind if I turn him loose?"

Monroe shook his head. Gulliver patted the pilot on the shoulder and said, "Thanks for the ride, Lieutenant." Then he and Monroe started moving away from the helicopter.

Canh paused uncertainly, then scrambled aboard his ship. He was the sole crewman, but the two Americans heard him go ahead and yell out his warning anyway—"Coming hot!"—in English, just the way he had been taught to do in whirlybird school at Fort Rucker, Alabama. Gulliver and Monroe exchanged grins as they watched the helicopter lift off.

When it was away, Monroe gave Gulliver a strange look and said: "You're up awful early this morning, my man."

Gulliver nodded. "I'm trying to hook up with some people from my shop. Are they here?"

Monroe shook his head. "Un-uh. They were up even earlier than you. Left about half an hour ago."

"Shit! By helo or by boat?"

"Boat. Why?" Monroe was giving him the odd look again.

"I need to catch up with them. It's important. Where did they go?"

"Hey, you should know, man. Your number-one Veet-namese was with them. Your man Dang."

"Yeah, but I don't. So where did they go?"

Monroe shook his head again. "Why don't you go in and see my P officer," he said. "Maybe he can tell you."

"Maybe you can tell me, Lester."

"Hey, man, if you don't know, then it ain't my place to tell you," Monroe said. "That Steelman's a mean motherfucker. He would have my ass."

"I wish I could say that if you don't tell me I'll have your ass," Gulliver said. "But you're too big to believe it."

Monroe grinned and nodded.

Gulliver was quiet a moment, then said: "Look, Lester, I'm going to spare us both the ordeal of me trying to run a load of bullshit by you. But I do need to find them, and I can't tell you why and I can't go through your boss. This is strictly back channels all the way. Your PRU and mine have pulled enough joint ops together for you to know if you can trust me or not. I'm asking you to trust me on this one."

Monroe scowled at him for a long moment. Then he said in a nasty, booming bass: "Repeat after me: Green Beanies eat shit."

"Huh?"

"Say it, man. Green Beanies eat shit."

"Green Beanies eat shit."

"SEALs are the greatest."

"SEALs are the greatest."

"Okay," Monroe said with a grin. "Now, what can I do for you, my man?"

The drop-off point was the tip of an island at the edge of the great swamp, an hour's run downriver, and the sun was well up in the eastern sky when Gulliver's small boat pulled in to dock alongside the sleek craft Steelman and the others had come down on earlier that morning.

Gulliver was rather grateful to have made it at all. The best that Monroe had been able to talk out of the Vietnamese Riverine skipper had been a *chu luc,* a leaky converted junk with one .50-caliber machine gun mounted in the bow and a .30-caliber amidship. More important to Gulliver's purpose than firepower was horsepower, and the engine had seemed better suited to a lawn mower. The trip seemed to have taken forever. The junk came with a four-man crew, most of whom had been pirates before they had been shanghaied into the Navy, and they had eyed their passenger the whole way, as if they would have liked nothing better than to kill him for his wristwatch and dump the body overboard.

Steelman, Swain, and Dang had come downriver in style on an American-made Monitor boat with a belt-fed M–70 grenade launcher mounted in the stern and a flamethrower in the bow, along with the usual complement of heavy machine guns. The five-man Vietnamese crew was lazing on deck, and fifty yards off, their American adviser, a Navy lieutenant, was squatting at the river's edge, having his morning bowel movement.

Gulliver could not wait for him to finish. He jumped ashore and asked one of the Monitor's crew: "Which way did they go?"

The sailor lazily pointed to the inland wall of growth and Gulliver could just make out the fresh track cut into it. He made for it on the run.

Monroe had told him that the island was ten kilometers long and badly overgrown, the largest piece of solid ground in the area during the dry season. "The perfect hideout for a VC colonel wanting to defect," Monroe had said. "But I still don't understand why they didn't just take a helicopter in. Slam-bam-thank-you-ma'am, in and out, slicker than shit on a Simonized floor. Sheee-it, they didn't even take a radio with them. Who was in charge of planning this amateur hour anyway? That cracker Army lieutenant?"

With the half-hour difference in starting time and the additional half-hour he had probably lost on the river in his slow boat, Gulliver estimated that he was a good hour behind. His only chance was to make it up on the trail. The track was already broken and he was finding the going relatively easy. He just might have an outside chance. He had not had time to think about what he would do if he did catch up with them. He would have to play it by ear.

Steelman had asked for Monroe's expert advice on the most

direct route to take, so Gulliver had some idea of where Razor planned to spring his surprise. About three miles inland was an oasis of waist-high grass, an island within an island, and it was there that the "defector" was supposed to be holed up.

The grassy plain was supposed to be nearly a mile long, and Gulliver did not know precisely where Steelman would make his play, but he was hoping that he would wait until they had crossed the field, would wait until the last possible minute. Even Razor could not be looking forward to it.

Gulliver went as hard as he could. The sun was high now and as hot as any he had ever felt, as hot as it had been on the day they had walked half-way round Nui Giai Mountain.

The sweat poured down his face and the camouflage paint on his hands and arms streaked and ran, rearranging into new patterns, as effective as before.

He pushed on, his legs growing heavy but his spirits becoming increasingly lighter. The wall of jungle was not very tall but it was abnormally thick. It had to be slowing them down to a crawl. The more he saw of it, the more his confidence gained ground. He was making good time. He was going to make it.

His whirly brain, still in the lingering grip of the pills he had taken earlier, was wiped clean by the sound of gunfire. Three shots in quick succession—*pop-pop-pop*—and then one more. By the time the fourth and final *pop* reached him, a single thought, searing and certain, had rushed in to fill the vacant space in his head. Dang was dead!

26

BENNETT STEELMAN HAD NEVER KILLED a man before, but he was far more curious than nervous about the prospect. As he saw it, there was no cause for nerves. He was an expert with firearms, the Browning automatic pistol in particular, and he would have the element of surprise going for him. He did not anticipate any trouble.

His immediate problem was the terrain. He had never seen anything like this damnable island: saw grass and bamboo side by side with canopied trees and vine-tangled undergrowth; a botanical laboratory with nearly impenetrable walls. That he was inappropriately dressed in a safari suit and a pair of Chinese jungle boots did not help. The boots had looked great when he had bought them from the street vendor in Saigon, but they had already started to come apart at the seams. The spongy earth—not quite swamp, but not quite solid ground either—sucked at his foolish shoes with every step.

There was supposed to be a trail. He had spent a great deal of time poring over the maps before choosing a spot—a clearing three miles inland, well away from the river and the waiting boat crew from Moc Hoa—and, goddammit, there was supposed to be a trail. On the map, it was well defined, a veritable boondock boulevard. On the ground, it was merely the subtlest of hints.

Up ahead at point, Captain Dang was using a machete to transform the path from a suggestion into a reality. Right behind him came Lieutenant Swain, providing cover in case of ambush, his own Uzi at the ready and Dang's AK–47 slung over his shoulder. Both of them were wearing their VC-lookalike uniforms, the black pajamas and rubber-tire sandals of the PRU. Steelman, in a shoulder holster and his Tu Do Street leisure wear, brought up the rear.

With half a mile to go, Steelman was already exhausted. He was not accustomed to this sort of physical effort, or to being out in a heat that could boil blood. His clothing was plastered to his body and his long hair hung from his skull in clumps, like wet hemp. He kept his head up as he stumbled along, scanning the overhanging foliage. He figured that the island must be subject to occasional flooding, because while there was no standing water to be seen, half a dozen leeches had already dropped out of the trees on him. Just thinking about it made him shiver.

But apart from the unforeseen physical discomforts, the operation was going as planned, even better than planned, for he had made one minor but useful change. Swain was supposed to shoot Dang when they reached the far side of the clearing. Then, of course, Steelman would shoot the unsuspecting Swain. But when he saw Dang take over the machete and hand Swain his weapon, he decided that he would shoot Swain first, then deal with the unarmed Captain Dang himself. He would already be in position behind Swain, who would be preoccupied with the plan as he knew it, psyching himself up to take out Dang, his eyes and his mind on his target.

Bennett Steelman smiled, cocked a thumb and forefinger, and flicked a spider off his arm. It was all simply a matter of taking advantage of the tactical opportunities when they presented themselves, he told himself with satisfaction. It was the ability to make quick adjustments in the field, not slavish devotion to a plan, that separated the professional operations agent from the amateur.

They moved slowly but steadily. Steelman watched Dang swing the machete, first with one arm, then the other, never missing a beat, never stopping to rest, and marveled at the man's endurance. He would have to be careful with Dang. He wiped the sweat from his eyes and unsnapped the strap of the holster at his shoulder. He took out the automatic and, for the umpteenth time, checked to make sure that the clip was securely seated. He thumbed the safety to the fire position and put the pistol back in its saddle. He did not refasten the holster strap.

Twenty yards in front of Steelman, Harry Swain also was laboring. He still was not used to the tire sandals and his feet were giving him trouble again. New blisters had pushed up from the ruins of old blisters. In an incredibly short time they had grown large and mushy-looking and had erupted. Swain could see blood on his feet. They ought to give any man who was forced to wear the fucking things an automatic Purple Heart, he thought irritably.

But in spite of his pain, Swain was not an altogether unhappy man. There was only one more hurdle ahead—pulling the trigger on Dang. The prospect did not please him as much as it once would have; ever since the mountain, he had developed a grudging respect for the tall gook. But after that it would be nothing but smooth sailing. By this time next week Harry Swain would be out of the Army and into the company. He would be transformed. He saw himself in expensive Italian suits, in long hair. He saw himself as Mai would see him.

There had been a couple of rough spots, but the Trung Affair had worked out pretty well after all, Swain thought. It had brought him closer to his company "Chinaman," to Mr. Steelman. They were in this thing together, and what Swain was about to do for Steelman would cement the relationship fast. Swain felt a little like the way he used to feel when he went hunting with his father.

An hour later Bennett Steelman saw Captain Dang hesitate in mid-swing, and suddenly there was a doorway of bright light in front of them. They had come to the field, a grassy plate, flat and wide, with only an occasional tree to ruin the view, the inviting illusion of freedom and fresh air.

Steelman had told them that the colonel, their defector, would be waiting for them in a bunker on the far side of the clearing, and Dang did not stop or break stride, just picked up the pace, knifing through the waist-high sea of grass like a motorboat. To Steelman, the fact that Dang was unconcerned with the possibility of trip wires or an ambush was just one more piece of proof that he was VC. He probably *knew* whether or not his fellow travelers were on the island.

They were moving in single file, twenty yards apart, and now that there was no longer any need to cut their own track, Steelman knew that Dang would be asking for his weapon back at any moment. He decided not to wait.

Steelman quickened his stride, reaching for the pistol even as he debated whether to shoot for the head or to go for the proverbial broad side of a barn, Swain's thick trunk, and when he had closed the gap to five feet he brought up his arm and put three quick, tightly grouped shots into Swain's wide back.

The three separate reports seemed to fuse into a single sudden shattering noise. Frightened birds came winging up out of the grass in a series of violent, flapping explosions. Monkeys screeched hysterically from the rim of the jungle. Dang, supposing an ambush, went flat. Swain, who had in fact been ambushed, remained upright. He staggered forward a few steps, dropped both the weapons he was carrying, and slowly turned around to face Steelman.

A slack, bovine look of incomprehension filled Swain's face. He tipped his chin to look down his pajama front at the dark splotches where two of the three parabellum bullets had gone all the way through him, then gingerly poked at each hole with a tentative finger, as if he were counting buttons on a shirt. Then he looked up at Steelman and, in an awed voice, said: "Jeez!"

Steelman, panicked that three shots had not downed his man, fired again, hitting Swain in the chest.

Harry Swain took two faltering steps backward and went to his knees. He took a last, curious look around, as if he were trying very hard to figure out exactly what it was that had tripped him up, and fell over dead.

Gulliver felt a hollowness, as if his insides had been suddenly scooped out, and also a hatred, black and pure.

The feelings were contradictory, pulling him this way and that. He wanted just to stop there, to take some time to grieve. He wanted to go after Razor.

A soldier's instincts settled the issue; he was already in motion. He took off in a dead run, paying no mind to the cuts the stalks and branches left on his face and arms. He sprinted for two hundred meters before he was suddenly out of the thick growth and into a sunburst sea of grass. He stopped, went into a crouch, and looked around wildly. There! Off to the right he caught a quick movement; someone had just vanished back into the tree line. He took off again, running straight up.

Gulliver spied the black object in the grass and hurdled it all in one reflexive motion, losing his balance and almost going down. He lurched to a stop and went back. A pajama-clad Swain rested on his knees, his cheek flat against the ground, his rear end stuck up in the air like a sleeping infant's. A swarm of flies was already at work, laying its eggs in what was left of his bloody back.

He touched the corpse with a booted toe and it toppled over. The narrow, swinelike eyes were open, no more vacuous in death than they had been in life, but the bushy brows were at rest at last. They had found their final statement, cocked forever in a question mark.

Gulliver did not stop to pick up the weapons lying next to Swain's body. He scanned the surrounding area, looking for a second body, then took off at a sprint, his blood pounding with the thought that Dang might still be alive, slowing only when he came to the wall of jungle. There was a narrow door, the mouth of a trail, and he slipped through it. Once he was inside, where noise would be trapped and funneled, he stopped to listen. He heard a sound, voices, low and muffled, and followed it.

He found them fifty meters down the path, in the pocket of a glove-shaped glade. He might have blundered right into them if he had not heard Steelman's reedy voice, loud and near. He jumped off the trail and began circling, homing on the voice, looking for a good place from which he could see and size up the situation. Armed only with his K-bar, he could not go barrel-assing in like Errol Flynn.

He worked his way through a patch of wait-a-minute vines and crawled into the line of squat, broad-leaf nut palms that surrounded the open space. He eased a frond aside for a look.

Dang was on his knees, tethered to the ground like a cow pony, handcuffed to a handy root, a tendril that arced up out of the ground like a ropy rainbow and went back in a few feet farther on. Steelman was squatting in front of him, just out of his prisoner's reach, pointing a pistol at Dang's head and talking.

Gulliver backed out and resumed circling, needing to get closer, taking a chance that he had the time, that as long as Steelman was talking he would not be shooting. He covered his movements with their voices, listening as he went.

Steelman: "I *am* going to shoot you, Captain Dang, so you may as well answer my questions. The more of them you answer, the more time you have to live."

Dang: "Then I can only hope that you are a very curious man, and have many questions."

Steelman (laughing): "You're a cool one. I will give you that."

Dang: "I will answer as many of your questions as I can, but only because it amuses me to do so. But I will not tell you anything that might compromise my associates or current operations. If that is what you want, shoot me now."

Steelman: "We will see about that. For the moment, I'm more interested in you personally. Your file says you mostly worked on the Cambodian border, both with the VC and later, when you became a scout for the Americans. Did you happen to know a man named Nguyen Tu Vuong?"

Dang: "I will answer that only because Vuong is dead and safe from further harm. Yes, I knew him. He worked for me."

Steelman (excitedly): "When you were with the VC or when you were working for us?"

Dang: "Both."

Steelman: "I knew it! I knew there was a connection! You were running agents! Even after you came over to us, you were running agents!"

Dang: "Yes, of course."

Steelman: "The Green Berets . . . the B–40 Detachment . . . you were the one behind their mission problems?"

Dang: "Yes. And Vuong. He fed me intelligence, I passed it on and helped coordinate the appropriate counteraction."

Steelman: "It's going to give me a good deal of pleasure to shoot you, Captain Dang. You and your friend Vuong caused me a lot of trouble. He was my recruit, you know."

Dang (pausing): "No, I did not know. Then that would make you the man they call Razor."

Steelman (sharply): "Razor? How do you know about Razor? Who told you about Razor? Gulliver?"

Gulliver was back among the nut palms, directly behind Steelman, five or six long paces away. That he had managed to get so close did not really surprise him; Steelman had spent too many years behind a desk. Nor was he much surprised that Dang spotted him immediately. He saw Dang's eyes graze along the tree line, pause a heartbeat, then move back to Steelman.

If Gulliver had any doubts that Dang had seen him, they were dispelled by what happened next. Dang smiled. Instead of answering Steelman's questions, he smiled. It was not much of a smile, little more than a brief flash of teeth, but it was a smile, the first Gulliver had seen from him. And it seemed to infuriate Steelman as much as it amazed Gulliver. Steelman walked over to stand on either side of Dang's manacled left hand, aimed the pistol straight down, and fired.

Dang did not make a sound, and at first Gulliver thought that the shot had been strictly for show, a crude attempt to intimidate Dang into answering the questions. Then he saw the blood spattered on Steelman's trouser legs. Gulliver came to a crouch, unsheathed the K-bar, and stepped out of the trees in one seamless motion. He closed the distance to Steelman in four long, smooth, unhurried strides.

Steelman's first clue that he was not alone with his man came when something slammed down on his wrist and knocked the Browning from his grasp. After that, it was all sensation and impression. A knee in the small of his back pushing his torso forward. A hand in his hair pulling his head back. A flash of metal. A cold burn on his throat. Something with him, behind him, an unseen terror. All scored with a hideous soundtrack: Dang's hissing voice. "Kill him, Sandman! Kill him!"

Only then, when Dang gave name to the unseen terror, did Bennett Steelman know for a fact that he was going to die. He screamed—a drawn-out, mind-tearing scream—but the notes hit a wall in his throat and stacked up there, unable to get around it, unable to escape. For one terrifying moment he was afraid he might choke to death on them. Then the pressure was suddenly eased, the blocked passage cleared, and his scream hurtled out, just as he felt himself being thrown roughly to the ground.

Steelman lay on his face in the dirt, crying and sucking for oxygen, his hands cradling his neck protectively, like a mandarin's collar. It was several seconds before his mind was working again, before he knew he was not dead after all.

Still sobbing and gasping, he opened his eyes and found himself looking right into Dang's face, only a few feet away. Dang's teeth were bared and his eyes were rabid. He strained against the handcuffs like a leashed dog trying to get at an intruder and said again: "Kill him, Sandman! Kill him!"

"Kill him, Sandman! Kill him!"

It was hearing the name, that and Dang's hissing voice, as urgent as escaping steam, that stopped him.

Gulliver took the knife away from Steelman's throat and threw him to the ground. He stood over him, breathing hard, his muscles still quivering, slowly coming out of it.

He had come within a blink of cutting Steelman's throat, strictly out of instinct. The blade had already broken skin, drawn blood, dug into the side of the neck to start a track, a monorail for the smooth glide to the other side. Carrying through with it had seemed like the most natural thing in the world to do.

Gulliver found the Browning where Steelman dropped it. He looked around for the K-bar Dang kept in the sheath at the small of his back, but didn't see it. He picked up Steelman's pistol and stuck it in his web belt. Then, his K-bar still in his hand, he crossed over to where Steelman cowered on the ground and leaned over him.

"No!" Steelman screamed. "Sweet Jesus, Sandman, please!

Nooooooo!" His terror-filled eyes were glued to the knife in Gulliver's right hand, to the blade already stained with his blood.

Gulliver patted Steelman's pockets and found the key to the handcuffs. He straightened, looked down at the cringing CIA officer, and said: "It's like I was telling you. There is no Sandman. He retired."

He moved over to Dang but did not unlock the handcuffs. One of Dang's fingers was gone, the ring finger on the left hand, and he thought it might be better if the hand was tied down while he tended to it. He reached for the chain around Dang's neck to pull up the morphine tube.

Dang shook his head and said, "No, I want to stay clear of mind." Gulliver hesitated, nodded, and reached into the first-aid pouch on his web belt for a dressing.

Dang did not flinch when Gulliver began working on his hand. He kept his dark eyes on Gulliver's face. "You made a mistake, my friend," he said calmly. "You should have killed him."

"There's been enough killing," Gulliver said without looking up.

Steelman was on his feet, still shaken but feeling much better, feeling more his old self. Some of the old arrogance, the old confidence, had returned.

He walked over and, careful to stay out of Dang's reach, stood over Gulliver. "You certainly did make a mistake," he said. "You are in trouble. Big trouble. Obstructing policy. Attacking a superior. Giving aid and comfort to the enemies of the United States of America. And do not delude yourself into thinking you can get out of it by resigning. Oh no. It's too late for that. You are going to prison. That's a promise, old boy."

Gulliver was dusting Dang's hand with sulfa. He paused long enough to look up. "Steelman, when I'm finished here I'm going back to bury Swain. If you're still anywhere around, I'm going to bury you alongside him. That's a promise too, old boy."

Steelman blinked, and believed him. Gulliver was still staring at him, his face closed and expressionless. Steelman could still feel the burn of the knife on his neck, could still feel the awful sensation of not being able to breathe.

"Don't you think we should talk about this?" he said.

"No, I don't," Gulliver said in a quiet, deadly voice. "I thought I was rid of you once, but you wormed your way back into my life. Well, I'm rid of you now. If I ever see you again, the Sandman is coming out of retirement for one last job." He paused, then said, "Do you understand?"

Steelman licked his lips once, twice, then turned on his heel.

He walked slowly down the path that led back to the sea of grass, trying not to run. When he was out of sight of the glade, he ran.

Gulliver spent another ten minutes on Dang's hand, and when he was done he backed off a few steps, drew Steelman's pistol, and tossed Dang the key to the cuffs.

Dang unshackled himself and stood. "What happens now, my friend?" he asked.

"I'm taking you back, Dang. You're going to stand trial for the murder of Nguyen Khac Trung. You've got to pay."

Dang held up his bandaged hand. "I took Trung's finger and now I have given a finger. He and I are exactly even."

Gulliver shook his head. "No you're not. It's you and I who are even. You saved my life on the mountain and I've just saved yours. But you still owe Trung. He's dead; you're not."

"Bich owed Trung a life. The *Trung Uy,* Swain, owed Trung a life. They have paid their debt. I owed only a finger."

"Bullshit!" Gulliver exploded. "It was you who put it in motion. You let it happen. All of it. The old man. Ti-Ti and the others on the mountain. The students in the streets. And now Bich and Swain. Even Cameron. Yes, poor harmless Cameron. He's yours too, Dang. They're all yours. Every goddamn one of them."

Dang nodded slowly. "A long, sad list," he agreed in a soft voice. "Almost as long as the Sandman's. Our struggle-group commander in Ban Me Thuot was a poet and a university professor before the war. He had six children. Our political cadre in Hue was a social worker, a man who built orphanages. He had eight children of his own. Our indoctrination cadre in Dalat was once a bonze, a teacher of the Way. He did not have children of his own, but hundreds of people in Dalat looked to him as a second father . . ." Dang paused and added with a shrug, "As your great General Sherman said, war is hell and you cannot refine it."

"You can quit it," Gulliver said.

Dang shook his head. "You can quit it, I cannot. You are going home. I *am* home."

They stood silent, facing off. Then Gulliver said: "Tell me something. Why didn't you kill me when they told you to? I was number one on your hit list. The One Who Comes at Night."

"Because you stopped," Dang said. "At first I let you live because I needed information from you, but then I became curious about you. You stopped killing. You even refused to do Fat Minh's 'specials.' I wanted to know why you had stopped, *how* you had stopped."

Dang paused, then asked: "Do you remember the story I once

told you about how the communists came into my village and pulled the eyes from the children?"

Gulliver nodded. "Another one of your fairy tales, no doubt," he said, his voice bitter. "I've talked to Nhu. I know you come from near Ben Tre, not Dong Ha."

Dang shook his head. "Not altogether a fairy tale, my friend. The part about them killing my father was a lie; he died many years ago, when I was a boy. And the village was in the *nambo,* the Southern region, not in the North. But the VC did come into the village after the American doctors, and did take the eyes of the children. I was the commander of that VC patrol . . . I gave the order."

It was a confession too terrible not to be true. "Jesus, Dang," Gulliver muttered.

"Yes," Dang said quietly. "It has been in my mind and in my heart for many years. Yet I felt nothing at the time, only the righteousness of my cause." He paused, then said, "So you see, my friend. I thought I could learn from you. How to pull the scabs from my heart and feel again. And the more I worked with you, the more I came to admire you . . ." He stopped again and shrugged, uncomfortable. "But if you had accepted another Sandman mission, just one, I would have killed you without hesitation and without remorse."

Gulliver did not say anything, and after a long silence Dang said: "I am going now."

Gulliver steadied the Browning. "Dang, you take one step and I'll blow you to hell. I swear to Christ I will. You're coming back with me."

Dang smiled. It was an honest smile this time, one that spread his broad face even wider and gave him an air that was almost benign. He shook his head. "I will miss my friend the Sandman . . . he was a good soldier," he said. "But I think that I will miss my friend Jake even more . . . he was a good man."

He gave Gulliver a little bow, then turned and walked slowly toward the trees.

"Dang! Get your ass back here!" Gulliver yelled after him. "Dang! I mean it!"

Dang did not stop. Just before he disappeared into the trees, he held up a hand—a gesture of farewell—but he did not turn around. Gulliver let him go. It wasn't his war anymore.

He threw the pistol as far into the jungle as he could, then sat spraddle-legged on the ground and used his K-bar to dig a hole.

When the hole was a foot deep, he pulled the beret from his

head. He stared at the soft, dark green hat for a long time, kneading it, smoothing it, then threw it into the hole.

He wiped the long blade of the K-bar on his thigh and, without ceremony, threw it into the hole on top of the hat.

Then he scooped the dirt back in and tamped it down with the heel of his hand.

He moved away from the mound and sat with his back to a tree. He reached into his pocket, shook a bent cigarette from the rumpled pack, and lit up. He smoked with his eyes closed, and after a few minutes his face seemed to change slowly, to lose its edges and furrows, its hard, angular lines.

When he finished the cigarette, he opened his eyes and looked at his watch.

He wondered how long it would take Dang to catch up with Razor.

ABOUT THE AUTHOR

NICHOLAS PROFFITT, a former journalist, made his auspicious debut as a novelist with the critically acclaimed GARDENS OF STONE in 1983 of which United Press International said, "[It] may very well be the best novel on the Vietnam War. . . . It earns Nicholas Proffitt a place alongside James Jones and Norman Mailer." The son of a military family, Proffitt served as a sergeant in the 1st Battalion, 3rd Infantry of the U.S. Army—The Old Guard—which formed the inspiration for his first novel. He has been a correspondent and later bureau chief for *Newsweek* in Beirut, London, Nairobi and Saigon, and has won two Overseas Press Club Awards for International Reporting for his coverage of the 1973 Arab–Israeli War and the fall of South Vietnam in 1975. Mr. Proffitt is married with three children and makes his home in Wilmington, North Carolina.